To Jack
With Best
from
Sacher Torte

With Broken Wings

Sacher Torte

Local Legend Publishing UK

Sacher Torte © Copyright 2010
www.sachertortebooks.com

All rights reserved

No parts of this publication may be reproduced, stored in a retrieval
system, or transmitted in any form or by any means, electronic,
mechanical, photocopying, recording or otherwise without the prior
permission of the publisher.

A Record of this Publication is available
from the British Library

ISBN 978-1-907203-18-3

Local Legend Publishing
Park Issa
St Martin's Road
Gobowen, Shropshire
SY11 3NP, UK
www.local-legend.co.uk

Cover Design by Titanium Design
www.titaniumdesign.co.uk

Cover illustration courtesy of
Steven F. Cooke, Chartered Designer - all rights reserved.
Email: cookehq@gmail.com

To all my special people; thank you for being you.

About the Author

Sacher is retired from teaching children with complex special needs. She lives in Mallorca where she now writes full time. She has three sons all living in the U.K. and a husband who is the illustrator of this book cover. Anyone wishing to contact the author may do so by emailing her at: sachertortebooks@hotmail.com

Her debut book is *With Bells on his Toes*, published by Local Legend Publishing in January 2010 and available from leading book stores and online, ISBN 978-1907203-10-7.

www.sachertortebooks.com

Table of Contents

One

Mally Kenyon was only lightly intoxicated as he came out of the Dog's Bed Inn in Lower Quinton still chuckling under his breath at a joke that Tock, the landlord, had told the gathered assembly. It was shortly before midnight on a very cold April evening; a wind with saw teeth almost cutting him in two. About him the town lying quiet under street light; its inhabitants driven indoors early by the very same wind. No lingering tonight for those with decent homes and warm firesides to go to unlike the man whose lonesome path would lead him over the road bridge, down the dark streets to a place of cold comfort. Going home for Mally Kenyon was never an easy decision to make. Not when he looked ahead of him to an empty bed, a cold hearth and a lonely existence in the pig sty he rented, not more than a half mile into the estate itself; a series of circular roads and cul-de-sacs making it dead end perfect for the thieves and dealers of which Mally Kenyon was one.

Finishing the last cigarette in his packet of twenty he ground it underfoot before turning his jacket collar up, cursing the thin material when he should have worn a fleece. Then he held his work-toned arms tight against his lean length to retain what little warmth he had in his inadequate clothing, shivering as the chill breeze frisked through the thin jeans and washed out T-shirt under the lightweight zip-up, knowing that part of his cold was caused by hunger. Living on beer and cigarettes was taking its toll. Hair dull and lifeless. His whiskery face sunken into hollows. The unkemptness about him making him look much older than his years. He sighed heavily as the effluence from his cigarette wreathed his face in drifting smoke, his countenance only for a moment showing worry for tomorrow's God-given grace of having enough work to keep the wolf from the door.

Then the police van and the dog appeared within his vision. Unexpected. There on the road bridge in front of him. The sight of it stopped him dead. A big man, gaunt of frame but still standing over six feet in height, Mally knew that there was no trying to pretend he was invisible as he noted the marked van parked with its bonnet pointing towards his own direction on the opposite side of Bridge Twenty-Eight which spanned the Whemley Canal. The van with its back door open to reveal the dog which had been set on guard duty. One moment lying down licking its bits, the next ears alert to Mally's noisy intrusion into its privacy after he had let the pub door clatter behind him. The dog slowly rising to take up the space in a sitting position to the rear of the van. Wolf eyes upon him.

For several moments Mally found himself unable to think. Not about the things in his pockets, which he would rather not be found on his person, but what to do about the dog. His fear of the large animal had caught him unawares. He felt himself weakening as an uncontrolled panic poured through him like a river in flood. Where was the handler? being the first coherent question in his head. The dog was unrestrained and the rear door to the van open. Then the flashes of recurring visions which had created and exacerbated his fear of German Shepherd dogs from being a child. Very sight of one sufficient to make the hairs on the back of his neck stand on end. He could no more creep away, at that moment, than he could do the impossible and run. His heart began to pound. His breath shortened as his panic mounted.

The dog's head went down further.

Mally held his breath. What he would have given in that moment to be somewhere else. Lifted up and hoisted away by winged angels as the dog's snout drew on the air between them across the width of the street, eyes glinting deep as it smelled the entrails of his fear. Though it remained unmoving, the dog had sensed his panic. A low growl emanating from between fanged teeth. Futile to try to escape. Stand still, he told himself. Defiance on his face, now, as he held his aversion at bay; barely.

Magdalene watching, too, from her bedroom window. He saw her in the upstairs window of the houses which backed onto the canal, looking out, trance-like, as if unaware of her view of the bridge. Too distant to guess her thoughts but ever hopeful that she might be thinking of him. Face keened to the glass. Was she looking in his direction or beyond him? All the more reason to keep his fear contained. It was not for Magdalene to know that she was his other weakness. Always had been and always will be; a woman too virtuous for her own good. Went to church, kneeled before the altar and said her Hail Mary's, as directed by her priest, while her mother shuffled the Tarot cards and looked into the crystal for her own direction, mumbling runes and worshiping the Earth itself. She had foretold the future when she had drawn The Tower and laid it before her daughter as the symbolic representation of Magdalene's disastrous marriage to his twin brother, Bass, now deceased. A daughter born to them before Bass had departed life and the child taken into care. Bass had had no God. Neither had Magdalene, then. Not as now.

Mally neither. No belief sufficient enough to save him now from his biggest fear: that of dogs which looked like wolves and could hunt in packs. Stuff of his worst nightmares when they never failed to hunt him down. Snapping at his heels as he tried to escape them. Omens, perhaps,

marauding untamed through his dreams. Terrible howling visions of bared
teeth which could have him waking in the night from his own screaming
cries. Sweat dripping off him and nothing else to do but rise, stare into a
fire, and take something to ease his mind. Even one lone dog enough to
petrify him and scare him witless.

The only thing to save him now came into his vision as a moving
figure between the van and the parapet of the bridge, which spanned the
canal some fifteen feet below, where the uniformed police officer must
have been standing, looking over at Mally, seeing his respect for the animal
written on a fearing face. No respect returned.

Seen! The dark figure in a dark blue uniform, beckoning him, flat
hat crushed under his armpit as he turned from looking down into the
canal water, with a shimmering, silver dog chain in his hand. Then, as if to
denote some other tangible reference for Mally to fear, he raised the hand
that held the dog chain and shouted to the now whimpering, obedient
creature, "Stay, Timber!" At the same time, his face flattening with some
form of recognition, revealed by the ochre glow of the bridge lamp. "A
word if I may!"

Eyes on the dog still, Mally kept to his own pavement for several
paces before crossing over. No inkling what the man could possibly have
been looking for over the bridge parapet when all that would be visible was
a long, narrow, and stinking, weed filled ditch of stagnant water, amputated
like an infected, flesh rotted limb from the reclaimed canal branches that
ran through the centre of Quinton. He looked behind him. The leaded
windows of the Dog's Bed Inn steamed with the breath of whoever had
hidden himself behind a curtain, looking out.

Mally took his time crossing the road, senses alert still, fear of the
dog causing him to walk cautiously. No reason apparent to Mally's thinking
for the police presence as far as he was aware. In the main, the police
stayed out of Lower Quinton and in particular the Dog's Bed Estate; a
place divided from civilization by the stinking cesspit of abandoned
rubbish and carelessly shed litter in a pool of slimy water that even the
majority of people from the Dog's Bed stayed clear of.

So why was he here? Why the dog? The police rarely visited and
only when they had to, choosing not to get trapped by the narrow bridge
and beyond the one-way warrens of dead end roads and alleyways between
the high rises. When they did venture in, they came in greater numbers, in
riot vans with Perspex shields and armed to the teeth. Unless they were
called here for the sake of an accident or someone missing, that is.
Sometimes to discover the decomposing remains of an old person not
seen for several days. Otherwise, let the low life police themselves or kill

each other in the process, their backs turned to even the worst of the criminal element as long as they were confined within this delta of flat land, both trapped by and exposed to the long, low hills behind.

"Move a bit quicker, lad. This is urgent."

Where was his mate? Mally looked about, keeping the van and the dog within his peripheral vision.

"This isn't to do with you, lad. Just a simple question."

A voice came up from below the parapet of the bridge, heralded by the golden, arced light of a randomly sweeping torch beam; female. "There's nothing here, Serge. False call, I think."

The copper on the bridge turned to Mally again as he came under the same ochre street lamp. Mally felt exposed by his expression, quickly looking down before he was caught by his own telltale silver eyes. "Thought I knew you. Mally Kenyon isn't it?"

"What if it is? Done nothing."

Mally saw the dog lead in the officer's hand being jingled as he thought on Mally's infamy. Then he folded the dog's restraint and gave one clacking slap against his own gloved palm, piercing what small hold Mally had on his inner controls, like the spike on a tin opener to his inner can of worms.

As if his flesh was infested, Mally could feel his nerve ends writhing as he placed his shaking hands deep in his pockets and dug them into the mishmash within, letting his neck sink into his turned-up collar, detesting his fear and thinking that his memorable face was part of the Kenyon curse. That curse being their physical likeness to each other. More the Kenyon eyes than the broad shouldered, fair-haired tallness. Eyes the colour of darting, silver fish in murky water; curious, too, despite being fearful of an obedient wolf-dog. Eyes that when angry flashed hot like the molten metal within an alchemist's crucible. At their most dangerous and deepest, the solid grey of cold mercury at the bottom of a thermometer before the slow rise of the clenching fists that most defined Mally's social ineptness. His worst trait being a sudden and unpredictable temper which could take even himself by surprise at times.

But not with a wolf watching. Mally set his face into a cooperative blank, taking care not to scuff the heels of his steel toe-capped, builder's boots as he crossed over, followed now by Tock Bartlett, landlord of the Dog's Bed Inn; Magdalene's father. "What's going on?"

Mally, eyes as hard as polished steel, now. "I've done nothing!"

The officer nodded to the man he knew by sight, already. "Never said you had. We've been called out to solve a mystery. What's this about a child being stuck in the canal, under the bridge? Got a call at the station."

Mally shrugged. "News to me. You sure you heard right?"

"This is Bridge Twenty-Eight? Someone pinched the number plaque off the bridge. Something about a child under the water."

Mally shrugged again. What did he care? "Kids are always falling in the canal. Can't be above a metre deep at its deepest, any road."

"Sure it's not a false call-out?" asked the landlord.

The voice from below was hesitant now. "There's something moving under the water but I can't make out what it is. Get down here quick."

The copper took the brick steps down two at a time, leaving Mally free to go if he should so choose to do so. It was the landlord's hand on his shoulder which went against his better judgement, "He said something about a child in the water. Best check it out ourselves."

Mally went with the propulsion of a hand to his shoulder, following on behind with a puzzled frown at his own obsequiousness but away from the dog which had now turned itself about and was watching him intently through the cage bars, looking over between the front seats. With access to the canal bank, he might get home another way.

Under the arch, on the opposite side of the brick tunnel, the water rinsed a wide, greasy, undulating line over the noxious ditch.

"Something's causing the water to move," said the female officer, torch beam roving through darkness. "Something made a splash. God! Look at the filth."

Pity she was a pig. She had the kind of breasts Mally liked to worship; large and pendulous.

"Stinks!" The torch roving to linger on their faces in order for the policewoman to see who had accompanied her colleague down the steps. Her eyes rolled at sight of Mally Kenyon; local thug, often to be seen at the station, hauled in from the back of the drunk-tank, fighting drunk or out of his head on drugs. She smiled vaguely at Tock.

Mally saw nothing other than an escape plan...a slow walk...a light jog...a fast dash at a suitable moment. Recalling the geography of the towpath: left, to Quinton. Right, the towpath changed sides; only the bridge linking one side to the other, but his access that way clear as long as he crossed the canal by wading through the water, as filthy as it looked. He needn't pass the dog again.

Thinking about it, he let his eyes roam with the torch beam. He didn't like being under bridges. Not here with this stench. Needles and condoms amidst a dumped stew of other discarded rubbish...bike wheels...the legs of an old armchair standing up above the stagnant water like an installation of modern art. Showing daily. Admission free to the discerning public. Bring your own nose clip, Mally thought. That arch above his head reminding him of something to do with the wolf of his nightmares. Didn't know why, though. Yet another thing of menace from a menaced childhood.

"There. Look. Centre, more or less. A sack. It's moving in the water."

Mally journeying closer to the officers he would have to pass before taking off for the allotments. The wolf was still up there. Safe!

The policewoman bent to shine her light on one area where the water was undulating slightly. She had no interest in Mally. The male officer likewise distracted. The chain, looped on his wrist, now, never stopping moving.

Mally made another couple of side steps to get past them.

"There's something recently been thrown in. Maybe it's just the air coming out and causing the water to be disturbed."

Mally looked up and down the towpaths, summonsing his night eyes. No one about now but themselves and a dog beginning to whine fractiously with its handler out of sight. The dog lead now being thrashed around on a spin cycle behind his back as the officer leant to look at concentric rings of disturbed water in the torch light.

Mally and Tock hung back, purely onlookers, watching the so-called protectors of the people at work, while standing in the criss-crosses and circular patterns in the mud, under their respective feet. The circles of light travelling over the black, brackish water. There was no sign of a child. "It was there a minute ago...something moving under the surface...a sort of wriggling sack just under the surface."

Mally looked, despite himself, as another step took him towards their group. Water just undulating quietly. Then it thrashed. There was something moving in the central beam between the arc of the bike wheel and some floating upholstery, central to the rings of disturbed, viscid, dark liquid as if something living was trapped under there.

"Can't be a fish. Probably kittens," Tock breathed into Mally's ear, following him as closely as if he had a button caught in Mally's jacket. "Who'd phone up the police about a few kittens in a sack? A water rat, maybe," the landlord offered, making a case for leaving sacks in clogged up canals to keep their secrets.

Mr PC Plod, no doubt, an expert on the wildlife to be found in the stagnant, rancid, rubbish clogged canals of Britain. "A rat wouldn't cause a disturbance like that...more a wake. They keep their noses above water most of the time when swimming."

It takes a rat to know a rat, Mally felt like saying.

So who was going in then? Her or her dog-chain-jangling superior? Now doing up and down waterfalls of the supple, silver chain from one gloved hand to the other.

She folded her arms on her own unspoken decision and looked at her superior officer with a feminine query concerning his manhood.

The policeman read her thoughts. He, obviously, disagreed with her unspoken proposal. No way to get a man who wore starched collars and shined his shoes to a mirror finish, probably using his own spit and Cherry Blossom Polish on a warm spoon, into the filth and stagnant pestilence of what remained of the Whemley Canal. A source of diphtheria or cholera, perhaps. Might even be arsenic in the silt at the bottom. Tetanus bacteria on the sharp edges of rusted cans. Rats and leeches.

Tock winging his moustache with the back of a hand. "Better make sure, hadn't you?"

Insulted, Serge stood upright, his face saying that he was pulling rank, as he clacked the dog chain once, very sharply, to denote his considered opinion. "I think we've been had. Bit over the top to send for a team of frogmen, don't you think? False call out."

Mally sneered. What if it was a child in the sack after all, as reported? They seemed to have forgotten their initial brief, even if it was just a bag full of bobbling footballs bleeding air.

Why did he say it? "I'll wade in if you won't." If he got out on the other towpath he could be off that way through the parkland. Why not? Mally considered himself to having been in worse trouble than anything the water could offer. Coat off, he passed it to Tock with a telling wink. Then his watch which Tock pocketed.

Sliding in, he started wading, waist deep. Things trailing and dangerous wrapping themselves about cold legs as he made to where the sack now wriggled with an increased motion, just under the surface of water only to be described as a filthy, gritty, noxious, thick soup of bog slime with hanging weed, bottom filled with what Mally felt to be glass bottles and old tin cans under his boots. He kept his arms high because he had no wish to dunk his hands until it was absolutely necessary. Until he came to the floating, wriggling sack. There was nothing else for it but to get his hands wet. Concern already deepening. Something strong banging against his thigh. Feeling queasy now as he drew the moving sack close enough to lift it up and break the surface. That was when he felt the weight of a solid wriggling body mass with four limbs, a torso and a round shape which suddenly seemed to understand his presence and urge itself towards him. A wolf nightmare grabbing at his clothing with a sound like a gurgling drain as whatever was within fought to take in air.

Fear such as he had never felt in his life before travelled like ball lightening through to his disbelieving brain, wiping out everything in its impact but the need to get this wriggling thing he had in the bag out of the water. Panic saw him attempt to hurry even as he felt the energy drain from his arms and legs. What could only be a human hand latched itself onto his T-shirt through the sacking, accompanied by a noise that bellowed like a fog horn of dragging sound, on and off, on and off, the sack draining of water. A drama unfolding in the beams of stage light.

The sack had a loop of string at the neck. Mally steeled himself to undo it. The wet string not separating freely, he had to tug, hearing cries from behind him. His brain heeding only his own volition.

It was as if he had opened up the catch on a jack-in-a-box, for suddenly the small gasping face covered in hanks of streaming hair and running with filthy water, sprang up before him, gasping for breath; a child's face; a girl's face, drawing air in deeply with a dragging panic. The fog horn of her struggle continuing...her mouth a big O. Dark, angry, pale coloured eyes as wide as a landed carp gaped back at him. Her face a thunder cloud; blaming Mally, as she flipped and bucked against his length to scramble as high up his frame as she could. Scrambling desperately to increase her grip on his clothing, rise above the water level completely, her shoes digging into his thighs as she raised herself upwards, her chin hard on the top of Mally's head.

Mally almost overwhelmed by the shock of her coming up and at him like that. Had she been a rampant weed and he an oak tree, she could have brought him down, given time enough. It was strength, not weakness that she had over him. Pandemonium going on behind him.

When she bit him, the pain came through cold, shocked numbness; her incisors cutting like hide punches into a layer of his scalp. Blame came upon him in the small hands that dragged at his hair, pulling so hard in her fury that he felt the roots tear away. As if he was her attempted murderer and not her saviour.

When she found the hand that attempted to stem the pain of his head Mally joined her banshee screaming. The sound of his cries cut her struggle dead. She had released his hair and scalp from between her biting teeth, transferring the incredible pain to the soft flesh of his hand between thumb and forefinger. He had to press his hand deeper against her teeth for her jaws to open and let his hand go. In that moment they looked at each other. Silver eyes into silver eyes reflecting the yellow torch light; a wizardly mingling of base metals which in Mally's impoverished breast and stunned mind, took on the lure of pure gold. The child was beautiful.

The pain remained like a baptism of fire as he carried her without faltering to the people waiting on the tow path. Never before had Mally Kenyon felt anything like this... a starburst of joy deep within his belly. Angels singing in his head. An incredible joy and happiness flowing through him, its warmth flowing through every vein, every capillary, through every hair follicle, his shortest whisker and the smallest flake of his skin. A joy of such proportion that stunned and enraptured him, taking his breath away. Even the wolf on the bridge forgotten. A change taking place created by a fountain of the sweetest, purest, most innocent pleasure. A gush more satisfying than any drug as he handed her up and over, then stayed in the water looking on the profile of the celestial cherub he had pulled from a cesspit.

The policewoman took the child into her arms, her face squashed to plainness with emotion. The torch she held up-lighting the brick arched roof of the bridge.

The dog chain jangled as it swung loose from the policeman's wrist. "This is the worst thing I have ever seen," he muttered deeply. "God strike dead the beast that has done this." The dog lead was shaking so much as it swung unattended from his trembling wrist that it jittered a sound like small, tuneless, musical bells.

In that moment the child wriggled out of her keeper's embrace, her breathing settling. As soon as her feet touched the cinders, she sank down onto the towpath, sitting on her haunches, hands hanging between her legs, fingers spreading flat, legs parted, silver eyes down to the dog handler's feet. The child shut down like a switch being flicked, retreating into herself, filthy dirty and dripping rancid water onto the cinder towpath. Her eyes moved to the clip end on the dog chain. She wore a red spotted dress, now blackened with the fetid silt from the canal water, the same colour as the blood pouring from Mally's head where she had bitten him. Her frilled socks blackened on legs running with the watery weeds she had dragged with her from her watery grave. Red leather shoes with buttoned fastenings totally ruined, like Mally's brown suede work boots would be.

Tock. "God almighty!"

The policewoman. "We'd better get her cleaned up and dry."

Mally. "Call an ambulance."

"No need. She can walk." The officer, gathering his dog chain in and depositing it into his pocket.

The policewoman, with children of her own, tried to lift the child again but she remained a solid, doubled shape on her folded haunches, staring at the pocket where the chain had been deposited.

Made incoherent...Mally having forgotten his intentions...they shared their looks of shocked fascination. Awe even. How long could this child have been in the water? It had to have been several minutes with five added on. Had she survived on a pocket of air until the sack had slowly filled with water and her body weight taken her under?

In the aftermath of shock there was anger on the faces of the officers, even a growing fear that they had very nearly left a child to drown. It had taken a villain like Mally Kenyon to save her. A man who now had tears to be denied as he looked over every inch of the child before him. It had been like seeing back in time to his own angry eyes in the mirror when she had bitten and beaten her way into his fortressed heart. A fragile, sensitive boy, wanting only to be loved; a lone dog kicked and dragged through a hard, cruel life. In his confusion, she was he and he was she, but reborn of a hessian sack and he her deliverer. His shaking hands had been the hands that had caught her and brought her to safety; this child, a beautiful, magical, mystical changeling whose rebirth, as his own, had happened in the moment that she had sprung, like a sprite, into the deep, bottomless well of his unguarded feelings.

Mally, lowering his head to hide his tears, saw that the sack was draped against him, still. It contained something that had shared her boggy grave; something else that he might save. With his tumultuous feelings settling, he opened the sack and looked inside. The other victim was a rag doll. He drew it out wet and limp; a doll with orange hair and a freckled face, its clothes just as stained with the putrid canal water as his and the child's were.

He handed it over to the policeman, seeing that the bite mark on his hand was becoming a livid, red welt into which the indentation of her teeth was embedded like rosary beads. Mally had nothing to say because words failed him.

He would never, again, be the same.

Two

Mally and Tock had departed the dark canal bank, moonlight only offering a meagre illumination to the shapes and shades of blackness about her. It shone on the ruffled surface of the canal and the glass roofs of the greenhouses to the rear of the adult, female form which emerged from a gap in the hedges, just a short way from the bridge; a shapeless figure bringing with it a container on wheels, gripped onto tightly by the handle. A small suitcase swung at her side as the woman turned to look towards the bridge.

The van which now had the extra passenger in the form of a loudly shrieking child was quickly disappearing into the dark night. It had already made a U turn and driven away. There could be no doubt that the slow moving figure and its accoutrements which came to stand by the water's edge was following the sounds of its departure and watching the van's progress away towards the centre of the town. There could be only one way it was heading. Only one destination; the police station.

For those who might have seen her standing alone and forlorn on a canal towpath after midnight her clothing might have suggested her to be after a concealment of identity not usual to her daytime self. That such clothing was no different than the garments she always wore would only be known to those aware of her occasional venturings out of the front door of her Lower Quinton home. For Serena Collins was draped from head to toe in voluminous clothing; a head scarf concealing her face, her coat fastened from neck to knee and her sheepskin boots allowing not even a glimpse of her white, fragile skin. Her gloves were sheepskin mittens which worried now at her hidden face as she clutched the tissue she needed to stem her weeping eyes and runny nose as she looked about carefully with wide sweeps of her head, cowering into her clothing, a dark stain beginning to show through the pale wool of the scarf which had been tied about her head in a way to stand out from her cheeks and forehead. A hand reaching up to the place that had so recently smote the stony path as her handbag had been snatched by its strap from her thin shoulder and she had been propelled forward by the unexpected attack. The jolt, as she had hit the banking, had been severe enough to jar the breath from her body and cause her brain to rattle in her skull. Even as she stood recalling, with a sense of disbelief, what had happened, she felt disorientated, still. So filled with fear and shock that she felt physically ill. The dark, spreading stain on her headscarf was that of her own blood. She had been mugged. Yet far more had been lost than merely a handbag.

Hard to think that only a few minutes previously, before being set upon, her intentions had still been as planned. Serena had just reached the bottom of the flight of brick steps down to the canal bank on the side which would allow a straight journey to the train station in the town centre when she had been so cruelly felled upon from behind. She had been so engaged in the carriage of a small suitcase in one hand and a cumbersome shopping trolley in the other, with her handbag suspended from its strap about her shoulder, that she had allowed herself to withdraw from the vigilance that might otherwise have kept her from trouble. Not usually out at so late an hour, she had considered herself to be unwatched, despite the drinkers still crowding the bar in the public house as she had passed by as unobtrusively as the trolley would allow, their sounds of laughter ringing in her ears as she made to come down the steps on the other side. She had guided it as carefully as she could because the trolley was heavy and its cargo precious. She had been so vastly tired, her muscles drained of energy. She had paused in her journey after bringing her burdens down the last of the rises in order to catch her breath, a pain in her side from the exertion. It had been then that the tall, strong assailant had struck her a brutal blow from behind. As if he had been lurking in the shadows of the bridge, waiting for some such opportunistic moment. A woman seemingly alone. Foolishly walking a canal bank late at night with a handbag and a shopping trolley and a small suitcase in which there could only be valuable things. As she had fallen the red bag had been snatched from her shoulder. The heavy trolley had stayed stubbornly upright while the suitcase had clattered against the brick wall and then become lost to the shadows.

For a moment, she had been stunned and disorientated. The need to protect her delicate skin causing her to pull the scarf further under her cheek as it had lain against the rough cinders. Shock could sometimes bring on a convulsion that would make her writhe for its short duration and while this did not happen, her fear of losing all consciousness took over from the fear that the man might rape her or continue an assault in a way that might reveal her identity. It had seemed so important not to be identified. He must not know her. Or look inside the trolley. Fear had coursed through her like forest fire. He must not take the trolley. Let him take the suitcase, instead. It was an exertion of massive proportion, just to speak. "Go, go," she had called, breathlessly, to her attacker. "There's money in my bag. Take the purse inside it. Over a hundred pounds in there. The suitcase has new clothes within. You will be able to sell them. Not the trolley. Please, not the trolley."

Anything rather than do what he did next. She had been unable to see his face, just his tall, gaunt frame, yellow lined with the faint ochre light coming down from the bridge lamps; a cruel, tight mouth, biting hard on clenched teeth. Fair hair hanging unkempt over an unshaven face which bristled with tiny silvery hairs as the light defined his silhouette. The smell of unwashed desperation. Dark, matt, suede builder's boots on his feet with steel toe caps; large feet with large boots covered in a pale powder, maybe cement or stone dust.

Then she had realised his intent. Hearing her own desperate voice, again. "Dear God, no!" she had cried, as his shaking hands, fingers work-worn, with nails bitten to the quick, deftly undid the buckle to Caitlin's hiding place. "No, please, no! Leave it," as he had pulled back the lid and put his hand to the hessian within.

The wriggling sack rose and his own shriek broke the sound of his heavy breathing. "God, a dog!" before he dropped it onto the ground, raising a foot as if he would kick it into the water which licked and lapped in the slimy ditch under the brick edge of the towpath.

"No! Not a dog...a child...a child...please, leave her."

His gasp had been admonishing. His face spread wide with a disgust that not even a man such as he could deny feeling. "A child...that's a child in there!" The sack abandoned, space made as he had backed away because the sack had taken on a small, human shape; crouched, hands feeling, head straining against the sacking; unmistakable.

All might have been well, save for what happened next. Caitlin taking up her leaping-frog position within the sack which had been tied with string to keep her in; a new skill, one she had practised in her daily games. Her agile body tense and then springing, froglike, as she sensed her own opportunity to escape. The splash had been enough to inform her jailer and their assailant that she had leapt the wrong way. She and her rag doll within the same sack had gone into the stinking, slimy water.

Even as he watched, the assailant had taken himself towards the bridge steps, walking backwards, knocking his heel against the suitcase as he went so that it took on the dust transferred from his boots, her red handbag clutched in his fist with the strap hanging, then turned to run as if being chased by a demon from Hell to the bridge above.

She had listened to his rapid footsteps as she had tried to struggle against the giddiness which threatened to take her into unconsciousness while the sack had thrashed with its thrusting contents, causing Serena to feel the splashes on her face as they bled through the thin wool of her scarf. The blow to her head, while not serious to someone of a stronger disposition, had been seriously disabling to a person as weakened and frail as she had become in recent months. Even so, she might have followed Caitlin into the water to try to save her except that a voice, which could only have been his, came deep and low, like a rumble of faraway thunder to her ears, as she lay stiffly on her side, unable to move, under the bridge arch. He was speaking from the parapet of the bridge above her. She could hear his words, clearly spoken; the last place she thought that he would call.

"Police? There's a child under the water at Bridge Twenty-Eight of the Whemley Canal...by the Dog's Bed Inn...under the bridge. Get here quick. This is not a crank call."

She had had to crawl away, then, leaving the sack with its head still just proud of the water where she could only hope that it would stay, standing with stiff and painful difficulty, allowing the now empty trolley to give its assistance as she had dragged herself to her feet and made to find somewhere where she might think clearly, picking up the suitcase as she went.

While urgently searching for a place of secretion amidst the vegetation and bushes to the side of the path she had looked back constantly, even as panic for her own exposure gripped her, seeing the rippling light rings which Caitlin's thrashing arms and legs were making inside the sacking. No sound, as if she had been concentrating hard, trying to find something to grab which would keep her head above the greasy, black bog. Hearing the car coming and knowing its intention to stop on the bridge even before it did so; a blue light pulsing on the roof of the van which she saw travelling the street at great speed towards the bridge. A rescue vehicle on an empty, midnight, weekday road without other traffic. The sound of it stopping on screeching tyres filled her with even more anxiety as its blue light cancelled. A flashlight pouring over the canal banking, the beams failing to reach her hiding place. More doors clicking open, a dog whimpering; "Stay Timber. Guard the van." Then to a companion, "Better get down there with the flashlight. You never know in a place like this."

She had found her hiding place; through and behind a privet hedge, with her back to the side boarding of a garden shed, carefully bringing the trolley round to be hidden also, keeping a tight grip on the small suitcase, when the police van and then the policewoman had appeared, slowly to be followed by the others who had proceeded to do what she had been unable to do: to save little Caitlin from the result of her own mischief. How hard she had listened then, praying, tears beginning to swill against her reddening lids. Stemming her cries of desperate anguish.

When she had looked back to the canal water, there was no outstanding shape to suggest that Caitlin was still above the water, alive and breathing, though she would know to hold her breath. Time so short since the call had been made. It was as if the police van had been waiting, close at hand, ready to be directed to the next troublesome place. The High Street, maybe. Police parked there, late at night, watching out for the men who would creep within the shadows of the backstreets, pressing themselves against rear gates and leaning on car door handles for those owned by people foolish enough to leave their property unprotected. Property, not people, that which mattered most. No protection down here where danger lurked on a nightly basis. Sometimes vagrants and druggies under the bridge. The place where the man had lain in wait. She should have known better than to come this way. Should have gone some other way. Only she had been more frightened of being stopped by a policeman seeing her walk the darkened streets. Wanting to look inside her trolley when she would have represented an unusual sight as she wandered the pavements of Quinton at gone midnight.

She had been going to catch the night train west, you see. The one that might have served her best with its empty carriages and few people to question why a disfigured woman with a small child might choose to travel into the leafy countryside of Shropshire before the morning light. The fewer to see, the better, CC had said. Though he might have driven them in his car had CC been a man with consideration for others. A man to know his responsibilities. A man decent enough in his heart and mind to know that Serena was doing only that which was best for all of them. She should have realised her own vulnerability in a place which had a reputation for harbouring the criminals who would think nothing of preying upon a weak and disabled woman walking alone. The kind of man who had thought nothing of striking her hard and pushing her down. Yet one who even in his depravity would be so repulsed by little Caitlin's mode of travel that he would drop her like a hot stone and call the police to have her saved from her own naughty foolishness.

Was it the same man who had attacked her? He who had accompanied the police down the bridge steps, followed by Tock Bartlett, the landlord of the Dog's Bed Inn? She could not recall sufficiently the detail of his appearance to make a sure identification, over the distance, though he looked to be both similar and familiar. Maybe, maybe not. If it was the same man, he would not fear her, now, as much as she should fear him. He might uncover her identity from the contents of her handbag if it was the same man and he of a will to hand the handbag over. Bills with her address at the top; a diary, the school papers, her purse, her crucifix. Not worn today because she did not want to feel that she was asking unfairly of Him. As she had removed it to place it in the handbag, it had been like breaking her connection with the Master of all things. He would not hear.

He would not see. He would be looking elsewhere. At the same time thinking that if she had asked, He might have allowed her to do this last thing for Caitlin...to get her away safely to a different world...a different life...to her inclusion instead of her separation. That was what Caitlin had failed to understand. The rejection was for her own sake, now that she, Serena, was ill. Now that she was dying. Now that soon she would be gone.

Now, her silhouette moved slowly as her head dipped low, a hand rising to put a tissue up to wipe a running nose, once again. From the same gap, pulling to her side in her free hand, the large, reinforced, shopping trolley on small, sturdy wheels which had been Caitlin's carriage just a few short minutes ago. A carriage that, hitherto, had always carried her safely with restraint, to avoid her presence being known. Looking out through the eye from within, as long as she was quiet. As long as she was still.

Now, silently, she manoeuvred the carriage on its small wheels, this way and that, making criss-cross patterns in the cinders, same as those when she had positioned the carriage at the bottom of the bridge steps, before the attack. An innocent looking carrier for heavy goods; darkly plaid in the ochre light from the bridge lamps, moving upright without noise, until it was tilted at an angle of forty-five degrees, ready to be dragged from behind using the handle which she gripped onto tightly in shaking fingers, crying softly into the scarf about her face.

Sounds like the flaps of rough linen were laid over the soft, dark velvet of the night as her own whispering voice cut through the dark quiet. Now the place where Caitlin had leapt was without movement; the discarded rubbish still standing proud of a glistening slick. "Dear God, in your goodness, help me, please! Hail Mary, mother of God, help me, please!" Head bowed, words sincere, she staggered slightly as if her knees were about to give way, the mud on her legs and sheepskin boots and down the front of her woollen coat, seeping through her outer clothing to her skin beneath. From out of a mouth wrapped up within the folds of the enveloping, woollen scarf, a short, sharp breath picked a frayed edge into the mantle of restored peace. A short walk and the bridge swallowed the silhouette up like a dark mouth before it could be seen again under the ochre lights of the bridge above.

Raising the now lightweight trolley up in one hand, the suitcase in the other, she made a quiet ascent up the bridge steps. There was no other way in which to attain the opposite towpath, after the bridge, on the Lower Quinton side, the illumination from the tall lamps casting its yellow outlines over her silhouette but keeping secrets, still.

At the top of the steps, she crossed the road bridge over the canal to the other side of the parapet, stopping only to look at the forms of the two men drinking tots of whisky at the bar, seen through the windows of the Dog's Bed Inn, one of them draped in the landlord's jacket. Serena recognised it, eyes under the low brim of her enveloping scarf narrowing with a long familiarity when he was not a man to be constantly changing a comfortable old coat for a different one. Tock Bartlett, a man of good reputation. Magdalene Kenyon's father, pouring from a full bottle instead of his optics, and winging his moustache with a flicking hand as the two men talked, heads close together, otherwise the pub deserted and in darkness.

Her head tilted in thought of the other man. Was he her assailant as well as the same man who had brought little Caitlin from the water? Mally Kenyon! She recognised him, now, too. Knew all of the Kenyon tribe by sight because they were distant relatives, yet not to be acknowledged because of the social divide. Cousins of cousins, these days, but all sharing branches of familial connection from the same Quinton root. Such was why her sister dare not allow her Quinton connections to become common knowledge. That, and Serena's gross deformity, of course. A matter of family shame. Catty had never been able to embrace Serena's ugly oddity. The obscenity of her face, indecent in its mutation from the regular features of the human form, perhaps because it heralded a genetic cause. Catty had always feared the recessive genes of abnormality which had rendered her sister a human curiosity from birth. It was within the human condition, was it not, to require perfection? Catty was perfection. Catty was all that Serena was not. Clever, suave, sophisticated and beautiful. Powerful, too; a woman who had dedicated her life to her own ambition, while Serena had been incarcerated within the parental home, hidden under veils. Too ugly to be looked upon. 'Poor Serena,' they said. How Serena hated their pity for the undeserved afflictions she must suffer. Keeping the anger trapped within. A reason, perhaps, for the rampant disease which had now invaded and was sapping at her strength, taking all her vitality for itself, feeding upon her like the parasite it was. Serena feeling the old, lonely, bitter anger, now, as she worried for Caitlin whose physical beauty was that of an angel so narrowly escaped from her recall to Heaven, itself. For what should have been her sister's child, fate had passed over to Serena. Little Caitlin; an aborted foetus, banging her tiny, finger-sized arm against the side of the galvanised metal pail where she had curled with the afterbirth, still attached by the cord of life, her heart beating and her breath pulsing in her tiny doll sized chest. Refusing to die, just as Serena had refused to die, when all had said that it would have been for the better had she, herself, failed to thrive. Little Caitlin who, because of the man on the barstool inside the Dog's Bed Inn, lived on, in a different place than Serena had intended her to be. Blackstone School was where Serena had intended Caitlin to be. Now she would be at the police station in Quinton. Dear God! Just to think of her being so close to Catty was unbearable. Something would have to be done! Her sister being none other than the Chief Constable of Quinton Dales and District Police yet entirely unaware that the child now being taken into their care was, in fact, her own daughter...the child she had never wanted but which Serena had secretly kept. Happily so, until to continue had become an impossible wish. Caitlin had, in recent months, become so very naughty and difficult to contain.

Under the bridge lamps was where she found the mobile from her pocket. She scrolled to find the number so very rarely used. Little point when, as expected, her whispered explanations and pleas for help were refused. As she had known they would be with CC, in his self indulgence, drunk or sober. What use was a drunken man at any time, let alone one such as this? Incapable in his intoxication of understanding the dreadful predicament they were in. For his name, as well as Serena's, were on the forms she had been taking with her to Blackstone School. C. C. Watson named as Caitlin's father. For once Serena's illness took its toll, someone would have to accept responsibility for her. Though, maybe, that might happen now, sooner, rather than later!

Unless, there was something to be done! Surely, something might be done to get little Caitlin back before she could go look for *the lady with the golden trumpet*. It had been Caitlin's way of giving Catty a name other than *mother*, a name so apt when it described Katrina Collins perfectly, to Serena's mind. A name that only a child could invent with such accurate information for Catty was in all ways *the lady with the golden trumpet*, a woman blessed with a big voice and such self importance!

Taking the most direct route homeward now meant going down the steps on the other side of the bridge to gain the alternated towpath which led to the gate to the playing fields and the pathways to Lower Quinton. As she went, Serena kept her head down in collusion with her thoughts, dragging the rumbling trolley over uneven, root infested pathways in the night dark of a park where tree boughs whipped newly laden branches in harmony with the gathering wind, its whistling music playing loudly, tossing notes of sound as the branches swung close to her bowed head, as if she was walking up and down the crochets and quavers of the same sheet of music; tragic and sweeping and wild like her feelings. So impossibly fearful that she felt as if her heart was about to shatter from its crescendos as she walked around the reed-filled lake. At its

26

circumference, shining yellowish silver in the moonlight, like a giant, on-looking eye with its island centre as dark as a distended pupil beyond which lies the knowing mind.

Within the centre was the reed-filled place, where a pair of nesting, white swans might yet come again with the summer. Serena had a desperate hope in her heart that they would return. For this place had been where they had known the cruelty of those who would come to run them through with spears, kill their signet, and drive them to live in fear within the reeds and bracken of the island. Serena had seen them rise before the moon and spread their long necks against the winds which would carry them on their painful journey to some other place. A symbol of hope in the midst of despair for they had survived despite their broken wings. Within her mind, she was as one with them, now, as she watched the buffeting wind scud the bright waters of the mere under the sweeping oars of the sailing moon. For this had been the place where her own end had started. For here was the bandstand, over to the far right of the parkland, where the bandsmen came to play on lazy, late summer days just before the swans departed. This place where, in her foolishness, Serena had revealed to Caitlin the true facts of her birth as Catty had played upon her beautiful golden trumpet and the seeds of change had been planted in little Caitlin's head. "Caitlin! Caitlin!" Some things, once done, can never be undone.

Her home was but a short walk from the gates of the old, derelict park. Across from the park railings, on the opposite side of the street. A house mid-row of a terrace where now the lights of evening had been turned off, all in darkness and the drapes at upper windows drawn.

Serena let herself into her home using the key from under a plant pot. Her own lights were not switched on until after her downstairs curtains had been drawn. Such rules being those that had governed her own childhood as well as Caitlin's. No one must see in as she disrobed and then went below to the place where so much joy and happiness had been won and was, now, cruelly lost unless some way might be found to avoid the inevitable. What must be avoided, at all cost, was her sister finding out.

It was within the same street, some thirty minutes after the attack, no lights apparent, now, in her house; the street in darkness save for the streetlamps, that her attacker stood by her gate with a damp, used paper tissue in his hand. With him, a large, stocky, Bull Mastiff shared the lead which passed between them. It sat, now that its task was done, to denote that the scent which the dog had followed was within. The squat, grey, muscle-bound, short-haired dog had followed her home, using the scent from a dropped tissue, bringing its master with it. It panted on a hunger pain in its belly with its tongue lolling out as its owner considered his thoughts, noted details of the house, looked up at the curtain-less, boarded-up, upstairs windows and the general air of poverty to be seen in a once proud street. The man noted her address as 34, Park Road, Lower Quinton. In his pocket were her money and the crucifix. He had stashed the handbag with its bulk of papers in the waste bin behind the Dog's Bed Inn; papers within that might, now, tell him who she was and just what it was had prevented her from waiting upon the arrival of the police. Strange behaviour under the circumstances. The woman had something to hide.

As it was, behind the boarded-up bedroom windows, while ignorant of having been followed home, Serena Collins hardly slept.

Three

Gina Mon had been called out in the early hours of the morning to help identify and provide for the immediate needs of an abandoned and severely abused...indeed, lucky to be alive!...child, who, despite seeming to be old enough to know her name and address and be able to recite it, remained mute to who she was. As the Child Welfare social worker on night duty for that week, it was her shout. She had been called out by the Night Duty Doctor who had examined the child at the station.

She was not alone as she parked in the lamp lit street to the front of the building in the early hours of the morning, herself in a metered space which would not require feeding until nine a.m., her trusty Fiat Punto looking glad of the relaxation as it rested on small tyres and sagged under rusting wheel arches . The other woman parking her very shiny four by four in a space reserved entirely for her convenience, where no parking warden dare approach, had about her uniformed bearing an air of prosperous authority. The white painted letters on the tarmac to the side of the building, over which the other vehicle purred quietly before the creaking handbrake was applied, should have stated the space to be reserved for the Chief of Police but, thanks to the ministrations of some clever dick with a pot of black paint, now proclaimed was the private parking area for the Chief of --lice.

Their differences of dress, bearing and importance were obvious to Gina as she prepared to enter the building with a canvas bag slung over her shoulder. The other woman would be marching inside with a black leather briefcase brought off the polished black leather seats to the rear of the top-of-the-range Range Rover where another small case declared that, perhaps, she would not be going straight home that evening. Gina, considerably younger also, had a scuffed leather jacket on the back seat of her battered Punto. She wore jeans and white trainers where the other woman looked crisply starched and smart in her navy blue uniform, with polished brogues over unsnagged, black tights. The tightness of the belt about her thickening waist the only indication that this other woman was passing out the other side of youth and into the prime of middle age.

Gina let her go ahead while she lingered behind because, otherwise, she might feel obliged to open the door for her, salute as she passed through, bear a cold and distant smile of acknowledgement but otherwise share no familiarity because the woman had not a clue who Gina was and, hopefully, never would. In the nine years that Catty Collins had been referred to as Ma'am by her Uncle Simon Mon; Desk Sergeant on night duty within, she had caused him for the first time since he had been awarded the Baton of Honour for his training, over thirty years previous to her appointment, to see his own face frowning back at him in the polish on his boots. If he and his uniformed colleagues referred to their boss as *Big Bertha* it was not to do with her size. If anything she was petit for a police woman, at least in a physical sense. Her likeness to cannon being more to do with her fixed positions, the long barrel bearing the iron ball of her will and a highly political mind which seemed to know instinctively where to point itself and fire with deadly accuracy.

An impressive woman if ever there was one. Gina watched her enter through the front glass doors of the building as she, herself, lingered over locking her driver's door with a well worn key about which bounced a collection of pointless keepsakes. Ma'am simply pressed the button on the device in her hand and gave not as much as a backward glance as she entered the station. Gina did not liken her to cannon, like Uncle Simon, more to a figurehead that she had once seen on the wooden prow of a sailing vessel; a renovated, carved and gloss painted masterpiece of mermaid folk lore, eyes coldly focused to the depths of the waves or the distant horizon, immaculately calm, her blonde tresses contained in a net to the back of her neck, make-up discretely but perfectly applied, carving a steady way through the turbulent waters all about her. Gina assumed that, like herself, she had been informed of something requiring her urgent attention to bring her from a warm bed at this time of the morning, though she would remain unaware that it was her habit to arrive at her desk before six and that she was merely an hour early on this particular day.

Neither would she allow the same cold-eyed woman who always wore large, light-responsive spectacles the kindness of assuming that her early presence could have anything to do with the life and welfare of one, insignificant child; the same tragic child whom Gina had been summoned to attend the station for. Not unless it represented a failure on the part of Quinton Dales and District Police Service which would require a cover-up. It made Gina so angry at times when it was her personal theory that to attend to the needs of children first and foremost might lessen the crime figures, eighteen years later on. The lack of attendance towards the appropriate funding of child care issues within the Quinton Authority, other than towards the protection of children against paedophiles and physical abuse, caused her blood to boil at times. She had written such in an article, printed in the Quinton Globe, following an article printed in one of the Out and About columns of the Daily Evening Clarion. Its investigative reporter, Cubby Watson, being the perpetrator of a blatantly provocative article concerning the babies of criminal parents and the need to use harsh, prevention tactics if they were not to grow up emulating their parents. In his opinion, the innocent infants should be fitted with a tracking device from birth; an implant which would keep track of their whereabouts like a GPS system, as if a newborn might be guilty of inadequacy and criminal intent from the moment of their birth. Such unfair discrimination had prompted her reply through his main competitor, The Globe Weekly News.

And so war had been declared. He had broadsided her retaliation that children should not be treated as dogs with the results of a so-called independent survey of his readership which voted, in the main, in favour of making lepers out of children before any disease was present. She had quickly realised that he had been deliberately provoking controversy to sell newspapers but only when it was all too late and she had allowed herself to be used as part of his personal promotion campaign. He was using her anger to raise the profile of his family-owned newspaper; a fact only realised when they shared a ten minute debate on a local radio programme with the presenter a disappointed referee to a one-sided contest. Gina had been so overawed and incapable of rising to the occasion that she had hardly been able to speak. Her cheeks still burned red with recall of how he had wiped the floor with her, not because her arguments were not watertight but because she had lost her confidence under the pressure of the occasion. Tongue-tied hardly described her incapacity of speech when it mattered most to her. She had been unable to find the words to counteract his incitement of what he put forward as the opinion of the greater mass of law abiding people which, to Gina, went against the desperate needs of the very children she sought at all times, through the vocation of her work, to protect. The bible she preached from being her own At Risk Register which was full of the names and addresses of children in crisis, mainly designated within families in problem areas such as the Dog's Bed Estate. While child abuse, in general...kept better hidden under more expensive covers in the higher social classes might run like a fault through the whole of the fabric of society...the Dog's Bed Estate was still the way she steered her car most days, ever on the lookout for children kept off school to hide their bruises, left out to wander unsafe streets in the rain, locked into filthy bedrooms at night without any food or clean and adequate clothing. Neglected and abused and battered urchins who deserved no higher level attention than that of a struggling team of poorly paid social workers of inadequate numbers to try to combat the worst of it. Never enough money in the budgets, placements bursting at the seams and too many politically correct PR men wanting to pretend that Quinton

Dales was a crime free, drug free, slum free environment with a hundred percent employment, backed up by the powers that be. Part of Catty Collins's job being to make the pretences necessary to justify her role; falsify the figures, do a bit of creative accounting when it came to producing the facts and figures presented to her own Police Board as the benchmarks upon which her performance might be judged. It was a fine balance between upping the rates of detection using the crime prosecution figures and, at the same time, showing her constabulary to be effective, and the crime prevention measures in place. This when, Gina knew, a lot of Lower Quinton residents no longer called the police to more minor incidents of lawlessness within their homes and immediate neighbourhoods. This because of all the attention it brought upon themselves; the residents of the Dog's Bed Estate being the ones least willing to attract any form of police notice for the most obvious of reasons.

She hated to admit it but on some issues her arch enemy, Cubby Watson, had a sharper stick to poke the fat, parlour cats of Quinton with, than any of the other local papers had. And did! The trouble being that in his vitriolic obsession with pulling the rugs from under the feet of local politicians, service providers and fund managers, he was in danger of toppling the very walls on the flimsy house of cards which was all they had to shelter under. The man was a fool and an idiot. A dangerous idiot at that! Incapable of appreciating the bigger picture. Out for his own ambitious, selfish ends and no one else's. What had he had the effrontery to call her? *Nursey-Nursey!* With a first aid kit, doling out sticking plasters, dishing out aspirin and dabbing the spreading sores of society with a small bottle of iodine. All to try to make it better for the poor things!

He had caused her blood to boil and especially when his words carried clout. If anything their fund managers had used the same attitudes to reduce, not increase, her budget as if the effectiveness of their various teams were in question. This by a man who, without qualification, referred to himself as the *People's Champion*. This when, already, her own department had not the money to provide all the care that was needed in a place like Lower Quinton which was like a dry, thirsty sponge of public need. The single placement and supervision of a 'looked after child' often costing many tens of thousands a year. More if their needs had to be catered for outside the local authority. Authorities simply did not have the money to pay.

What he paid no heed to, and this was a personal rather than a professional opinion of Gina's, was that empathy and understanding could sometimes do what ample budgets and a sharp surgeon's knife could not.

The pure and simple seeds of tolerant kindness, Gina had long marvelled, could heal from within as long as the recipient was of a mind to receive the comforting balm and allow help to be given. Such as that offered to the deprived children of Lower Quinton and, particularly, those of the Dog's Bed Estate, in grains of hope, no bigger than grains of rice but which might swell and swell given the right conditions to something worthwhile. Simple help and kindness such as that which she strived daily to offer through her own efforts and the ministrations of Magdalene Kenyon, who worked with Father Turner, so that children might have an enhanced beginning. Sufficient to see just one struggling plant turn its face to the sun and thrive. Her friend Magdalene Kenyon being one of them; come so far from the shadows of her drug addiction to offer the same hope to others. Magdalene had had to see her own child taken away from her before she had dedicated her life to putting candles into jam jars to offer a guiding light to others.

Not that now was the time to think about Magdalene! And most definitely not Cubby Watson! Gina refused to think about him at all because to do so gave his puerile opinions credence. She cast him out of her mind like balling a used tissue and depositing it in the trash can. This even as it struck Gina, her feet following the same route as the woman more powerful than she might ever hope to be, that perhaps this particular case, because the child was still unidentified never mind her torturer not apprehended, might have a higher profile with Ma'am than initially considered. Maybe it was the child that had brought her cutting through the shallows so early in the morning, before daybreak, to follow on from the doctor who had already examined the little girl and consulted Gina by telephone when he could not wait for her to arrive at the station and discuss his findings, face to face.

As Gina put her own white trainers in the direction of the same front steps as the Chief Constable of Quinton Dales and District, seeing her through the glass doors entering the lift to her lofty office at the top of the building, she brought her mind fully to bear on her own reasons for being there. That being the child they had brought out of the stinking canal waters which cut the Dog's Bed Estate off from the mainstream of Lower Quinton and the more affluent areas of Quinton, itself.

As she walked she reminded herself of the results of his basic medical assessment. Overall, he had declared the child to be healthy despite her ordeal. Seeming to have no sensory deficits other than a tongue which the child had tied into the tight purse strings of her clamped lips except when eating a bowl of cereal. Gina would get a written copy of his report in the morning but, presently, she had his verbal report still within her head, declaring her to have good sensory responses and certainly not deaf, as might have been initially suspected by the police officers who had brought her in. Apparently, she had seemed not to hear their words as she had struggled and screamed on the policewoman's knee, in the van, before the dog handler's German Shepherd had barked loudly to quieten her.

The doctor had observed, as an onlooker, a chastened child being cleansed of the foul water drying on her person and the provision of clean clothing by the same policewoman who had helped in her rescue. Apparently, he had refrained from touching her when she had bared her teeth at him. The WPC ministering, had elected not to touch, either, letting her see to her own needs from instruction only. While she had not been bitten, herself, she had full recall of the blood running down the face of Mally Kenyon and the teeth marks on the hand the child had bitten when he had brought her out of the water. Instead, the doctor had obtained his observations from the way she had followed verbal instruction while offering herself, willingly, to the cleansing procedures necessary to rid her body of the stench of the Whemley Canal.

Following that, the child had been able to indicate choices in the food and drink which she had imbibed slowly, without greed, her eyes, however, watching warily with a scowl that indicated that she was confused and unable to understand her unfamiliar environment. The only word she had uttered had been a barely audible *Thank you* as she had been served with something to eat, spoon in hand and seated at the table in Room Three where all stray or troublesome children with a wait at the police station were either interviewed or entertained while parents were telephoned and their attendance politely demanded. In this case none had come forward.

He had determined her age as a physically small but not malnourished child of approximately seven years of age. This mainly determined from his obeyed request that she open her mouth so that he might examine her baby teeth.

As the WPC had directed her showering, he had used a body chart to plot any bruising or injuries. She was surprisingly free of any marks to indicate that she had been severely abused previous to her entry into the water, except for some rough skin around her neck which seemed not to have disturbed her vital functions or caused infection. Indeed, he considered that she had not been physically abused in any way, with any discernable consequences, despite having been tied into a sack and thrown into stinking water. There was no sign of blood, contusion or bruising about the tops of her legs or anal passage to indicate that she had been penetrated. She was able to wash herself with the soapy flannel passed over by the police woman, showing no specific concern for those parts of her body that a sexually abused child might focus upon, obsessively.

Her self help skills were developed and efficient in a child of her age. She had been able to clean her own teeth. Assist in her own undressing and dressing, using the towel provided to wipe herself dry. She had even availed herself of talcum powder and the brush and comb provided. Her gross mobility skills were assessed as agile.

However, her hand-eye coordination had been a strange mixture of ambidextrous swapping over from one hand to another. When she had been given a kaleidoscope which the WPC had offered to her as a plaything, the doctor noted that while she put it first to look through using her right eye, guided by her right hand, she then swapped it to her left hand but placed it, not to her left eye but to the bridge of her nose and the centre of her forehead, through which, of course, she was able to see nothing. This action, causing him to raise the question of her intellectual status.

His report, verbally given to Gina, on the telephone some half hour before when she was still trying to shake the sleep from her head, had indicated no conclusions other than that the child appeared from initial, superficial examination not to have suffered from her time under the water. A considerable time in the water, in fact, from the time the anonymous call had been reported to the time when Mally Kenyon had pulled her out.

Mally Kenyon, of all people! The Kenyons, as a clan, were well known to Gina. That time having been assessed as more than the five or so minutes it had taken, with the blue lights flashing on the dog handler's van, to get to the stated bridge in Lower Quinton and then make a torch light investigation in order to find her. The very surprising and remarkable lack of water within her lungs he had put down to the instinctive responses of any small child to hold its breath in water, without panic. If the large, cloth doll had been held under her chin when she had entered the water it was possible that her head had been floating on an air bubble long enough for her to take in enough oxygen before her body weight had taken her under. She would not have been able to stand in the short sack, it had been assumed on inspection of the same, that having been brought back to the station with the doll as evidence though the string which bound it had been cast away by Mally Kenyon. All in all, what might have ended as a murder enquiry...child murder to be exact!... would become one of locating a possible paedophile or child abductor who had sought to silence the only person who could give evidence against him: the child herself!

All this to the forefront of Gina's mind as she pushed open the cold glass door of the station and ventured within seeing nothing out of the way for an early Wednesday morning in an average town in central, northern England. Even having a child howling in a corner of the large, rangy, closed mouthed, modern building was nothing new even at this time of day. A noise which travelled from beyond the closed door she would go through as soon as her police sergeant uncle, on the desk, presently trying to cope with the drunk who had sprawled himself over his counter and was mumbling something about having been locked out of his house, caught her eye and winked. Almost five in the morning and knots of concerned looking people waiting dourly on the interlinked seating in the foyer with a sour eye to the *No Smoking* sign over their heads. As with all public buildings there had been a ring of cigarette butts ground out on the pavement by the front door and a vapour wall of stale cigarette smoke to get through. Gina waving to her uncle who directed his younger assistant in Gina's direction. She only ever coming into his domain in connection with the juvenile waifs and strays which had been rounded up by the night patrol or school welfare officers. All ending up at Quinton Dales main police station.

Her route was already known to her; Interview Room Three on the ground floor, through the locked green door with a swipe card entry system. Drunks and wrongdoers hauled out of marked cars to the rear and taken straight to the cells in the basement. Reports and charging to the ground floor and basement. Call centre, CID and administration on the two floors above. Big Bertha housed in the pivotal position at the top, looking out over the town and guarded from invasion by her uniformed secretary, Sandra, a woman who watched everyone who passed in and out of the Chief Constable's office with a cynical grin despite constantly asking questions in her voracious need to know which of her fellow townsfolk were failing to behave themselves. Sandra had a sniff louder than a cocaine addict's!

Quite unaware that he was flirting with his immediate boss's niece, the very appreciative young police officer came to Gina's rescue with a swipe card as well as the usual request to fill in the next line on the willing visitor's book. She filled it in quickly using the cracked ball pen attached to a length of string with a ball of very sticky, sticky tape...Name: Gina Mon... Designation: Child Welfare Officer...Reason for Attendance: Abused Child Investigation...Time: 4.57 a.m. If she failed to be receptive to the hungry eyes which lingered on a pair of shapely legs lagged in tight fitting denim as he followed her, needlessly, along a quiet corridor to the door of Interview Room Three where the crying had emanated from and was, now, thankfully stopped, it was because Gina was distracted with her purpose.

As he drooled from an advantageous height upon a brace of impressive breasts clad in a pale blue, angora sweater as she turned to thank him for his attention, she remained distant in manner as she put a finger to mewed lips and whispered. "I'll slip in as quietly as I can. Don't want to excite the child any more than necessary."

His stolen moment over and disappointment clearly visible on his face. The current fashion might be for female emaciation but what a man dreamt of was something else again. Gina possessed curves in all the right places; an hour glass figure saved from dumpiness by a pair of impressively long legs. His pheromones responding to her scent of pear drops with a hint of warm vanilla. It was with regret that he returned to a counter where imagination was unnecessary as a trio of hard-eyed prostitutes, which the night patrols brought in, waited for him, familiar sneers on garish faces.

"Hello Carl. In a bit later than usual. Fancy a freebee?"

He was these days, like Sergeant Mon, past blushing.

Meanwhile Gina's moment of quiet reflection was spent with her head to the door of Interview Room Three, listening. The child seemed to have settled as sobs and hiccoughs diminished and she could hear an adult, female voice talking soothingly. She kept her eyes down as she prepared herself for what she might find inside, quite unaware that she had caused a young man to wish for things that could never be. Herself longing for her bed when she had suffered two, sequential nights of disturbed sleep. This being her week for assuming the role of Duty Officer on the emergency night rote. Already two call-outs to rescue children from homes where parents, drink and drug fuelled, were after killing each other. The others in such a stupor that they had been entirely unaware of the children who had taken an axe to the furniture. Still with a weekend to go!

How she entered the room would be important and so she gave herself a few moments before opening the door and entering to get rid of the cold outside air which clung to her clothing and call on her own inner quietness. The latter not always a fully stocked resource despite her strivings to keep her inner larder of calm replenished. She could not recall the last time she had filled the bath with water softening salts or foam, lit the tea lights and had Josh Groben all to herself for a half hour or more. She could not afford massages and needed all her energy to do her job instead of wasting it at the gym or running the streets at dawn, though such a release of tension might have sometimes helped her to bring a more tranquil attitude towards some of the barbarian cruelties inflicted on children which, day after day, she had to cope with, with as much calm as she could muster.

Bringing her own anger before the distressed children she sought to protect was not a good way to deal with their problems or situations. It exacerbated rather than soothed. Passion never calmed or cured anything, she knew, and Gina carried as much emotional baggage of her own around with her as everyone else did. One of her oft heard carps being that if she didn't care about the lost and abused children placed in her care, no one else would. Indeed this was Gina's vanity. She saw herself as the dispenser of the burning candles in jam jars, much like Magdalene Kenyon, leading a way out of cruelty and despair. Suffer the little children to come unto me.

Like the child fished out of a stinking cut. The same child as the one now before her as she quietly slipped inside an overly warm, brightly lit room then closed the door behind her. Creeping and avoiding eye contact yet acutely aware of the child whose wet eyes were momentarily distracted from the same WPC who had brought her to the station. She was engaged in what appeared to be an attempt to entertain her with a collection of small dolls. In fact, the dolls were the props of most Child Protection Officers to wheedle information in a way in which a child might remain unaware of as interrogation. From the look on the child's unhappy face, for the moment, she was having none of it.

The same WPC of Mally Kenyon's female breast obsession, her uniform soiled with the dried on silt from the canal bottom and blithely unaware that someone else had quietly entered the room was waggling her friendly set of pipe cleaner sized, communication dolls just a few inches from the child's face. "What shall I call this dolly? She looks a bit like you." This a blonde-haired doll in a frilly pink skirt which she held in her left hand as a companion to the dark haired one dressed in jeans and a T-shirt, within her right.

Gina took the time to examine the child's facial expressions further. What she saw fascinated even as the child scowled, her left eye shutting and her right eye opening wide to focus upon the waggling doll. Rarely had she seen such perfect features; a small nose, cupid bow lips, a delicate curve to her cheeks. The features combined with an unusual grace in a child as agitated as she seemed to be. Her platinum hair now washed and most probably brushed by the WPC as a welcome grooming, shone like threads of silver and gold in the hold of two glittery pink bobbles, either side of her head.

Clean and well groomed, the child looked spruce and wholesome. The scent of lavender soap and talcum powder was telling of the shower she had taken shortly before while the doctor had observed her and noted his findings. Most probably the WPC's own toiletries, Gina thought, out of her personal locker. Same as the fluffy pink towel over the chair back at the desk where Gina quietly went to sit.

The rag doll, brought with the child out of the stinking water, had been similarly dealt with and was now drying on a radiator, its head of bright orange thrums hair dangling down, its face to the heat, its boyish body steaming as it flopped, body bent, arms hanging down, with its feet trapped between the wall and the radiator. Gina had a sudden whiff of pine disinfectant.

The child with the head of the doll on a level with her own flashed silver eyes at Gina again, frowning deeply with a suddenly pensive look of grave disappointment as if she had expected someone else to be the one to enter, then wiped her eyes on the backs of her hands. She was wearing pink, ankle length boots with rainbow coloured laces, legs bent as she sat in her corner, back to the wall, as the policewoman plied her with dolls in vain attempts to illicit an identity. While the delicately slim child sat hunched over her own legs in her corner, the WPC had perched herself low on a moulded plastic chair pulled up close. Gina thought her to be too close. She was actively invading the child's space and causing the mewing lips and stubborn light in the glittery eye which turned from Gina and settled back on the laces she was pulling and twisting, repeatedly. If the child had gone to sit in a corner of her own volition, Gina considered that action to be self defensive. In her estimation, the WPC was taking an unnecessary risk. The child's body language was asking to be left alone in this particular moment as she pulled the unfastened laces tighter and tighter onto her small feet, her legs straining against her own insistence to raise them, as if fighting her own compulsions. Body taut. Head low.

The child was severely agitated. Her eyes had a luminous quality; one slightly different in expression from the other as if they might be different hues of a very light grey; one almost silver and the other matt pewter.

The WPC put forward the same doll which the child had frowned upon with her left eye closed again, the right one held wide, almost silver in colour. As if seeming to look with both eyes working independently of its partner, she turned her head to present her left eye as wider than the other. Gina wondered whether she had a problem of vision to resort to this unusual behaviour. This eye was darkly wary, too, but not as aggressively focussed as the right one. Then she turned her head again, shutting her right eye and opening her left, her expression altering as she did so, from anger to calmer concern and then back again. This, she did repeatedly as the dolls were shoved at her and waggled to attain her attention.

As if entirely unaware of the child's distress, or perhaps, ignoring it, the WPC presented the doll in her left hand and continued her one-sided conversation. "I've called this dolly, Wendy, because she was found in the water on a windy night at Bridge Twenty-Eight of the Whemley Canal. That's her address if anyone asks her for it. Her name's Wendy Bridgewater. Which dolly do you want to be? This with no name or this one I've called Wendy."

The child presented her left eye as the one leading her decision-making before she put a tentative, left hand, index finger out to the pipe cleaner doll with a name and tapped it. A smile dappled, momentarily, like gentle fingers of sunlight on the, otherwise, darker shadows of the child's face. It was as if the voice she found was buried very deep inside herself; a very small, tentative breathy voice. "Is here where the lady with the golden trumpet lives?"

Gina making a mental note of what the child said. She slid into the seat at a table holding a computer, a cylinder of pens and colouring pencils, with thoughts to prepare herself for some note taking. Behind her was a bank of filing cabinets which she knew held an assortment of useful toys and occupations for drawing children into discussion. This was where the WPC had found the communication dolls along with a variety of children's books which she had spread around the child. The books had seemingly remained unopened. The WPC had left the drawer on one of the cabinets open a couple of inches. She ignored the child's question.

"Shall we call you Wendy? Wendy Bridgewater then?"

The child was frowning again. Her nod came slowly and thoughtfully after it had been turned left and then right, left and then right again, as if a difference of opinion was being consulted and an agreement made within. Again, a small voice eventually forced itself between small, pointed teeth. "Wendy speak to the lady with the golden trumpet, please."

The WPC, with a flick of her head, now seemed aware that Gina was sitting silently at the desk behind her, switching on the computer, accessing the internet, bringing up her own, personal email account on Hotmail which she would use to write her own observations before emailing it to her other email address at the Child Welfare Unit. She was as surprised as the child's interviewer was by this sudden change to cooperation. The child had just as suddenly stopped pulling on her laces and looked, pleadingly, up from her position on the floor, in the left side corner of the room, opposite the door, at her uniformed guardian.

Encouraged, the WPC continued to indulge a fantasy situation in which the child seemed willing to have become involved. Ignoring the child's question, she presented the doll in her right hand. "Would this little girl like to play a trumpet? We can buy her a toy trumpet to play if she tells us her name."

The child's right eye came to focus intently on the doll with a cold, angry glare. Her head shook from side to side. "The lady with the golden trumpet!" she shouted, now. "You're not the lady with the big hat and the golden trumpet!" anger building. She put an angry right hand up to her own chin and turned it, closing the left eye, so looking up at the WPC with a Cyclops stare. "The lady with the golden trumpet in the big, black case...in the summer with the sun shining...listening to the band...in the cart...then she came..." Then she stopped speaking and turned her angry eye away.

Gina looked up from her perusal of the resource bank of possible emergency, respite homes on her screen. She had scrolled the list for an available place while listening and looking. Maybe her presence was what was disturbing the child, again. Why was she so demanding in her insistence to speak to a lady with a golden trumpet? The cold right eye informed her that she was being watched equally as closely as the WPC and the waggling dolls. It was perhaps an inappropriate moment for her to intervene when, as an observer, initially, she might make a few preparatory notes to guide her interviewing technique, later. Though first of all what had to be her first priority would be to find the child some safe shelter. She stayed at the desk but said in a friendly voice, her face smiling softly, "Hello, Wendy."

The policewoman seemed to resent her interference. Better not to speak again until invited to.

Keeping her email account open she scrolled again through the lists of possible care homes for one with a night duty staff with the right training and resources when it had already been reported to Gina that the child had badly bitten her rescuer. She brought up a suitable respite facility called Roseacre which just might, full or not, take another child of such desperate situation even though by doing so it countermanded its own rulings. As usual, every single bed in the unit was taken. It would be a matter of falling on bended knee and pleading. Either there or the children's ward of the local, psychiatric hospital. Roseacre was her best option. If necessary taking the child before making the request and letting her situation speak for itself while she pleaded for just a few hours respite from people suitably trained in intensive child care.

Come the morning, she would give the child's case her full and undivided attention, seeking somewhere more appropriate for her to be cared for unless the child's parents came forward in the meantime. It was not impossible that the child had left home while her parents were sleeping and been attacked while roaming the streets, unsupervised. They would not realise her missing until the morning and be horrified at the abuse their daughter had suffered. Neither was it impossible for the child to have left a car at a petrol station, say to use the toilet, and her parents, in ignorance, had set off again on a journey which might not avail them of knowledge of her abandonment until they arrived home after a long journey.

Gina was deep into solving what was often the hardest part of her role as a child welfare officer when the emergency respite care units in the area were severely under-funded and poorly staffed, also.

Her attention was solely upon this pressing problem when she looked back at the child and began to realise that the situation had changed abruptly. The child was dragging at the heel of her right boot with both hands while her face took on an expression of black thunder. Then she was looking at Gina with hating eyes. She found herself included in the anger that grew in her facial expression. A swill of fear tightened the nerves in her somersaulting stomach and caused her to sit upright. Something deeply disturbing had been transmitted. Gina felt the hairs on the back of her bare neck stand on end. Warnings were being metered out. Her experience was telling her to beware; an experience that had many times taught her that a frightened child can harbour as much anger as an adult and be surprisingly effective in expressing it.

In that stare, for the first time during the few minutes in which she had sat in upon the interview, she was reminded again of those of the Kenyon Clan with a very similar eye colouring. Yet she was sure that she had never seen this child before when she did the rounds of the local infant and junior schools to do her whole school counselling sessions using a puppet theatre as the props for educating even very small children in ways to ask for help or advice. This despite understanding that children very often had no wish to leave even the most gruesome of parents. The Kenyons, in the main, being more neglectful than abusing, with listings on her 'looked after' children's register if not her 'children at risk' register.

As far as she knew, the Kenyon children were all accounted for in terms of registration at birth, clinic checks, social welfare support and all the related services that families like the Kenyons drew towards them simply by virtue of their surname...cousins, nieces, nephews, sons and daughters...who Gina knew, mainly, from personal contact.

Obviously the silver eyes were a random trait and not a fixed feature. Although most of those who came to the forefront as troublesome teenagers, in particular, shared the same genetic link between silver eyes and wild behaviour. Certainly the criminal element did. The likes of the three Kenyon brothers still living on and terrorising the Dog's Bed Estate as a prime example though she refused to think that her own observations, in part, were in support of Cubby Watson's insistence that social dysfunction had a genetic link somewhere.

Gina knew more about the Kenyons than any of her fellow social workers, her friend, Magdalene, having been married to Bass, the deceased brother, Mally's twin, in fact, and as silver-eyed as the rest of the siblings in that particular family grouping. Bass's death having provided a salvation when no one escaped unscathed from a Kenyon relationship, or so it seemed to Gina, their women folk all seeming to her like battle hardened, war horses. Magdalene had only seen her own salvation arrive through the lifebelt of an intense and personal religious belief and her work within the community. This only after her child had been wrested from her and taken into care.

Not this child though! Not possible! That child being, now, all of seventeen, maybe eighteen years old. A girl. The other brothers being Bass's twin, Mally, of course. Then Woody and Benny; all silver-eyed. All disaffected. All dangerous.

It had been Mally Kenyon who had brought the child out of the water! Accusing thoughts swimming in Gina's head as the child's boot was slipped off her right foot and, using the laces as the sling shot, was propelled in a circular motion, until it was a spinning missile. It did not even leave the child's hand as it was directed into the face of the unprepared WPC with a splash of bright red blood streaking through the air from her shattered nose before the weapon clattered to the floor. Before Gina could rise, the other boot followed suit, directed at the same target, before the child was on her feet and running to shove the WPC backwards so that the chair she now slumped back against was pushed over to take her with it, the pipe cleaner communication dolls, still in her hands. A look of terrified shock on her face. Blood spilling everywhere.

When her head cracked against the floor tiles with the sickening thud and more bloody spillage, Gina had a moment of blind panic when all she could do was to look on in horror. She was aware of crying out as she realised that she was to be a follow-up victim. The child's glittering, menacing eyes turning to her, now, with nothing but a desk top between them. Gina's panic slowing her attempt to push back a chair which refused to slide so that she might stand, the rubber caps on the end of the legs caught on the square of restricting carpet. Gina's own legs like jelly, her arms having lost all of their strength, as the child squared herself towards Gina and made a clear intention.

Later, Gina was to think of herself as a sitting target. She had been stupidly, totally unprepared and in denial of everything she had already noted, this being that the child was both agitated and angry with her questions unanswered. She was also capable of extreme aggression if she had caused Mally Kenyon to suffer an assault which caused him to be injured.

The attack was over and done with before Gina could do anything to protect herself. She was at the desk in a split second, pushing off the computer screen with a resounding crack as it hit the floor, screen shattering. The attached wires to the user ports taking the rest of the associated equipment with it. She had her hands to the edge of the desk before Gina understood her intention and began to push it towards Gina with an incredible strength. In her rush to try to extricate herself from her chair Gina used her feet to try to release the chair legs from their grooves in the carpet. Unable to do so the action facilitated the tipping up and then the toppling backwards of her chair as the edge of the desk ledged painfully under her ribs. Like being propelled helplessly on an out-of-control fairground ride, the lightweight, plastic chair guided by her own weight, sent her head striking against the sharp edge of the open cabinet drawer. She rolled off the seat with a gash to the back of her skull and her own bright red blood smearing the investigative hand she put there as she lay supine, as shocked as her compatriot who was now moaning and crying out for some help to come, quickly

It was as the child...small, slim, female, delicate, seven years of age by the doctor's reckoning...brought the chair into her own hands and swung it upwards with the clear intention of bringing it crashing down on Gina's head, that the door opened. Doctor Tommo Thomas, on his way down to the cells to collect one of his teenage runaways from the secure unit of Greengates House, caught an arcing chair leg just as the angry child would have brought it full down on Gina's prostate form. Never in her life before had Gina been more pleased to see anyone. It was Tommo who saved her from the angry aggression of a seven year old child. She would be eternally grateful as he used his expertise to control and contain, through restraint, a child who would have attacked him the same.

Four

Upstairs at the very top of the building the Chief of Police for Quinton Dales and District was at her desk reading, with some horror, the copies of the reports of the police dog handler and the WPC who, to her astounded disbelief, had fished a small, seven year old girl from a fetid sewer where she had been thrown to drown and done nothing more than bring her back to the station, clean her up, ply her with refreshment, call a doctor to examine her and an emergency-placement social worker to arrange for her temporary care. This when there remained loose a demented and highly dangerous paedophile who had struck once and was highly likely to do so again. No immediate reinforcements having been called for. No guard put on duty at the crime scene to ensure that any evidence remained uncontaminated. The crime scene should have been cordoned off, footprints examined and other necessary forensic investigations ordered, even if they would have to wait for daylight. Why had no action been taken to assure the area of a police presence when news got around the Dog's Bed Estate? Something visible through sitting room windows such as men patrolling the streets, even if they did have to go in twos in that area with a dog for protection, while an appropriate and rigorous investigation got underway?

While reports had been made they had not been processed but had got stuck into an absentee's in-tray. There should by now have been a Rapid Response Team in place and operational. It took little for her imagination to work out what the critics would make of it. If there was one thing to arouse the anger of the residents of the Dog's Bed Estate more than anything else, it was child cruelty even when their kids ran around neglected and unsupervised, got clattered about the head on a regular basis for just being a nuisance and were allowed to stay up till the early hours of the morning. They would, in the morning, when the news spread like wildfire, be like baying dogs, out for the kill.

At this time Catty Collins was firmly of the opinion that the child could only be one of the offspring of one of the many feckless families living on the Dog's Bed Estate. Parents not even aware of the child's predicament when no one had come forward to claim her. The type of people, however, the press liked to support as underdogs victimised by police discrimination. Had a child been found in the Upper Quinton area, it would have been different, they would say accusingly. The police would have been overrunning the place, turning every stone looking for evidence and poking every bush to winkle out anyone hiding in the undergrowth.

The press would have a field day and quite rightly so. No matter her personal opinion, the police had a duty to provide protection without prejudice. This awful, repulsive crime had to have happened there, hadn't it? The very place she would have gladly put a time bomb under, given her own way. Even while she had had enough of Cubby Watson's inciting clap-trap in the Clarion newspaper, she privately agreed with him on some things. The thought of placing ASBOs on whole families at a time if the law would but let her, was vastly pleasing, so saving the taxpayer a great deal of money when yet another single-handed, petty crime spree followed in father's footsteps. So dissipating her manpower and budgets which might, otherwise, have been directed towards the real, hardened criminals who fed upon the very weakest of society in the first place.

Catty Collins was heartily sick and tired of the lawlessness of the place and its never ending drain on her resources. She had become a parrot in her debates with local counsellors with repeated appeals for the slum to undergo some radical architectural restructuring. Better still total demolition, with a divide and conquer intention. It had become almost inaccessible in terms of effective policing without her officers being stoned by the estate children, spat at and ridiculed within the warrens of alleys and backstreets and the tight enclaves of the buildings, particularly the high rises which allowed runaway villains impenetrable escape routes. Time and time again, false alarms raised. Time and time again, police cars petrol bombed while her officers were within a house, following up an enquiry. Time and time again, her own position compromised when she dare not speak in a discriminatory manner about the problems endemic to that locality to the press. Dare not respond to the likes of Cubby Watson and his constant stream of vitriolic criticism against the police...the fire brigade...the hospital trusts...housing departments...counsellors and the dignitaries who ran the authority. It would have been like giving him a tin opener to tear a jagged opening into the lid of a can of wriggling worms which, as long as she did not reply to his demands, had a chance of remaining both shelved and unopened. The man was like a mosquito feeding on her flesh; a disease carrying insect and just as irritating.

Expecting what? She knew what...heads on chopping blocks, that was what! Even while at the same time knowing that like the manager of any football club she was only as good as her weakest team player. It was she who would carry the blame. In this case the blame for a child being thrown like a sack of garbage into a stinking ditch, probably by one of the many paedophiles in the area already known to police but still with rights concerning non-harassment. Either that or cruel torturing from a gang of children from the estate when the child had presented herself to them, alone and defenceless.

And nothing done about it! It could cost her her job whether she had been informed of the incident at the time of its discovery, or not, unless she could turn the situation around so that it looked as if the police had been involved and actively at work from the very beginning.

She was pacing her office carpet even as she demanded the dog handler and the WPC's immediate presence along with that of the Rapid Response Team Organiser, whose job it should have been to tick-box the incident against a list of specified criteria, come to the conclusion that a heinous crime had been committed which called for a Rapid Response Team to be assembled, organise the team, equip it, and then implement the required procedures from fixed guidelines, with some urgency. Either she or her deputy should have been immediately informed due to the gravity of the situation if only to be ready with press statements and to assure the public that they were taking the matter very, very seriously, indeed.

As it was, it was only by chance that Chief Inspector Catty Collins had been early at the station before the press got wind of it as a piece of luck rarely afforded. Thoughts of Cubby Watson with a dagger raised at her back causing her breath to rattle in her throat, eyes to go heavenward and her head to shake while saying a quiet, "Thank You!"

She had been in early and at her desk in order to trawl through left-over paperwork, scan the incident sheets for trends, sign documents and write memos...her work, in the main, a sixteen hour a day commitment...before leaving for a conference in the south of England where she might have taken an opportunity for a much needed break, played some music as the best relief from stress, with old friends, before travelling back home, refreshed and ready to take up her commitments again. She could not relax in Quinton even if she did occasionally play her trumpet with the local police band at formal functions. The friends she enjoyed most, being the former band members she no longer had time to be in regular contact with from her days with the Met, before her appointment as Chief Constable in the very place that she had been raised in. Her job was, these days, of necessity, a lonely position of total responsibility. Katrina Collins had worked her way up from the very bottom rung of the ladder to the top. There were things in her background that had had to be hidden.

It was not public knowledge that Catty Collins had been born and bred in Lower Quinton and, indeed, still had a sister living in the house where they were raised. All that her curriculum vitae gave away was that she had been born within central, northern England, had been educated at the Manchester School of Music before entering the police force at the age of twenty-one. It wasn't public knowledge that Catty Collins had gone to school with some of her contemporaries who still roamed the beat, not least because she had become known, due to her fondness of cats as Catty, instead of Katrina. Her own personal presentation had changed greatly in the twenty five years she had been away from Quinton, working within other precincts.

Then there was Serena, her sister, to consider. Serena was grossly disabled and in need of her protection from unwanted publicity; a recluse, in fact. One who needed her privacy due to her gross deformities of person, in line with that which had been deemed appropriate for the whole of her life. Or so Catty fooled herself. It was a sad and regrettable fact that Catty had never been able to accept Serena without feeling humiliated by her difference. Serena's disfigurements demeaned her own strength. Her sister would be used as a weakness exposed. The power of her position was all that she had, sometimes, to make her feel special. How could a woman so terribly deformed be suitable family for a woman of her elevated position? If she fooled herself that it was for Serena that she kept her childhood links with Quinton Dales and District low profile, she liked to think that she was doing it for the most noblest of reasons and especially now that their parents were dead.

Living alone, Serena was vulnerable. Catty told herself that it was in fairness towards Serena that her own position should not create a situation of discomfort for her reclusive sister. This despite no estrangement. More a lack of visiting each other with any frequency than anything caused through disagreement, the separation having been initiated by Catty spending so many years, prior to her current appointment, working away, moving about the country to improve her opportunities of promotion before gaining the appointment she now held which entailed having very little time to spare. Her sister remaining in the house of their parents by family agreement... in the same house where they had grown up, in fact, in Lower Quinton...not the notorious Dog's Bed Estate...facing the parkland and the mere where the swans came each summer and where the bandstand presented an occasional venue for the local police band. Catty occasionally joining their number, even if not always welcome, when she was able to escape the more serious demands of her work.

How could she acknowledge a sister as socially incompetent as Serena? There was an element of shame in having a sister living poorly on benefits when her afflictions made it impossible for her to work. Catty was grateful for the fact that Serena was discrete in her habits and careful never to mention that her sister was the Quinton Dales and District Chief Constable mainly because she had no friends, sought no company and shunned visitors. Easier for them both, in the long term.

And then that, of course! A painful, shameful memory, still! The reason being better forgotten even if it still plagued the private woman within. The one whose lonely existence was populated mainly by the beloved cats that had given her her nickname. She had filled her apartment with them and regarded them as all the kith and kin she needed. Regarded them as her children...the children she had never been able to afford herself, due to her position. That and the lack of a reliable man who was able to support, rather than resent, the strength of her ambition and the power of her position. Most of the men who had shared her life, from time to time, having proved themselves to be unwise choices. The last one being the worst. Cubby Watson's father, no less; Chief Editor of the Clarion Daily Evening Newspaper, husband of the owner; his cash cow and bread and butter. When, these days, Catty had no choice but to meet him as part of her civic duties, she had to steel herself even to smile coldly at him. His wife had known why, of course, as the wives of cheating men always did, yet still carried on living with them. Why it was that Catty could spot a criminal a mile off but not an emotional cheat and a silver-tongued liar cheek to cheek remained unanswered. Especially when C. C. Watson's reputation had come to her ears before him. It had been the need in his blue eyes, of course, that had been to blame.

Enough of all that! She had a *Delayed* Response Team to organize in order to make the best of a bad thing. Even as she paced and thought of other things, she put a spoken message into her pocket Dictaphone, stridently given, for all her unnecessary appointments for the day and the coming weekend to be cancelled by her secretary, Sandra, the moment she arrived in. She could feel the storm brewing like an approaching earthquake shaking the foundations of the very building she was standing in unless she managed to make a show of the police response that should have been made some five hours previously.

As it turned out there was no one within the building to actually carpet after phoning down to speak to the Duty Sergeant. The dog handler had been called out again, reports duly written and handed in. It was as she spoke to the Desk Sergeant that she was informed that the WPC in question had been seriously attacked by the said child and had had to be ambulanced to hospital along with his own niece; the on-duty social worker who had come to find her an emergency placement in a care home, the parents not having showed themselves. The Rapid Response Team Officer, who should have brought her from her bed immediately he had been aware of what had transpired at Bridge Twenty-Eight of the Whemley Canal had gone home with a dose of the runs no sooner had he turned in for duty and before the incident was first reported by an eyewitness who had refused to give his name over the telephone. He had not been replaced by a designated person authorised to put a fast response team together because it was such a rare occurrence...both his diarrhoea and the severity of the incident! Sergeant Mon, who had collated the incident sheets, could not be blamed either. He had taken the required photocopies of all reports handed in to him, sent the copies through to their various appointed destinations in the hands of his gofer, to the in-trays of all who might have picked up the need for a rapid response, herself included. Unfortunately, with no one in situ to act upon the information until she had arrived to read the reports on her desk ready for her early morning briefing meeting which, as ever, was called for seven.

However, by the time she had finished making calls all hell had been let loose at Quinton Police Station. Teams were being assembled with some rapidity. Riot gear authorised for no more reason than that it was never wise to attend the Dog's Bed Estate unless prepared for affray of some kind. Cordons agreed and an incoming team of frogmen applied for along with a dredging machine to start searching the canal just in case what had been found in the water was the fortunate result of a dire repeat performance and more bodies of drowned children were to be found under the filth.

Before she had finished lighting fire crackers and throwing them at the heels of her officers she recalled that the child must still be somewhere on the station premises. She phoned down to the Desk Sergeant, again. "Where is the child, by the way?" she enquired of Uncle Simon.

"The expert on juvenile bad behaviour, himself, just happened to be here. Tommo Thomas took her down to the cells with him. He was here to pick up the lad who had escaped from his minder at the secure unit and was running wild for most of the night. Jacko Bennett was apprehended and brought in about a half hour before the child was. Tommo was on his way downstairs when he heard the child attacking WPC Hannon and Gina Mon, who just happens to be my niece. They've both had to be carted off for treatment, though WPC Hannon seems to have got the worst of it. Who'd have thought that a child of seven could cause such injuries! Never mind wreck a complete room. The computer in Room Three is beyond repair, I gather. Two of the chairs have been buckled and the filing cabinet drawer is refusing to close. Blood everywhere."

Ma'am was flicking back through her own mental filing cabinet. Dr Thomas? His was a name always tagged onto the juvenile and adolescent tearaways of Quinton as the man who was allowed to provide the last sympathetic profile of why they misbehaved before the police threw the book at them just as they came of age. Underage thugs, mainly, with an incapacity to tow the line after a great many warnings. Some too young for the kinds of salutary lessons she would have preferred to meter out in light of the public stocks being no more than a tourist feature in this day and age. They were damaged goods by the time they came before her and then on to the local Juvenile Magistrates' Court. Some with such tragic backgrounds that it seemed, even to her, on the victim end of things, that they had been programmed through violent upbringing to end up as what they were; young people disaffected from society, dangerous even within their own communities and often mentally ill.

However, ever after her own ends, her further questioning was to assure herself that she had in mind the right person. "Dr Thomas is the designated psychologist we are obliged to use as a consultant, is he not, when we feel that there is some concern why a holding cell is unsuitable prior to juvenile charging and sentencing?"

"That's him." It was obvious to Uncle Simon that Ma'am was thinking to off-load the feral child they had been landed with. She had been taken down to the cells and locked in, in fact, at that very moment in order to calm her down and before she did any further damage to those very people trying to protect her. He had seen the injuries to the WPC as well as his niece and been appalled by them. "Has a personal interest if I remember correctly. Back twenty years now, maybe more, he..."

Not to be diverted Catty's voice cut through the man's aside impatiently. "He's already a listed member of the multi-disciplinary, juvenile offenders' assessment team in Quinton. I would think...in light of a police cell being an inappropriate place of containment for the child...it would be within our remit to ask him to take her off our hands until such time as we can advise social services of the situation. An assessment of her state of mind, in light of such a cruel experience, would be appropriate. It will be of use to the Crown Prosecution Service when we apprehend her attacker and charges are made against him."

"Or her!" Uncle Simon resisting telling her that there were others she might ask who would be able to inform her better than him. "He's the person we contact at first base, yes, with repeat juvenile offenders who exhibit self harming or overly aggressive behaviour...danger to themselves and others, in other words."

"The secure unit takes them off our hands for assessment?"

"Not seven year olds, it doesn't! Just the adolescents. I've already tried Roseacre and the children's ward at the psychiatric unit. They can't take her. Least not before her needs have been assessed and the paper work in place."

"I'll have a word with Brian Ghould at Social Services first thing. Meantime we'll see if Dr Thomas can accommodate her, temporarily, of course. Greengates House is our only available option in the midst of an urgent police investigation to find and arrest her attacker. Alert the press team to such when they arrive in. Warn them to pass the onus of placement onto Social Services."

Uncle Simon was beginning to realise what should have been apparent immediately she was brought in. Someone had messed up, somewhere, and failed on an immediate response in the follow-up. He put his own lack of action down to skeleton staffing on the night desk when a never ending procession of people, most of whom he knew better than he did some members of his own family, had traipsed, stamped, staggered or sat through the filling of page after page of his well kept report book. It was not his duty to oversee the manning of any other desk other than his own. He hoped the dog handler suffered from deafness and had a thick skin. As far as Bongo, the RRT Officer was concerned, when you got to go, you got to go. Best excuse ever!

"It will be Social Services' responsibility to fund her placement. Under the circumstances, her aggression considered, Greengates House is our only recourse as things stand." Talk about hammering her point home!

"Ask Dr Thomas, if he's still downstairs, to contact me as soon as possible on this extension if he's still on the premises. Otherwise, get me the phone number for Greengates House."

Her first task after she had put the phone down was to leave a message on the recorded message service of the Head of Child Welfare at Social Services; Gina's boss, Brian Ghould. Her mode of presentation was to tell him first of the tragic circumstance of his Child Welfare night duty social worker. Secondly, the child's predicament. Thirdly, her own predicament and her decision to use Greengates House as a temporary play pen. "Let me know what your recommendations will be regarding the child's placement, Brian, when you're able to take charge of her circumstances. No one has come forward to identify her, as yet. By the way, you'll have to be the one to raise the order for her stay at Greengates House. Expensive accommodation, I gather." She would get someone else to absorb the hole it would make in a tight budget, if she possibly could.

With that she had taken appropriate steps to offload the child with the appropriate agencies in her estimation of the total picture, even if Greengates House was not suitable to the needs of a seven year old child with rights scripted in law. The fact that two women had been severely assaulted, and also the child's rescuer, sufficiently for two of them to be hospitalised was but grist to her mill. She had yet to realise that person being Mally Kenyon; a well known, local petty villain. She cast them not another thought as they had been suitably processed, also, via her chains of command, into the receipt of the attention their injuries seemed to have accorded. Quinton Police might be regarded as having acted swiftly, efficiently and appropriately under unpredictable circumstances.

Her next call was to the officer who had now been tardily appointed as being in charge of the gathering response team presently traipsing in full of sleep but with hungry looks in their eyes. Mally Kenyon's name was being kicked about as a chief suspect and Ma'am was informed firmly of that assumption. A possible scapegoat to the initial lack of police action? Ma'am saw in Mally a smokescreen to her force's lack of diligence. It would do no harm to bring him in, use him as a high profile example of Quinton Police doing their job. The man had a trail of convictions to justify bringing him in. Her men were more than ready to tackle bringing in the Devil, himself, as operational fever took hold and the adrenalin kicked in. These were the occasions they had joined the police force to deal with. Excitement was building.

As orders were signed for firearms, ramming devices, back up vehicles and riot gear, there was a growing tension tinged with a tangible pleasure. This was what each and every officer had envisaged as the job they would be doing from the first application they had filled out at the beginning of their careers. It was a rare chance to be on the sharp end. They were eager. She was setting up her skittles nicely!

It was now going on for seven a.m. In two hours she, as Chief Constable had, single-handedly, arranged for what would later culminate in her writing out her own resignation using the same pen and paper presently so neatly stashed within her tidy desk. The last thing she did before ringing her deputy…her battle plan in place and one for which he would be unable, as things presently stood, to snatch some of the glory…was to determine that now was perhaps the time to show the residents of the Dog's Bed Estate her most determined intention to clean up the streets of Lower Quinton. The Dog's Bed Estate in particular, with a police presence second to none. What better excuse than a very necessary response to a child being put into a sack and chucked into a stinking brook, there to drown? To that end, she justified the cancellation of all leave of absence until after the weekend, her own included, though she would have no need to mention that to anyone else. Catty Collins was, in fact, a law unto herself.

She had, if only she had but realised it, declared the Dog's Bed

Sacher Torte

Estate a war zone. People have a habit of fighting back!

Five

By seven a.m. that morning Wendy Bridgewater, for want of a better name, had been officially designated by the Chief Constable to be a suitable client, even if not yet delivered as a temporary Ward of the Authority, into the care of Greengates House; a secure unit charged with the profiling and assessment of disaffected youth.

The unit was never short of clients. Always another naughty boy or girl coming in as the last went out to face his or her fate before a magistrate or judge. Its senior representative being Dr Thomas; thirty-four years old, dark, straight, chin-length hair ever falling into shy gunmetal grey eyes behind silver rimmed spectacles which suggested a quiet and diligent nature. The troublesome hair forever being swept out of the way by thin, bony fingers which had a habit of drumming against any surface available, nails bitten to the quick to express an inner restlessness otherwise not apparent. This usually a forerunner to putting a finger to the bridge of his glasses and shoving them back up the bridge of his nose where they would slowly slide back down again.

This very early morning Tommo had risen before his alarm call following an informative phone call from the local police station concerning the whereabouts of a runaway adolescent within his care. He had been roused from slumber shortly after five in the morning. His ceremonial rising from his very neat, single bed entailed slipping himself like an amoeba from between unruffled bedding where he had spent five hours barely moving as it was his habit to sleep as the dead and then extricate himself from his tomb with as little air disturbance as possible. To that end, he had folded back the perfect, equilateral triangle of quilt with a precise eye to its neat formation before sitting on the edge of the mattress to put on his glasses and take a moment to get his body in motion with a long, silent stretch. Here was a man who not only wore pressed, cotton pyjamas, habitually, but fastened every button and matched the length of the drawstrings before fastening a symmetrical bow to keep them about his waist. His night clothes were always grey and grey was Tommo's favourite colour. They had no pattern to denote any passion or lack of it. Pattern being something Tommo spent his working life trying to analyse within the deviant behaviours of his adolescent clients. He preferred to give no hint through which others might analyse his own, if at all possible, outside of the meticulous order which governed his life.

Standing, now, amidst a room where the furnishings were devoid of any colour other than plum, grey and black and any texture other than smooth, Tommo prepared himself for an earlier start than usual well before first light, moving quietly so as not to wake his assistant, Gary, in the room next door. Had Tommo looked therein, the untidiness would have seen him picking up, folding, depositing and giving one of his disapproving stares. Tommo had a compulsive drive to straighten anything disarranged. He had particular trouble with the fallen leaves of autumn in public gardens, car parks and anything unevenly spaced or unsymmetrical. Therefore, the necessary remaking of the single bed was a series of sweeps, tucks and shakes which followed an exact sequence before all was assessed as being to his satisfaction; none of the long edges visible and his pillow bearing no indentations to suggest that this place was where his head had lain. Such behaviour; the eradication of all evidence of his having availed himself of any particular place, air supply, tool or receptacle, being common to the existence of a man who washed cups immediately they were used, stowed away, tidied up habitually and had a place for everything and everything in its place. If Tommo could tidy the world of all its detritus with a dustpan and brush, he would. The orderliness within his environment being the tool he used to define his own state of calm and wellbeing. Having spent most of his life in institutions with such requirements, he managed the unexpected as best he could.

Therefore without time to carefully fold his pyjamas against the rule of his forearm, checking and tucking, before laying them in an exact formation under his pillow, he chose to leave them on under the clothing he would have to select quickly to get to where he had agreed to be not a minute early or a minute late. That his sleep pattern had been interrupted would later cause him to regret a lack of forward thinking that he should have allowed himself an extra two hours by taking himself off to bed early once it was clear that Jacko had legged off to a temporary freedom, over the fence. Now, Jacko had been hauled into a police station cell and was awaiting his deliverance back to Greengates House after the completion of certain paperwork which would have to be completed prior to that event taking place. That Tommo had slept at all in light of this shortfall to his usual exact and carefully diligent practise was unusual. In fact, he had merely closed his eyes, gone down one floor behind closed eyelids and lain there like a corpse with little sign of life until the call had brought him back up on the elevator to wakefulness to see his hand reaching out for the telephone receiver by his bed. Tommo even slept tidily. His life in its limited but well managed fields being as measured, weighed, statistically evaluated and recorded in exact detail as that of his clients.

Having remade his bed with a last tuck and smoothing gesture to ensure perfection he went to drag his pants from the crossbar of a hanger in a wardrobe that held his only suit; grey pinstripe. Yesterday's clothes now having been relegated to the wash basket or carefully folded and replaced within his drawers after careful scrutiny for even the tiniest blemish.

After struggling into their cold linings without removing the pyjama bottoms he donned socks which he failed to note as being odd, followed by casual deck shoes and a denim shirt with a frayed collar over his pyjama jacket. Here, in the selection of his clothing, Tommo strayed from all the other concepts of category and sequence which strictly overruled his life. Indeed, such was his usual choice of mismatched dress, for while Tommo looked all about at the straightness and orderliness of his environment, he never looked at himself. He had no idea what he looked like from the neck down other than to be very aware that all his buttons were fastened, collars and shirt tails tucked and shoe laces symmetrically fastened with the same care with which he had fastened the drawstring on his pyjamas. This sad neglect being due to his appearance never being something he judged in a mirror, combined, as it was, with short sightedness and colour blindness.

Of medium height, quiet and unassuming of disposition until his need for ultimate control was threatened, a Bachelor of Science degree, PhD in philosophy and a doctorate in psychology lay somewhat preposterously upon the shoulders of a man who seemed to have the utmost difficulty in the pairing of matched socks and the careful blending of the colours and styles of his clothing into an acceptable format. It was sufficient merely to feel himself suitably covered and correctly fastened in as he prepared to go fetch Jacko Bennett back to the very place from where he had escaped; a lad born to chaos, aggressive defiance, supreme anger and absolutely no ability to understand the complexities of emotional turbulence, either in himself, or others.

Trying not to awake the other two members of the staff who lived in, like himself, on a quiet way out of the building by the side door from Angie's tidy kitchen, he snatched up a voluminous dark blue, serge mackintosh which covered the greater part of his clothing mistakes, save for perhaps the odd socks; one navy, cotton weave and one, ribbed black wool, soft top.

As a normal course to his own strict code of practise he left a note on his office desk, on a grey sticky, for his assistant, Gary Silvers, presently loudly asleep in the bedroom upstairs next to Tommo's; the one that looked as if it had been hit by a clothing hurricane. The caretaker, Harry, as the only other member of the live-in staff, being flat out in his basement lair, cellar-deep in slumber.

No other clients in residence to make a night duty necessary once Jacko had made his leap for freedom, Tommo left the premises quietly, going through the small gate within the large high railings and fences that surrounded the house. He took his own humble but shiny Corsa on a short journey to Quinton Police Station. There, he fed a parking machine despite there being no need to at that time of day because the habit was entrenched; not to have done so would have lasted as a lingering worry. Then made quickly into the building by the glass doors to the front when, at any other time of day, he might have been allowed a quicker entrance to the cells from the back. He had parked, in fact, right next to Gina's Fiat Punto; the back gates to the car park being locked at this time of darkness to anyone other than the arresting officers taking their captives into the cells. The large four wheel drive of the Chief of --lice, still where she had left it with its suitcase upon the rear seat; a somewhat careless lack of thought in a place like Quinton. One would have thought the woman to have known better, in her position!

As a familiar face...indeed the one to have called him, earlier...Uncle Simon waved him through and Carl went to present the register for his signing in, followed by the opening of the interior door using the same swipe card. Carl hadn't the slightest wish to escort Tommo to the downstairs cells where his charge awaited, though he had taken note of the strange clothes and the air of distraction which Tommo used to shield himself from the unwanted approaches of strangers. Appraised by his line manager, Carl thought that Tommo seemed a least likely person to affiliate himself with the gross and often heinous behaviour of the youths who came in a never ending, single file procession through the police station doors before ending up at the unit where Dr Thomas practised.

Indeed it had gone down as a first at Greengates House for a client to scale the heights of a ten foot high, chain link fence in one desperate scramble, after which he had legged it off to rob three shops, get smashed out of his brain on vodka and Vallium, upon which sad loss of intelligence, he was quickly back into custody again.

Hence Tommo's presence at Quinton Police Station in the early hours of the morning, the reason for him walking past the door of Interview Room Three, and his saving of a woman from a wild and angry child who had just been about to bring a plastic chair crashing down upon her head. A child who he had quietly taken at arm's length, face forward, kicking at air, bucking and screaming, red-faced and shouting insistently that she wanted to see some lady with a golden trumpet. She would see the lady with the golden trumpet! Blood spilled, even, to drive her point home to anyone who doubted it. He had thought it best to extricate her from the situation so as not to allow her to savour the extreme damage she had inflicted and so had carried her thus down a flight of steps, greeting those returning to their desks after a coffee break with the smile of someone carrying nothing more demanding than a bad tempered pet monkey and deposited her in a cell with the first door open and the cell empty. It was the Charge Officer; the man who had the key to the cell Jacko Bennett was trapped within, hanging from a chain on his belt, who locked up after her, also.

"You usually take them away not bring them back, Tommo," the Charge Officer smiled. "Whose is she? A bit younger than your usual clientele. Not a daughter your baby sitting, by any chance, and needing a lesson to sort her out?"

Tommo glowered. The remark causing him to cringe and shiver. The last thing he ever wanted for himself was fatherhood. "She seems to have inflicted quite a bit of damage in Interview Room Three. A broken nose and cut heads. There'll be a lot of clearing up to do." He dismissed the horror of the disarranged room from his brain; the child he could tolerate but not the mess she had created.

"Better find out what to do with her. She can't stay here." The Charge Officer phoned up to the main desk, to be told to keep her where she was for the present. It was pandemonium up there. They had had to call an ambulance to take both women to hospital. Alert the Chief, too, who was in early. Big Bertha in her gun tower, already!

"She's got the reports about that one on her desk. We'll get a message down from the Battery as soon as she realises that Bongo's gone home with a bad case of the runs and the rest of us are run off our feet. Fancy a char, Tommo?"

"Don't mind if I do," Tommo smiling affably at a man he met with some frequency. If not this man, then one of his long-standing colleagues who manned the same post, on the day or evening shifts, who filled him in with the most pertinent information about the lads he hauled back to Greengates House, usually in handcuffs and attached to a handling belt. Info such as the graphic, verbal descriptions of what had really happened to bring his clients to a cell in the first place, how they behaved in confinement and what they were likely to do when they found out that they were going to be transferred to a secure, assessment unit where they would be the only *guest* for the short duration of stay before they would be standing before the magistrate's bench. The official reports were usually stilted, toned down and ambiguous when, often, the arresting officer had to stand up in the Magistrates' Court and defend his own actions; he himself would be challenged in his own defence. So Tommo appreciated the more lively tales as likely to have been more the case of how his clients behaved under duress, though always slightly exaggerated. It was usually the loneliness and constant attention from Tommo and his assistant, Gary, which brought out either the worst or the best in them, sometimes leading to additional conflicts and sometimes to a complete emotional breakdown. If Tommo failed to have a physical presence to incite the rutting stags, it was to his advantage. That and being an expert in Strategic Restraint Procedures who regularly underwent the courses needed to restrain his clients from physical violence should they start to break up the furniture. Jacko had, only a day or two previously, hauled a pine wardrobe over the banister rail to render it to matchwood, so making the training in restraint procedures very necessary to Tommo, along with Gary Silvers, who had worked with Tommo for the previous five years. Even the caretaking and housekeeping staff was trained in the careful handling of their more violent guests at Greengates House. If they needed back-up, they called in the caretaker, Harry Groves, and when really pressed, Tommo had known Angie, the housekeeper; his own surrogate mother, to intervene with some old fashioned *mother-henning*. Angie could nag like no other woman he had ever known; a sure antidote to rutting stag syndrome. She also never failed to achieve, with her Spotted Dick and hot custard, what he and Gary couldn't, which was a reason for his clients to behave in those ways asked quietly of them. Angie cooked the best food in the whole of Quinton.

Even though he could hear Jacko banging and dragging his enamel cup on the metal grating and calling him to hurry up Tommo had things to do before Jacko would be going anywhere. In fact he had already forgotten about the child and was thinking more of the tea, the offer of which he had gratefully accepted even while she continued to kick at the door, howl and scream, still shouting the same demand, over and over. "Wendy speak to the lady with the golden trumpet. Now!"

Tea drunk, Tommo had forms to fill in which would require signing and counter-signing before Jacko Bennett could be released into his custody, once again. The paperwork entailed in this handing-over procedure being horrendously time consuming. It was only when all went quiet that he found himself wondering what she was doing. "Shouldn't you check on her?" he asked the Charge Officer who was now sipping at his own brew and dunking a digestive.

"Nothing much she can do to herself in there. No loose objects, no seat on the loo and nothing to injure herself with."

Tommo wished he shared the same confidence as the mobile, counter phone rang, so distracting the Charge Officer and taking him away from his refreshment to raise it to his ear, flicking eyes at Tommo and the cell where the child had been incarcerated, as he listened. When he replaced the receiver it was to inform Tommo that he was requested to contact Ma'am with some immediacy. "She's on the warpath, I gather, because no one was available to mobilise a Rapid Response Team to the child's situation. Her in there! Someone tried to drown her in a sack. If you ask me it's likely to be a case of attempted infanticide by parents at the end of their tether. Some folk shouldn't be allowed to have kids. Cubby Watson's got a point, if you ask me."

Just to hear mention of Cubby Watson's name brought a frown to Tommo's face. He accepted the mobile and was told the internal numbers to press. "Big Bertha's got her ear to the floor, extension one, two, one. Wants to speak to you about her in there," nodding his head towards sudden silence. "About time, too! Give me fighting mad lads, rather than screaming girls, anytime."

Ma'am was all charm and grace when her voice came silky smooth to Tommo's hearing. "How fortunate, if not fated, that you are on the premises just as you were needed, Dr Thomas. Thank you for intervening in what was a most unfortunate incident."

It was as the child's predicament was being explained to him in a quietly, imploring voice...which failed to fool him for a single moment...that Tommo's nose perceived a familiar but distinctly repulsive smell. It was coming from the same cell where he had deposited the screaming, kicking, red-faced angry child, now silent. As the Chief Constable continued to put her case for the child's psychological profile to be assessed with some expedience and Tommo having been so readily available, her request couched in language of great persuasiveness...the child's young age and vulnerability...the trauma of her experience...her aggressive behaviour which had resulted in her rescuer being badly bitten...one of her officers, and a visiting social worker, being seriously injured...all to be considered along with the child's safety and personal needs, of course, as the prime issue...in light of what would appear to be parental failure. One could not rule the parents out, either, as suspects to her attempted drowning. Though Tommo in his cynical mind replaced *safety* and *needs* with the words *police convenience*. Even as he set his footfalls in the direction of the cell, where he had placed her earlier, his mobile to his ear, the Charge Officer reclining on his office chair, once more, feet up on a stool, dunking biscuits between slurps from the pint mug of strong, steaming tea in his hand...the first quiet of a night that had seen his cells almost full and the paperwork piling...Tommo had a suspicion what the child was doing.

Pulling back the metal cover over the grill, Tommo made an

immediate decision to take her with him as soon as he could pass Jacko onto the court jailers and then come back for her. The child was crouching, the straps and pants of her dungarees down about her ankles. She was digging excrement with her small fingers from her own backside and smearing it in a ring all about her; a two inch wide ring of greasy, brown, smelly body waste, turning on her haunches to fill in any spaces in her ring of defence as she did so. The look of terror on her face was heart rending.

"I'll take her."

From behind him, he was aware of the Charge Officer retching as he came to stand behind him. "The kid's feral. I ain't going anywhere near her, that's for sure."

"Someone has to," was all Tommo said, a huge sadness within him, for within her disgusting act he saw her final statement. "I'll have to see to Jacko first. I'll have a few phone calls to make because I won't be able to take her without a female care assistant to see to her needs. In the meantime get someone to clean her up. Let me in and I'll have a word with her."

As he entered the cell, on the sound of the key turning in the lock, the child raised begging eyes, her small chin quivering as she stood with soiled hands raised towards him. "Wendy see the lady with the golden trumpet...please?"

Six

It was Gary Silvers who rang the Employment Agency in Quinton town centre at shortly after nine that morning. He was in need of a female support worker. Qualifications were not as important as temperament. It was a temporary post but the applicant would be required to work with an aggressive child with complex and extreme special needs. Some training would be given in restraint practises. The female supply person would be mentored and closely supported by himself and Tommo. She would require a current CRB certificate to say that she had no previous convictions for the abuse of children or, indeed, any criminal record to deny suitability. If the candidate did have qualifications in Child Care, all the better, but Gary was not prepared to be too fussy on the latter. If they could find a younger rather than an older applicant who ticked the right boxes, more because the child would require energy to be expended if her support worker was to keep up with her through a long and tiring day, all the better. What was imperative, however, was that for the duration of the short term contract, the female supporter would have to live in at Greengates House. Certainly for the following few days and over the weekend. This, needless to say, cut down on the availability of a suitable person for obvious reasons. Also, an immediate start was vital. They would be unable to bring the child from the police station to Greengates House without a female support worker in attendance.

It was as the employment agent in Jobs Direct disconnected the call and was scratching his head in wonderment as to how he might go about immediately finding someone suitable to the requirements of Greengates House that Holly Hargreaves walked into his office straight off the street, her clipped strides in very high heels covering the floor quickly. He immediately saw her potential as she plonked herself down on one of his plastic chairs, brought together her long, bare legs, gave a bright smile to the lady sitting behind her and took a copy of Parent and Child out of her purple, plastic shoulder bag.

His smile was immediately welcoming though not returned as Holly, with ingenuity, looked about so that his eyes might travel freely over her slim form while she took an interest in the work notices on the walls. Mainly dogsbody stuff; not quite what Holly was looking for. She had come in to ask if there were any live-in, nanny jobs going. It was imperative she have both a source of income and a place to stay, until she had orientated herself and settled on a way to gain her purpose. She had already spent most of her job seeker's allowance on the plastic earrings and cheap market clothing which adorned her person. The thick slick of her long, dark hair shone with healthy vitality where it hung over her shoulders, tied back as it was with a prim, shell pink scarf. If she wore too much make-up it was so that she might be considered more mature than her years; all eighteen of them but each one from the age of seven double packed with experience. The man, had he but known it, was about to fall into Holly Hargreaves' man-trap of seductive manipulation for no other reason that that he was a man. She wanted a live-in job and he would give her one.

Holly Hargreaves waited a moment while she perused an interesting advertisement for a picker in a biscuit factory, took a quick preview of a caption on one of the inside pages of her purloined magazine and made as if to wait her turn with patient equanimity. When she did allow her own warm brown, interested eyes to join with his, she knew herself to have him eating from the palm of her long-fingered hand as she returned his grin with full eye contact, sat up smartly so that her young, firm breasts shaped her silhouette against her tight clothing and pulled the hem of her short skirt down her slim, bare thighs to denote a primness not hitherto known in the teenage girl who had just arrived in Quinton on the last bus out of Manchester city centre.

The beast already trapped, she replaced the copy of Parent and Child magazine in her bag now that it had served her purpose. He had seen it. Her second prop was the plastic bound, red folder with gold lettering within which she had managed to acquire all the trumped-up qualifications she considered she needed to get her fixed up with paid work, free food and some living accommodation before the day was through. There was something about the way that he was focussing on her that told her that she had more than just looks to draw his attention firmly her way, away from the middle-aged woman in char-lady garb who was sitting over on the seats by a door marked *Interview Room* or the man who was obviously on a stake-out for first shout on any job marked first come, first served. She was about to quickly achieve her goal, even if it had been a hard pick between baby minding, hotel work or squatting and shoplifting, at least until she had a man in tow. The first choice in her selection having come about because at her latest education establishment...Special rather than Mainstream... she had managed to acquire a basic child care certificate as her only NVQ.... a lack of literacy skills being a major problem. They had told her that she was dyslexic; a slur which Holly deeply resented. Only people with brain damage were dyslexic in Holly's reckoning. Something to be strenuously denied. No one learnt quicker than Holly Hargreaves when she had a mind to. The *mind to* bit usually being her worst downfall.

Boring! Not that anyone would have thought her anything but an accomplished student on looking over the certificates as proof of her qualifications in the Record of Achievement she now laid on her lap in a protective plastic folder, as she waited. If she had embellished them with an impressive array of her own pre-designed, computer printed certificates to denote a selection of educational courses passed satisfactorily, it was no more than could be expected from a girl with bright, intelligent eyes and an alertness to all that was going on around her. Not beyond the impossible, even if Holly had never managed to get much beyond page one of any text book and had fallen into daydreaming at the sound of a teacher's voice.

Resourcefulness was, however, one of her most useful aptitudes. If she had changed a few letters on a purloined CRB certificate then such was a recommendation in favour of her own, very resourceful nature. The alteration had been a simple change of Haley to Holly, the surname staying the same, when the certificate had been honestly granted to an elder sister, via adoption, who had dropped child care for flight crew, long before Holly had found herself back into care. If he questioned anything, all she had to do was to say that she had changed her mind, get up and leave. No harm done, was there?

Holly smiled brightly again as if pleased with everything about her and all well with her world. Her puppy brown eyes flashing with bright intelligence at the employment agent whose eyes had lingered long enough on Holly to give her a hopeful feeling.

He in turn, thought that his problem might be solved. The girl looked, from first glance, to be perfect for the job that had just that minute come in. A bit young and inexperienced but the brief had been more to find someone young enough to deal with a child with extreme, special needs and not some old butty with arthritic knees who would spend all their time complaining. A bit gaudily dressed but that was how teenagers dressed these days. The employer would no doubt provide a dress code. Not that he disapproved of the white nylon zipper jacket that clung to her curves. Or her high heels and short skirt. The current, female fashion for revealing legs as long and slim as hers made his journey to work worthwhile, as nothing else did. A man could dream. In his thoughts, he was George Clooney; international film star, not Peter Parkin; Employment Recruitment Personnel.

However, in this instance, Peter Parkin would solve Holly's immediate dilemma where George Clooney could not as, in absent manner, she let her skirt ride up her long legs and laid them together, on display, in a way that only a woman with model legs can. She made her brown eyes twinkle and smiled sweetly at him. As he gestured for her to come forward to take a seat, she pegged him as one of those sad men in mackintoshes who pushed prams with kids in about rainy streets on weekdays but then went boogying in nightclubs at the weekend with their chest hairs showing. They knew all the words to *I will Survive* and tried to smooch at every opportunity. How sad was that then?

"I take it you're looking for work?"

Holly nodded. "I'm hoping for one where I can live in and look after children." Holly opened her Record of Achievement to show him her only genuinely achieved vocational qualification in basic child care. "Love kids, me."

"I think that I have just what you're looking for."

Her corns were killing her. She couldn't wait to change into flat shoes but they were worth every twinge. "Just point me in the right direction."

Seven

Cubby Watson woke from sleep with a start, eyes roaming gimlet black in the early morning gloom over a bedroom which had his innate untidiness marked all over it. There, he continued to rest like a fox within a lair. Or indeed any other sharp-toothed, hungry creature which must, by virtue of its predatory nature get out into the undergrowth and lie in wait for an unsuspecting breakfast.

At this first moment of a new day, Cubby was savouring the expectation before him; a sense of excitement building as he lay within a tangled heap of crumpled duvet, floor strewn with discarded clothing, surfaces heaped up with the clutter of his distracted existence, over all a film of the dust of Quinton town centre which had risen up from the silent streets, four floors below. It wasn't as much that Cubby enjoyed his own untidiness; merely that he never noticed it. Cubby Watson cleared up after no one, not even himself. So many other better ways to spend one's time and especially when there was something about this day that made it feel special. He did not know why; it just did. The light having established itself outside when it was barely seven in the morning shone about the dark rectangle of his tightly drawn curtains like beckoning fingers as Cubby turned his ears from side to side to listen to the morning quiet, below which something buzzed indefinably.

He sniffed the stale air of his bedroom sensing rather than scenting a disturbance on the way. Lungs tingling with expectation. Something already rippling the surface of his grogginess as he turned over and shook the grubby pillow upon which his stirring senses told him that this day would be special in a way not yet apparent. He had a feeling; a gut feeling, that today was his day. A day when he would fly, levitate, beam himself right into the epicentre of his ambitions. Those ambitions being to drag the Clarion Evening News off its death bed, through the donation of his own hard work and aspiration. Give it a healthy heart, a sharp brain and a revitalised circulation.

He could feel something coming like an imminent, as yet undetected, earth tremor. Like a vibration sensed but still not apparent in a disruption to the stillness about him. Tired as his body might be from his never ending exertions of the day before, and each and every day that presented itself, his brain refused to rest. No point, now, in trying to catch the coat tails of sleep, Cubby considered, as he reached out for his pack of cigarettes, already making space within his day for the investigative reporting which was inspiring his imagination with double sized headlines, scoops and adulation. Already he was delegating the tame column concerning the disgusting states of local, restaurant kitchens to his mother even if she would tone down the accusations, water down the blame, use inference instead of reported evidence to tell the people of Quinton what they had every right to know; that they shared food with a nightshift of mice and cockroaches in most establishments and ate boil in the bag when believing their choice to be cooked from fresh...all things his mother would prefer not to know in the first place about the hostelries she frequented.

Telling his father what to do these days, too! Today, Cubby would tell CC, as he was popularly known, to ask the questions needed to shake the dust off the public ledgers to reveal the illegal land sales being conducted by council agents; land which had been designated green belt. Tell him! Not ask! Tell him! This despite his father's title of Chief Editor but, as far as Cubby was concerned, gone to the dogs, burnt out, and wasted. The gist of his days lost in his growing inability to make courageous decisions, spit in the face of tame objectors, fend off the law suits and do what a paper should do...defend the people!

Cubby Watson was a young man fired with a mission. He regarded himself as someone to be feared by the local powers-that-be like a guided missile heading towards their unguarded bunkers with its warhead activated. As lead reporter at the Clarion Evening News, that mission gave no quarter and took no prisoners. Mopping up operations he left to the victims of the sharp dagger he used for a pen, usually with the blood stains impossible to remove from their parlour carpets. Cubby, never for a single moment forgetting who and what he was; the founder's grandson, heir apparent and destined for every moment of his waking life, to chase news, report it in hard copy and then get it out there; quick and fresh, bright and alive, with all the punch of the people's champion he considered himself to be. His columns these days getting more and more vitriolic, even spiteful, as he set his blood hound nose to the ground of public liability and roped his opponents into his own boxing arena. If they did not own a pair of boxing gloves and a gum shield, hard luck, them! Glass-chinned, most of them. Local politicians, civic dignitaries, service trust managers, high powered business men such as those doing the land deals for bribes. The corrupt to fall under his merciless pounding until they lay flat on their backs, knocked out for the count.

When his mobile squawked and vibrated, pulsing an aura of rainbow light over the other debris of trouser pockets, spilled there the previous evening...business cards with telephone numbers scrawled along the edge in his spidery handwriting... a receipt for his lunch at the

Italiana...another for his laundry which he usually managed to drop off once a week at the launderette on his street corner to be processed for him...loose change...a packet of tissues...a lighter put to the cigarette in his hand...Cubby knew that he had awoken especially to receive it. He had no sooner lit his cigarette than he ground it out in the already overflowing ashtray. Knew it because his guts had a connective intelligence in a three hundred and sixty degree radius, like ley lines travelling out from his consciousness. An instinct that he was about to receive news of something important.

That it was barely after seven in the morning might also have been a clue. Also, that it was one of two mobiles he carried for entirely different purposes. This one, lying next to its brother which when activated trumpeted out a tame clarion call, he retained entirely for communications with those who would be better not to declare an association with Cubby Watson; Investigative Reporter on the Clarion Evening News. The names and numbers within this phone were all his undercover informants. Sneaks and back-biters in the main. Ill minded people desperate for money or just plain greedy for what life otherwise denied them. The odd, conscientious whistle-blower, thrown in. They were dotted in a network all over Quinton and urban district, many of them in places that afforded an insider knowledge which their contracts of employment or personal ethics, if nothing else, should have forbidden them from trading. Some people were incapable of keeping secrets, so why not get paid for it!

The first of two calls coming one after the other had his own code name of 'Panda'...a truncation of Police Sandra, to be exact. Her message was quick and to the point, cryptic but clear in its direction. A female whisper: "Dog's Bed Estate. A cordon of men to make an arrest. Battering-ram equipment out of stores. Marksmen and divers there already. Mally Kenyon. Carlton Close. Just come in for duty to find the place in uproar. Ma'am's on the warpath."

No sooner had Cubby disconnected than his phone was irritating the palm of his hand and casting more rainbow beams over the thumb and curled fingers of his left hand. Cubby being left handed in all things save for making love to a woman. Another call which his mind accepted as his confirmation, taking it impatiently even as he arose buck naked from his bed, scratching at his bobbling testicles and rolling member, then up and along his pubic hair line, thin fingers with ragged nails leaving red tracks over his white, freckled skin which the cold, April air, after a warm bed, was rapidly goose-pimpling.

Cubby was itching with his own anxious excitement because all his nerve ends were buzzing as if infested with lice. Something big was coming in! Not that he wouldn't chase any smoke signal, no matter how vague the whiff of smoky vapour, if it promised him a sensational story. If he had nothing better to do he chased ambulances, police cars, fire engines for a scoop. Failing that, which had yet to happen, he would not have put it past his own self admission to consider setting the fires himself that brought the vermin out of the haystacks by making exposures of information concerning the personal lives of the town's elite, just for the sheer satisfaction of doing it. In the main, people he detested for no more reason than that they detested him for his cut-throat honesty and bald determination. The smug and the powerful, himself excluded. People like Catty Collins; Chief Constable of Quinton...a woman he hated because he had never seen her stripped of that pair of light reflective glasses with tinted lenses which made her impossible to read. That uniform of hers which rather than make her look like a bag of Jersey Royals flattered her braided position of power and pomp as nothing else could. Not to forget, either, the polished, hardwood stick she carried under arm and brought out like an epee from time to time to labour her points with. She had once poked him in the chest with the sharp end when he had stood too close at a press conference, asked too many aggressive questions, demanding that she explain herself when her answers were insufficient or, more to the point, hiding something. From that day on, she had become one of his hunted and would be until the day she was put from office, which could not happen soon enough for Cubby Watson; rogue, roving, sole, investigative reporter for the Clarion Evening News. On sale five nights a week, circulation rising. Nobody treated Cubby Watson that way! Caitlin Collins, Chief Constable for Quinton Dales and District Police Force; dedicated to her own ambition, and no one else's, would regret the humiliation she had served before his fellow professionals, that day. One day she would regret it because he would use all and everything in his power to humiliate her, in turn.

Cubby filed the question as a mental memo of whether a cordon on the Dog's Bed Estate would be a legal procedure if it inhibited the rights of the innocent population to be about their daily business. Especially if all they wanted to do was arrest a pathetic no-hoper like Mally Kenyon; a name recalled from his days as a young, probationer reporter sitting in the gallery of the local Magistrates' Court while his mother plied her other job of town magistrate.

This equally familiar, heavily accented voice, made no introduction, either. Code named Hero, short for the substance which made its prisoners anything but. A man who frequently robbed from his own disorientated friends and family to feed his habit. A sewer rat from the opposite end of his information chain to Panda. A sallow-faced, veins punctured, sore-infested skeleton with a tremulous shake to his desperate voice, speaking softly but with ill intention, as if to keep his words from anyone listening in. One whose real name was Benny Kenyon "'S'me! Get here quick before they lynch him. Our Mally. Twelve Carlton Close. Didn't do it but try telling the fuzz that. That kid in the canal. Fifty to be left in an envelope behind the bar at the Dog's Bed Inn with the barmaid...not Tock...he'll grass to our Woody. Winnings."

Cubby listening behind the words, heard the mayhem going on. Outside noise, not inside quiet, coming through to his filtering brain. His mind wondering but knowing already that what was occurring on the Dog's Bed Estate, was, most likely, an indication of public riot if the police had gone prepared with battering rams and were ready to put up cordons. Not second-hand reporting, either, from a background radio or TV set but sounding as if it was all happening in real time. Out on a public street. Women cat-calling and chanting mob rhymes. Someone talking through a megaphone in an appeal for calm, before the call was disconnected.

This was what he had woken early for as he made like a headless chicken to pick up discarded clothes from the floor. Then dress with urgency, cursing when he could not get his socks on quick enough. Leaving shoe laces unfastened. Stopping only to scoop up the debris of coins and bits of paper from his bedside table to deposit into the same pockets emptied the night before. Leaving his chestnut-coloured hair to riot in its natural, tangled curl which his mother chastised him for as if her having the same was a denial of her responsibility in the first place. Making sure that he had pens, notebooks, charged camera, keys. Money, too, because nothing oiled a stiff tongue better than a twenty pound note did.

Inconsideration to those still sleeping, being one of the most noticeable lapses in Cubby's list of social graces, he slammed his way out of his own apartment in the block of flats and noisily whined his way down in the lift to the basement where he kept his car. Using his zapper to speed operations as he got into the small, red sports car with the hood down, despite the April cold, he raised the entrance door to the parking area using one similar and then backed his vehicle out as if the subject of a car chase, wheels already spinning because the car was both lightweight and powerful.

Quinton at that time in the morning was a ghost town of empty streets, green lights on the main thoroughfares and empty commercial buildings as he put his foot down to the low floor of his road-rage-red racer, burning the rubber off a new set of tyres, leaving the tread on the tarmac behind him as he took the direction which would take him to

Lower Quinton and the Dog's Bed Estate. Buses passing into town loaded with shop staff, clerks, bank tellers, and market traders; little traffic passing out in the same direction as Cubby was travelling, his chestnut-coloured curls flying in his own wind. Past the police station, left at the lights onto Lower Quinton Road, past Greengates House where a man who had a criminal record himself now championed the cause of the thugs Cubby would sooner see hung, drawn and quartered than given excuses. Pleaded their case, he did, did Tommo Thomas, asking for soft options from Cubby's mother who beaked her nose on the magistrate's bench and, as usual, wavered from raising the guillotine to let it fall, without mercy, to chop off their vermin heads. So to put their decapitated skulls on the spikes of the railings outside for public declaration that others misbehaving would get the same. Some people in positions of judgement, his mother included, too soft in their thinking, these days. People to be taken advantage of because they thought a villain could be saved. Cubby, scathingly, recalling himself standing before his private school headmaster; a soft touch if ever there was one, cap in hand, head bowed, wanting to titter, saying; "Couldn't help it, Sir!" Lying through his sharp, pointed, little teeth. Damned well could, help it! These days, squirming inside at his own lies even while sneering at the gullible pomp of his head teacher; a man better suited to being a shoe salesman than moulding the morals and ethics of future generations. Cubby's mischief all planned and meticulously thought about before whatever he was getting into trouble for, had been committed. Then, carrying it out with the same determination of purpose which only Cubby could bring to an act of defiance. Usually, some preposterous, seemingly funny, adolescent piece of senseless tomfoolery, instigated by the insatiable curiosity that had seemed to govern his whole life.

A quest for truth, even then, even if his purpose had been a mindless, invasive intention to discover the form and colour of the knickers of every girl affiliated to the enclave of *Nightingale* in the girls' school down the road. *Nightingale* only because they had their dormitory windows to the ground floor. He had even illustrated the garments for his friends' amusement and published his findings with a descriptive piece under a column name of *The Naughty Knickers of Netheringham Nightingales* of which he was now thoroughly ashamed. Especially when he sometimes bumped into the very owners of his first penetrative attempts at journalism. He had even known the form and colour of the kecks worn by the, now, leader of the Conservative Council. Who would have thought that fat Debbie Carstairs had worn red lace thongs with a split crotch and had known at the age of fifteen, already, where to squeeze a boy in all the right places. He appalled that he could ever have thought his fellow pupils would be remotely interested in what now seemed to him like gutter press antics, though he had not been afraid to broadcast the information, then, as he was not afraid to broadcast the results of his more serious investigative reporting, now. Not until he had found a pair of similar nether garments in the pocket of his father's trousers. The encrusted stain as dried hard as a glue spillage had smelt to Cubby of his own wet dreams before he had replaced them back where he had found them, much as his mother had done just a few moments earlier.

He had been an adolescent boy no longer when he had witnessed the pain and torment on her face. Thereafter, to withdraw further away from his parents into his own adulthood save for his adoration and emulation of his maternal grandfather; Cuthbert Barton; the founder of the Clarion newspaper. It had taken his mother's hurt to see that he had something of his father in the way he was heading and, thereafter, shied away from it. Some areas he kept sacrosanct, these days, though people might be surprised to know it. For there lay his vulnerability; his right-handedness, the place where his feelings lay; a hand caught and tied at the wrist because he would not do to any woman what his father did to his mother. Who would have thought it!

With no traffic on the roads to speak of he took a little over three minutes to come to the Dog's Bed Inn, on the near side of the road bridge, which was milling with people at a time of day when usually curtains were still drawn and milk bottles still on doorsteps. Something going on of extreme importance. Staccato noise coming to him and a feeling of disturbance causing himself to shout out loudly; "Yes!" when he saw the police cars on the bridge.

This was the stuff that made headlines. Men with diving suits going down the brick steps to the canal bank. Cordons of blue plastic duct tape printed with the words *Police. No Entry* just about to be looped across the road bridge as he slipped through on a thrust of throbbing acceleration just before the estate was isolated. People everywhere as if the knocker-up had been round every door. Children in pyjamas on doorsteps. Men leaning against fences. Mothers in nightdresses with coats hastily dragged over polyester frills, fags in hands covered with the stains of nicotine while pulling their offspring against their flimsy skirts instead of shoving them away, as was more usual. Carlton Close being a cul-de-sac leading only to allotments which bordered onto the canal. A street already known to Cubby Watson as his hard, black-pea eyes took in the excitement.

"Yes!" again.

Mally Kenyon; Hero's brother, had one of the houses on the frail looking terrace of pebble-dashed dwellings, every one built to exactly the same specification. Each made out of pebble-dashed grey concrete. Frontage onto a pedestrian-only walkway. Rain-washed fences to the rear. Doors to the side of those on the end of each terrace with an extra bit of dumping ground, lucky things!

Hero, better known as Benny and his brother, Woody...all named after the brands of cigarettes with similar life expectancies in ground-out endings... sharing a silver-eyed, fairness. Big men, yet weak with malnutrition and drug abuse and the hollow-cheeked, unkempt appearance their lifestyle engendered. Cubby's eyes sought to ferret them out of the throngs. A family that had come here like so many others when the wafer thin concrete sandcastles had been newly built. They had been celebrated as modern sunshine homes with indoor toilets under the towering, stack-'em-high-and-pack-'em-deep structures of the tower blocks rising behind. When it came to adding the cement to the concrete with which they had been built, someone had hived off the other half that should have gone into the mixer and used it for a foreigner down the road; the way of all cowboy builders, Cubby knew, big or small. They always had a smaller *project* on the go, preferably round the corner which, like a cuckoo amongst a nest of sparrows, cost very little for the real parents to raise in the long run, at the expense of the health of the blighted fledglings which had every right to be adequately fed. Concrete everywhere; whole rivers of it having been poured to cover what was geographically the delta of an old river course which had supposedly got diverted but which, Cubby suspected, had simply been forced to spread itself around the foundations of the houses. It bled itself into the Whemley Canal. The whole place had a smell of damp about it. Puddles lasted well beyond the time when the land beneath should have acted as a natural soak-away.

But then what to expect from a place where the dregs of society had settled like brown, mouldy sludge at the bottom of a percolator which had been used and then forgotten about. Cubby, recalling with satisfaction the article he had once published on how this rat infested slum of dead end roads with grass verges, instead of pavements, had become the chief council tip for the human trash that had been deposited there. No one in their right minds, save for their local priest, could ever choose to live there. These days ruled not by the old prideful, vigilante mafia, but petty thieves and drug dealers, inadequates and opportunists. That bitch at the Social Services office, Gina Mon, Team Leader of the Child Protection Unit, having failed to give the support he had expected of her, of all people. *Little Miss-Nursey-Nursey* in her dressing-up uniform, playing at being Matron in a game of hospital, as milksop girls will do, along with

Magdalene Kenyon whose work with the bedraggled kids and homeless of the estate, he grudgingly admired.

While he had talked in searing terms of demolition balls, re-housing and divide-to-conquer tactics, in order to lay guilt and blame on the heads of those who should claim responsibility instead of deny it, Gina Mon had counteracted by taking the forum offered by the Quinton Globe and blasted him for ripping off the healing plasters she and her teams of social workers slapped on the enlarging, infected abscesses of an estate with terminal illness. Crutches doled out, instead of amputation and prosthesis. A dab of iodine when radical, major surgery was needed. A place brought to its knees by social cancer would be better served, put to sleep, forever, Cubby believed.

Cubby moving on in his head because he had felt like bedding the bitch to show her what her place was, though he didn't like being reminded of it because such thoughts placed him, with full recognition, as being his father's son. The suspicion that he might actually *be* an ingrained chauvinistic pig, as described by the gift of a tie covered in the little blunt-snouted porkies given him by the girls in the typing pool at the Clarion last Christmas, not lying all that well with his self image. When it came to women, be they friend or lover, Cubby preferred instead the types who did as they were told, never argued back, and fluttered their eyelashes at him. Women with blank opinions upon which he might scribble his own graffiti to his heart's content. He detested most the superior attitudes of some of the girls he dated because they seemed to expect him to accord them the right to intellectual independence. Though he had some conviction towards the suggestion that they should not all be like his mother; door mats their husbands wiped their feet on! His father seeming to tramp in his filthy boots all over his mother's clean, inner house. She, always stupid enough to get on hands and knees to scrub up after him. Pail after pail of scummy water as she sanitised his existence to her own satisfaction...inebriated car crashes...indiscrete affairs with women who thought he had made them promises when he wasn't capable of knowing what a promise constituted...sordid business deals...so many scrapes that his mother sorted for him as if she had been put on Earth for no other reason than to bail C. C. Watson out of his own pan of shit. God alone, knew, that she put up with enough of his habits. Not least those which wore black, lace thongs like the pair which, as a teenage boy, Cubby had drawn from his father's trouser pocket. Not his mother's white, cotton boilables, that was for sure! Marriage and commitment being the biggest mistake any man could make according to Cubby. A harsh prison sentence in solitary confinement, thereafter. A total incompatibility guaranteed when no woman was telling Cubby what to do! Not that he did not sometimes think of the irrational, tantalising thought of holding a child in his arms, of his own making. It would have black-pea eyes and chestnut coloured curls and be everything he wanted it to be instead of the randomly sorted, hybrid product of DNA as Mother Nature made them. You get what you're given! Not if Cubby could have a choice. He would miss his own father out of the genetic chain of gene contributors so to produce another Cubby exactly like himself. No mother selected yet, though, for the impregnation. What was she anyway other than an incubation vessel?...a greenhouse? Better still, a cloche would suffice his purpose. Didn't take up the same space and was handily stowed away when not in use to the back of the potting shed!

Where would he find one, anyway? Certainly not here, in this hell-hole of the Dog's Bed Estate; its proper name the Carlton Manor Estate with its suggestions of noblemen's houses and fiefdoms. Mally Kenyon, not a fief but a thief, proven time and time over. Cubby recalling, again, those hours as a junior reporter gathering court appearance details in which the Kenyon name was a major reason, according to Cubby, for compulsory vasectomy or the tagging of new born babies when born to those of a low, means tested status combined with a criminal record, both of which controversial options he had later presented to his readership with more approval coming in than disagreement. One of his first blinding conversions to the fact that sensationalism both affected opinion and sold newspapers.

That and naming names. The Kenyon name ever recalling Crown and Magistrates' Court judgements, social welfare orders, broken council promises concerned with poor schools and under achieving children of which the Kenyon Clan were prime examples. ASBOs, conditions of bail, jail sentences, all reported. Mally Kenyon being one such ...what?...victim not a suitable word...product, maybe. Thinking no further than the next fag, next fix, next fuck, and next bucket of cold failure chucked at their deserving shoulders. Cubby getting so mixed in his metaphors sometimes that he could argue himself about to the opposite opinion of those to be best regarded as the ethos of the People's Champion. Yet never a liar! That was where his pride lay: told it as it was! Said it as it came! Truth, the whole truth and nothing but the truth, so help him! What had God got to do with it? Or anyone else, for that matter? Cubby had the staunch and unrelenting belief inside him that he was unquestionably right in all things. In the end, he would be all that he wanted to be because he deserved to be so!

What he really wanted was to be a newspaper owning magnet just like his grandfather. Wanted it with a hunger that was like a burning fire within him. The newspaper having almost sunk under before Cubby had been old enough to pick up the broken rod which still bore the tattered flag of the Clarion Evening News. For that state of affairs he blamed the ineptness of his father who always had his eye on a pretty pair of ankles rather than the reputation of a once glorious journal. Cubby would repair the rod, splice it strong, again. Raise it high, again, with his own profile upon it. The paper would be his and no one else's. He was the Clarion, these days, and the staff, as well as their readership, knew it. A local journal heading for bigger things with stories like the one unfolding before him and he the only journalist in sight, yet, as far as he could reckon. Certainly no one with a zoom lens camera the size of a bucket to make his own look like a disposable. Front page news in the making was well in progress. Number Twelve already apparent as a mob of chanting women, shouted in unison, "Let us at him!...Paedophile! Let us at him!...Paedophile!"; a chant guaranteed to raise the hackles of the whole community and the possibility of extreme public disturbance if the angry women had their way.

Trouble was brewing and no mistake. The police allowing it, too, even while protecting the offender's front and back gate and the side door, a battering ram in the hands of one officer seemingly not needed as the gates stood open. Cubby could see heads within the house through the windows with the closed door intact and not splintered. Then, maybe, Mally Kenyon would fear more the opinions of his neighbours and in particular the angry women hanging about the gate. One of them carrying a noose formed of a washing line. Another a rolling pin. Another a sweeping brush to batter the heads of anyone they disparaged enough to risk seriously injuring them. Aids to domesticity but still weapons when wielded by angry women; the police seemingly unconcerned.

Cubby parked carelessly in the centre of his lane, unable as he was to get closer for the rampaging crowd and not prepared to waste time trying to do so. Camera out and snapping before applying the handbrake. Shouts and cries erupting all around him. Standing high then to maximise his height with shoe laces trailing on the polished black leather of his driving seat as the women milled about a scuffed back gate that came directly onto the pavement; a phalanx of them, chanting still.

Cubby used his camera eye to snap police cars, policemen, and then his target. Just in time! Seconds later and he would have missed it. Mally Kenyon...could be no other...with a blanket over his head, in hand cuffs, being led out of his disreputable side door inside a ring of coppers and for once him not objecting as he was dragged along by the arm. The policemen with loaded, black bin bags in hands, as if they had been gathering evidence.

Snap, snap, snap!

The women surging like hyenas for a road kill. Policemen forming a cordon to push them back as the hooded figure in jogging bottoms, bare footed and barely able to walk without assistance, covered by a blue striped blanket, was hauled down the overgrown path and pushed unceremoniously into the back of a waiting vehicle. Someone else carried clothes which, presumably, he would be given to dress himself with at the station.

What the hell had Mally Kenyon done to a child to have his own neighbours turn against him, like this? Had he abducted it even when his brother had said that he was innocent and had, indeed, tried to murder it? He could not trust Hero to be correctly aware of what was happening about him when he was perpetually under the influence of some drug or other. It all needed confirming and with some urgency as the camera was dropped to hang on the cord about his neck and a pen and notepad appeared in hand to denote his press status.

"Here, mate!" Called to a passing stranger with an angry pursed mouth. "What's he done this time?"

The man spat a bright green golly into the gutter, face twisted with disgust. "Taken a child...abused it...put it in a sack and tried to drown it!"

"What? He's a small time crook...!" Then, having to believe the accusation if not the assumed guilt that went along with it. "Tried to drown it?"

The man nodded. "We don't suffer paedophiles, round here. Or child murderers."

"Which child was it?" This while snapping the car with its hooded passenger being driven away.

"Taken from elsewhere. None of ours missing. He'd have been dangling dead on a gibbet had that been the case. Ask the Kenyons. Bastards, the lot of them. Except for Magdalene."

That's when Cubby spotted Magdalene Kenyon and immediately knew her. Next to her mother, Nan Bartlett, suffering a barging from the lynch mob about them. Woody and Benny; Mally's brothers, standing behind them as if for protection and looking perplexed. At the same time worried for themselves, also, though Benny's eyes met his and nodded. He wanted his fifty quid.

It was Woody had a large, muzzled, bow-legged Bull Mastiff on a studded, leather collar and chain. Whatever he had to say to his brother, was angry and bitter as judged from the pinched, white creases about his wormy lips.

Benny nodded, looking away.

Magdalene had her hands on a rosary, looking stunned.

Nan Bartlett would no doubt be sticking pins into dolls; later.

Mother and daughter, linked with the Kenyons through marriage only. Mally's deceased twin brother, Bass, having been the link. It was as if they were standing with the Kenyon brothers to offer support. Either that or for their protection. Magdalene was, these days, respected within this community because she had come through her own Hell in order to run a charity aided playschool under the auspice of the church, organise the hostel for the homeless and a charity kitchen to feed those to whom Father Turner dished out a meal ticket. All her time spent at the church community centre, if not on her knees before the altar, working for the betterment of this abject place.

There was a look of disbelief on her face as she watched her brother-in-law being carted away. Cubby spent a moment wondering himself if Mally had that kind of cruelty in him. There was no doubting that he was the most physically abusive of the Kenyons but what would he gain from harming a child in that way? If he mugged anyone it would be for money to feed a habit or his hunger with the same pathetic desperation of the poor and depraved who passed by his mother's bench in a never ending stream. But even out of his brain on drugs, he was more likely to be pathetically mellow; a lesser danger to society than more so until the drug roused a craving for more. What he would need then would be money not the twisted satisfactions of a paedophile. There was nothing within his past that Cubby could pinpoint to indicate that he was a child molester. Still, even the most unlikely of people had proved to have that trait when caught at it. People who in seemingly pious respectability filled their computer screens and private moments with the obscenity of violated children.

Cubby raised his snapping eye and quietly put his finger to the button; one click, two; a rare family group this. Save for Mally, it had never been known before for the Kenyons to gather for a family portrait. They tended to prefer the small, full-headed, dated and numbered, individual, miniature portraits taken at the police station, following arrest. Magdalene at one time, too, if not her mother, though she had been known to disturb the peace on one occasion as a run up to divorce, following an altercation with her ex-husband, Magdalene's father, Tock Bartlett, which had spilled over into domestic violence. Her doing the battering! Thereafter, Tock had packed a suitcase for her and shown her the door. It had always been his name over the door of the Dog's Bed Inn and not hers. She had had no choice but to go. Or so he had been told.

Cubby knew Magdalene's mother more because of the tea leaf and Tarot card readings which were often advertised on his mother's *What's On* page of the Clarion. There had been remarkable occasions when his readership had reported an accuracy that defied logic in her mystical predictions, but always reported to him after the event, so impossible to prove.

Cubby took all aesthetic belief with a pinch of salt, anyway, seeing it as nothing more than an alternative to the unproven powers of supernatural providence. Nothing more than another word for hope. Why should the established churches hold the franchise on predicting the future? To Cubby, it was all futuristic gobbledegook, each persuasion's promises being as unlikely as any other, in his opinion. Being agnostic had a practical purpose in Cubby's life, also. He need not fear the afterlife if he did not believe in it. Especially when what he wrote was of a challenging nature and always strongly refuted by the accused. God was always brought into a sworn testimony, somewhere, even when people were lying to their back teeth. Truth, the whole truth, and nothing but the truth, more his forte as the ethical approach he brought to all things, at all times, to all parts of his existence. Cubby never lied as a point of principle. If what he said proved not to be truthful...rarely so...he could stand up, hand on heart, and state to the world that no malice had lain behind his reporting. He had simply printed what was before his own eyes as it was before anyone else's. People deserved to be questioned if they took public office or made public statement. Honest debate could not be anything other than good for everyone affected by the issues. The issues being what mattered, not the individual. So let battle commence on the front pages of the Clarion newspaper. He would always win, in the end, because his readership liked nothing better than a good scrap. Nothing sold print better than a prize fight between giants and Cubby knew it. Threats, law suits, acts of retaliation, were all scoops to Cubby Watson and scoops sold newsprint.

Now this! A scoop! A first! The Clarion would be first to print the story with photographs after which he would sell them on to the nationals if they found the story worthy of national interest. Cubby felt victorious. Joyful. Gleeful. Sated. He needed to locate where he might gain some information on the child. What better place than the notorious Dog's Bed Inn, itself?

Sliding down into his seat again he decided to drive back there. When he arrived, the cordon had now been removed from the lamp posts on the bridge, the arrest made and Mally Kenyon driven off to face the music at Quinton Police Station, the last of it being removed as Cubby parked his car on the estate side and crossed over the road bridge.

However, the police presence was far from subtle as the armed policemen patrolled the bridge with an arrogance guaranteed to get backs up, stopping cars going out and coming in, asking questions of people who would rather cut out their tongues than talk to policemen.

Something roaring and clanking was making its way down the canal bank, looking like an ambling, long-necked, small-brained dinosaur; a mobile crane on caterpillar treads with a large scoop attached.

Cubby had seen plain clothed men and women walking pathways and knocking on doors. He considered the anger which was present in the very air he was drawing into his lungs. He felt himself rise like a meerkat on back legs to sense what was approaching; a warning instinct which raised the hairs on the back of his neck. The knots of people gathering, were talking loudly and resentfully about the antagonism they felt when the police had lingered long after what they had come to do was over. They should have been following Mally Kenyon back to Quinton Police Station but that was not happening. They were staying on to ask questions yet not solely about the child that had been so badly abused.

Cubby saw and sensed that people were becoming fretful and anxious. The sniffer dogs were out in numbers, too. Their handlers letting them follow their noses to trouser pockets, clutched handbags, up pathways, down steps and into alleyways. It all seemed to be a bit over the top to Cubby. Why so many police? Why this show of strength? Why, if they had got their man were they lingering and looking in such an invasive way at the residents of the Dog's Bed Estate? They had been after one man and presumably got him for the crime in question. If they were remembering that same business and not using their presence as an excuse to clear up a backlog of cases never resolved from years back. There was something else going on, here, and Cubby sensed that it had nothing to do with the child or any paedophile rings operating in the area.

The estate people disagreeing with each other, too. Cubby, the meerkat, picking up snatches of conversation, here and there, as he pushed through the crowd of people milling on the bridge pavement. Some strident in their opinion of Mally Kenyon being guilty. Others talking them down because druggies and petty thieves were rarely paedophiles, they said, just sad arsed cowards in the main, unable to cope with life. Living in a bath of warm water when under the influence or wrapped up in a drugged baby blanket; the paedophiles in these cases being the drug dealers who hung about the school gates and gave tokes away to ten year olds as free samples. While all the Kenyons were considered estate vermin, even amongst those who used themselves, they had never been aware of them selling to children.

Catty Collins was up to divide and conquer tactics, Cubby

surmised correctly. Already people were feeling threatened. Lock-ups might be searched. Cellars investigated. Stashes of stolen goods discovered. Hoards of drugs money uncovered. Criminals on the run prized out of the woodwork. All kinds of illegal deals, trades and contracts exposed and set before the Crown Prosecution Service for the glory of their noble Chief Constable. She would be having a field day. Having got her toe in the door next would come her knee and then her shoulder. Then the door burst right open for a full force, full frontal invasion.

Before the time for school registration arrived, Cubby could imagine a few cars set on fire. Stones being hurled. Abuse shouted. Kids running wild. The kids were always the ones to pick up the tensions first and foremost and react in ways they had yet to learn would sooner or later, inevitably, lead them up before his mother.

The restlessness and upset was still present despite the man whom the police considered to be guilty, or at least suitable for questioning, having been taken away.

Which had come first? Cubby considered this like the chicken and the egg question when he would have to gauge the best attitude to report with if he was to get the Clarion readership behind him. Had the community, itself, pointed the finger at Mally Kenyon? Or was this community aroused to such anger because the police had come for Mally Kenyon, trespassing into their estate, for once with a right to be here and using it to their own advantage. People, initially, seeming to be fully supportive when the law enforcers did have good reason for investigation, in this case. Not so supportive when they hung about, as unwelcome guests, long afterwards. Didn't they have any other business in Quinton Dales and District? Like parking offences and speeding tickets to hand out…shoplifters in need of collaring…normal, everyday, breaking and entering…a good old bank raid…or a quarrel between neighbours that had got out of hand, to attend to!

The police were not going away, were they? Even after an arrest had been made. They were staying to question, poke and pry, strip the community naked. Picking on them. The residents becoming confused and frightened in themselves. Reacting like hysterical rabbits under the glare of car headlights as the beams got brighter and brighter, and more focussed. That's what people did when something frightened them, Cubby thought; they initially became paralysed before deciding what it was exactly that had caused them to feel unsafe and unsettled, in the first place. They then hunted it down in packs; man being a pack animal. Only afterwards considering whether what they had sourced and eradicated had been the real source of their fears. The same scenario as people fearing wolves and snakes and sharks when really what they feared was night dark, long grass and deep water; unknown territory. The very destructiveness of mans' nature wreaking havoc when the ecology of their world as a single unit, was threatened. What was it? The Chaos Theory? When butterflies in an Amazon jungle flap their wings and the collective effect is felt as a hurricane over central Europe. All this might spread to the whole of Quinton...the whole of the north of England...the whole of the world, even. Cubby's imagination never having been lacking in taking his thoughts to the most preposterous of endings.

Did Catty Collins realise the anger that her invasive tactics were engendering? Cubby could imagine the Home Guard swatting in with tanks and missiles if she went too far just to cure the unrest her random but exposing investigations were causing. Too far being exactly what he was witnessing!

Was Mally Kenyon guilty? Or had the excuse of the child being so terribly tortured, and Mally Kenyon being a possible suspect, been exactly the reason she had needed for a criminal cleansing campaign on the Dog's Bed Estate? She seemed to have forgotten that her power was dependent on her ability to take a political stance for the public good. They had lost the last Chief Constable to a vote of no confidence after his son had been caught with a male prostitute in the men's toilets at the bus station in Quinton. The man had been laughed out of office when he was after a major clean up of the same red light district where a respectable woman dared not walk at night, alone, for fear of harassment. Cubby could not help but think that the exiting Chief had been framed by the very people who were there to support him. Those directly below on the same top rungs of the ladder. No other way to the top, was there, but following on, one from the other, standing on each other's fingers, save for the one at the top? That was why those at the top had a habit of selecting their own second in commands from the young and inexperienced and those who could be easily manipulated. Catty Collins's deputy was a butter-headed, malleable idiot she used to promote her own iron will; her stooge in other words. She was not one for the underdog, either, as far as he could see. And maybe there lay her downfall!

Cubby wondered what would happen if Mally Kenyon could be proven to be innocent. The underdog being one of his recurrent themes when it suited; an innocent cur dragged out from under the table and made to take the blame just to appease the bloodthirsty. The thought amused him as one by which he might; just might, see the back of Catty Collins. Yet another interesting thought! Maybe he might sit on the fence over this one; report sides with equal factually. He had yet to make his mind up.

Whichever way, Mally Kenyon had probably been saved from the angry mob of women who, in their fear of acute attention turning against themselves, had risen against him just to get the police out of the place. The men slower to rise, but Cubby smelling the fear in them, seeing the anger, feeling male aggression coming to the fore in raised shoulders and legs apart stances; injured innocence; defiance; revolt and revolution against the police antics in the air like would-be gunslingers taking on all comers. All it would take, he surmised, was a carelessly discarded match for the whole place to go up in flames. The police were not helping matters, that was for sure.

The thought intrigued him as his shoes with laces trailing crossed over the threshold of the crowded pub. The bar was thronging even before eight in the morning, the landlord serving coffee, hot rolls and butter, bacon sandwiches, giving change for the cigarette machines and offering a version of his own story. Between serving he winged his moustache and leant his elbows on the beer pumps even as he spoke, watching the police presence as if he, himself, was being frisked and taken to book for profiting from the situation. He would be an idiot if he didn't because someone else would.

Cubby listened, looking through his pockets for change as the landlord explained to his audience that it had been the police, themselves, who had ordered him to open up in order to allow the use of his public bars as their centre of operations. Laptops fitted with mobile modems for internet connections which were up and running on his taproom tables. Reports being filtered by officers with heads together. People dragged in from cars and questioned. Not good for business in the long term, was this, but what else could he do, for the time being but serve people as they requested? Tock Bartlett knowing which side of the law his bread was buttered on and it sure as hell wasn't the side of Quinton Constabulary, that was for certain.

More than one arrest, too, the landlord advised the crowd before him. They, mainly men, having to make do with coffee and soft drinks because not only did Tock Bartlett not have a licence for selling alcohol so early in the day, he made more profit from coffee and snacks. This while curious people lingered with any excuse to watch the proceedings from the very heart of the operation.

Cubby listened as Tock explained authoritatively that he saw no reason to think Mally Kenyon guilty. He had witnessed, himself, what had happened and told people so. Seen how the lad had been upset and shaken by the cruelty of it. Seen, too, the fact that he had been moved to deep emotion on being the child's saviour when, had they obeyed the coppers, the child would have drowned and no mistake. He had gone home in the early hours after having talked it through with Tock and asking over and over again, "Who is she? Kenyon eyes. Not mine. At least I don't think so."

Tock had stated his own reply. "By blows don't count, son. Them brothers of yours have sown enough seeds to grow a wheat field full of Kenyons. Kids are the woman's responsibility, anyway. Has to belong to someone and no one come forward to claim her, by all accounts."

Tock had seen a staggering Mally go home with his own coat draped over his shoulders, still upset, still enthralled by his own actions in saving the child. Probably the first gallant, selfless act, Tock had surmised, that Mally Kenyon had ever done in the whole of his life. How could he have been guilty?

Tock had presented himself as a voluntary witness to this effect but it was as if they didn't want to have anything said, at this point in time, to divert them from a bigger issue. All they did was make a note and say that he would be invited to attend the station at the appropriate time when they would gladly take his statement.

Cubby, thinking deeply, kept his own council as his eyes swept over the police presence to the rear of the bar area. They had taken over the tables by the swing doors with laptops functioning nicely, questioning people as they went in and out, making a nuisance, being openly provocative. Cheeky, even!

Cubby listened, buried incognito as he was amongst a group of taller men so that the give-away of a professional-quality camera went unnoticed as the landlord explained that the first he had known about the police coming to arrest Mally Kenyon had been a phone call from his daughter, Magdalene, these days an early bird at rising. She had seen them coming over the bridge from her bedroom window, shortly after seven; a procession of fast moving police vehicles, lights on against the grey mist of early morning light. It had been a milkman who had appealed for the explanation of their presence and the rumours then spread like wildfire.

Cubby slipped himself outside the yammering knot in order to light a cigarette then went round the gathered crowd to order a drink from the barmaid who looked at him questioningly when he palmed her a fifty pound note and mouthed, "For Benny Kenyon. Winnings. Banana milk shake, please."

It went down the front of her blouse; not the most secure of places by Cubby's reckoning before she turned to complete his order. Cubby never for a moment stopping listening. It was his skill to be able to listen to several conversations at once, even when seemingly fully engaged on other things.

The landlord was going over old ground for new custom. "I was with them when they brought her out. No way did Mally know what that sack contained. He was more shocked than I was. Tears in his eyes."

A variety of responses met Cubby's watchful eyes; nods, shakes, shrugs, tuts, chins jutted, eyes raised in thought as if the answer lay within the ring of their own halos.

The man standing next to Cubby banged his fist on the bar top as Cubby accepted his glass of banana milk shake and passed over a two pound coin. "Would have if he was guilty. The only time you see a Kenyon cry is when they're bound over. I was in here last night, remember. He went into the gents before you started telling the joke about the man with a frog on his nose, probably listened to it while peeing in the urinal. Either that or he'd nipped out the back, more like. Then next I see him he's out there unable to believe the police were on to him already. You've already said the little girl was petrified of him...bit him and kicked him and pulled his hair. You don't do that if something saves you. Mally would have been livid enough to drop her in again, unless he deserved it."

The barmaid had the cheek to ask Cubby for another fifty pence. The drink was good, though, as he drank in deeply; cold on his thirsty tongue as he sucked through the straw; banana flavour, a favourite. He had not eaten breakfast so, while he was being attended to, he asked for a bacon sandwich, took back his two quid and gave her a fiver as a covering amount. Then reminded, gave her the two pound coin as well. "Keep the change." A friend in the right place as things were happening at the moment. In with Benny Kenyon, too. She might be a useful source if Benny and Woody got nabbed for possession when the police knocked on their door. Though Cubby thought that he wouldn't fancy being in the shoes of an arresting officer with that Bull Mastiff of Woody's at the door. An ugly, aggressive looking beast!

Tock guffawed, shaking his head but, nevertheless, looking unsure. "Nah! I mean she did go for him and kept trying to wriggle away before she was handed over. I'm sure he was at the bar when I told that joke. I'd just finished when I heard the swing door clatter. It was him going out. That's when I saw the police van on the bridge. He'd been in here all evening except for about a half hour when he went with Benny to meet someone..."

"You sure he went with Benny? Benny's a smack head. Mally dabbles. He'd have been more for getting an eye full of that daughter of yours when she walks back home from the church usually about nine o'clock in the evening. Later, too, when she stands at that bedroom window of hers before drawing her curtains. Does it every night like clockwork. He goes out to look on her, like clockwork. My missus reckons he coveted her for himself when she married his twin brother."

The landlord's face darkened. The last thing he wanted for his daughter was more truck with a Kenyon. Not that Bass had been as much wicked as weak and easily victimised. Magdalene, too, before Father Turner had got his claws into her and she had converted herself to Catholicism...sack cloth and ashes...rosary beads and Hail Marys by the daily dozen...head bowed and hands locked together, placid and beseeching of His mercy...praying to the greater power in her subservience. Down on her knees in pious obedience in other words!

She had a dependent nature, did his daughter, religion being as powerful a control as any Class A drug to those indoctrinated. Not out of the woods and never would be out of the woods if she had anything to do with Mally Kenyon, who was the spit of the man she had married, though Bass had had the meeker nature of the twins. Mally was renowned for having a temper on him like a sewer rat when cornered, even if he had never been known, unlike Benny, to thump women. Took up a melon off his own kitchen table, Benny had, and smashed it over his wife's head for nagging him as soon as he had got out of bed and before he had downed his morning Methadone. Then came in the Dog's Bed and bragged about it. The battered woman had worn a neck brace for weeks but then been compensated when Benny had claimed it was whiplash from a crash he had engineered. Five grand in his pocket. The spree had lasted for six weeks before she had the sense to pocket the last grand and skedaddle back from whence she came.

Bass had been the best of the Dog's-Bed-Kenyon-crop but, even so, it hadn't stopped them taking Tock's granddaughter away, aged seven; a dark-eyed, pretty little thing like her mother. She had had to be withdrawn from heroin addiction the moment she was born, having been nurtured by a placenta that had been feeding it to her. Last he heard she had been adopted down Manchester way. Best to leave well alone when the report had come back to them from Gina Mon, then a rookie social worker, that she had settled well with new parents. He and Nan had split up by then, anyway. Magdalene in recovery, but fragile. Nan, not the best of advertisements when she even dressed like Petrulenga. A scarf full of silver sixpences over her head in order to advertise her services wherever she went. That crystal ball in her handbag and never a set of Tarot cards far from her shuffling fingers. She had been known to give readings to total strangers on public benches in the middle of the shopping centre. They were always mindful to cross a gypsy's palm with silver or know a day's bad luck. These days, Nan lived off her earnings off other people's hope.

Not that Nan and his daughter agreed with him entirely about little Holly being better off where she was. The child whom he still thought of as a little, innocent girl of seven with a stuffed monkey in her arms as she had played in the old Wendy House in a beer garden, now, long gone. They had stated that if the child ever wanted to come back into the family fold, when she was eighteen and old enough to decide for herself, they would welcome her. However, she had turned eighteen years of age, already, and still not turned up. Not likely, was it? Not here, any road! Not to the Dog's Bed Estate after being used to the posh life, elsewhere. The Dog's Bed Estate was the pit of all pits and they all knew it. Why come here? Like the kittens he had thought were in the sack, why save them just to become feral? More hope for the lass away from the place than there would ever be here. The shortcomings of her paternal family being one of the main reasons for his opinions. Best leave it be.

His reply was terse. "Magdalene's clean and's got her head sorted these days. I still can't see how Mally could have done it."

"How much time do you need?" someone else offered, impatient with excuses. "Got spotted taking her by whoever tipped off the police. The informer grassed on seeing him as we all would have done. Too frightened to reveal himself or herself. Named him probably. Thought he'd got away with it. Could have had that child in that rancid house with him for days. Maybe that's where he went for that half hour he was missing. Went back to tie her up in a sack and took her to hide her someplace close, like the allotment sheds."

His invention gained another eager supporter. They would all clap to see the Kenyons depleted in numbers. "Before he dumps her, he leaves here, nips down the steps, chucks the sack in the water and comes back in here. How long would that take?"

Someone else joining in with a bark of laughter. "Tock takes an age telling them jokes of his. Works with sacks, too, does Mally when he can get some labouring work. It had probably had building sand in it. Carries his tools in a sack, too, bound with string."

The landlord shook his head. "Nah!" Thinking, though, that there had been this look of fear on Mally's face when he saw the copper looking over the bridge and then asked him over. He shook his head and mewed, the handlebars of his tash hanging low. "Known Mally Kenyon a long time. I have to say that I've never seen him as frightened of the long arm of the law before. Sort of blanched as if the police van on the bridge was the last thing he expected to see. Guilty of something, maybe, but not that."

Time for Cubby to slip away, the bacon sarnie temporarily forgotten about. Then at the door he saw a black plastic briefcase left open. The copper who seemed to be the owner was busy taking down a statement, his back slightly turned as he claimed an easy chair and nibbled on a packet of pork scratchings, legs crossed and looking as if he owned the place. The case open to his files, the edge of a photo a few inches proud of the rest of the papers as if hurriedly deposited between; a child's photograph. It might have been the policeman's own daughter when all Cubby could see was a blonde head of hair and a frowning forehead, but Cubby saw an opportunity not to be missed. He also had the excuse to crouch close to the open briefcase in order to fasten his shoelaces, letting his coat fall open so that he might pick up the sticky print, slide it under his armpit, from where he would examine it later. The policeman paid him no heed as he did so.

He then slid outside through the clattering door, walking quickly back in the direction of his red sports car which surprisingly seemed to have remained not interfered with. Usually, it was too much of a temptation for wandering street kids to ignore. More than once he found them having removed the top cover, standing on the driver's seat, putting dusty trainer prints all over the black leather while they made imaginary journeys via the steering wheel. Not today, though!

The roaring and clanking noise coming from the side of the bridge drew his attention. Raising his camera and removing the dust cap from the lens, he passed on to the mid part of the bridge towards the estate where people were watching what was going on below with interest. He took several snaps while noting that the crane with a scoop on the end of its hydraulic piston was dredging the bottom of the canal from its place on the tow path, to the Quinton side of the bridge. It was raising a stink as it lifted a collection of watery objects inside gripping jaws which, when empty, would come together like a sealed bucket. Now it worked like a giant grabber to dump the rancid trash before the men in stained white suits and slime covered Wellington boots, heads covered with white hoods, wearing nose masks, as they waded through the heap as if to find another sack, another body. This time, a dead child instead of a live one. Looking to find some concrete proof of Mally Kenyon's guilt, maybe, when to Cubby, none had yet been suggested from the evidence put before him. According to the facts of the matter, Mally Kenyon had saved the child not harmed it.

Yet what a horrible situation for the child to have been in. The stinking water struck Cubby's nose as the smell of rotting flesh might have done, though this analogy was provided entirely by his imagination. He found disgust and revulsion rising as nausea; the milk shake curdling in his stomach even while he regretted having forgotten about his bacon sandwich. He'd go back and ask for it to be put in a bag to take back to the Clarion offices where he would arrange things so that he might work on the front page display, between following up different leads on the same breaking story. This was by far the biggest feature he had tackled as a front page spread. He needed to check facts. Find out what he could about the child. Focus deeply on the style of presentation. Choose words carefully in order to write an article which raised questions concerning Catty Collins's rights to set her ambitious sweeping brush to the dirty corners of her own living room, fill a bucket with hot water and soapy detergent so to swill out the places better not interfered with for the present, when she should be putting the whole of her force's energy into getting to the bottom of who had done such a repulsive thing to a small, helpless child.

Cubby found himself truly horrified as he looked at the stinking black silted garbage as yet another jaw full was retrieved and deposited on the canal bank. The child had been thrown into that! Tied into a sack and thrown into that! This as frogmen stood about in wait, ready to venture into the same place themselves once clear of its hidden dangers. From out of this heap, someone picked out a bright red handbag looking like a splash of blood against the white of his clothing. Soggy wet and dripping but looking as if it could not have been in the canal for long. Anyone's guess! Cubby took a snap of it using the automatic zoom function on his camera. He would probably not use it unless it came through as a reference for evidence against Mally Kenyon.

Suddenly it came home to Cubby in a sweep of livid anger as he looked down upon old bikes, broken furniture, supermarket shopping trolleys, rusting tin cans and broken bottles, what the child must have suffered. Not just a few items, either, but bales of discarded junk, dead reeds and an assortment of the rotten paraphernalia which had collected in there over the century and a half that the canal had been an artery to the industrial heartland of Whemley. Now, almost as dead as a dodo as far as local employment was concerned. They would probably be dredging from the viaduct right down the disused canal to the old locks, the pile of effluence ever growing.

How she had survived, was another question to be answered. To still be alive meant only one thing: She had only just been thrown in before Mally had brought her out again. Changed his mind, had he? Or not been guilty in the first place? Whichever way one looked at it, it had been an awful thing to happen to a child.

The child should have been the main reason for all this public expense and police activity, but Cubby doubted it. Catty Collins was after removing the fleas from the dog's bed, washing the bedding, replacing a Pit Bull with a clipped and manicured Poodle and pressing the button on a can of rose scented air spray to take away this stench. On paper, it would look entirely justifiable to pull the old dog's teeth and maybe put it to sleep altogether, but a child's suffering was at the heart of all this. Quite a few villains would be heading down to the cells at Quinton Police Station today which would be nothing to do with the repulsive treatment of an innocent child; merely a fortunate by-product. Was that why she was ignoring the need to find the child's parents? Find out who she is? The child had been the victim of an attempted murder, for Christ's sake!

With evil cruelty to the forefront of his mind, he separated the priest, Father Turner, from all the people looking over the parapet at what was happening. The old priest was readily identifiable in his vestments and intent on watching, looking over the parapet as if looking on Hell itself, eyes open but his fingers working the holy cross about his neck. His large Labrador, happy-faced and tongue lolling, paws up on the bridge, was looking over with him as the priest's hand went to its head and began to scratch at a spot between its ears. The stench seemed to be to the dog's liking as its tail wagged. Not so Father Turner's; his being a picture of lugubrious sadness as he worried for the sins of his fellow men.

Cubby thought to have a word. Maybe the gentle eyed, softly spoken priest could put a perspective on what was happening to inspire a popular tone for his writing. If anyone knew the background of the Clan-Kenyon and Mally Kenyon in particular, Father Turner did. His church was in the very epicentre of the estate. He would have talked to a lot of people this morning, already, and had knowledge of the groundswell of opinion, Magdalene Kenyon's included. She was, after all, still Mally Kenyon's sister-in-law, despite her husband's demise.

The priest was the first to speak in his soft Irish twang, recognising Cubby immediately. "First of the news hounds, Mr Watson. It's a terrible thing. A terrible thing!"

Cubby took the hand offered to him, appreciating its dry warmth. "Do you think Mally Kenyon did it?"

"I prefer to think not. Someone did it, apparently, but not of here. She is not a child of the estate, I gather. At least, none are missing. Tock says that he didn't recognise her and all our children are accounted for. A silver-eyed child of about six or seven years of age."

Cubby's eyes widened. Silver eyes! The stolen photograph was smooth under the grip of Cubby's armpit. He looked about before retrieving it, wanting to look immediately so that his suspicions could be examined in a view of the child's features. It was the first thing he looked at but the angle at which the photograph had been snapped allowed only dark, glittery slits to be noticeable.

The priest looking on shook his head. "If that's the child, I don't know her."

The child stood against a white wall, her photograph numbered and dated, cleanly dressed and groomed in red dungarees and stout boots. She carried a rag doll which she held at arm's length, away from her, towards the camera. The doll looked to be sodden and stained but the photo suggested to Cubby that she would not relinquish it as her comforter. A child of unusual beauty.

If he had but taken the trouble to look closer he might have seen something else. However, people usually find only that which they are searching for. He was not looking for family likeness; some familiarity about her mouth, maybe; a small mouth shaped like a cupid's bow, quite escaped him. A small nose similar in shape to his own. Had he taken more of an objective view and seen what there was to see within the child's facial characteristics he would never have done what he was about to do. It might have stopped him in his tracks, there and then, in his growing quest to go to any lengths to find out who she was. The need was becoming urgent within him to do what the police were failing to do in his estimation. To find out what had happened to her! Who was to blame! More than anything…who she was. A child abandoned and still unclaimed.

Then his thoughts were interrupted as a cry went up from the crowd about him. Catty Collins, herself, chin raised, aloof in her bearing, was getting out of a car to his rear. She was slipping off the rear seat of a police crested limousine after having been chauffeur driven to denote her importance. As usual, looking like she had been turned out from a mould, newly come off the end of a moving conveyor belt. One of a batch of spanking new, Spode Pottery figurines, referenced as Ma'am; never anything but high gloss porcelain and showing every detail of her braided uniform. Moving as if she was wheeling herself along, smoothly, instead of walking on her own two feet into the front door of the Dog's Bed Inn. If it did not clatter behind her it was because someone was holding it open, deferentially. That polished hardwood stick under arm, one glove removing its partner from the other hand with neat, quick, short jerks. Behind her a cavalcade had brought a posse of other journalists, cameramen, a van for TV coverage already running leads, unpacking lights and boom-sounding the crowd which was already surging about them. They might beat Cubby to national publication but they would not have the shots in his own camera, or at least, even if they found amateur footage, it was unlikely to have any quality sufficiently good enough to make it preferable to his own.

It was Father Turner who gave a hefty sigh. "What's the woman playing at if not using this tragic situation to generate her own publicity? A press conference, here! Mark my words, she'll have riot on her hands if she uses this for anything other than to try to locate the fiend who has done this to an innocent child." Then, looking at his watch. "I'll have to go. I have a visit from the bishop before the prayer group meeting Magdalene has asked for. The bishop and the man to give advice about the debts of the parish." Here, he shook his head on other sad things. "So disappointing to know that people will no longer dip into their own pockets to support the church within their community. What will happen to us? What will happen to any of us? It's a day of reckoning, so it is! She isn't helping anything."

Cubby did not hang around to hear what she might have to say, either, in an address to the nation as the cameras rolled and her prepared speech was issued with confident authority, directly from memory. He had noted that his own phone had failed to ring in invitation, his hands gripping into fists as he took the slight onboard. Instead, he got in his car and left the vicinity. He had enough information to start his own investigation.

Eight

Cuthbert C. Watson, ever known as CC, sat with seeming importance at the helm of the Clarion Evening News as Editor in Chief. This while knowing full well that, these days, it was his son, rather than he and his wife, Marjory...she being the major share holder...who had been responsible for the recent and ever growing revival in popularity of the time-served, evening newspaper, the Clarion Evening News.

In the previous five years, since Cubby had served his apprenticeship following university, he had seemed to promote himself to higher and ever higher status over and above his mother and father which relegated CC to a position of no real strength. Indeed, like everyone else employed at the Clarion, he was expected to follow orders as opposed to giving them. If he sometimes brooded that his son as office tea boy in relation to his own extensive experience was peas-above-sticks, it was the way of things in a modern world where ignorance was needed to tramp a way through unmapped, snake infested, swampy forest while experience took a more circuitous and careful route.

Maybe he should not have allowed Cubby to take over the orienteering but no one working at the Clarion was in the slightest doubt of where the drive and power lay, using his own inimitable style of bullying which was simply to barge people out of the way.

Then his son's journalistic style was refreshing to a readership which had had middle of the road reporting for far too long. He had a way of making words sing in newsprint. Even the paper printed upon felt crisper. What were old fashioned manners, anyway, but old fashioned? Political correctness Cubby ignored totally as something that had little to do with truth and was often the excuse which masked other reasons for public appointments and civic actions. His attitude of print it first and *then* let the tricky-dickies try to wriggle out of it had made even the nearly-dead in their seemingly safe mausoleum sit up and take note. Cubby dug over old graves and drove over anything standing in his way. The JCB of his huge personality being big enough to tear out whole strips of Quinton undergrowth and leave it as matchwood. If CC had, perhaps, once played a pivotal role in the Clarion's popularity as a journalist of merit, along with a staff of cub-scout reporters happy to report on local football teams and petty crimes, while his wife sat in judgement in the local Magistrates' Court between writing on bland women's issues, he had been carried along on the last rush of the waves from times gone by. Any popularity they might have retained had waned with the death of his father-in-law, Cuthbert

Barton; a mould breaker himself. He having been the original founder and a driving force to be reckoned with within all spheres of his long and productive life. The man Cubby most took after. A man who had privately despised the very ground that CC walked upon even while paying off some of the worst of his gaming debts when, like his daughter, his family reputation mattered more than anything else.

These days, wisdom coming with age, even if reform hadn't, CC tried to keep the baser actions of his existence to himself and, in the main part, considered himself successful. However, God forbid that Marjory should discover his latest predicament. Last night's disaster! The one that he had spent the previous seven years keeping under wraps. He was dependent on her for every penny in his pockets and could not exist without her. Even his salary from the paper Marjory doled out with her hand to the purse strings. He had his own bank account but even so there were times when he wondered how she knew that he had bought socks from Crestfalls, not Trimbles, or had lunch at the Italiana instead of the Crown Carvery. Black truth being that she bored the living-hell out of him even as she held the reigns of his restraint. And now this predicament!

His son, someone to be ever watchful of, too. The trouble being that Cubby had laser eyes even better at seeing through darkness than the mother he physically resembled. A moralist, like Marjory, he banged his own drum loudly and preached from his own stern bible. CC had long found it necessary to carefully cover his tracks from his son as he did his wife.

As for himself, he had no moral virtues and despised those who considered themselves to be life's worthies. That he was suffering the ravages of time was the penance he served as recompense for a life lived to the full. These days CC was overweight, his shirt always a good inch smaller than the girth of his waist. Blue eyes bagged and red veined from drinking too much, late at night, after Marjory had wound a sober way to bed, she never more than a single malt imbibed at any one time. If the phone rang with a call from one of his forbidden amours, it was usually after midnight when Marjory was fast asleep. Last night it had rung just as he had been about to stumble up to bed himself, with news of what had happened to Serena and Caitlin. A rare call when Serena knew that she should never phone him at home.

Now, Marjory was looking at him from her desk to his right hand side, her black-pea eyes hard upon him. Cubby, not at his desk because he was chasing breaking news. CC feeling that he was in a goldfish bowl as all the Clarion reporting staff shared the same room. He was tired of asking for some screening so that, occasionally, he might put his head on his hands and go to sleep. Marjory sensing, perhaps, with a weaker radar than Cubby's powerful receptors that he was agitated and distressed under the sick pallor he was feeling, refusing, as he was, to call it fear. What would she do if she found out that eight years ago he had fathered an illegitimate child; a girl. A daughter! A daughter who, last night, had escaped her sensible restraints and was now detained at Quinton Police Station while they sought to discover her identity.

Not that Caitlin would tell them who she was, he considered, despite her appallingly bad behaviour of late and her loud, vocal demands to be taken to see the lady with the golden trumpet...the mother who had wanted a child even less than CC had wanted her. Not this child, anyway! Not Caitlin! These days, ever screaming and shouting when order and quiet had to be exacted and Serena had had no choice than to put the collar and chain on her neck to quieten her. A child for whom the trained, haughty sophistication of a spoilt princess had peeled away as her behaviour had deteriorated. A spoilt brat of a child whom Serena had indulged shamelessly in her wish that the child have everything her heart desired. Was it any wonder that Caitlin had become excessive in her violence and tantrums since she had been foolishly told that she was to go away to school? Fear in her eyes just to hear of such a place. Little Caitlin could not be kept secret forever.

Now this! He was thinking with sickening clarity, now, of the things that had occurred last night, coming up to midnight, with all the horror of someone looking back on happenings only vaguely remembered due to the alcoholic haze which had clouded his brain. Recalling Serena's thin, dulcet tones as she had informed him of what had occurred, over the telephone.

Her tale had been barely believable, anyway. Mugged! Her purse taken! The child discovered but escaped into the water! Taken by the police after the mugger had called them! The cloud of whisky vapour had been too strong in his brain to heed anything else but his own need to sleep as he had laid down the receiver, stumbled up to his own bed and, promptly, slept. Recalling nothing until he had opened his eyes to the lost memories of the previous night and it had all come back to him in a rush of sickening realization without the anaesthetic of drink to numb his own worst nightmare when he had heard the very same reported on local radio as soon as his radio alarm had switched itself on...

Seven thirty. Quinton Radio News Special. Last night a girl of about seven years of age was reported to have been brought out of the Whemley Canal at the area popularly known as the Dog's Bed Estate in Lower Quinton. She had been tied into a sack and left to drown. The child's parents have yet to come forward. Anyone with any

97

knowledge of a missing child should ring Quinton Police Station as quickly as possible. It is understood that a man has been arrested early this morning and taken in for questioning.

His hands were still shaking. His mind in denial of accepting any responsibility towards a situation he had not sought for himself...at least, not in its timing, or the route Serena and Caitlin had taken to the train station in Quinton from where they should have travelled to Blackstone School. It had been Serena's decision, not his, to move the child at night just in case she decided to make yet another bid to run away. So many already attempted: through the cellar window; out the cat flap; up through the lid of the trolley, when even the dog collar and lead was strained to contain her, these days. At other times, cowering into the cellar corners and refusing to go anywhere. Never to school. Not into an outside world full of other children and strange situations. Throwing tantrums of such massive proportions that it had all become too much for Serena. She had become physically ill and emotionally drained when Caitlin seemed to think that her birth mother would want her where Serena did not. Truth being that it was the child's worsening behaviour that had triggered a reversal of Serena's health. One minute morose and the next violent. The child had become so much a mess of confusing contradictions that he had had no choice but to agree with Serena that she must, now, be weaned away from the small world in which she had, until six short months previously, seemed to be so happily contained. They had agreed to bring her schooling forward from the autumn to the summer term. Now this! Come the morning she would have been at school...free...integrated...if only she had not fought against it and taken such an unexpected opportunity to escape.

Then, most concerning, now, in the cold light of a sober morning, the mugging of Serena, her words coming back to him on waves of freezing consciousness. *My handbag was taken, CC! It has my address inside...yours, too. He took it with him. Inside, the school forms filled in with our contact information...you and I, both named! You do not seem to understand how vital it is that you help me in this situation, CC. The papers must be retrieved. Caitlin must be returned to us. What if my sister discovers the truth!*

The telephone on his desk was droning like a wasp boring into his petrified recall like a stinging tail as he stared at his outstretched hand while it rang, again and again. Marjory was casting him glances as if wondering what was preventing him from answering it quickly. She had a way of looking at him that was ever critical, ever suspicious, ever accusing. He forced himself to pick up the handset rather than let Marjory's brow deepen further with questioning glances when he had still to look at a single article in his in-tray because he lacked the concentration upon anything but Caitlin. His agitation would not be contained. His hand shook as he raised the receiver to his ear.

Marjory noted it.

The receptionist from the front of office, below, who also manned the telephone extension system and entertained visiting clients until someone could get down there had a shrill, little voice that twanged upon the pain in his temple. "Cubby for you, Mr Watson."

"Put him on." The last person he required a conversation with at that precise moment. He lit a cigarette, the nicotine increasing his feeling of nausea while creating a modicum of mental relief and watched Marjory mew at him. She nagged him about his smoking habit a million times a day in different ways.

When he heard his son's voice, eager and all fired up, his heart began to bang and leap in his chest despite the nicotine hitting home. He knew with the inspired pessimism of a man about to meet his own Armageddon that what his son was about to report was in connection with the very thing he would have preferred that he stay furthest away from.

"Hold the front page, Dad. Major news breaking. That child nearly drowned in the Whemley Canal…!"

CC's hammering heartbeat took a greater leap and threatened to come smashing through his chest wall to land at Marjory's feet. His face must have paled. He turned from Marjory's narrow-eyed expression so that she could no longer read his face. "What of her?"

"She'd been tied into a sack prior to being thrown in that stinking ditch like a bag of garbage. Most likely off the bridge near the Dog's Bed Inn. Catty Collins swanning about doing national press interviews from the threshold of the Dog's Bed Inn. She says they'll be going door to door, doing everything they can to put those guilty away for a very long time to come. They're on the lookout for a paedophile ring, I gather, from what was said on my car radio. Enough of a police presence on the estate to cause a lot of unrest. Mally Kenyon taken in for questioning."

CC's eyes closed. Mally Kenyon, the mugger? The one who had, in fact, called the police? How could it all have been so wrongly construed? What should never have come to public knowledge was blowing wide open as if primed with explosive…national news, even! One small child jumps into a canal of her own volition, be it inside a hessian sack, and it becomes a paedophile investigation of national interest. The sack, tied lightly at the neck, had been nothing more than a way to keep Caitlin within the trolley while in a state of mild sedation. A better proposition, it had seemed, should she make herself known by wriggling and calling than the dog collar and chain. There had been no cruelty intended. That Serena loved the child too much had ever been the problem.

"I'm coming straight in. Phone the police station and try to find out what's happened to the kid. Save the front page. I have photographs of the arrest and a photo of the child, too."

CC felt about to retch. A photograph? A photo of Little Caitlin, as Serena often called her! He ran a worried hand through his hair so that it stood on end in places. He remained unaware of his comical appearance as the rest of the observant staff in the news office tittered under their breath. As far as they were concerned, CC was drinking at his desk again from the hip flask in his back pocket. It had become almost a daily occurrence.

Then the real questions hit home. Would Mally Kenyon be able to provide a description of Serena? He considered it unlikely that the handbag would come to light as it would, now, be evidence of guilt of the mugging itself. More likely, already disposed of away from the scene and its contents never to be considered of any real importance. It would be unlikely for the likes of Mally Kenyon to admit any involvement came the reply to his own question. Kenyons never admitted to anything as a point of principle. They even denied their own shadows as belonging to themselves if questioned. Always done unto, never doing against, also. Except, maybe, because of the seriousness of the situation. A description of sorts could be made of Serena from her clothing and the shopping trolley alone. Perhaps Serena was the person he should worry about, not Mally Kenyon? Though, just now he was incapable of thinking straight. Marjory was not only watching him but closing in on his conversation with his son...a son who seemed hell bent upon squeezing as much news and drama out of the situation as was possible.

"Fine," was all CC said with some breathlessness. "I'll rearrange the layouts." He knew that there was a note in his voice which Marjory would pick up on. Maybe a trip home was called for in order to prepare for a visit to Serena. One that might have been better to have been made after her phone call last night had such been possible. He had to admit to himself that he had been grossly incapacitated again. Drink was what had led to most of the problems in CC's problematic life yet he had never managed to contain his addiction to it. Was it any wonder with Marjory's eyes constantly watching over him?

He could feel and see Marjory's eyes turned towards him now. A wise habit to keep her in his peripheral vision when in the same room with her as she took up the printed hard copy, fresh from her own printer, and brought it over the few yards which separated their working relationship.

He watched her walk towards him like a thin, black widow spider. Her clothes always black, white or grey, as her life was. Her hair a crested tuft like that on a beaky bird. The only colour about her was in the short curls; a rich chestnut shade like Cubby's. She always reminded him of an old black and white, hand coloured photograph of a sour-faced woman from hard times, long gone by. She would be the one with sufferance in her eyes, who could not raise a smile even for a photograph. The same black-pea eyes as his son, only Marjory's were ever coldly accusing, rarely fired and lively as Cubby's were. Always steeped with intelligence, though, when he was sure that she was reading his thoughts because they ran like ticker tape over his eyelids. The same thoughts, now, to be gone over again and again in repetitive motion like a never ending loop on a video recording, endowing Marjory with the same sixth sense as his son, if the message was repeated often enough. Cubby only having to look at him hard to frighten the life out of him.

A sweat was forming on his brow even if the press office was always cold first thing in the morning, because Cubby was on his way in. Cubby would soon be filling the office with his presence. There would be nothing else to do but to brazen it out. It had not been he who had placed her in a sack and tied the string. He smiled at Marjory even though his lips stuck to his teeth.

Marjory looked at him with a question in her eyes as he wiped his brow, coughed and took a sip from the mug of cold tea on his desk. She placed the paper close to his overheated hand. Her own hand ever radiating an icy coldness which no amount of rubbing could improve. She placed the articles in his in-tray along with several others that had been lodged there from the other more junior reporters. They made up a fat wad of hard copy still not processed. Usually by this time in the morning he had edited and shaped the articles and advertisements using the format of an off-the-shelf publishing programme which greatly simplified his work. The one about illegal land deals would have to take third page, now.

"Was that Cubby on the phone?"

CC nodded, refusing eye contact. He could not bear to look into Marjory's eyes because of what he saw there. "We're to hold the front page. A child brought out of the canal, seemingly brutalised by Mally Kenyon."

"Do we know who the child is?"

CC shook his head. "Just some kid. Probably someone he picked up off the street."

Marjory went back to her own desk with some mewing of her tight, small, little mouth which pursed and relaxed over small pointed teeth. As a youth, Mally Kenyon was one of the accused before her bench with great regularity. "I would not have thought him capable of such a thing. Benny, maybe. Woody at a push. Not Mally, though."

"People are capable of anything if desperate enough," was his only reply, snatching up her copy and seemingly concentrating on the limp article she had written. Then he recalled Cubby's request and picked up the receiver of his landline telephone. He phoned to Quinton Police Station and was put through to the press room. They would be getting a photograph out for publication, most probably late afternoon. The details he was given were minimal. Nothing new was released for the press coverage except her place of safety; Greengates House. CC's eyes widened. Tommo Thomas's assessment unit for very naughty girls and boys; usually adolescents only. That could only mean one thing. Caitlin was displaying all the aggressive, disgusting and potentially harmful behaviour she had been indulging in ever since she had learned something of her beginnings from a few careless words spoken by Serena, and the terrible prospect of her going away to school.

Some few minutes later they could both hear Cubby bowling in and bringing the cold morning air in with him, his face as animated as a hunting dog's, telling the whole office to sit up and listen, take note of his words. "I have the fate of Catty Collin's right here in the palm of my hand," he told them, his manner arrogant, forceful, even gleeful, as he stripped off his jacket and threw it carelessly onto the pegs, rolling up his sleeves and tucking in his shirt, ready for business. "Just you wait and see, Dad. All of you! The bitch's head will roll for this one. There's an uprising afoot on the Dog's Bed and it's all of her own making." He then threw himself into his office chair and turning it to face the way of his gaping audience sent it skidding back towards his father's desk with practised skill. "What's happening with the kid at the station?"

CC passed over a slip of paper. "Still at the station. Just about to be transferred to Greengates House, I gather."

"But that's a secure assessment unit for adolescents."

"Deemed to be suitable for some unknown reason."

The photograph which Cubby flung onto the desk before his father caused CC's stomach to turn over with a giddying jerk. CC knew that this was the first photograph of Caitlin ever taken in the whole of her seven year plus, life span. Impossible not to notice, either, that Caitlin was holding the rag doll which he had purchased for her at Serena's insistence from the Christmas Fair at St Andrew's Church, which Marjory had made him attend, pretending it to be a donated raffle prize for a charity he supported. He had funded quite a lot of Caitlin's clothing and play things, in fact, even if he had spent very little time with her for no other reason than that it was ever at the back of Serena's imperious beseeching to tell.

To tell Marjory. To tell her sister if little Caitlin needed something that a father should provide for his secret daughter and seemed unwilling. She never used overt threats, but Serena had a quiet way of achieving all that others might demand through blackmail or extortion through the use of inference. There had ever been about her a determination of purpose which belied her situation where Caitlin was concerned. Caitlin would have the very best of everything she could have to make up for all that her restricted existence lacked. The child was spoilt by material possessions to an extreme.

He was quite sure, however, that the doll was untraceable even if he had registered his name with the cheque to pay for it. He had promised to buy something to support the fundraising for Marjory's church. The Clarion had provided the hamper prizes. They had advertised the function widely. The rag doll for Caitlin had merged in with the rest from several being sold for charity at the same venue. Marjory had smiled at his munificence. Anything to keep Marjory happy was CC's maxim.

However, CC was deeply troubled as he watched his son scoot his office chair back to his own desk and switch on his computer, all his movements quick, rapid and precise while CC's hands trembled, uncontrollably. His eyes once again settling on the photograph before him. That of his daughter, Caitlin. She was looking right into his eyes and holding out to him the doll he had bought for her, as if an object of reference for himself alone. CC needed a drink.

*****

Marjory had noticed everything. When CC slipped off home...a mere ten minute drive each way...Marjory was perfectly aware of where he had gone, though why was intriguing. She took the opportunity to take a better look at the photograph which had seemed to perturb him so, her face spreading into a sneer. When he returned she noted that he looked to be more worried than even before. He had brought with him his mackintosh and his Homburg hat. That could only mean that CC planned to go somewhere other than his usual afternoon spent partaking of a leisurely lunch at the Crown Carvery next door to the Clarion offices. She, herself, would be heading in the direction of the local, Juvenile Magistrates' Court after a short trip home to change her clothing. Today a young, well-known thug called Jacko Bennett was down for sentencing, followed by a parade of minor offenders, many of them resident on the Carlton Manor Estate.

Though Marjory, unlike many, was not foolish enough to think that virtue was the bedfellow of social standing. More often than not it was ignorance combined with a lack of parental supervision which brought the young hooligans before her bench. Richer, more attentive parents ensured that there was as least opportunity for their underage offspring to get into mischief, in the first place. When they did so, it was often possible to take remedial steps to put right the effects of the offence by applying suitable resources to the problem. Looking after CC was often a bit like looking after an immature child, also. It was usually down to careful observance and then crisis management. It was what she had done for all of their married years.

CC had only just returned to his desk when Marjory left for home.

Nine

There was a small core of local people gathered for prayer before the altar at St Saviour's Church on the Carlton Manor Estate, otherwise known as the Dog's Bed Estate, which Father Turner had called for ten o'clock that same day. He had earlier had a meeting with his bishop and the church accountant concerning the debts of the church. Their proposals had at first alarmed him so they had left him to think them over. However, he now seemed to Magdalene to be more relaxed concerning the bishop's proposals than he had been earlier. Whatever had transpired was removing a great weight from his mind, Magdalene thought, as they placed their chairs in a circle before the altar. The bishop and the accountant would be returning later to conclude certain arrangements. They would then have a private blessing. Magdalene was beside herself with envy. She would consider herself blessed, indeed, to kiss the hem of His Holiness, the bishop's dress.

This was not an open congregation but a private gathering of those few whose faith was strong enough to believe in the power of concentrated prayer. A prayer that when conjoined with the prayer of others magnifies and swells in strength to become a force of reckoning as all the emotive energies interlink like an invisible chain of silver paperclips combining to make a direct-line, two-way, radio connection to He who is omnipotent, the all powerful, all seeing Son of God Himself. He whose light of life lies in the aftermath, but takes its gravity from those who are believers on Earth.

It was Magdalene Kenyon's rock solid belief that Jesus and the Holy Mother would not ignore such collective wilfulness for His help at such a difficult time. For His truth to find the light. For His intervention in the case of the possibly unjustified arrest of Mally Kenyon. And especially after what her father, a direct eyewitness, had told her when she had telephoned him with her observation that the police were coming in numbers to the Dog's Bed Estate at just gone seven, that morning. And in light of her own knowledge of Mally who, to her reckoning, might get into fistfights and let that temper of his lead him into all kinds of destructive behaviour...but to harm a child? No, not Mally! As if Bass was telling her so from the afterlife, shouting it at her. *Our Mally, never! Woody or Benny, maybe. It was them used to pin frogs down on the canal bank and strap them till their innards burst when me and Mally walked away...* Echoing words, repeated in her head ever since she had been stunned with the disbelief of it. He had been the child's saviour. He was her deceased husband's beloved twin. Bass had loved him. Even when his emotions had been numbed by the drugs that had killed him he had only trust and love for his brother, Mally. As Mally had had only trust and love for Bass.

Later, the accusations of their neighbours against Mally had turned to fear and now to hysteria. The police had come in force and not gone away. Anyone with reason to be suspected of something or anything – as well as the repulsive molestation and attempted murder of one small girl – had been questioned, fingerprinted and if reason substantiated for any sort of crime having being committed, arrested.

Even as the prayer group gathered, DNA swabs were being taken from all those willing to allow themselves to be so accounted for should the child have been infested with her assailant's body fluid, so allowing for their being discounted from the police investigations. The police telling them that it was better to be eliminated from their enquiries than to be kept on a list of possible suspects. They might as well have painted a bloody cross on some doors and not on others so that the Angel of Death would know who not to contaminate when the plagues arrived as imminently expected.

Old convictions were being dragged up and paraded openly as the police went from house to house, knocking on doors with commanding authority. Rapping hard on windows if there was any delay to open up when they were sure that the householders were within. Car registrations were being checked for ownership and payment of insurance and licence. More than one bicycle had been confiscated because it had an invisible name or registration which showed up under ultraviolet light as not belonging to the person riding it. Absconding school children were rounded up and the educational welfare officers informed. The parents would be prosecuted for failure to ensure that their children were in school as the law demanded. Lock-ups were crowbar opened and the contents investigated. Swarms of uniformed police were on the streets and, so it was rumoured, would shortly be reinforced by those from neighbouring stations. Questions remained unanswered. Just what were they looking for now that they had taken Mally Kenyon as a suspect? More than one father packed a suitcase and skedaddled leaving a family in distress. Wives left to shoulder the full burden.

People were gathering on street corners and talking heatedly of provocation and harassment. While Magdalene would pray for the real perpetrators to be discovered, she would pray for peace within her community. She would also pray for Mally Kenyon.

Magdalene could not, in her true heart of hearts, believe it to be

Mally who had done such a terrible thing. The twin brothers had been identical in looks and speech and mannerisms and, while some might say that Bass had been as bad as Benny and Woody, Magdalene knew, now, that what he had suffered from was not badness but the same, pathetic weakness as herself; a disorganization of spirit and purpose, exacerbated by declining ambitions as the drugs took their hold. Her own addiction had been a gradual decline also exacerbated by a hyperactivity of mind and an accompanying disquiet of temperament that only a narcotic drug would quieten.

As a teenager, Magdalene had gone from being a nervous, jittery but conscientious and studious girl to a drop-out layabout, too numb to care about anything but the next fix of the drug that soothed her disaffection with life. By the age of eighteen she was living in squats, getting money in any way she could. Bass the same. Working the markets, selling handmade soaps and candles. When the drugs kicked in to spoil the effects of their efforts they might melt the wax down and start again. Which profit went on drugs and little else.

They had clung together like lost souls even as their daughter had been born and the commitment of marriage had been made because, even as inadequate parents, they made desperate attempts at convention which never lasted. Her parents more often than not taking the child in until their own marriage had split asunder under the strain of a daughter they could never agree about. It had ever been the other who had been responsible for Magdalene's latest lapse from grace, fingers pointing at anyone but themselves. Who had allowed her too many freedoms? Who had not sought the help that was needed when the problems manifested themselves? Who had failed to give enough love and attention when she was growing up? They had both been too busy running the pub. Why had they both been looking in an entirely different direction when she had been down on the canal bank sharing a bong with a group of friends they had believed to be suitable company for a girl destined for university and better things? Of whom Gina Mon had been one! The pub, a constant source of contraband and trafficking, but her father ever vigilante to the use of his toilets and never afraid to ask the more overt dealers to leave his premises, fast. This while Magdalene had been meeting them where they openly traded on street corners, under lampposts, the drugs getting harder as her habit began to kick in. Until the final break-up when a girl of seventeen thinks that she can live a romantic life on the streets. Until the weirdoes close in. Until the cramps become a morning sickness and the body won't stop shaking until it's had its fix. Until a man dies after choking on his own vomit and a child is taken away. Even against all the warnings of the same friend who had once giggled over a toke in a tidy bedroom, but then chosen a different way. A friend who, in her professional role, had been the one to come for Holly, age seven, and take her away. Then return to place her arms about her friend, cry together in their grief, promise to help and support as long as there was a contract never to be broken. Magdalene must never even in her darkest, most pain-filled moments of despair, ever *use* again.

The journey had not been an easy one for Magdalene in the days when she had yet to understand, as she did now, that it had been her own lack of self purpose and self responsibility that had seen her so abysmally fail; a natural victim to a lump of brown substance, in her case, inhaled as vapour and not injected.

In his own way, Mally had wished her well, too. She had seen his dreaming watchfulness over a distance. She had known that when the tempters had come closing in he had seen them on their way. She had been aware that as she walked home from the church, each evening, he stood guard along her journey. As he had done even when she had been lost to consciousness, with Bass. It had been Mally who had sat cross-legged, in some hard place, watching over them.

But when Bass had died and Holly had been wrested from her, she had had nothing left inside her to love anyone with, least of all herself. Her mind had become a hollow shell of numbness. Her body wretchedly old and tired, her limbs stiff. It had been Father Turner who had arranged that she go to the place where her addiction might be treated. The withdrawal had been careful; no highs, no lows; no escape from the inevitable understanding that she was at a crossroads which she would never be allowed to stand at again. As slowly she was brought back to a state of non-intoxication, even then Mally had come to support her over the distance...flowers on a wall...a CD in the post...a bottle of fruit juice...little tokens left in her path for her to come across. Never a word, though. Never a single word. For Mally had none himself that could be spoken. His emotions had become as incapacitated as her own with the death of Bass, his brother; his own twin soul.

She had known for as long as she had known Bass that Mally loved her. If love was longing. If longing was love. However, she dare not risk being ripped from her moorings, now. Not when she had a lifeline in her hands and all about her the storm-tossed seas of her undulating cravings...the need to have her daughter back, included...like the dragging troughs and perilous swells of rolling breakers when problems shook the buoy and tugged at the lifebelt which kept her head above water. Even now she might be tempted to let go her hold on her own self government and drift away as Bass had done, under the waves to the bottom of the ocean where so many lifeless bodies dragged along the sand. Not now, though, when within her heart and understanding she held compassion and hope for herself as well as those whose lives had become equally blighted within the community where she had been raised. Her vocation was, above all else, the children.

Her faith was within her as a kindness for herself and for others, now. Through her staunch beliefs, Magdalene now considered that life might have some chance for fairness, after all, within the accountability which comes with consciousness, either now or in the afterlife, as surely as the sun rises and the sun sets, the tides roll in and the tides roll out, again.

Kindness and forgiveness for her lapses must begin inside herself. Father Turner had taught her that.... "Love yourself first, Magdalene. Only then can you love others. The love of God should come last, not first, as many of my brethren would have it. Even then, it is the fellowship of the flock, rather than the praising of the Almighty, that should be our work at hand. It's why I stay here. It's the work that God set me to accomplish upon this soil. The vocation matters above all else."

Some criticised him for it because he allowed so many sinners through the portals of his church and affiliated himself with them. Those who had yet to repent. The likes of Mally and Benny and Woody Kenyon when their lifestyle rendered them too feeble to look after themselves. The church hostel for those in need being part of the fabric of the building, its crypt always left open to shelter the needy. There was many a knock on Father Turner's door gone midnight. He never failed to get up and open it.

Which perhaps accounted for the tiredness in Father Turner's eyes as he started the prayers. "Let's hold hands together, please. Spend a few moments in silence, eyes closed, heads bowed in order to cast off our outer concerns and tune in to our spiritual core. Nan, you may care to follow your daughter who understands the ways and purpose of our prayer group."

"Yes, Father. I'm willing to chip my five pennyworth in. I don't think Mally Kenyon is guilty, either."

Eyes were rolled. Few, other than Father Turner and Magdalene, cared about Mally Kenyon. Nan was missing the point. The point being that they were unsettled in themselves and feeling victimised, harassed, unsafe in the very place where they thought they knew everything which might create a danger. Now, snakes were loose in the house. They were gathering closer to the mantle of the Holy Father and pressing themselves within His folds where serpents are toothless.

The unrest was pulling the rug from under the feet of their

community. Their normal cycles were being interrupted. Neighbour was resenting neighbour if that neighbour brought the police into their street or onto their floor in the high rises. People were arguing instead of keeping opinion to themselves. Small affrays, no more than happened every Friday and Saturday night outside the Dog's Bed Inn or on the street outside the row of metal shuttered, graffiti decorated shops, caused those disturbing the peace to be grabbed in a headlock and thrown into the back of the police riot van to take back for questioning.

"It's the truth that we are supporting, Nan, not the individual in this case. As well as for peace to be restored within our community."

"Though we pray for the souls of all when they have stumbled," someone else explained.

Arrogance if ever there was any, Nan considered, privately, as Magdalene poked her, warningly, in the ribs.

"We all have to live here and get on together as best we can. We have to learn to accept that the police have a role to play and this fiend must be caught. People, who have done nothing wrong, like us, should have nothing to fear. We pray for the souls of all heathens and sinners."

Nan sniffed at that one, also, with a face like someone imparting a silent curse. Herself included, no doubt, amongst the sinners and the heathens! She might have let the arrogant speaker know a thing or two at any other time than this. Magdalene to her left, or Magdalene not to her left! As she was at this very moment with her foot pressing against the painful corn that had been giving Nan most gip; a sign if ever there was one that something portentous was coming. People having told her for many a long year, now, that she was a fairy-headed nutcase for her enduring embrace of spirituality from the earth up and not the heavens down.

Nan, being the only heathen present at the group prayer meeting. If she had but known, allowed there by the majority only to make up the numbers. She was the only one to be unsure of what to do as they obeyed Father Turner, finally, and dipped their heads, holding hands, in a conjoined circle. The rest seasoned, as was Magdalene these days, to prayer group meetings at St. Savour's, usually once a month with more ordinary quests in mind. Someone's illness made bearable such as that of that poor, deformed woman who lived across the canal, over the playing fields and across from the park, in the terraced houses on Park Road which overlooked the park railings. The same one who Father Turner visited occasionally, in order to say the sacraments and give holy communion to, in the dark cloister of her own home where she shut herself away so as not to offend the sensitivities of people who preferred not to witness such suffering. They had a right to be protected from it, hadn't they?

Lots of other good causes they prayed for, too. Someone's need for a job granted. Someone's financial hardship, eased. His help to raise the funds for their next trip to Lourdes which was always a good jolly and free to the helpers even while taking the handicapped and terminally ill in wheelchairs, which was damned hard work because they were so demanding. Or to call for the blessing of someone moving off the Dog's Bed Estate and into the mainstream. The equivalent of a move to Outer Mongolia in most people's point of view.

Please God to let the Wilkins' get a mortgage so they can escape. Bobby Masters to stop fighting so he fits in with his new schooling. A decent repair to be made to the church roof, if we can raise the money.

This when the estate was full of cowboy builders who put a third again to the final bill on every estimate. Ordinary, normal, everyday hopes that Nan disagreed with using precious prayer for. Fancy calling on the Almighty for a lower gas bill! Father Turner's desk in his vestry was piled high with bills. He worried about them constantly. If it was God's duty to pay them then He should pay them for everybody, Nan considered. Not just them that went to church.

The Prayer Group, now holding hands, shoulder to shoulder, eyes closed and trying to relax enough to loosen the girths on their spiritual souls. Little more than a séance in Nan's opinion. If what they were asking for was peace on Earth, it was a bit of a tall order. Same as asking Mally Kenyon to have his innocence celebrated instead of his guilt proven. With his track record, they would have sufficient offences in which he was named as the possible offender to keep him temporarily in custody for the next five years. Not that she considered him to be guilty, though. Mally was no child offender, of that she felt certain. And Mally did matter! Everyone matters! Arrogant buggers were these church zealots.

Then, knowing her own scathing disrespect for the rights of others to believe freely and sorry for it when they all meant well. *Now, now, Nan, be tolerant! Naughty, Nancy Bartlett! Give your own hand a good slap!* This said to herself and knowing her own arrogance in being so scathing. She knew only too well from her more usual experience how people needed the comfort and protection of an inner circle even while...as someone had just said of herself...points were being missed. They were missing the point that an innocent man was being treated, without evidence, as if he was guilty. A whole community was being punished, also. It wasn't right! It wasn't fair!

A joyless lot, though! Too serious...too Godly...too without a sense of humour. God's greatest gift in Nan's opinion. Get you through where nothing else could even in the most tragic of circumstances. She had known her own circle to bring questions to the spiritual forum which appealed to her own sense of wicked fun, but which often brought her a recognition which helped line an empty pocket with a voluntary contribution. Questions like: "Can your spirit guide tell me where I put that new pair of shoes I bought last Saturday? Can't find them anywhere!"

"Try looking in Bunny's Pawn Shop where your Vaughn's probably taken them to get a sub on some beer money." Nan knew because she had seen him through the crystal of her own front window hiking off over the bridge with a lady's shoebox underarm.

This circle of overly zealous bigots without a scrap of fun on offer. Tea and biscuits, neither. Light full on as the sun streamed in through the long windows to warm the back of her head. No mood suggested other than sombreness. No theatre to offer a hushed excitement. No action to mesmerise. Nothing two-way about it. Just dreaming hard into blank space and no one knowing what anyone was actually thinking about. Even if their focus was the same. She would have bet her last penny that Father Turner was planning where he would take that dog of his for his afternoon walk...out into the fields?...up the lanes to the top of the hill?...anywhere away from this godforsaken place! A place, where, she had to admit, the tensions were combining like knit one, pearl one, in too tight a stitch. You didn't need to be a mind reader to feel it!

If only she might consult her crystals and Tarot cards, even amongst the disbelievers, for them to see what she was getting proof of every time she brought them from the little wooden box in her pocket...the one which bore her Tarot cards wrapped in a square of purple silk...to show the castigators the signs she was receiving that a powder keg was about to explode. Nan felt that they might have some proper tools of prediction to play with then, instead of just wishful thinking. She had been having some powerful warnings lately with her Tarot cards forming Celtic Crosses full of Wands to signify people with fair features combined with the Devil card of the Greater Arcana. A Kenyon combination of cards if ever there was one. Only this morning, she had drawn the Tower; a symbol of adversity, disgrace, deception and ruin, along with oppression, imprisonment and tyranny, reversed or not reversed, of little difference in its forecast of calamity. This with the Moon card coming up with great regularity...hidden enemies, danger, calumny, darkness, terror and deception. Things badly misconstrued, to her mind, yet just what was wrong, failing to materialise in an otherwise bland array of Pages signifying illness, discord and disquiet.

If she showed them where her own predictive intelligence lay, they would soon have her stoned to death. She even looked the odd-one-out in her refusal to close her eyes completely, grip onto the hands of those next to her by anything other than her purple painted fingertips, digits full of silver rings and, of course, the colours and style of her bizarre clothing. Wearing, as she was, the long, gathered, cheese cloth skirt with a collarless blouse of the same fabric. Also a waistcoat with sequins to match the silver sixpences which adorned a purple headscarf, tied with a knot to the rear of her long, curly, dyed, auburn hair; sprouting white at the roots, under the headscarf.

Nan liked to feel comfortable so she wore sandals indoors, summer and winter, alike. They avoided the chaffing of a full shoe so to protect the painful corns which no amount of ointment served to eradicate. Along with a bunion the size of a large shallot on both big toes, she had corns on each and every one of her smaller digits, also. Today, they were jumping with the cold inside an unheated space the size of a small gymnasium. The austerity of the building was not much to her liking, either, save for the patterns and colours in the one long, narrow, floor to ceiling, stained glass window and the icons behind the altar. The church was a modern, shabbily built, open plan edifice of the same fifty or sixty years of age as the flimsy, cardboard dwellings round about. Its central spire of grey clay shingles dwarfed only by the high rises to the rear of the estate. It had a clapboard frontage supported by light coloured brick which required repainting with extreme regularity. Its facade had more the look of a converted Tesco supermarket than a solid, sure house of God. Its pillars having been moulded of concrete in wooden shuttering – not chiselled with sacrifice and sweated from natural stone – a few slaves having been done unto death in its making, so to up its value. Its altar but a smooth, oak door, placed on trestles and hidden by a starched white cloth, though the chalice was pure silver, polished carefully by Magdalene on a daily basis; a labour of love, along with maintaining the burnished brightness of the holy cross of gold and the pewter communion plates which gleamed in the sun streaming in through the tall, glass windows. The one with the stained glass the only one to lay upon the floor a long stripe of rainbow colours, the rest casting bands of plain light over the polished floorboards. Magdalene's care evident, everywhere.

Nan was proud of her daughter, these days, as she let a peep of her own dark brown eyes take in the troubled beauty of her daughter's face. She was like her father in his tall slimness and like herself only in the shield shape of a pointed face with dark features. Her beauty ripe despite her previous life and the sorrows and the heartaches that had followed. Wanting to claim back the daughter lost to her, yet knowing that it was better to let sleeping dogs lie until they rise and stretch of their own volition. Over eleven years now since the child had been taken. Her granddaughter would be eighteen years of age. Nan imagined her to be as ethereal and innocent of sin as a drifting angel because she had been saved from the ultimate indoctrination of the Dog's Bed Estate which stripped away all innocence and made children old before their years. A brown-eyed, dark-haired beauty Holly had been, like her mother. Maybe one day she might come to find them. Such would be Holly's choice. In that she agreed with Tock, reluctantly. Yet Nan shared Magdalene's fervent wish that she would return, someday, of her own volition from a place where home was in a tree-lined street with manicured lawns and flowerbeds leading up to a glossy front door. Whenever she imagined it, she saw the number seven in polished brass. In a respectable street where people kept themselves to themselves as they went about their business. Doffing caps politely as they passed on the pavement. Walking Poodles and carrying handbag dogs instead of scruffy owners, mutts themselves, being dragged along by untrained Irish Wolf Hounds or small brained Dalmatians. Pit Bulls with jaws capable of biting a child's arm off. Alsatians and Rottweiler's matched for temperament with their owners. Holly would, maybe, be off to university now. Just as she and Tock had so hoped that Magdalene would when she had been developing the right qualifications. Now to be nothing more than a skivvy for a kindly and well meaning but interfering priest who spent most of his time trying to drag a straying flock back from escape through the breaches of a church which had insufficient within to entertain them. Settle bills for which no money was forthcoming. The church, Nan knew from Magdalene, was in financial crisis.

Peeping about her, now, she saw that Magdalene had done her best to make the place as cheerful as an empty stadium could look to those who worshipped there. She had arranged the individual chairs in diagonal lines with wide spacing like a pattern of dotted lines to use up the arena. The congregation was poor, these days unless whatever function occurring inside the open plan space promised to offer something other than spiritual guidance...a jamboree or hot gospel choir for a change, a potato pie supper and bingo, a children's Easter Parade. Faith and dogma mattering little these days. Life on the estate lived in material aspirations instead of spiritual richness...satellite dishes...tellies the size of cinema screens...computers with enough memory to hold the life story of every person ever to have lived there...game players taken to school and listened to through ear pieces instead of attending to lessons...mobile phones which took photographs and booked cinema tickets at the Odeon in Quinton as well as sending texts and emails. These days, Nan reflected, worshippers kneeled on cold wooden flooring to offer prayers for the make-over TV shows, elbows against their cheap stapled-together furniture covered with thin upholstery and faux fur cushions. Life on the never-never. Debt and hardship because of it. Why pray for what could have been prevented through education? Budgeting on lower incomes never having been on the curriculum at Carlton Manor High School. Contraception, neither, if the number of unmarried mothers pushing prams was anything to go by. The place gleamed coldly and smelt of lavender from Magdalene's polishing.

Father Turner's voice carved into the quietness; gently, softly spoken. "Hear our prayers, oh Lord, this day. For we hold fear in our hearts that our community harbours within our trusting bosom the fiend that has brutalised the child thrown into the canal in a sack, late last night. We ask only for Thy truth to lead the police to those who are guilty and deserving of punishment. Hear our prayers, oh Lord."

Nan's voice could be heard in full support. "Here! Here! And get the blue fuzz out of our hair. They're doing my head in."

The pressure of Magdalene's foot on her mother's painful corns made her whelp.

Only Father Turner said, "Amen."

Magdalene shook her head. Sometimes, she thought her mother to be in league with the Devil himself. Then she looked to the windows which gave a view of the rear yard of the church. "The bishop's here, again, Father," she said. "He has someone with him carrying a big black case. Not an accountant again, I hope. Twice in the same day. We are well supported by our mother church, are we not?"

Father Turner got up to go. "So we are. We are to discuss matters in private. After you have served meals in the hostel make sure to go home. We might all be better to batten ourselves in against what is happening out there."

"We will see you later, Father?" Magdalene asked. "A simple stew but you will be welcome to join us."

He nodded. "Usual time, around five-thirty?"

Nan nodded along with her daughter to denote her own permission for him to eat with them. "Make sure to bring that dog with you." Then, more conspiratorially. "Magdalene tells me that the church has financial worries. What you need to do," she chirped, brightly, "...is to charge so much a head for your services. Five pound in the plate from each of your customers, every Sunday, should see you straight."

Ten

Holly Hargreaves was hanging about the foyer of Quinton Police Station waiting for a Dr Thomas to arrive with someone called Gary Silvers who would be the man showing her the ropes. Meanwhile, she sat leafing her way through the Child and Parent magazine brought from her shoulder bag to fill time, smirking at all the pompous advice of a particularly obnoxious author who gave prognostic descriptions of difficult, childhood behaviour along with suspicious advice to worried parents on a range of child rearing issues. All of which Holly had direct experience of. Mainly because she had caused more grey hairs to sprout, before time, on the heads of her carers than she had had hot dinners. No need to tell Holly Hargreaves about what constituted difficult, childhood behaviours because she considered herself to be the subject the so called experts were writing about in the first place. Fat lot of good they had done her!

The magazine had been of great usefulness to her purpose, though. She had been thrilled to know that as a stage prop, along with her invented qualifications, it had been worth the risk of its purloining. She hadn't had to say a word other than stating a love of children in general which was as far from the truth as a lie could possibly get. So easy to get away with being dishonest, too, when the man in the job agency had not even photocopied her invented qualifications. One swift look and she had been hired. Just the kind of work she had in mind, too, which would mean that she could delay the inevitable of hanging around a few bars and public houses to reel in the man who would quickly find himself with a lodger in need of looking after. The uglier, the better, as far as Holly was concerned because he would be less demanding and more likely to go on bended knee when she paid him with the only currency she had to hand; her body!

If the temporary work which promised to be sufficient to allow her time to orientate herself in a town she had but scant memory of was to be that of a support worker to a seven year old girl, who was being assessed within a local secure, assessment unit, she did not tell the man that she most probably had the appropriate experience, already. If not exactly as an inmate of a secure, assessment unit then certainly the next best thing; a juvenile remand centre where she had been sent for reformation and education, mid-way between a failed adoption and a traumatic fostering, followed by a spell in a residential special school from where she had been expelled after repeatedly running away. Holly had loved nothing better than the ride back to a school in uproar on the rear seat of a police car with her own policewoman as a support worker, all to herself.

So what the heck! What did they think they could do to her? The latter place of correction being the one that had provided her with her only genuine NVQ. The one in basic child care, as if washing a doll and putting a nappy on it was anything approaching the real thing. Carrying around a raw egg in a cardboard cradle for a day had been the daftest thing she had had to do for its achievement. When she had broken the egg...it had simply rolled out of its carelessly held container and smashed on the floor within the first hour of its nurturing...she had been asked to link it to the neglect of a newborn baby. Her sweetly spoken answer...*because newborn babies are fragile and vulnerable, Miss*...had gained Holly a credit she felt that she did not deserve. Such obvious reply seeming to be sufficient to get her an A grade despite her carelessness. She had refrained from using some profanity to explain her disgust to the bullshit teacher who had thought her too naive to understand the full implication of dropping a baby upon its head before the salutary lesson had served to teach her something. Or say what she had felt like saying because it would have brought her yet another detention and a loss of the points which allowed her to opt for certain treats come the weekend. That being: *Dolts, the lot of you! The kid's dead. I commit infanticide and all you can do is praise me!* Which proved to be the case when her teachers, generally full of themselves but trying, struggled so hard to build a chimney of self esteem within a house with no foundations, along with the undeserved reward of the certificate itself.

Not that there was not a positive side to everything, all considered. Holly was good at squeezing what she could from life on a daily basis. Oft painfully to those whom she contracted into her everyday relationships. Entirely one-way affairs as far as Holly was concerned, mainly due to the fact that Holly saw other people as being there entirely to serve her own purpose. The art of people-puppeteering having been learned along the stony way. Holly having people management down to a T if it suited her purpose. She was particularly talented in modes of manipulative behaviour which ensured that she had her own way, the application of emotional undermining with which to dominate her opponent and the expert skill involved in playing one person off against another, with Holly as the piggy-in-middle, when she fancied claiming all the attention for herself.

Her ace card was the one to place before the wider public when she might otherwise be found out for being the deceiving, little cow she knew she was underneath. The one which best described her rejection by her family and her subsequent life in care as the failure of society, in general, to protect all innocent children. The fact that she possessed survival techniques second to none after leaving the said institutions was the ace up her sleeve. If she had managed to stay clear of the loonies and weirdoes it was because she had gone to the same educational establishments as they had. The ones that had the ethos of *The Fuck You School of Hard Knocks. Nothing to Learn. Know it all Already. Get Lost, Prick!* (as proved by the hardened attitudes of those pupils who had amassed substantial experience in predatory skills for survival. Holly Hargreaves passing out with a final qualification of being Head Girl).

The counselling had been a laugh a minute. What the hell could an academic know of how a child felt when every home she had been placed in had rejected her? A round peg in a square hole and not a square peg in a round hole, at that! The latter with a chance of being whittled to fit, if not the former.

Holly Hargreaves recognised herself as an outsider; one of life's rejects. It hurt. Little wonder that Holly had lost her temper in frustration almost on a daily basis and had had to be restrained by three staff with full training with the added benefit of knowing that she would be safe in letting off steam because what they dare not do was to hurt her or to allow her to hurt herself. It got her out of all kinds of situations where she might have to admit that she had not been attentive on the day they had covered that particular concept in school. A useful resource whenever she was being tested and in danger of making a fool of herself. Better to break a few things than allow her contemporaries to become aware that she was unable to answer a question or complete most ordinary, average tasks. Exams in a sin-bin are impossible, also. So who said she had failed every exam she sat, Miss Thicky? Never sat any to fail!

Thus being the way of things for an intelligent but skill/knowledge-impoverished child for whom the constant protection and enduring love of a caring family had ever been denied. Holly trusted no-one, these days. Done it too often in the past. Been let down too much. Ever since she had been amputated from a life as Holly Kenyon. The one she could recall little of, save for playing happily in a beer garden inside a Wendy House. Which special place had had a toy monkey within upon which she had done some nappy practise. The woman she had called Mummy, then, had done a lot of sleeping. As had the man she called Daddy. Dopey folk whom she would later come to recognise as drug addicts. Still, Holly wondered. Who am I? Where do I come from? She had managed to steer well clear of drugs because Holly Hargreaves was a control freak. Start that shit and the only people who control anything are the dealers.

Holly had become Hargreaves, nee Kenyon, through a change of name by deed poll on the insistence of adoptive parents who had later realised, somewhat too late, that the one thing their other children did not need was a cigarette smoking teenage sister with an attitude problem.

These days, she was a girl on a mission. She had come to Quinton for only one reason. She had to know why she had been put into care. Had it been her own naughty behaviour which had put her there? So many times flinging herself on the floor in a tantrum and screaming fit to burst. Jumping up and down on bouncing, clacking, rickety beds when her nan...at least she thought it had been her nan...had come thumping up the stairs, shouting that she was about to bring the ceilings, in the tap room below, down on the heads of the drinkers. *For God's sake, you naughty girl, behave yourself!*

Had she disappointed her parents because she had always found it hard to write with good spelling? Nothing made someone seem more utterly stupid than that person being unable to spell. Her teachers had ever been on to her nan to tie her to the kitchen table and make her recite the alphabet over and over again until she was blue in the face. Though she knew, now, that her main problem had always been that she never read enough to absorb the very patterns of the words. Hence the young teenage love stories far too idealised for someone as streetwise as Holly Hargreaves which she hid from the world in an effort to do some catching up. She didn't want anyone to think that she had gone soft in the head and started to believe in love and romance. So many teachers and foster carers humiliating her with their pressured one-to-one lessons to try to make her acquire something she had developed a mental block against. Not that she was unable to read! She could read but what she could not do was spell very well despite an innate intelligence that often allowed her to problem solve better than her teachers.

Holly smarted, even yet, with a deep and abiding loathing of all the do-gooders who had poured through her life in a never ending stream. What did they know about rejection? If she had one more air-head tell her that it was time to move on and forget about her beginning she would scream. What beginning? She had no beginning because there was nothing in her inside thoughts to link her to other human beings who possessed any sort of solid identity. Who cared anyway? Answer: no one! So why should she?

Angry thoughts hidden, she smiled at a young policeman on the desk as she tugged at her short skirt, the waiting room beginning to fill with people asking questions, almost swarming, standing instead of sitting, demanding to speak with the Chief Constable. Holly keeping a low profile, turning pages. One white, peep-toe stiletto shoe swinging off her blue painted toenails as she crossed her long and very shapely legs so that he could take a better look. Not wanting to be lost within the milling crowd of people. As if she ever could be! She was waiting for her new employers and wanted to be immediately recognisable as the qualified person the employment agency had sent to work with the little girl in question. She would not be flashing her qualifications at anyone else so they were now deposited safely back into the small suitcase at her feet, next to her shoulder bag. The one she had reclaimed from where she had stashed it with a very friendly looking lady at a launderette on the corner of some blocks of flats in the town centre, who had made a crude gesture at someone flashing by in a red sports car, with words to the effect of *Arrogant little toe rag!*

The launderette was opposite the bus station, next to the employment agency which had been so very handy when her first intention had been to find a live-in-job. Failing that the dog of an eager boyfriend who would allow her to share his living and his living space free of charge for the time being in exchange for rampant sex.

Holly was not the type to be dependent but she was the type to see a boyfriend as a facility to be used to her best advantage with a bartered return. Only if that failed would the idea of a squat and some furtive shoplifting provide a final solution to her current homelessness. She had left Greater Manchester owing six weeks rent and with an eviction notice in her pocket having sacrificed her shelf-stacker's job for the satisfaction of telling her line manager where he could stick it after he had changed her aisle from books, CDs and magazines, to tinned peas, soups and baked beans. Where was she expected to purloin her hobbies from, thereafter? That's where her copy of Parent and Child had come from.

Holly was a fussy girl! She had already turned her nose up at the job offer in the launderette window when the requirement was to spend all day folding someone else's underwear for minimum wage. Though the lady had been kindness itself in giving her directions to the police station where she had now been set to wait with a letter of introduction in her pocket, she could stuff a job like that.

Quinton, quite a busy place from the look of it, too. The police station certainly was. There was a lot of complaining about police victimisation going on somewhere called the Dog's Bed Estate. The name rang a bell of familiarity inside Holly's head. She pricked up her ears and listened. The square accent was familiar. Voices came into her head which spoke over a long distance. Not unkind, either. Voices that called her, *Our Holly, love!* The same flat vowels were within the voices of the people she listened to, now, as their owners crowded the counter to make loud complaint. "We shouldn't all have to suffer harassment just because someone hurt a child, as repulsive as that is…."

"You've been pulling people off the streets right left and centre and they've done nothing…"

"Where's my Georgie when he was hawked by the neck into the riot van and driven away?"

A woman in tears.

A man seriously angry as he was restrained by his friends from letting a punch fly in the direction of the young policeman Holly was considering for leading dog. Trouble was he had wiry, ginger hair.

Others saying little but supportive as backup.

The voice cutting through her attention to what was going on over by the police counter was quiet and easy; a big, slack man with his hands stuck in his pockets, smelling of stale beer and roll-your-owns. Middle-aged, a tweed jacket with a dog lead hanging out of his pocket. His smile was friendly. "Just a guess. You Holly Hargreaves? Got a daughter of my own of about your age."

Holly stood tall, smiling back at a father figure. A smiling moon face, he had bread crumbs stuck into the crease at the side of his mouth. "You're Doctor Thomas?" Holly asked handing her letter over.

"Gosh, no. Gary Silvers. Care Assistant. I won't say Leading Care Assistant but normally there's only me and Tommo to make up the assessment team. That's Tommo over there, signing us through."

The man he indicated was standing at a lectern, writing into the big book using a splintered ball pen tied onto a hairy string with a ball of sticky tape which he seemed to find irksome for some reason. He glanced at her and smiled but vacuously as if he had seen her but not seen her. As if she didn't matter. Holly bristled. She could see by his air of distraction that he was not as beguiled by her looks as most men were. As Gary was, even though his attitude was essentially paternal. Strange dress sense too. She had him twigged in a moment; a psychologist. Holly had had a lot of experience of psychologists wandering into rooms where she sat waiting, carrying files with her name on. Such files having started their existence when she had been nine years old and her attention seeking behaviours had started to drive her adoptive parents and harassed teachers potty. He would have a briefcase full of case files somewhere. By the time she had left school at sixteen, or been expelled being more to the point, they had been four inches thick with incident. So many of them having come into her classrooms at various stages of her disturbed schooling trying to look part of the furniture, sitting at the back of the room and watching her indiscreetly as if she was the only child present. Holly deliberately putting her hand up to answer questions and, for once, the teacher choosing her to answer. A real give away, that, when she had usually been ignored unless creating mayhem. Usually Teacher's Pet selected, instead, because correct answers always gained a good mark on the weekly score board. If Holly gained none in the first place she had none to be taken away. They did not work in minuses.

Holly had started the downward spiral in her junior years and hit rock bottom before she was twelve and first year at secondary school. So what was this one kid to someone with her experience? One naughty little seven year old girl! Holly knew how to deal with every trick going because she had been a naughty girl herself, up to every trick going. Treble trouble, not double trouble! She could still raise the roof upon occasion.

The man she now knew to be Dr Thomas became the subject of his colleague's conversation. "Tommo likes us all to be on first name terms at Greengates. Call me Gary. Then there's Angie and Harry who look after the place and make sure we get fed and watered. You'll find him a bit on the quiet side until he gets to know you. I'll be showing you the ropes as soon as possible. Though he always insists on the initial mentoring of anyone new to the unit. Likes to lecture, a bit, does Tommo. Likes things done as he likes things done, does Tommo."

Holly nodded. So did she! She'd soon have things arranged to her own liking. "Can I pop out later, for a few things, if that's okay? I need some toothpaste and a few bits and bobs so's I can settle in." And find out where the nightlife was happening!

Gary nodded. "We are aware of the short notice, though you won't be allowed to leave the child alone except at night. As long as Angie can cover for you it should be alright. Our clients are never to be left unsupervised unless they're in their room and the door locked where we monitor them by CCTV."

Holly's eyes grew wide; the term *secure unit* very reminding. "Will I be sleeping in the same room, with her?"

Gary shook his head. "She'll be locked in. I'll be waking you if need be. She has to have female supervision for all her needs and that means you...no one else. Angie's not strictly just cook cum housekeeper but she has her own jobs to do. She's been at Greengates forever. I live in these days as Tommo does along with the caretaker, but Angie lives out. We all muck in when necessary because it can get tough at times. There are certain ground rules that Tommo's a stickler for. He'll explain all those himself, later. If we need an extra pair of hands, Harry the caretaker isn't beyond wading in. Angie, too, sometimes. Can't see that that's necessary with this little one, though. She'll be a change from our usual raging bullocks."

Interesting! That meant that Holly could have some time to herself. She would soon have the kid doing her bidding. Things were looking up. Because of its unsociable hours, the job, temporary as it was, would pay enough to get her started. She imagined herself with a leg over a windowsill, shinning down a drainpipe at first dark opportunity, nipping over a fence, no one any the wiser. Not back till dawn light. If she had to tie the child up during the day while she got a bit of kip, she'd find some bribe or other to keep her quiet...set her on look-out, maybe, in exchange for not being thumped. Way of the world according to Holly Hargreaves and necessary under the circumstances. That lad with her meal ticket in his pocket would be waiting somewhere in a Quinton night club. Once she had him eating out of the palm of her hand she could set about her real business of tracing the family who had put her into care. The one that couldn't give a shit! The one that Holly hoped to have the satisfaction of spitting some hostility at before heading back to Manchester. Maybe, after that, she'd choose a stud to have a baby herself because being a single mother meant that she could claim a council flat and they would both be looked after by the State. Only she'd dedicate herself to its welfare. She was already getting fed up of this lark of working for a living. Eighteen months in a supermarket stacking shelves was enough to piss anybody off and put them off, for ever more, from working for a living.

"Better get on then. The kid's ready and waiting, I gather. Needed showering again and changing before transferring."

Cargo meat, Holly thought. That's what she had been for most of her existence.

As they got up to go and meet her temporary boss, he was beckoning over the young, ginger-haired policeman from the centre of a throng of complaining people still finding issue for complaint. The name she overheard, again; Dog's Bed Estate caused Holly to frown in vague recollection. For some reason the name Dog's Bed Inn came to mind; the place of the Wendy House with the stuffed monkey where she had always felt safe, even when her grandparents were rowing their heads off. A place called Carlton Manor Primary School, too, where she had been happy enough until she had had to start to learn writing, letters jumping about on the pages of her exercise books like fleas on a mangy dog.

"I believe the child has been cleaned up. Some new clothes will be provided by Social Services. Her social worker will be taking them round there. She'll meet us there." Holly not really listening. Instead, she was pulling her shoulders back so that her breasts stood out against her white nylon zipper. Despite his ginger locks, she smiled at the young PC invitingly as she followed Gary and the unfriendly Tommo through the door which the policeman opened with a swipe card, her high heels clicking as she followed on, lingering just long enough in the open doorway to let him get a whiff of Born Wild. Somewhere in her suitcase was a pair of flats she would put on later. Holly suffered from corns though she had a grin and bear it attitude and refused to complain about them. Her feet were killing her.

Last through the door, Holly smiled a goodbye at the young PC as he turned away and she saw a look of longing cross over his face, so restoring her confidence in the face of Dr Thomas's lack of appreciation. Maybe ginger wasn't too bad, after all!

Tommo and Gary went through the door ahead of her so that Holly had to hold it for herself. The result of the modern manners those dolt-brain feminists had brought upon themselves. One day, though, when she was famous and had the whole world eating out of the palm of her hand she'd have doors held open for her. Holly finding excuse for the young PC to take another peep at her legs as she held the door open for longer than was strictly necessary. Mayhem on the corridors here as well. People everywhere.

In a crowded inner hallway a man was walking hurriedly towards her wearing a flat, grey cap over untidy fair hair. The navy blue reefer jacket looked too small for him, showing bony wrists and a cheap watch; suitcase crap with the gold worn off. She noted the bandage on his hand, too. He had his head well down while his hands dug firmly into the pockets of dirty jeans. The smell came before him. She caught sight of an unshaven face and a flash of silver grey, panic-bright eyes before he lowered his head further. She smelled his pong as he slipped through the door she held open; a smell like stagnant water having dried on his person. Barging her slightly as if in a controlled hurry with the side of his left arm rubbing against her right one as he passed.

Holly had the impression that she knew him. Knew the eyes he flashed at her from somewhere and recognised the pleading look in them. Then she recalled where. The man she had used to call Daddy whose death had been the impetus for her being given away had had silver eyes, too. She closed the door after him, unaware that the hive of activity before her was unusual. People going in and out of numbered rooms, some in handcuffs, others looking stunned and white-faced. While men in suits accompanied them, files under arm.

It was then that two, uniformed officers came quickly to the top of the steps where Tommo was, now, leading them in a small convoy, about to go down. One of them spoke loudly and sharply. "Anyone seen Mally Kenyon? That kid opened the door for him from the outside. We'd left him in the Holding Room to cool off. Someone pinched my coat and hat. Can only have been him."

Holly stemmed a gasp. She had just let him through the door and closed it behind him. His name! His familiarity! A Kenyon!

Neither Tommo nor Gary seemed to have been aware of him. "Mally Kenyon, here?" Tommo had been one of the same gang as Mally, long ago, so knew him well enough. Not that Tommo was known for clear sighted observations of what was happening directly about himself in the course of everyday life. The jolly green giant could have stomped past him and he, most probably, would have remained unaware even if he'd been tapped on the head and barged out of the way. The news yet to break outside of the Dog's Bed Estate that Mally Kenyon was, actually, now named as the man the police had arrested in connection with the attempted drowning of a little girl. "I thought he'd been a hero, for once."

Gary surprised, too, when he had been looking with curiosity into an interview room and recognising an old client of theirs just as the door was slammed closed. "Wasn't it Mally pulled the child out of the water?"

The policemen scratching their heads, looking round. "He's done a bunk. Knew we should have kept him cuffed. How the hell's he got out of the place?"

Holly kept her own counsel as the policemen went the other way intent on a fruitless search of the building. He had gone out the front way into a crowded foyer. Easy then to slip through the front glass doors and away. A Kenyon!

Holly felt as if things were moving a bit too fast for her as memories began to kick in. As if a small window into her long and distant past had been opened. Memories of a public house with black and white wood around the upper windows. A place with pebble-dashed houses crammed tightly together. All the same as each other in street after twisting street. Grass verges instead of pavements to the rear of them. Walkways to the front. High rise flats to the back of a spired church where the land rose, beyond. She and her friends from school had gone there to play amongst tiny streams and brooks, collecting buttercups and daisies to make fairy necklaces. She recalled a row of shops where the wind had blown her scarf away one day while she was wearing new red shoes. It had caught on a red pillar box just as she went tripping over the toes of her stiff new shoes, cutting her knees and hands to ribbons. Being lifted, tears wiped and then a lollipop to compensate. A tall, thin man with a moustache who she called Granddad, but others called Tock. As in tick-tock-clock; memories coming back of a fob watch consulted out of a waistcoat pocket. All this somehow linked with a pair of silver eyes and a pub called the Dog's Bed Inn, on the Dog's Bed Estate in Lower Quinton.

Holly followed on, mindless to her surroundings or the child who waited for them.

Eleven

Indeed, the child was waiting for them in great expectation...a child, quiet and patient, now, having folded her own, now clean hands firmly together over her chest as if to keep them out of trouble. Silver eyes looking this way and that under blonde eyebrows; one bright, the other dull. The calm, dull one seeming to be the one to lead the child's reformed mood after the station housekeeper had had to put a bucket of hot soapy water in a swill over the cell floor where the child had been contained and get to work to stiff brush the brown ring down the drain because the cell was needed for a different occupant. Then shoved her roughly under a tepid shower with only a stiff, green, plastic curtain between her and the corridor where the cells were, with a nail brush and a bottle of shampoo, offering her the boy's clothing that she was wearing because her other clothes were soiled.

She had then been sat on a big chair behind, but to one side of the Charge Officer's desk, as the station became more like a railway station than a police station with people in uniform heaving about other people in handcuffs; up the stairs and down, into the cells and out, through doors that banged closed behind them.

She needed to be good, to be gone, if she was ever to find the lady with the golden trumpet. Though she did not know where. Like Chicken-Licken looking for the king. You just had to ask and ask until you found who you were looking for. She put her head down and directed her mind to being part of the chair. She could feel its hard, spindly, upright support like a backbone against her own, the seat digging into the back of her calves.

She didn't move or look up even as someone came down the stairs and put the rag doll on her knee though her hands crept to hold it tight. Oswald had become her favourite because he was agile. He could bend any which way he wanted and not break. When she had first thought to go look for the lady with the golden trumpet, it was Oswald Rag Doll that had first taught her that escape was all about being able to tumble fast, go with the pull on a leg upside down if maybe, be tossed against a wall and absorb the shock as he slid down into a heap onto the floor again. To be amenable. Oswald was always ready to flop, not fight. Last into the toy box and first out of it because he always made sure that he fitted in whatever spaces were left, lying flat. She put his orange head to her ear in case he might tell her things. He had been in the room, upstairs, when Caitlin had done those naughty things. Naughty, that, Caitlin. Stay in! Let Wendy deal with things in a quiet way, like Oswald. He had nothing to say but to lay softly against her shoulder, her only friend in the whole wide world. Save for the lady with the golden trumpet. Please, save for the lady with the golden trumpet!

When the Charge Officer changed, she seemed to become forgotten about. A child set to wait for the man to come back again to claim her.

Then the man with the silver eyes which were the same colour as Serena's! She had seen the man who had brought her out of the water as she emerged from the shower, washed and clean again. Their eyes met just for a fraction of a moment. Her own sorry now. His keening, a pleading look and sudden hope on his desperate face as he was pushed into a room and the door shut on him; a door with a high handle on the outside. When he came to bang on the door and shout. "Ask the child, she'll tell you! I'm innocent!" she knew that he was locked in. Like in the cellar room and her bedroom with the boarded window and the eye her only means of seeing out. There would be a handle on the outside but not the inside. Only a special key might open it from the inside while the handle would open it from without. She thought carefully, her two hands in partnership and still for a moment as he continued to shout and cry from within. "Ask the child. I'm innocent, I tell you. For Christ's sake! She'll tell you...she'll speak."

Slowly, she had shaken her head. No matter how they had asked and asked who she was, she hadn't told them anything more than the police lady had told her to say. She would tell no one about Caitlin even when she was causing so much trouble. She was Wendy Bridgewater now, not Caitlin Collins who nobody wanted. Her address was Bridge 28, Lower Quinton, not 34, Park Road, Lower Quinton. Wendy, if not Caitlin, had been new born of the hard edged, stinking water by the hands of the man who had saved her and brought her up and into the air again.

The police lady with the dolls had told her who she was, now. Police ladies told the truth, the whole truth, and nothing but the truth even when they did not listen. But no matter how she had asked, or how naughty Caitlin had been, she had still not been naughty enough to come before the lady with the golden trumpet. The only person who could save Caitlin from Blackstone School. Because Caitlin would not go to Blackstone School. "Never, see, never, no! Go away, Serena! The cellar is where I want to be!"

But that had been naughty Caitlin Collins and now she was good Wendy Bridgewater; a happy girl, nice to know. Clean once again. In old, rubbish clothes that felt scratchy and hard. Clothes Caitlin would never have worn. Caitlin had to have the soft fabrics with pretty lace and silky bits because Caitlin was a little princess. Said so on her clothing. Wendy did not mind the ill fitting, baggy and scratchy clothes as she watched all about her for the lady with the golden trumpet, when she had been so sure that she would be in this very same place where she lived because of her uniform; all hell breaking loose as grown-up people and adolescent youths were being dragged in through the Charge Room doors and thrust into cells the same as she had been until Wendy had come to their rescue and had agreed to make the magic brown ring to set them both free again. The naughty people come for a telling off. Caitlin was naughty. Wendy was good.

Naughty people everywhere, here. No other little girls, though. They would all be in that room upstairs with the little dolls, crowded together, like school would be. Wendy had to stop thinking about that so that Caitlin wouldn't get mad again. That's where they put the naughty girls, though! They got brought to the police station and locked up in Room Three, never to escape, trapped in a corner by a lady who wouldn't listen. Serena had told her from being a tiny baby when she would not be quiet in the cellar. When she wanted to break from her restraint within the cart or bang on the boarding which covered the window glass where the eye was and go watch…never to play with…the other little girls who sat in the grass by the lake, in the park, across the way, where the swans glided…that little girls who were noisy and bad ended up at the police station.

Only she had not known then that it was where the lady with the golden trumpet lived. She wasn't here, though, when she had looked so very hard at every passing face. It was Wendy, not Caitlin, had scanned every face that passed as she sat on her chair and waited for the next stage in her adventure. Wendy would never stop asking until she found the lady who would want her where Serena didn't. Her real mummy would keep Caitlin in the cellar where Caitlin was happy but let Wendy out to play. Then they would both be happy. Wendy looking closely at everyone who passed, especially the uniformed females, while she waited, legs dangling from her oversized chair, in big, boy's clothes and socks too big for her. No pink boots now with rainbow laces which Wendy had liked so very much and Caitlin had flung away. Just some soft galoshes as she waited for the man to come back, take her to some unexplained place, maybe where the lady with the golden trumpet lived. She no longer asking over and over, of everyone coming and going, where was the lady with the golden trumpet, please. No one had answered her, anyway, just looked at her funny. Caitlin beginning to scream in her head because Caitlin would be answered and no one would turn away, blank-eyed, from Caitlin. Caitlin would never be ignored.

Quiet Caitlin! Let Wendy lead the way. Patience, patience, Caitlin! Quiet, Caitlin! But Caitlin never had been patient. Clever Caitlin but never quiet Caitlin. Angry Caitlin ever since she had been told that she was to be sent away from everything she knew and loved. Flinging toys, breaking and spilling things. Bringing Serena to her knees. Caitlin smacking her hard over her head where the skin was sore. Seeing the blood come. Puckered chin but not saying sorry! Then the magic brown ring, because it was somewhere she could go to feel safest. No one ever followed her inside the brown ring.

Wendy shut her mouth against the angry sob that might have escaped her. Caitlin's angry sob; not her own, because Caitlin was spoilt. That's what she had heard the man say, once. Caitlin needed putting over someone's knee and her bottom slapping he had said. Serena had shown him the door after taking the money. When she had taken off her veil her eyes had been fizzing in her head and two red patches had grown on her paper skin but then it had all been forgotten about. "We must see you properly prepared for the outside world," was all she had said. "The uniform is expensive."

That had been when the lady in the big hat came. The one who gave Serena money but never came inside the house. They met on the street under the street lamps when the dark came, then went across to the bandstand in the park to chat because Serena would not be seen on the street. Serena had never played out, either.

Caitlin had seen the clutch of money pass over and then she had a new computer and a new programme called "Out and About". Caitlin had had to try to name all the different items. Serena had told her that she must be able to name and then recite the names of all those things she didn't know already...shopping trolley...shelves...aisles...chill cabinet...freezer units...check out. Read price labels...count the money out...pack the shopping items in the plastic bags that ripped as Caitlin got angrier and angrier and snapped the baguettes and threw the bits at Serena and stamped her feet and yelled and screamed and cried until her cheeks were red hot buns and Serena was crying, too, and pleading with her to be good. "You are making me ill...so ill...my darling, cherished child. Please, to be good!"

She had, indeed, been the one to open the outer door to the room where they had taken the man she recognised as the same to have brought her up out of the water for Wendy to be born. Stood on her chair to do so to reach the high handle after carrying her chair across the floor when the man at the desk went to bring in yet another of the angry boys and men in handcuffs; the one who had been shouting and dragging a cup on the grating having gone off with Tommo; the man who would be coming for her.

Sorry now for hitting and pushing the ladies and hurting them and then making the brown ring which seemed to make other people as angry as it did Serena. Sorry, too, for hurting the man when he had helped her. It was naughty to bite but Caitlin had been so desperate and wild and angry. So very frightened when the water had come over her head. She had bitten his head and his hand and kicked out at him because she had not understood, at first, what was happening through the dizziness, red lights flashing in her head. Never been touched before by a man, not even the man whom Serena had, sometimes, let into the house. The man who had been making all the arrangements for her going away to Blackstone School. On her way to Blackstone School, in fact. The man that Serena said was her daddy only he was nasty and had had to be made to pay for Caitlin's schooling. The only one ever to touch her having been Serena whose funny hands were kind and soothing, yet who was not to be dissuaded no matter how much Caitlin tried to convince her to let her stay. "It has to be my darling child. It has to be." Soft, silver eyes running with tears.

But Caitlin wasn't going to go away to Blackstone School which was why she had taken her only, last opportunity for escape. She had put herself in the water after being lifted from the trolley, inside the sack, and dropped again on her feet, remembering the man's voice as it had echoed and come back to her, shouting; "...it's a child?...a child in there?" A voice deep with astonishment before the tragic leap that had nearly drowned her. He had smelled of dogs as she had been up against his hard boots and could feel his legs through the sacking just for a moment, like the dogs with hot, bad breath that came sniffing at the trolley when she had been kept within.

For a long time, Caitlin had thought herself to be a dog because they all wore a collar, too, and had to behave when they were attached to the chain, just as she had been. Now she thought that she must look like Serena; beautiful in animation. And especially when she smiled with swirly love in the watery pools of her silver, fish bowl eyes and her luscious, red lips trembled with emotion. "I wish...Oh, my darling, Caitlin, how I wish...!" Twirling her around, laughing and dancing together. So very happy!

Until it had come to being sent away to school. She knew why Serena had tied her into the sack because it had been the only way to get her into the trolley when she refused to ride in the cart as she had once so loved to do to see the bright busy world from which she and Serena must hide away.

She had fought Serena all the way in its prevention but then became happy-sleepy in the sack...*Just a game, Caitlin, my darling. Just a game of hide and seek!* Her slack, warm body lying at an angle of forty-five degrees and so soothed by the rumbling of her carriage. Only frightened when the gathered neck of the sack had been grabbed and she had been raised up and then dropped just as suddenly.

She knew that she had jumped the wrong way into the water without knowing where she was going. A slow struggle under, not upwards, because the sack had pulled her feet underneath her bottom. She had been ledged against the round and pokey things in the smelly water. Oswald, under her chin, having helped her to breathe until the last of the shapes had moved away and she had finally gone under.

Then, after the man had lifted her out, she had been so frozen with fear. She had seen the dog lead in the policeman's hands; the sign for total obedience! She had wanted so to be taken to the lady with the golden trumpet. She had been glad of the shower and the nice clean clothes; red dungarees, like boy's wear and the pretty, stout, pink boots with the rainbow laces and having her hair up in shiny, pink bobbles. So happy to see her rag doll safe, also. Her Oswald, got for Christmas. Showered just as she was and then dunked in the stringent fumes which would take the germs away. Put to dry on the radiator. Happy to have him back again.

Why hadn't they listened when Caitlin had remembered her manners, spoken nicely, as Serena had taught her, asked her question, clearly, over and over and over again, using the name the police lady had given her, "Wendy speak with the lady with the golden trumpet, please?"

And now Caitlin was inconsolable so that Wendy had had to take over. It had been the police lady's idea to have Wendy speak for Caitlin who was angry still, stamping her feet inside her head, shouting at Wendy in that loud and demanding voice of hers, trying to get her hand away from Wendy's even as Wendy calmly and quietly held it, trying to comfort her other self. There, there, Caitlin! There, there!

Then she recognised the feet coming down the stairs; the brown deck shoes and the odd socks, one black and one navy blue. The striped trousers and the big, blue mackintosh. Eyes of a dark, moody grey flecked with bits of brown that hadn't screwed themselves with disgust when she had made the brown ring. Like he knew its magic and understood it. A man with a long finger that kept pushing his spectacles up his nose and sweeping back the curtains of his brown hair.

Wendy had yet to know what colour her own eyes were as she tucked the now dry rag doll down the neck of her overlarge jersey so that she had two heads to represent herself; Wendy, and Caitlin, too, in one body, going everywhere together. Though she would not try to define which was which as she smiled at the man who came to claim her.

She smiled, now, most beguilingly because this was the same man who had carried her down the steps from the room where Caitlin had lost her temper and held her fast until Caitlin had begun to calm down inside her. He had explained that he would come for her, later, and so he had. He had come for her with a man with black, scuffed shoes with frayed laces whose socks were plaid and hung about his ankles because the tops had grown too big. She could see them in wrinkles under his baggy trousers as he walked behind the deck shoes, down the stairs. His jacket old and comfortable. Caitlin knew nothing of men save for the man with the very blue eyes who looked at her with blame. She didn't like them.

They both said hello. The man with the crumpled, hairy, woollen jacket smelled funny; of dogs and tobacco and boiled sweets like cough drops. He said his name was Gary and ruffled her damp hair with a big hand which covered the whole of her head as he messed up her hair where she sat on the chair, ignoring her other head with its orange mop as if he did not realise that it was a part of her. She noted the dog lead in his pocket. Time for Caitlin to behave.

Behind them was a lady with long, bare legs and white shoes with tall, thin heels. She had blue toe nails and wore a short, dark skirt and a white, nylon zipper jacket which clung to her shape. She had long dark hair brought back from a colourful face. Dark brown eyes. How strange! She kept looking behind her and frowning. Did she know that Wendy had opened the door for the man to come out, take the hat and coat off the peg and walk away? He had looked about as if to see anyone but her then blown her a kiss and made for the stairs. She had still been standing on the chair next to the open door when the policemen had come looking and followed him up. Wendy could not understand why the man was here when he had not been naughty. Or at least not as far as she knew. He had been a good man. He had saved her from the water.

Wendy considered that she had done the right thing so she did not feel bad inside as she might have done had what she had done been a bad thing. Letting people go free could never be a bad thing.

Also, Serena had always taught her that if people were kind they should be kindly treated in return. This when it had been pointed out to Caitlin that Serena had never been anything but good to Caitlin and treated her as every little princess should be with graceful care. This would be important if she was ever to find the lady with the golden trumpet. Wendy understood that, even if Caitlin didn't.

Best to keep one's distance, though, if secrets where to be protected, as Serena had used to say to Caitlin, because the neighbours must never see her or know of her. She would be telling no one the secrets other than the lady with the golden trumpet. Not this lady who had yet to do anything but give her a surly glance and curl one side of her mouth up. She wasn't the lady with the golden trumpet, either. Disappointment filling Wendy's mind, again. Yet so sure that she remembered correctly the features of the one she was looking for. The special one was an older lady with blonde hair tied in a net to the back of her head, who wore the dark blue uniform of a very smart and important police person. She carried a leather case in which was the golden trumpet which Caitlin had seen her play in the park when Serena had taken her in the cart to the bandstand that glorious summer day, when the swans were gliding and Serena had told her things that she had not known before. Then, that same night, all had changed. The swans had been attacked and their wings broken. Their fluffy, baby chick stamped on until it was dead. The lady with the golden trumpet had come to knock on their door and nothing had been the same, again. Caitlin had watched her from the secret, hiding place under the stairs where the trolley lived. Seen her beautiful face so different from Serena's beauty. Sisters. They were sisters. Serena had told Caitlin that the lady with the golden trumpet had been the one to give Caitlin to Serena because she had not wanted her for herself. Only she did not know about Caitlin. She was their secret and should always be so.

This was not the lady with the golden trumpet. Too young. Too dark-haired. Silver eyes meeting brown. Yet knowing something because the girl...not a lady...a girl...had a secret, too. Wendy knew about secrets. Wendy understood secrets. Caitlin's life had been a secret...riding in the cart...happy in the cellar...doing all her school work...dancing and singing...listening to music...computer studies, too. Using the computer that Serena had got the lady to buy her because she would have to know how to use one when she went to school. Like the one she had trashed because she would not go to Blackstone School. Never! So there!

"Me, Wendy," she told the girl, with the friendly, babyish voice so unlike Caitlin's haughty way of speaking. She felt her own cheeks rise upwards as she smiled.

The troubled, brown eyes stretched at her in a surprised glare. She had covered her skin with an orange colour streaked with pink and mauve and turned her lips a funny shade of pearly pink, white teeth, glossy lips stretching. "Okay, kid?"

Caitlin didn't like to be called a kid. She wasn't a goat. Wendy was much younger than Caitlin, though. All of four while Caitlin was seven.

Wendy wasn't bothered how she was referred to. She wanted the girl and the men to know that she was not the same girl as the one who had done all the naughty things. "Me a good girl, now."

Holly's eyes widened, even further. What was all this? If the kid thought that she was taken in by a baby voice she would soon find out that Holly Hargreaves wasn't fooled for a single moment. "I'm delighted to meet you." Charm itself. About the only useful thing her schooling had instilled was the value of good manners when needed. "My name's Holly," she added with a mock-friendly smile growing over a derisive one. She offered a set of false, gel finger nails which the child ignored as she continued to sit with her hands laced together over her tummy. So the kid had to be told who called the shots, hey? Ways and means; always smile while doing something intended to make a point to be noted as she took the child by the laced hands with kind insistence, putting her head close so that the child's nose wrinkled against the smell of her cheap perfume. The unlacing of Wendy's tightly woven fingers was achieved with a knowing look.

Wendy felt the sharp, little nails of her right hand curl into the palm which Holly held onto tightly. Caitlin was after scratching. Holly seemed to know exactly what Caitlin would like to do. She watched as Holly shook her head from side to side, thinking better of it.

Very careful to keep her voice low, just for the child to hear, Holly bent closer still. "I wouldn't if I were you, kid. Them, yes. Me, no. You're safe with them but not with me. I got just the thing in my handbag to stop you from scratching anyone. Me, in particular. They're called nail scissors," was what she whispered for the child's ears only. "We'll hold hands, nicely, shall we?"

Wendy knew when compliance was necessary. She allowed Holly to take her right hand and hold it tightly while not moving from her seat as she relaxed the bag inside her that held the water in. When the bag opened it was warm and wet and swilled all about her upper legs.

Tommo and Gary were already ringing the counter bell, then getting on with the completion and signing of some forms left out for them.

Holly knew from her own experience that the forms would be concerned with signing for their charge's transfer to the secure, assessment unit until such time as the child could be found a more appropriate placement. Holly had been signed over so many times in her life she looked back on her past as if she had been a second-hand fridge freezer; mere cargo to be moved about from this place to that.

Wendy, understanding where Caitlin might not, allowed herself to be brought off the seat leaving behind her the wet puddle. Caitlin's doing, of course, not Wendy's. It dripped over the rim and onto the floor changing the colour of the wooden seat from light to dark. The retort, Wendy thought, seeming appropriate though Caitlin was up to naughty tricks again. Next best thing to the brown ring, as a warning. The lady had better watch out!

Holly considered the wet patch as the child's reply to being told how they would be playing this life game which lay ahead of them both with some serious competition between them. However, it would be game, set and match to Holly Hargreaves. Holly had started wetting herself again at seven, also. "Gets awful uncomfortable when it dries on your knickers, you know."

Brown eyes and silver-grey locked and held each other; both unblinking. Defiance on the child's face. Determination on Holly's after a sly glance to ensure that they were still not being watched or listened to. Both Tommo and Gary were now talking with a very harassed looking Charge Officer to discover something of why the station was almost bursting at the seams on an average weekday. She whispered again. "The first thing I'll be teaching you, kid, is how to wash your own knickers in the sink when we get to this Greengates House place." Just to make sure she reached into the child's jersey and snatched up the rag doll. "Understand?"

The child's right, glittery eye was presented. That was their rag doll the girl-lady had taken! It was their Oswald. It was important to them both.

"You'll get it back when you're doing what your told and not before." Yet someone else with glittery, silver-eyes, Holly thought, Quinton full of them. She was pretty though. Gritty, too. Determined, just as she had been at that age. Holly was reminded.

Tommo and Gary were not after waiting for them it seemed. Without a backward glance they were going out the door which had a guard set upon it. Holly dragged the child through it to the waiting mini-bus which Gary had parked in the car park close to the rear doors. Holly knew all about travelling in mini-buses as a contrast to the sedate, family saloons most children rode in. Knew what to do when inside it, too. She even sorted out the strapping to make it small enough as she buckled the child into her seat tightly. Then she took a seat herself. To be sure the kid behaved, she sat the doll on her own knee and wagged its head at Wendy.

Wendy's chin puckered.

"Sweet things are ragged dolls, aren't they? I always wanted one when I was a kid, myself."

Twelve

Greengates House was a hive of activity that morning, also. Young Jacko had been handed over in handcuffs for his last ride in an unprotected, police vehicle before sentencing through the Juvenile Magistrates' Courts. Most probably to the secure mental hospital where his deepening schizophrenia might be treated, as Tommo had recommended.

Now there was a new one coming in on the heels of the last. Angie was after getting ahead of her domestic tasks. There would not be the usual grace of a day or two while Tommo and Gary went out giving handling courses to professional groups who also needed to know an approved way of restraining violent youths other than engaging in frantic scuffles or felling them with a karate kick. Either that or some consultancy work when the demands for planning behaviour strategies with difficult adolescent pupils particularly, were much in demand. While they worked primarily from Greengates House which was run as an independent charity as far as its funding went – part of a national chain, in fact, with green gates all over the country – they were always in demand for their expertise in the careful handling of aggressive youths. Gary Silvers being part of the team approach and, therefore, as much a part of the teaching process as Tommo was. Tommo being, of all things, an old boy of the unit, himself. Gary being a man who had never known any different work so took all the angst and anger the job contained in his stride. He was happy to follow Tommo's strict directives. As they all had to follow Tommo's strict directives.

Even bolshy Harry Groves when he considered his caretaker's role to be independent of Tommo's control. Fat chance! There was only one master here to be obeyed and that was Tommo. Take the overgrown bushes which ran around the rear of the perimeter fencing. Harry had had to get them cut down, last night, before he dare get into bed because they had assisted Jacko's escape. Either that or Tommo would want to know why; bad back or no bad back! They should never have been allowed to grow so tall in the first place. Angie had smiled to herself...even enjoyed a snidy laugh...when Harry had had to present himself to Tommo, knocking for entry into his office for the rollicking, with mutinous glares. He had come out with his cheeks aflame and then gone straight away to get on with what he should have done weeks ago; tail between his legs.

They all needed a break, though, and so having a little girl in the unit for a change was as good as a rest. Angie had even been up in the attic as well as into the school room, already, looking out for girly play things;

paints, crayons, story books; not a doll to be found. Lots of squeezy stress toys though nothing much of anything else. But enough to get them going. She had had to warn Tommo that they had no spare clothing to fit a little girl. Unless she came with her own suitcase he would have to get onto Social Services first thing for some suitable clothing for the child of her age. However, Angie had brought from home what she could; a fairy colouring book and some ribbons and beads the child could thread with as long as she was provided with just a few at a time. Awful little things to have to pick up if they got spilled. Spilled or thrown being the same difference to Angie. It was what their clients did when they came to Greengates, destructiveness being more entrenched in their use of games and playthings than constructiveness and part of the problems that made them an ill-fit with ordinary life. Yet Angie seeing such behaviour as a symptom while Harry always had negative comments to make, usually concerned with torture chambers and boiling oil. He had only just carted away the results of Jacko's destructive behaviour. They would all be looking for a few days grace.

Not that Harry knew yet about their new client whom Tommo would be bringing in once they had a female care assistant in place. Tommo had phoned her at home, early, to tell her that they would be having a little girl for a change. Did considerate things like that, did Tommo. But then Angie was more than just a cook and housekeeper at Greengates House. Angie was the surrogate mother Tommo had come to know when he had come to Greengates as a client, himself. The one who had darned his socks and sewed his buttons on and fussed a bit too much. The caring mother he had never had because the poor thing had been a shambling wreck and frightened of her own shadow; sedative dependent, too, for most of his life but now remarried and living elsewhere.

Angie being the one he came to lodge with after his stay in a juvenile institution where it had been noted that Tommo was extremely bright academically; took to books like a duck to water. She had been the one who had phoned him up to ask how he was when he had been at university and it sometimes all got a bit too much for him. Working too hard to erase his past, maybe. No time to get out to the pub or to a football match. The occasional weekend river fishing being about all Tommo's social life ever extended to and that always a solitary pastime, well away from towns and other people. If he had ever had a girlfriend, Angie had yet to know about it. Women made Tommo nervous. Or at least more so than he was made to feel intimidated by natural inclination towards normal people and normal situations. Angie sometimes thought they were all institutionalised by working at a place like Greengates House.

But Tommo understood what it felt like to be in trouble and then have to go through the system of trial and retribution.

What he knew about children, though, was zilch to Angie's reckoning. She hadn't needed a doctorate in psychology to know a thing or two about people. Books, books and more books; whole rows of them in that office of his. Dust gatherers, Angie called them, because when she dusted she always did a proper job and it took her ages working one by one with a clean, yellow cloth. Even flapping the inside pages to get rid of the paper mites and rubbing up the bindings of his leather bound ones. Them with the titles stamped into the leather and painted with gold to make the lettering stand out. Did people actually read books that had a thousand pages and all the print so small that it gave her a headache just to look at it? Not much of a reader, was Angie, outside of the odd Mills and Boon romance which people shouldn't knock because reading was reading when all came to all.

But not like Tommo read books. Tommo consulted books as his oracle. It was Tommo who observed, profiled, and then wrote the detailed, forensic reports with recommendations to inform, if not direct, a magistrate. Sometimes a judge. Their clients had to have done something heinous and life threatening for that to be the case, though. They were usually up before the magistrate and then sent to a corrective institution when they were always under eighteen years of age. After that the judges and magistrates could throw the book at them when they had some damned big tomes of their own to chuck their weight around with.

Some tragic cases, too. Tommo had already told Angie something of the experience of the little girl who had been horribly abused before being rescued from the disused Whemley Canal; a stinking mire if ever there was one. Should have been filled in years ago when it was nothing but a dumping ground for all the town's rubbish. Not just that of the residents of the Dog's Bed Estate, either! The same little girl for whom the news reporters on the local radio kept appealing for parents to come forward. Indeed, anyone to contact the police if they knew of a little, seven year old girl being missing. Angie had already phoned round to all her friends and acquaintance using her mobile. They, in turn, phoned her when it became known that such a tragic child was to be sent to Greengates House. The only person she didn't phone was her husband who would be too busy digging holes on some motorway or other and had no interest in kids anyway. He preferred his racing greyhounds to children, any day.

Angie had already had a call from her friend, Nan Bartlett, who lived on the Dog's Bed Estate telling her that that nasty bit of work who was brother-in-law to her daughter, Magdalene; Mally Kenyon, had been taken in for questioning because he had somehow been involved in the child's discovery. Kenyons were a bad lot, in the main. Not all, of course, but the decent ones had been known to change their name or even wear them fancy, coloured contact lenses if they were marked by the silver eyes which never failed to give their game away. Albino, people said, but they were not so fair of hair and skin to lack all pigmentation; just eyes like them little silver fishes she used to find living in her fireplace but which now infested the walls behind the cupboards in her kitchen, at home. She'd find them dead in teacups, curled up. They turned to dust as soon as touched.

The Chief constable of Quinton Dales and District had been on the TV, too. What was her name? Catty Collins, all smart and shiny. She had said that the little girl had been placed at Greengates House; correctly described as a secure assessment unit, but only for want of a better placement. Also, she had stated that the girl had shown signs of being extremely traumatised by what had happened to her. Until she had had time to settle, assuming that her parents could prove themselves not to be guilty of neglect once they did come forward, she might go home again. That, of course, would be a Social Services decision. However, it had been her immediate priority, after consultation with the Head of the Child Welfare Department, with whom she was in complete and total agreement, to keep her separate from other children until her needs could be fully assessed by their consultant expert on behavioural psychology, Dr Thomas Thomas.

Angie had switched off the TV in the client lounge where she had been dusting and vacuuming at the time of broadcast, intent on following events concerning the child, further, as they happened to be reported but in need of getting on with other things.

Within her large and well appointed kitchen, with its views to both the front and the back of the house, where she regarded herself as on permanent crow-watch, she put on her local radio because she had a batch of scones to get in the oven for their morning break. Hopefully, Tommo and Gary being back with the child and a new care assistant before time because she did not much care for being asked to make pots of tea and hawk trays about the roomy house when the lunch needed preparing. Today, sausages and onion gravy with garlic mash and steamed cauliflower. They would have jam sponge and custard to follow. All eaten with plastic cutlery because they never had anything that might be used as a dangerous weapon in the rooms inhabited by the clients. Even the table in the dining room was screwed down to the floor and the TV set on a plinth so high it could not be tampered with, never mind thrown at anyone.

To Angie, it had become second nature to count even the plastic cutlery out and count the same plastic cutlery back into her drawers again. When they had a particularly volatile client in residence, they ate off waxed plates and served themselves from plastic dishes so lightweight that even full of food, if flung, they would be unlikely to hurt anyone. All furniture if not screwed down being bought for the same harmless qualities of being unsuitable as weaponry. Straight back chairs were on runners instead of straight legged. They did less damage when slung in anger. Anything that might be used as a cutter was also carefully assessed for the same reason. Only this time, as weaponry of client choice for use against themselves as opposed to directly venting their anger on Tommo or Gary. Kids would cut themselves with anything to hand when allowed to as a common symptom of the emotional stress they were under. Mirrors were all plastic at Greengates House. No razor blades allowed, anywhere. Gary complained, endlessly, that the electric shaver he was forced to use cut his skin to shreds. If he wanted a wet shave he had to take himself off to the barber in Quinton who had brought the old fashioned luxury back again. Doing a mint, he was.

She had put some washing in the machine and got the dryer going, also, when that radio presenter – the same one who had invited Cubby Watson and Gina Mon to discuss their differences of opinion on the local authority's policies towards easing the social problems of troublesome children within troublesome families – especially when collected together in a place like the Dog's Bed Estate...said that he was all for calling Round Two between the same protagonists, even if Gina had suffered a knock out as soon as the bell had sounded the end of Round One.

Angie had been with Gina all the way. She considered the same problem, now, her fingers tickling butter into self raising flour in a large, glass dish. Her husband and Harry, having sided with Cubby Watson. Though what did they know? Angie had a lot of good friends living on the Dog's Bed. She didn't tell her husband or Tommo but she went with some frequency to Nancy Bartlett's front room séances and card readings. Nan had seen things in her tealeaf readings that had made Angie's hair stand on end. But just to be safe, she always nipped into St Saviour's on her way home to put a pound coin in the collection box just inside the front door, there. The iron box had been screwed into the wall with a coach bolt otherwise she'd have given it directly to Father Turner or Magdalene Kenyon who never failed to ask why her attendance was poor, these days. The longer she stayed away the worse it got because she could not then confess to the lies she told when she always blamed her Sunday absences on her husband having the M6 to re-tarmac. She had fibbed when she said that she was dependent on him giving her a lift.

Not that Father Turner was not understanding. For a man, he was an exception to the rule in many ways. Bumbled through his services he did. What her husband called an old fart. Should have put himself out to pasture years ago. She preferred her priests to be closet gays, anyway, because they knew what it was to be discriminated against. Though anything to do with emotional wellbeing she would have preferred to be led by women. It was what women had been put on Earth for in Angie's opinion, as she looked out onto the rear garden and saw what an untidy job Harry Groves had made of cutting down the bushes that had just burst into glorious leaf. Instead of pruning them he had lopped off whole branches with a chain saw and yet kept the bottoms thick. He hadn't liked being blamed by Tommo for Jacko leaping the fence.

Fruit and sugar in, a dash of water and her scone mixture came together nicely with a few flicks of her wooden spoon. She was scattering flour and rolling while sorting out the ills of the world in her caring head. Indeed, if Angie had her way, women would rule and men take second place. It had been Angie had helped Tommo to change because she had shown him some affection and understanding where none had previously existed. In fact, few adolescent lads failed to respond to her kindliness when they were as rutting stags to the men who tried their best to offer empathy but usually only served to get the aggression flowing and keep it maintained. Everything a man did was testosterone led!

To Angie, there was nothing like a bit of maternal attention to calm the raging-bull behaviours of the endless stream of angry boys who passed through the assessment unit. She considered, privately...knowing her attitudes to be entirely unprofessional but thinking it just the same...that there was, in her own estimation, more potential in a caring hug and a sticky sweet pudding than any amount of handling belts and arm locks which was all that most men had to control the young offenders when they let their tempers blow and all hell was let loose.

If she had her way, all corrective institutions for naughty boys and girls would be manned by plump, big breasted women in aprons with no nonsense attitudes, such as herself. Not that Harry Groves agreed. According to Harry, she might think herself Mother Earth but she was dealing with prickly thistles, not sweet peas. She might have taken Tommo in and saved him and be known for her charity and positive thoughts towards people rather than extolling only their shortcomings...except for himself, whose faults were noted and well documented by Angie Meadows!...but she would not choose to be alone with a single one of them, as he wouldn't, either, given the choice. Neither would Tommo or

Gary. They all needed each other's back-up because these lads and girls were damned hard work even in single numbers.

Says him! Harry Big Mouth Groves got right up her nose, he did! If there was one person, she'd gladly see banged up for a life sentence and the key thrown away, it was him. So God help her for thinking wicked things and in need of a cross sign made with her flour covered hands to stem all her further bad thoughts where Harry Groves was concerned.

Then, she could see him through her kitchen window – speak of the Devil! – about to come in for his morning break when she would wish he'd go pester, elsewhere. Especially when the scones would be a few minutes late. He always had something to say when Angie was a few minutes late with the service as she put the scones in the hot oven knowing that they would be no more than ten or fifteen minutes. He was talking with some woman or other, anyway. A woman wearing a big coat which seemed to be inappropriate for a temperate April morning with a weak sun shining. Angie admired her green and black plaid shopping trolley which looked big enough to carry the weekly groceries for a family of five. All she had, herself, was a feeble thing on rickety wheels. Hers looked sturdy and reinforced.

Did Angie know her? If she did it would come to her soon enough when she knew almost everyone living in the suburbs of Lower Quinton, where she had lived for all of her own forty-seven years. She'd start with the alphabet and work her way through it even while she wondered why Harry Groves was talking to her. The woman to the other side of the railings to the front of the house. Him this and a big locked, green gate barring her entry. A woman with a headscarf hiding her face, sort of fastened close under the chin but then pulled right out. A neck scarf, gloves, sheepskin boots, also, when the weather was Mediterranean rather than Arctic. Angie thought she knew her well enough as someone she occasionally saw around Lower Quinton, her interest taking a bit of a turn when she considered them in close conversation.

Was the old goat having a fling? No wife to cuckold, of course, but he'd changed his spots if he was chatting up a woman; that half of the human species least to his liking. The only thing Harry Groves chatted to nicely was his pay packet and the two pints of beer he consumed every evening, work finished. Never a please or thank you for Angie doing his washing along with Gary and Tommo's when Harry and Gary...never Tommo who was compulsive in his obsessive tidiness...thought to do a pick-up off their bedroom floors. She drew the line at picking up after them. The clients, yes, but not the staff. Anyone would think that this was a proper, family home and not an institution with bars on the windows and locked gates which no one could enter unless with the approval of Harry Groves, the bumped-up caretaker who strode about like a real little Hitler.

Tommo with last say, of course, when he was here. Harry, now, flapping his hands at the woman in one of his *go-away-I'm-busy* modes. That putting an end to Angie's ideas that he might have advanced sufficiently as a human being to consider having a girlfriend even when he'd managed to the age of almost fifty-six all on his own. Nod and a wink!

What could the woman possibly want when she kept pointing to the locked gates and imploring him as she shook a dog lead at him? No chance, love, Angie thought, after assuming that she wanted in. When he really wanted to be awkward he refused to let even Tommo and Gary on the premises unless they wore their staff badges. Now, if that's not awkward, what is?

However, a quick look at his watch and he was on his way back to the house while the woman let her hands drop. Boiling water, now, on the tea bags in the pot, a last stir, scones just a few more minutes to be fully risen and golden and the pot on the table just as the back door opened. The dog sitting outside the open door with a hopeful look at Angie and a wag of its tail. Angie shook her head at it. Angie considered dogs unhygienic. At least her husband kept his greyhounds in a large pen in the back garden where they loped and played. Face on Harry Groves like an angry wasp as he closed the door behind him. Hadn't even taken off those dirty boots of his after digging in the garden. He was coming through the inner door and then into her kitchen just as Angie set cups and saucers and spoons to the table. As ever, his mood dark and bitter with some sour thought or other.

He had never been any different from the first day they had come to work at Greengates House together, upon its first day of opening more years previously than either of them would care to admit. It had been the 4th of January 1990 though he would have it that it was the 5th of January, one year previously. If there was no one for Harry Groves to argue with, Angie reckoned, he argued with his reflection in the bathroom mirror.

As usual, he trudged in that belligerent manner of his with his thick neck deep into the collar of his frayed shirt, his overalls unbuttoned down the front so that Angie could see that he had a button missing from the waistband of his trousers. The very slovenliness of him offended her. Angie thought men with buttons missing should be made to undergo compulsory courses as to how to sew another one on instead of waiting for some woman to do it for them. If she had never managed to train Tommo in the art of good dressing, he had a few excuses. Harry Groves had none; nasty little man that he was, treading mud all over her newly mopped floor and a stubborn look on his face as he flapped his morning paper at her as if she was responsible for all the bad news within it.

"That paper boy was seven minutes late, again." He had The Guardian delivered every morning by a fiend on a bicycle who chucked it over the railings instead of dropping it into the mail box. Same with the local Clarion Evening News, usually delivered about four o'clock each weekday afternoon. Greengates paid for them out of Angie's housekeeping budget. Pity anyone, though, who tried to read it before he had trawled his way through every word of every column and every advert. As far as Harry was concerned, he had first bagsy on it. Then Tommo. Then Gary. Then Angie, last, because what did women want with newspapers except to look at the adverts and read up on local gossip. Besides, she didn't live in the house so he regarded her as a visitor with no rights of occupation. Damned cheek of the man!

Not even a good morning! Heckling her, too! No other word for it as he slumped in a hard back chair at the table and spread his legs after hitching up his overalls. He'd been digging in the vegetable patch and there was earth falling from the turn ups of his pants onto the floor, as well as stuck in clumps on the soles of his boots. "Bloody do-gooders! Cubby Watson's right. Take that child, for instance, the one they pulled out of the canal...."

Why was he shouting? She was no more than a couple of yards away and there was nothing wrong with Angie's hearing! Such aggressive words were always Harry's way of starting one of his topics for discussion. These days he was closely following Cubby Watson's sensational opinions and agreeing with them all. Harry Groves, in Angie Meadow's opinion, was becoming brainwashed by Cubby Watson. Like Cubby Watson, Harry was sounding like a stuck record when even the thought of tagging babies at birth was the most stupid thing that Angie had ever heard. He'd been smoking them stinky cigarettes again. Her nose wrinkled in disgust.

Also, she considered herself to be a do-gooder and proud of it. She glowered at him, half guessing at what he would say, next. She saw the scones would do, extracted them from the oven on their very hot tray. Then scooped them onto a cooling rack using a fish slice. Ever since that journalist, Cubby Watson, at the Clarion, had started tub thumping Harry considered that he had a creditable back-up to his own extreme opinions, concerning children. He had yet to know that the child in question would be coming here...a trump card to Angie! He hated it when she knew things that he didn't.

"Dumped like waste in a trash can, she was. Should have drowned by all accounts. It's been on the TV and the local radio's full of it. Not charged anybody yet but it's just on the news they've got Mally Kenyon in for questioning. Whichever pig fathered her should be made to have the snip. The sow sterilized. If they can't look after her proper they should be stopped from having any more children by a surgeon's knife. Only stands to common sense if you ask me."

Angie hadn't asked him but she would have to hear it just the same! She rolled her eyes heavenward. How stupid can people be? Start that game and there would be no stopping the demand for the compulsory removal of body bits like they did in some barbaric countries in the Far East, even in this day and age. Hands chopped off for stealing. Eyes gouged out for voyeurism. Tongues removed for talking against the powers that be. What did they do with those who indulged in gossip, she wondered! Stitched their lips together, she supposed. That being the case, she would have been silenced long ago! Letting him get it off his chest, she remained mute as she found the butter from the fridge and placed that before him.

"Failing that she should have been tagged with a micro-chip at birth like Cubby Watson suggested. Whoever's responsible for her has dumped her onto us, the taxpayers. Like Cubby says in his evening rag, if they can do it to a dog and it's not thought to be cruel, they can do it to newborn babies. Bring back the old Means Test for parenthood, I say. They do it when people adopt, don't they?"

The man was mad! "There's tea in the pot. The milk's in the jug." She felt like feeding him some of Chester's dog biscuits instead of her carefully made scones; best butter and fruit in them.

"Get's my blood up. Where's Tommo and Gary?"

"Gone to pick up the very child you're talking about, as a matter of fact. Makes a change...a girl of seven instead of a lad of fifteen to look after."

Harry's face elongating as he slapped his paper on the table and drew out his chair to get his legs under the table. Gardening always did his back in.

"I thought Tommo was going fly fishing this weekend and Gary taking that daughter of his to visit his parents."

"They were. Tommo decided to take the girl in when he saw her locked into a cell at the station and no suitable accommodation available. Smearing, of course. Poor little thing scared witless. He was asked to take her as a temporary measure. No places at Roseacre. Gary will just have to apologise to that daughter of his, again."

"Smearing! Ye Gods! Not another one! The pressure washer's on the blink and the steam-clean device got smashed by that Rory who spent all his time climbing the walls and fouling up his bedroom. They'll need another female." Said with a distinct insult to denote his marked discrimination against women in general. "She can shift the shit when it's not my job, in the first place."

Angie's eyes rolled and her head tipped at him. If he wanted one of her scones, he'd have to wait for one. "Maybe all men should have the snip to stop fathers with stupid ideas from cloning themselves along with their daft opinions."

"Them scones look passable, Angie. I'll have two, if I may." Then his head jerked towards the front, kitchen window. "You know who that woman is out at the front who keeps pestering me about her dog being in the grounds? Has a shopping trolley and a pink dog lead. If I've told her once, I've told her a thousand times in the past half hour that it just isn't possible for her to wander in here. Says she's lost her dog and it's come under the fence and got in. A timid little thing. Fat chance! Not even a rabbit can burrow its way in here. Not without my permission, that is."

Angie had thought at first that she did not know the woman but then suddenly twigged. She'd reached S but then went back again to C. "Isn't she that woman from over the park houses? Always has that shopping trolley with her. Wrapped up like a mummy because she has some kind of extreme disfigurement. I've seen Father Turner visiting her sometimes." Angie lived quite close to the park, herself, but more towards the High Street.

Harry shrugged. Despite the fact that he had asked if she knew her, he scathingly wondered how women managed to have everyone pegged. "Whoever she is she's driving me potty. Been on at me since ten o'clock when I've been trying to get some carrot plugs in and the bean sticks sorted. I keep telling her that this is a secure unit. If she isn't naughty, she can't come in. No one comes in here, anyway, without a letter of authorization. If she had one I'd let her in, I tell her, but she'll still have to go through procedure...have her photo taken, for one thing. No dog in here, anyway, save Chester. I keep telling her but she don't listen. She says Chester's why her dog won't come to her when she calls it. It's in the grounds hiding because it's nervous of other dogs, cowering under some bush or other. As if a Cocker Spaniel's a Rottweiler or something."

"What breed is it?"

"The dog she's lost? Don't know. Didn't ask. Anything that wears a pink collar with rhinestones can't be bigger than a Miniature Poodle. Probably one of them wrinkled things with no hair and purple skin; spends all its time shivering in corners. If dogs do look like their owners that is."

The things the man said! "Poor woman can't help it. She was born that way." Angie turned away, a brooding look as she waited for her memory to come up with some more identification; none forthcoming. She wasn't someone she saw about much and had never spoken to even at bus stops because she always turned her back and dropped her head in a stand-offish way. Born deformed. It was all coming back to Angie now. Had a sister was a good musician. The sister had gone to the Manchester School of Music. Got her face in the paper with a trumpet on her lap. It was usually only ugly women with floppy top lips played trumpets. Couldn't remember her name. Though S and C still had a hook into her memory bank. Left Quinton after studying at the School of Music...the older sister, that was...lovely looking girl, slim and very sophisticated. The parents had always made a big display of the older sister just as they kept the younger one out of public sight, in darkened rooms, even boarded up the windows and made her wear a veil when people called or she went out, anywhere.

As far as Angie knew, the good looking one had never returned. Who could blame her? Quinton had nothing to offer unless you were well heeled. In that case a mansion up on the fells must be very pleasant, indeed. "She'll be off once she's fed up of asking. Some people get an idea in their heads and there's no shaking it," disparaging eyes on the back of Harry's balding pate, as she said it. She wished he'd wash his hands before starting eating or drinking, never mind touch her clean teapot. "Strange character if she is who I think she is. Lives a few doors up from my husband's first wife's, best friend, Deirdre, whose mother used to know her mother and was on speaking terms. Deformed from birth. Her face and hands and feet not right. Poor thing."

Harry poured his tea, longing for a pint-pot mug so as not to have to keep topping up, just a tip of milk added but spooning in three, generous sugars and stirring as if mixing paint, the spoon rattling against the sides of the bone china cup quite unnecessarily in his thoroughness. If she wasn't quick with them scones, he'd help himself and risk getting his hand slapped. He had his entitlements.

He was about to take his first sip of English Breakfast just as Angie made the hopeful gesture of reaching in an upper cupboard for small plates when a loud bell sounded through the whole of the building like an air raid siren giving warning of attack. The gate bell never failed to make him jump when he wasn't expecting anyone. He looked out through the front kitchen window; the kitchen having been built on to the side of the building like an annex with its back wall glazed, also, offering views to the back garden. He could see the high, green gates set in tall, narrowly spaced, green painted, iron railings as clearly as he could from his gardening shed to the right of the gates where he liked to lurk, these days. At least, when his aching back was at its worst. The same gates that had given the house its name and its trade mark.

The dog barked twice; two feeble calls like an invalid asking someone else to answer the door because the task was too much trouble, otherwise. Chester rarely went on guard duty, these days, because he was getting old and preferred his kennel. Except, of course, when walkies were on offer. Gary took it to the fields down the lanes, to the back of the unit where it could refresh itself with a few new smells; aromatherapy for old dogs as well as young ones, under the viaduct arches and along the canal bank.

He could see a grey Fiat Punto parked up against the bell waiting for his attention. A blonde-haired, woman driver at the wheel. She was holding her head, eyes lowered, as if she had a headache. Seen both the car and its driver before but for a moment couldn't remember where. Who was it? Someone not seen much lately but both the car and her tinkling on his memory bell.

Angie answered his own question, straightening her flower patterned apron. "Gina Mon. Not seen her for years and years. She used to come here before Tommo's time as Head of the Unit for case conferences. When Brian Ghould was Head of the Unit. Gosh! What brings her here?" Then she twigged. "She's the one bringing some clothes for the little girl. She works for Child Welfare, these days, I think from what was said on that radio programme when Cubby Watson wiped the floor with her, poor thing. I told Tommo we've nothing small enough for the little girl in our spares cupboard. Tommo said about mid-day, though. She's early." Then Angie tutted. "Shame she'll miss Tommo!"

Then Harry was guffawing. He began one of his running commentaries as if Angie didn't have eyes to see for herself. Nothing shut Harry Groves up once he'd started, though. "I bet she wishes she was elsewhere. Someone else pulling up behind her. Blow me! Cubby Watson. He's getting out. Left that car of his parked skew-whiff. Not even bothered shutting the driver's door. Typical of a man decisive in action. Seen his opportunity and taken it. Probably fancies her. Even I have to admit that she is a handsome woman and no mistaking it. Curves in all the right places." His chuckle was wickedly admiring. "Couldn't give a toss, could he? He's tapping on her passenger window, now. He'll have had news about the maltreated child being placed here. If we're lucky we'll be witnessing a punch up."

Angie saw the red sports car with its open door and the short but perfectly formed figure of Cubby Watson poking his head into Gina's passenger window and scowled. It had been he who had written an article against Tommo's appointment when he had taken over the unit. He had entitled it: *It Takes One, To Know One!* Tommo had never forgiven him for raking up his past and plastering it on the front page of the Clarion Evening News. This, the same man who was, these days Harry Grove's champion of people's opinion; the very ones she was sick to death of hearing about.

For once, he didn't mind his tea break being interrupted and especially when he saw that the woman with the shopping trolley had taken the hint and was, now, after a casual glance, nowhere to be seen. He hoped that if they were about to have a slanging match, they'd have the consideration to wait until he had his gate keys and could get out there, listening in.

As he went, Angie turned up the volume on the radio; BBC Radio Lancashire running up-to-the-hour news. The child had still not been identified. It was being broadcast, again, with some astonishment expressed, that Greengates House Secure Assessment Unit was to take in a child as young as seven until Social Services could provide a more suitable placement. Angie knew different. Nobody came to Greengates unless they deserved to be here. Tommo didn't waste his fly fishing time unless the client was in need of his services. That meant only one thing; the child had severe behavioural difficulties and emotional instability as well as poor, personal hygiene and most probably, an intellectual deficit. Seven years old and coming here, poor thing!

Angie got out her recipe book in order to make gingerbread men. If the little girl was good she could help Angie to ice them and put on the currant-eyes, jelly buttons, and cherry-lips. At the same time, she kept her eye on the kitchen window to the front of the building as Harry went to tell the poor woman, Gina Mon, that she would have to wait outside for Tommo to approve her entry if she did not have a letter of access stamped by the powers that be. No chance for that Cubby Watson coming in here, though, if that's what he expected, even if he was Harry's hero. He would be after a photograph of the girl, perhaps. Some more information on the little girl which none of them had at present. Angie hated newspaper men as much as Tommo did.

Then she saw Gina Mon get out of her car, hands on hips, her finger pointing and wagging. Telling that Cubby Watson a thing or two from the look of it as he went to face her, bold as brass. He even took her photograph and started asking something just as she made a grab for his camera. Not quick enough. Cubby caught her wrist, looking up at her. In her flat trainers, she looked to be a couple of inches taller than him. It looked to Angie that he was making some form of offensive proposition. Cheeky bugger!

Angie was shaking her head, turning, her peripheral vision catching sight of a sudden movement outside her rear kitchen window. Her first thought was of the woman's dog but there was none to be seen. Looking back, Harry was now talking to both visitors through the front railings so it could not possibly be him. He was making no effort towards letting Gina Mon inside by unlocking the gates when she dragged her hand from Cubby's grip and shouted for Harry to let her in. No one else but Angie in the house. Gary and Tommo out and Jacko gone off to be metered his punishment.

The woman with the shopping trolley had disappeared.

The feeling that she was being watched from the rear garden consumed her. Yet it wasn't possible. Like Harry said, the place was as secure to intrusion as it was to escape…Jacko an exception to the usual rule. Whoever wanted to come in to a secure detention centre, anyway? The clients were always desperate to get out. The fence was ten feet high and unbroken, also. One of Harry's jobs was to check it daily though Angie had observed that it was one of the jobs he had been shelving of late when he was walking badly with that back of his. At night it was electrified at its upper levels, which was when she was not here, anyway. She was home at that time of day, in her own bed at her bungalow, her husband snoring next to her like a blocked drain. Her home was just off the High Street in Lower Quinton. A short ride on a number thirty nine bus with Whemley Cemetery on the front of the bus as its destination.

Seeing things not there, was she? She could not believe that it was the woman's nervous dog, either. Chester, maybe. Sometimes the dog jumped up at the window if he wanted feeding or hared off to the bottom of the garden chasing an intruding cat. Though he was old these days and, like deterring other unwanted visitors, it was rare he bothered with the odd cat climbing in. Too much energy was needed for the objections to be made.

Maybe it had been just a tree bough moving or a bird skittering on the grass. When she went to the sink to close the slightly open window, bars to the outside, there was nothing to see but a garden bare of people. On the other side of the fence, the winding, hedged path meandered a lonely way down to the canal. Across a broken lift bridge, through the fields was a popular shortcut to the Dog's Bed Estate. The area was a dog walker's paradise. Not a breath of wind after the gale of the previous night.

Thirteen

Almost eleven a.m.

Gina Mon, rubbing her temples where a headache pulsed, was trying to ignore the man tapping on her passenger door, window glass. If she was pretending that he was not there it was to belie the fact that she had been aware of him as a red spot growing ever larger in her driving mirrors for some several minutes past, as she had made her way out of Quinton towards Greengates House. She had seen him in her rear view mirror slowly eating up the distance between them from some miles back. As usual, driving too fast and overtaking dangerously in that red bullet of his. Heading towards Lower Quinton as if being chased by a bat out of Hell. He had been almost upon her as she turned in before the closed green gates with no choice but to wait until they were opened for her.

His screeched halt had been sudden. She had been the reason it would seem because he had noticed the arrival of a car...not necessarily Gina's car...at the gates of Greengates House. Whether he knew that it was Gina driving that same car was a matter for speculation. His whole life must be lived on a fast track, Gina surmised, as a car travelling too close behind him had to swerve to avoid a collision with his back bumper before he brought the car to a slanted halt directly behind her. Horns blared. He had, in fact, hemmed her in.

Most probably, like Gina, he had already heard that she was to be placed in the secure assessment unit, at the very place where he just happened to be passing, at that very moment, because Quinton Social Services had a dire shortage of approved places for violent children in extreme distress. The very fact that his main column subject matter often concerned the allocation...or to be precise; the shortcomings...of public service provisions within the local authority trusts, would suggest that his criticisms had been correct.

Gina braced herself. She was in no position to defend the services provided by the Child Welfare Department. Not only was she not qualified to do so but she was feeling far too vulnerable in her weakened, physical state. The shock she had experienced some six hours before would take some time to get over.

In any scenario, Gina considered herself to be in the wrong place at the wrong time. Cubby Watson was the very last person she wanted to meet. She had been listening, herself, to the local news being broadcast from her own car radio. She had turned it off as soon as she was aware of herself being spotted and a finger jabbing out in her direction with the cry of "Wait!" With only one hand on his steering wheel before he slammed his foot on the brake, she had become the quarry of her arch enemy; the People's Champion, himself, once again.

Her tension headache was demanding that she relax instead of increasing with the feeling that she had become trapped. She was feeling not only shocked but also mentally assaulted, physically abused and very tearful. More than anything she felt demeaned. She had failed to notice the signs of distress building in a client and so blamed herself. Usually such batterings were verbal and from white hot angry mothers not harmless looking children. Even when she had worked with disaffected adolescents she had never been assaulted as she had been by a seven year old girl with undiluted hatred in her eyes. Not that she had suffered the same as WPC Hannon who would later milk the situation for all the compensation that she could screw out of a broken nose, cracked ribs and severe bruising to her torso. Gina had, in fact, been triaged as a much lower priority. Time enough to write up her report, place a message on Brian Ghould's recording machine and promise that she would call in before taking herself off, officially, on sick leave.

Time to listen to her radio, too, and be well aware that Mally Kenyon had been arrested. The latest development was being reported as if the police believed him to be the monster who had put the child into the sack and thrown her into the canal because she would be someone who could testify against him. His guilt being consolidated by the fact that he had sought to escape the police station instead of staying to confirm his innocence. He had simply walked out of the building before questioning. Maybe under the circumstances, Gina thought, Greengates House might be the safest place if not the most appropriate. Having said that, she could not align the crime with what she knew of the man himself. Things did not add up.

However, what had most concerned both her boss and herself was out! It was, now, public news that the child was to be placed in the securest accommodation usually reserved for violent adolescents that Quinton possessed, short of a locked cell. That the child would be on her own, there, and not subject to bad influence or the distress of others would fail to be communicated to a very interested public who would be avid to know what was happening to a little girl who had been so badly abused; a child that seemed with every passing moment that she remained unclaimed to be a Quinton child. Yet no one recognised her. No one had come forward to claim her. A child seemingly well cared for physically. It was all very strange.

Unfortunately, where else was there for a violent, demanding and potentially lethal child to be cared for within the placements available? Gina recognised the impasse Brian Ghould had been in. Not only was the child violent but also lacking the basic conditioning within her personal behaviour. He had explained just how the placement had come about when it had not been a decision of the Child Welfare Department but that of the Chief Constable, herself. Apparently, she had covered the police station cell in her own body excrement. So what was new?

Time had come, perhaps, for Mr General Public...the likes of Cubby Watson...to have their own noses rubbed in it if only to shut them up. Where did people get the idea from that human distress could be sanitised merely because it was offensive to the way they would prefer to envisage a disadvantaged child, perhaps, as no more than an empathetic, still photograph. Money, too, always money at the base of what might be on offer when the provision of suitable care facilities for anyone with extreme special needs in Quinton, was ever deficient to the demand. Not to forget the fears for litigation with which the western world had become consumed. It was not possible, these days, to shove juveniles in any old nook or cranny. This before the Health and Safety Laws which put red crosses through so many more flexible options which had been available in the past. Legislation had not helped the situation for children like Wendy Bridgewater. Not to mention the paranoid vetting of each and every carer to the point where promising candidates considered themselves unsuitable even if all they had on their police record were parking fines.

Greengates House *was* unsuitable as a holding point for a seven year old child whose care was now one of a Ward of the Authority until her parents could be located but truth was there was nowhere else. They all knew it at the Child Welfare Department but would the public understand why it was sometimes necessary simply to take the best of poor options because perfection, as ever, was a myth?

That would be what Cubby Watson would be after challenging her about, she surmised, as she had watched through her driving mirror the dramatic way in which he exited his badly parked vehicle and sprang, rather than slid, from the driver's seat with that mop of curly, chestnut hair shining in the sunlight. He could not be bothered even closing the driver's door so that it impeded the progress of passers-by such as the woman she could see halted, to the far side of the grounds where the caretaker's garden shed stood in front of the railings, partly concealed under the leafy boughs of a horse chestnut tree growing from the pavement. She was inspecting the contents of a black handbag as if looking for something, a pink, diamante studded dog lead in her hand and a sturdy shopping trolley propped up on its wheels. The bus stop was on the other side of the gates so maybe she was looking for change. One woman might not be an audience in a plural sense but she made Gina blush to the roots of her hair just the same because there was an altercation heading her way. Gina would have preferred, henceforth, to fight her battles with Cubby Watson in private and especially when she could see the length of his strides to denote his purpose in her wing mirror. The thrust of his leather shod feet describing his determination to speak with her. The mould of his short legs through the fabric of his expensive trousers catching her attention; all meat and sinew. Calf and thigh muscles moving with an agile, athletic grace. Wearing Armani from the look of the cut of the taupe coloured cloth but not impressing her much when his clothes had a slept in look about them. Either that or they had spent the night on his bedroom floor, his white shirt hanging open at the collar to reveal a hairy chest. A sage green tie looped crookedly over some incorrectly fastened buttons on his waistcoat and his baggy jacket hanging off his shoulders instead of being properly fastened up. Slovenly, being the word that sprang to mind. He was smoking, too, but then cast the butt away without extinguishing it; a behaviour which particularly annoyed her. The man had no consideration for the rest of the human race and certainly none for the bare paws of any animal which happened to stand on it.

Then, hard, black-pea eyes were pressing in on her through the passenger window, his fingernails tap-tap-tapping on the glass. He was short in height so that he didn't have to bend far, built like a hollow-faced greyhound with that chestnut hair and a pale, freckly skin. He had a skim of dark beard on his chin.

She turned her head the other way then regretted it because he would see the iodine still in her light blonde hair where she had had the throbbing wound stitched. When he smiled without pleasure he had sharp pointed teeth; very white and highly polished and a red tongue which licked at the corners of his small mouth like a cat. "Yoo-hoo! Miss Mon, isn't it?

Gina turned her head towards him because she knew there would be nothing gained by ignoring him. He was the kind of man who saw resistance as challenge. Yet when he smiled, despite the teeth, there was something remarkably virile about him. Someone short of stature but powerful like Napoleon, perhaps, with a strong charisma about him. It caught at her throat and made her feel breathless. It was the same intensity; an aura of vibrancy, which she recalled as being her real reason for having become so tongue-tied on the radio programme just a few short weeks before when she had been unable to defend her opinions against the strength of his own. His presence was both dominating and domineering.

His pink nails tapping on her passenger door window glass very demanding. "I need to speak to you about the child."

"No comment. Go away, Mr Watson."

She should not have been at work after having a stitch put in the gaping wound at the back of her head. The policewoman had been admitted. Her Uncle Simon had picked her up from the hospital after he had finished his counter shift at the police station and then driven her back to her car, still parked outside the police station but with a parking ticket under the windscreen wiper. Some days were shit from the very beginning! The four wheel drive belonging to the Chief of --lice had still been parked where Ma'am had left it at shortly before five that morning. Otherwise, nothing was the same. The streets in the town centre, with the coming of the morning light, had been buzzing with people. Uncle Simon had explained about the raid on the Dog's Bed Estate. Complaints were coming in left, right and centre. But for having just finished a ten hour shift he might have been implicated. They were already bringing in offenders caught with irrefutable evidence as part of the on-going raids and house-to-house investigations. "Big Bertha should have gone to a conference today and not been back 'til Monday. Maybe her deputy would have acted differently. It does no good in the long run to upset the very people one's supposed to be serving."

Gina had had some personal calls to make. Her mother had been informed and was having kittens in her panic to know what had befallen her only daughter. She had never wanted Gina to be a social worker in the first place because of the kind of homes she constantly visited, where she was rarely welcome, and the people she sought only to help were frequently threatening. She had certainly been proved right this day!

In fact, Gina had had no intention of going into work except for having previously written reports to hand in to her superior; Brian Ghould, a man whom she had the highest respect for. The paperwork, as in most public service jobs these days, being her biggest bugbear. Best to get it in and over and done with; take the long weekend which her injuries merited. All her files would then be up-to-date for someone to take over her caseloads should yet another emergency occur.

Her boss had told her that because of all the publicity surrounding the case, he would be taking a personal interest in the child and especially when the Chief Constable had taken it upon herself to place the child at Greengates House, prior to consultation. This should have been the last place he would have considered, preferring to find the money to send her out of the authority before making such a controversial placement. Only now, the arrangement seemed to have been chiselled in stone. Ma'am would not have her decision questioned. She had actually suggested that it had, perhaps, been the fault of his night-duty social worker for the child's aggressive behaviour. The child must have been provoked and mishandled for her to be attacked in such a way. Brian had told her this so that Gina might be prepared for the newspapers handing her the blame, also: Cubby Watson for one; the very person she was now facing. Ma'am, Gina had been told, was already laying all the blame on Social Services for what was, essentially, a case of extreme child abuse for which his staff seemed to have no adequate response mechanisms in place. They should know all the children in Quinton who were at risk of such gross maltreatment simply because they existed, usually, within families where such occurrences, even if not as severe, were, nevertheless, commonplace. Ma'am, it would seem, insisting that the unidentified girl had to be a child of the Dog's Bed Estate. That or considering the kind of crime committed and its location, she would be from within the wider area of Lower Quinton where the main perpetrators of crime were almost as industrious, if not quite as concentrated, as those on the Dog's Bed. This despite her having run her own checks on local schools and so far none having reported a child of her description failing to turn up for morning registration.

Gina had burst into tears; something else not usual to her behaviour. Not least because she was tired and had a headache. Her body ached where bruises were now showing under her ribs in particular, her arms and hipbone also where she had hit the floor after tumbling off the chair. The one single stitch holding the mouth of the cut together at the back of her head felt as if it had been stitched with tight catgut; far too tender to touch. Gina, thankfully, recalled Brian's words: *Take a couple of days off to recover. If you can call into Greengates House with some clothing for the child on your way home, I will appreciate it. Tommo rang earlier. Maybe you can introduce yourself to Tommo, too. One of my old naughty boys turned himself around and now has the same position as I once had as head of the unit. Wish I was still there and away from the politics sometimes.*

Gina had, therefore, done his bidding. She had gone to Trimbles and spent two hundred and fifty pounds on a set of three changes of clothing to fit a girl of Wendy Bridgewater's size along with a coat, two nightdresses and some slippers which she hoped would fit until she could get a proper measurement and equip her with a proper pair of outdoor shoes. No matter her real name, Gina had come to think of her as Wendy Bridgewater. Those silver eyes burnt into her memory as a firebrand of experience never to be forgotten. Her skull aching and throbbing just to remember the hatred on the child's face.

Now just as she was about to complete the last of her tasks, before getting home to her bed, her arch enemy was tapping on her car window and asking to speak to her in his demanding fashion. Suddenly her temper rose. She was ready to give anyone a piece of her mind if they were as rude and arrogant as he was. So out of her car she got, standing tall as she slammed the door shut with the sound of it reverberating in her overtaxed brain. She marched round to his side of her car determined this time to speak her opinions loudly and eloquently. That was when he had the audacity to take her photograph. The horror of what she must look like with her bleached cheeks, darkly ringed eyes and a look of annoyance and upset on her face, with her hair knotted and limp, no make-up, was the final insult.

How dare he? Her hand shot out to grab his camera. There was an erase button to the back of it and she intended to use it. Either that or strangle him with the cord with which it was suspended from his neck. That was when he grabbed her hand and pulled her closer. His strength of purpose wrapping itself about her wrist like a constricting snake. "Now, now! You look so pretty when you're angry! Anyone ever tell you that? Just the person I want to speak to, too. You can help me. I'm determined to find out who that child is. I want you to help me find out who she is."

Gina's mouth dropped open. He was not about to let go of her hand. His breath stank of stale nicotine yet strangely she didn't mind it. "Why?"

"Someone has to. The child has Kenyon eyes. She has to be local."

"I've never seen her in my life before. There has to be other people in the world with silver eyes and not just Kenyons. She might have been abandoned by people living miles away...itinerants...travellers who'd stopped to fill up and hadn't realised that she'd left the vehicle."

"I don't think so. I believe in gut feeling, Ms Mon. My guts tell me that we should know who she is because she's a Quinton kid. We should be looking after our own and making sure that Quinton is a safe place for our kids to grow up in."

"That's the ideology, Mr Watson, not the reality, unfortunately. I can't see how I can help you. Besides, it's the duty of the police to locate her attackers...and her family."

"Catty Collins is too busy, these days, blowing her own trumpet. She's using the situation to have a clean-up. She thinks the child gives her every reason to harass and provoke law abiding people when...if there's one case in which the residents of the Dog's Bed would be behind her every step of the way...it would be in finding the child's abuser. She's alienating instead of fostering. There's deep trouble brewing."

"So you see your opportunity do you? You will achieve what the Quinton police are unable to achieve because they have the wrong priorities."

"Bang on, Ms Mon. Bright girl!"

Gina felt patronised rather than flattered. "Why me?"

"Because you know the families on the Dog's Bed better than anyone except for your best friend, Magdalene, who happens to be a Kenyon. Father Turner's handicapped by his calling. You know that Mally Kenyon's skipped arrest, don't you?"

She had heard as much, yes. "They'll soon have him back again."

"If he's still around. If he's skipped it will be taken as an admission of his own guilt."

She dragged her hand out of his hold and spoke with conviction. "Not necessarily. Do you know what it feels like to be victimised, Mr Watson? Everyone on the Dog's Bed Estate is guilty before being proven innocent as far as Catty Collins is concerned. But then, what do you know? Private school educated...a job guaranteed...a silver spoon in your mouth. You're in no place to comment."

Cubby sneered even while thinking that the hospital smell clinging to her could not detract from a damned pretty women. Gutsy! He liked that. Before she had seemed more like a milksop even if he had admired her curves. "You know nothing about me, Ms Mon. However, I do know that you were one of the people the child injured last night."

"How?"

"I have my sources. Those packages for her? Trimbles! Not cheap. If she's off the Dog's Bed she'll be used to wearing hand-me-downs."

"Not all of the families on the estate dress their children from the jumble sales, Mr Watson. I just happen to have been born there myself. I have the best family that anyone could possibly wish for."

"I know. I know everything about you worth knowing. I made it my priority to find out before we met with a radio microphone between us. Know thy enemy is rule number one. I found it disappointing that you were off form that day. I like nothing better than confrontational debate. We could work together on this though. I'm going to find out who she is whether you help me or not. She has special needs from what I hear."

"You seem to hear a lot you shouldn't be privy to."

Cubby winked. "Three o'clock for last covers at The Italiana? I'm paying. Be there. We might be able to do what Catty Collins is finding impossible at the moment because she's after something different. We might be able to find out who this child is. That will mean that we will be part way to knowing who did this to her. The bastard should never be allowed near a child, ever again."

Despite herself, Gina found herself drawn towards his suggestion. "Maybe," was all she said, for the moment. "How would you go about it?"

"I may be able to gain access to her clothes...the sack...more photographs to offer more clues to how she was cared for before she entered the canal. You'll have access to the child because of your calling. I would be interested in what the child has to say about all this. Tommo Thomas won't let me near her because he's hated my guts ever since I told the public what a bad boy he used to be. Took a brush to his father's head and beat him dead. Maybe he was saving his mother from being raped and beaten but that's no excuse for murder, is it?"

Gina thought it was. "How old was he when he did this?"

"Twelve...thirteen, maybe. Used to run with Mally and the other Kenyons back then. A changed person, if ever there was one."

Gina thought herself better prepared to meet the man she had come to introduce herself to knowing something about him other than the few hints which Brian Ghould had already made. Brian had only praise for him. Part of her own empathy for the underdogs of the world was formed by suffering the same prejudices. People do change. People do adapt. People do take whatever opportunities are offered to better themselves. Magdalene's problems had been formed from an addictive nature...and Bass Kenyon who had been even weaker than Magdalene. Bass had been a nice man despite his weaknesses unlike those brothers of his, Benny and Woody, in particular. "I won't divulge any information considered to be confidential."

"So you'll meet me?"

Gina hesitated for a moment before shaking her head, the decision made. "No! More than my job's worth. Besides I need to get back to my flat to sleep. The police will deal with this. If people let them get on with their job they should soon find out who she is and who did it."

Cubby looked disappointed. "If you change your mind you know where to find me. Maybe I owe you a dinner just for the way I treated you, last time. My way of making an apology."

Gina was tempted. Close up and smiling his eyes were a mixture of many different shades of brown. From light to dark. From palest toffee to the deepest chocolate. Cubby had one of those grins which come suddenly to illuminate the landscape of an unusual face like bright sunshine through parting cloud. Every corner of his face lit up and made her want to explore it further.

Likewise!

They spent a moment just looking at each other. Until she saw the caretaker poking his ear through a space in the railings, listening in, eavesdropping. She recalled him from previous visits when she had been part of the Adolescent Offenders Mentoring Team. She turned herself away from Cubby abruptly, rudely even, and spoke to the man she recalled as Harry. "I'm from the Child Welfare Department with clothes for the child who's coming in. You maybe remember me? Gina Mon. May I come in, please?"

Harry had been about to refuse her request but then saw the white Greengates mini-bus pull off the road and come to a halt to the side of her, nipping round Mr Watson's very badly parked car. Gary driving with Tommo to the rear. The child and the new care assistant were centre bus. Fun over with! Gary was raising a hand to Gina. He used to work at Roseacre so they knew each other well. Tommo was dagger eyes on Cubby Watson who was taking pictures of the child through the window glass in rapid succession. At this point the child was quiet enough though she put her head down on seeing the enormous green gates and began to turn her gaze from side to side as if consulting two different opinions. "Is Blackstone School?" she mouthed.

Then the woman wearing the enveloping headscarf reappeared, the dog lead in hand, pulling her shopping trolley, a scuffed black handbag dangling from a shoulder strap. She started to tap at the window glass of the mini-bus with the clip end of the chain. She would have spoken through the glass to Tommo and Gary who had turned to look at her. "A word, please…"

Harry's annoyance spilled. "Be off with you, woman! If I've told you once I've told you a thousand times. I won't be telling you again. Next time I see you hanging about here, I'll call the police. Skedaddle!"

"My dog…."

Keys in hand and locks turned, Harry began the slow process of running back the large gates on their rolling wheels, bending to the work with his shoulder against the edge of the metal when the gates were heavy. "Step one foot over this threshold and I'll have you prosecuted for trespass. Want to be taken to the police station, do you?"

The woman drew herself up sharply, about to reply. She seemed about to say something then changed her mind. "No! I understand that what you told me earlier is final."

That was when the child inside the mini-bus began to beat with her fists on the window glass and smack her feet against the back of the seat in front of her. Wendy was screaming as if being physically beaten when nothing was touching her other than the restraining seat belt. Whatever was said to her by her care assistant or Tommo made no difference as she wriggled and bucked in an effort to free herself from the seat belt and howled like an abandoned dog between shouting. "Wendy see the lady with the golden trumpet, now! Wendy see the lady, now!"

Harry saw the woman lift her head with great bewilderment to look at the angry child as she flailed her limbs and bucked and screamed and shouted so that her enveloping head scarf failed to shadow her face. He caught sight of unusual, very wide spaced, colourless eyes without lashes or lids; eyes pooling with tears. The sinew of a nose that was almost non-existent. Her small, round thickly fleshed mouth stood open to reveal shards of jagged bone for teeth. Her receding chin shivered as she drew shallow breaths. Her face in its pale, shiny strangeness reminded him of something from a horror film. He could not help but grimace as she raised a gloved hand to her lips and then hid her deformity again within the confines of the woollen head scarf. She looked to have given up her insistence that she come into the grounds to look for her dog. With shoulders slumped she turned away.

Gina Mon got back in her car as her way was made open to her and drove through the open gates ahead of the mini-bus. She parked up in front of the yellow painted door with an opaque glass panel in a quite ordinary looking brown brick house with outbuildings. The mini bus followed suit and parked to the right, next to her.

Through her mirror she saw the woman's head turn to consult the traffic situation before rumbling the shopping trolley on her way over the busy highroad to stand at the Lower Quinton bus stop on the other side as Harry Groves rolled the gates closed behind them and securely locked them in.

Cubby Watson stood where he was on the outside, taking photographs of Wendy's entry to a place he deemed to be entirely unsuitable to a child who, despite her reported behaviour, did not deserve to be separated from her peers as far as his knowledge was concerned. He raised three stubby fingers using his left hand towards Gina's rear view mirrors. She knew what he meant. Despite her refusal he would be at the restaurant at three. Then he turned and took a picture of Harry as he locked the gates once more.

With Tommo out of earshot, Harry winked. "Keep up the good work," he said quietly. "Some of us think that the hard line's the best. Spare the rod and spoil the child is my considered opinion."

That had not been Cubby's argument but there was no doubting that he had a fan as he took another snap of the child and his attention sharpened. She was being manhandled out of the bus and hastily carried, even as she kicked and screamed, into the premises. They were let in by someone who had opened the front door; a matronly looking woman in an apron. The child was a slim, agile little thing in oversized boy's clothing. She was still bucking and twisting in the arms of the two strong men, her long blonde hair hanging down behind her as she arched her back and then tried to head butt them.

How he would have loved to have been a fly on the wall inside the house at that moment. Cubby wondered whether the caretaker might provide him with the mole he needed if Gina wouldn't play his game. Either him or the pretty, young girl who got off the bus after the others and then took a moment looking about at the locked gates and the bars on the windows, as if wondering where she had come to. The girl looked stunned as if not expecting what greeted her. Cubby suspected that she would have to change her clothes if she was to deal with a child in such tantrum when it took two fully grown men to handle her.

Pretty little thing even in a temper; the child not her teenage, female companion! Cubby had no interest in teenage girls who dressed to kill; child-women, without maturity or intellect as he considered them. But he was interested in Gina Mon as he watched her extract the shopping bags from her car while studiously ignoring him. The pale blue angora sweater with its bloodstains, the denim jeans which he hated women to wear, even her white trainers, could not spoil the delight of her hour glass figure. There was just something about her that attracted him immensely. Had she stayed around the last time they had met he might have asked her out…shared a lunch…got to know each other.

He didn't like it! *It* being this feeling of glad warmth inside him as he looked at her. His smile evaporated as he rubbed at his whiskers with his right hand, not his left, before coming back to his senses. What the hell was he musing over a woman for when he had so many other equally fascinating things to do? His purpose reinstated and that having nothing to do with a woman but everything to do with a small, vulnerable, little girl. He'd discover the true identity of the child if it was the last thing he'd do. Then he'd use his knowledge to bring down both Social Services and the Quinton Dales Chief of Police if the residents on the Dog's Bed Estate didn't do it first.

This afternoon's spearhead in Cubby's journalistic war was already written and remained largely unedited, as yet, by his father who seemed to have been so distracted by one of the massive hangovers he frequently suffered that, but for Cubby's intervention, the editing looked unlikely to get done at all. In fact, CC had yet to look at anything that had landed in his in-tray including the hard copy which had flown out of the end of Cubby's fingers in record time like automatic writing. He had gone home, in fact, for something he had forgotten and only returned shortly before Cubby had left the Clarion Offices with every intention of going as quickly as possible back to the Dog's Bed Estate. Afraid, as he was, of missing an important development. His mother had been on her way to the Magistrates' Courts as soon as CC had returned, her eyes curiously looking, taking in his outdoor clothing yet refraining from asking her husband why he should need anything heavyweight on a day such as this. As a parting gesture they had both tried to dissuade him from making the child front page news, saying that they thought it unwise to try to sensationalise happenings as indecent as a child being brutalised. This, even while Cubby was ordering his junior staff to keep track of what was going on through press releases from the police station because he was of the very opposite opinion; the more publicity this case gained, the better. The article, which would lead this afternoon's front page, had been written to incite as much unrest on the Dog's Bed Estate as he could muster without being directly accused of inspiring anarchy, but he had made his interest in discovering the child's identity clear.

He would discover the identity of the child; her real situation and her on-going needs as well as discovering whoever had failed her most, and by that route, her abuser. This would be his first and foremost priority no matter what his mother had to say in that quietly cutting way of hers. By that divide he would show Quinton that their illustrious Chief Constable was nothing more than a shallow, vain, empty-headed woman who deserved to be demoted. Either that or made to retire from the power and position of her exalted office. This, too, despite his parents both objecting loudly, especially his mother, to what they saw as something which would gain no credit for their newspaper. When his father had returned, coat over arm, and before his mother had left for her other work, they had had one joint, cowardly message to give him: *This is not in the best interests of the Clarion,* being their jointly spoken opinion.

Yeah! Yeah! Which was when he had taken the final decision and on his own head be it. Cubby had locked his print-face into the front page format with his own secret password so that it could not be altered. Or at least not until he returned and had another angle to the story which promised a better scoop. Time yet for it all to change; four hours, in fact, until they would have to go to print. But that would be his decision, not theirs.

It had been just as he was leaving the office that his grass-phone had rung, again. He had taken it while bounding down the stairs. Hero was reporting again. He wanted money, of course. "If you want to avoid scandal you better listen."

Cubby was on his own fast track and not to be derailed for anything. "Shut it, Benny. I already left your fifty with that barmaid at the pub. Know where that brother of yours is?"

"No. Gone to ground. I have something else for you if you must know. Something a bit close to home. I want twenty-five grand up front though."

Cubby smirked. "Twenty-five grand?"

"You'll be glad of the info."

"Nothing's worth twenty-five grand. What do you mean? Close to home?"

Hero started to speak but then the line went dead as if Hero had switched off his phone. Cubby shrugged. Nothing was worth twenty-five grand. Everything in the open as matters concerned him and no time for a new development as long as the story about the kid was current. If Hero did not know where Mally was Cubby could think of nothing worth paying above a hundred for. Or maybe he did but what did Mally Kenyon matter anyway?

It had been his phone call to the barmaid at the Dog's Bed Inn that had told him what was happening on the Dog's Bed Estate...cashing in for a tip time! Well worth a twenty more.

As predictable as night following day anarchy was raising its ugly head without any help from the Clarion newspaper. The residents were planning to build a barricade using all the heaped up rotting garbage which had been taken from out of the Whemley Canal and was being left in stinking heaps at the side of the canal, blocking the banking. The police had not even done the estate the courtesy of having it taken away. They could not even make one phone call to the Refuse Department on behalf of the health and wellbeing of the townsfolk. Already the flies were amassing. The residents were now talking about it over pints of strong ale and pledging themselves to the cause as the beer flowed, despite it yet to turn eleven in the morning. They were waiting for the last of the police cars to withdraw so that the fuzz were on the wrong side of the road bridge and then get building. The last of the house-to-house questioning and searches yet to be made. Then the militants would have their own say. Catty Collins had already had hers. It would not be contained to the local press, either. They would be alerting the national press not to go away as the residents turned out in force. The police wanted a stink! The police would get a stink! All the raw material they needed to build a barricade was there for them to use for that very purpose.

Cubby envisaged himself to be a very busy man over the coming few days

Fourteen

Tommo noted the Clarion's main reporter looking through the gates as soon as he got out of the mini-bus even while struggling, along with Gary, to get the awkwardly placed, fighting child into the house as quickly as possible out of Cubby Watson's camera sights.

Under any other circumstance they might have left her where she was, strapped in with the back-of-seat buckle to keep her in place, waiting quietly and patiently until she tired herself out. Later it would prove not to have been a wise decision to get her behind closed doors as quickly as possible where Cubby's camera could not follow even on zoom. Tommo making this decision to move her inside as quickly as they could...he and Gary doing the handling...Holly not yet having had any training in care and restraint procedures when a client was in need of containment. He considered that it would not take long for Cubby Watson to be joined by other newshounds just as eager to get sensational photographs as he was.

Some decisions just prove to be incorrect and nothing to be done about the result until after the event. He had not foreseen that the photographs they were about to provide would be the most sensational possible. Those provided by two, strong, adult men struggling to control one small, angry, female child. Both he and Gary might have felt as if they were trying to overwhelm a giant, slippery and exceedingly strong anaconda which was trying its best to inflict as much painful injury upon them as was possible, but to the rest of the world it would look more like they were using inappropriate strength to control one very vulnerable and weak, little girl. Like taking a sledge hammer to crack a walnut...applying unnecessary force...simply failing to respect her childish innocence as they manhandled her into the house. It would look as if they had abused her dignity and not the other way about.

The child's cheeks had been brick red and her squeals loud and carrying across the forecourt to Cubby Watson's ears as she had fought against their attempts to get her as quickly as possible inside the building, calling still for the woman with the damned, golden trumpet to come and rescue her, screaming it out in white hot rage until Tommo thought his ear drums would burst, as her hollering mouth with its biting teeth was no more than a few inches from his ear lobe. He preferred his person to remain intact, if at all possible.

She had already struck Gary with a head butt to his right cheekbone causing it to swell and then got her nails into the back of his hand where the veins stood out blue but ran copiously with his own red blood. The child had no such wounds yet, somehow, the blood had become transferred in smears to her own small face when her hand went to her mouth and her temper flared once again. She began to bite herself before they could prevent it. Her rage transferred onto herself with a suddenness which took them by surprise. It was when Tommo tried to pull her hand away from her mouth that he let go of her sufficiently for her to grab onto a porch post, bloodied finger nails gripping tight, her bloodied face set with a determination so strong that the image had to be the one which Cubby would later use on the front page of his paper.

Why bother, then, with his stolen image of a placid child dressed in dungarees and holding out the rag doll which he had stolen from the policeman's briefcase earlier? Her anger, the blood on her hands and face, all her body language in her will to get away consolidated an opinion that her objections were against entry into a unit of detainment; a secure unit, in fact, where she would be isolated, incarcerated, even imprisoned. What other reason could a child have for behaving in that way? The fact that she was yelling out. "No go to Blackstone School. Never!" seemed to have got lost in the melee.

The pictures that Cubby Watson would print later would be damning. They would travel nationwide on the front covers of the Clarion and then the tabloids, in particular, across the world wide web and all around the world. This was the age of immediate access to what concerned people most; child abuse, in all its forms, being one of them. They would become issues for urgent discussion amongst parent groups and those involved with any league of people whose vulnerable friends and relatives had occasional need of careful restraint at vulnerable times in their lives. They would be passed round council chambers and end up on the desks of the Members of Parliament for the Quinton and Dales District area. They would travel up through floors in important places. They would bring all eyes to Quinton and Greengates House, in particular. They would be tied in with what was going on at the Dog's Bed Estate; for people to wonder over the insult of its parochial nickname, damning even more the situation and the treatment of its residents by the police themselves; the true guardians of the people, whose Chief Constable was taking the opportunity to clean out her kitchen cupboards rather than find out who had most likely dealt with a child so cruelly that she had become as a feral animal, fighting against the very people trying to help her and they not helping her as they struggled to defend themselves.

Cubby was having a field day! Surely, there were better ways to handle such situations? He would have to move back again the scandal of green belt land being sold off cheap to selected builders offering brown envelopes to council land agents to page five as the topics from a single act spread and multiplied, like breeding rabbits.

Gina could not get Cubby out of her mind as she followed Holly Hargreaves over the threshold with a sad look on her face. Even those with the best training in child handling still had some situations that they could not control. She was glad that she was not a participant, herself. She could not have faced yet another confrontation with Wendy Bridgewater at whose hands she had, already, suffered gravely.

Instead of hanging around she handed the carrier bags over to Angie, being unsure who Holly was before turning to walk away, back to her car. There was something familiar about her but she could not say what it was. She would introduce herself to Tommo another day. The caretaker would just have to open the gates for her again. She would not stop to speak to Cubby Watson, either, who was still hanging about with his camera before his face. She certainly would not be meeting him at the Italiana at three p.m. She just wanted to get home to sleep, crawl into her own corner and lick her wounds as any injured animal will. She had no opinion on the violence that she had just witnessed, knowing that such situations sprang up like wildfires and Tommo and Gary had simply dealt with it as best they could. It was part and parcel of their work.

Angie closed the door as Gina left upon a hurried explanation that she would return later and Holly came through it. Ever perceptive, she noted the pallor on the young girl's face. Holly looked seriously concerned and disturbed by the situation, her eyes keened and frightened. The child had not been merely blowing steam as she had been oft to do, herself, but had become genuinely and violently distraught as if fighting for her very existence. Watching someone else in such distress was much harder to cope with, in an emotional sense, than being the one at the very epicentre of a temper tantrum and gaining the satisfaction of exacting vengeful retribution. It had been, to Holly, like looking back upon herself but from the point of view of those who had stood as bystanders, looking on. Nothing to admire. Nothing to be gained. Everyone involved upset and distraught by the whole situation, judging by the looks on Tommo's and Gary's faces. So why had she, herself, once behaved in that way? She found her empathy with the child almost impossible to bear while having no sympathy with the girl she, herself, had used to be. The one who thought nothing of making displays of abusive temper which had required her to be restrained. Neither could she pass blame onto the men who had tried their best to offer Wendy some dignity. It had been the child who refused it. All her own guilt showed upon her face as the kindly looking woman in the apron shut the door behind them.

"You'll be Holly," Angie said with understanding. "It's never as bad as it looks. Getting them here's always the worst bit when they think it's a place of torture, which it isn't. It gets better as they come to understand that we aren't against them. In fact if we can't cope with them, who can? Poor little thing, too. Her being so young for a place like this."

Holly found herself with very little to say.

"You best get on and follow them. I'm Angie, by the way. The chap who opened the gate is Harry. Tommo and Gary are in the second room on the right, now, with the little girl...nothing to throw in there and just a few mats to sit on other than the chairs always being set in place just for occasions like this. We call it the Exercise Room for want of a better description. You'll get used to it all in time."

Holly removed her shoes and put down her purple shoulder bag and the small suitcase. She clutched the rag doll to her chest before going into the room where three chairs had been set and the men now sat quietly trying to get their breath back with the child between them. She was weeping now, breathing deeply, red plums for cheeks but her struggles had stopped, her head down; defeated.

How many times had Holly been placed to *calm down* in a room like this in a similar situation?

Tommo looked at her and spoke without the knowledge that he was speaking to a girl with the ultimate experience of being the one at the centre of things but none at all of one who could only look on and feel threatened by the display of someone else's anger. "Now that you're here, we'll stand up and leave, locking the door behind us. She'll require a change of faces. You weren't involved so she won't attack you. The room has CCTV, as have all the rooms our clients use for different purposes. We have a bank of TV sets in the office. If she starts again we'll be here in a matter of moments." Then as if for incentive. "Sausages and onion gravy with mash for lunch, I think, Wendy."

Holly watched them go. The child was crying softly, now, her anger spent. She took a chair beside her. "It gets you nowhere, you know. Not if you want to be somewhere different."

The child sniffed and raised her head, her silver orbs deeply flooded with her fast running tears. Gary's blood still smeared on her cheeks. She sniffed them away and rubbed them off her cheeks with the backs of her hands. "Her sorry, now. D'is prison? You is a naughty girl, too?"

Not more than five minutes ago Holly might have replied, "You bet and proud of it!" Now she merely nodded. No point in lying to the kid. The adults, yes, but not the child. "Looks like it. Here...your doll. What's its name?"

"Oswald Thecil."

"Nice name for a rag doll with orange hair. Dinner sounds good. Nice smell."

The child nodded, sniffing deeply. "Wendy likes sausages. Caitlin doesn't. No healthy."

"Who's Caitlin? Your sister?"

Wendy put her head down, taking the doll from Holly and stuffing it down inside the neck of her jumper so that she looked to have two heads again; one a straggling blonde and wet with tears but so pretty of face that she pulled at Holly's heartstrings. Not that Holly Hargreaves would admit to having any. If anyone else had asked about her feelings which they never did. The other head was of white cotton with big blue plastic eyes, a freckled, drawn-on nose, a wide smile, and, of course, the orange strands of coarse wool for hair.

"Her no say. Secrets." Wendy had seen secrets in Holly's eyes, too. "You and me is friends?"

Why not? It would makes things a lot easier, that was a fact. "I'll help you get changed if you like. It's a bit smelly in here."

Wendy nodded. "Caitlin a naughty girl. No me."

"So you keep saying, kid. Is she your imaginary friend? I had one once. I blamed her for everything, too."

"D'is Blackstone School?"

"Same difference, maybe, from the grim sound of it. Greengates House, it's called. I had hoped to be able to get out now and then but it doesn't look likely unless I ask permission."

"D'is prison?"

"Might as well be." Then, to change the subject. "Let's have a look what's in the bags. I like new clothes. Do You?"

Wendy nodded, slipping off the chair gingerly, seemingly aware of the brown stain on her pants and her wet knickers from earlier. Holly's punishment! Yet going to join Wendy on the mat where they sat, together, other things on her mind. Holly loved clothes because they made her feel good. There was nothing quite like looking at something bright and colourful for improving her mood.

As Holly brought each garment from the bags the child sat cross-legged, looking with interest to ascertain what the bags contained. Holly unable to sit in any other way but like a mermaid on a rock because of the tightness of her skirt. First she brought out a pink track suit.

"I's got one of them already."

"Just the same as this?"

The child nodded, her voice lowering to a barely perceptible whisper, her silver eyes conspiratorial and friendly. "Trimbles. For riding the exercise bike. Caitlin likes exercises. Me no like exercises." Then her eyes lifted to the lens mounted on a plinth in the ceiling corner of the room. Then to another on the ceiling corner nearest to a window which overlooked the rear garden. She turned so that her back was towards the camera and mouthed the words clearly. It was as if she understood their function. "You's help Caitlin and Wendy, Caitlin and Wendy helps you."

Holly's eyes flicked up to the lenses wondering at the child's intelligence. She would not have thought her clever enough to understand what Tommo had been referring to before he left the room. If there were cameras there would be a sound pick-up, too. The men would be looking directly at them from this office place and hearing everything that was said between them except that which was whispered.

It felt strange to Holly to be on the other side of the fence for a change. She had probably been watched, herself, when she had been doing naughty things and thought herself invisible and invincible. Little wonder she had rarely been successful in her mischief. They might have heard all that little Wendy said, too, had she spoken the words loudly.

Then Holly saw the rough, red welt around her neck, her eyes drawn there by the strange position of the doll. *What had caused that?* she wondered. Like something that had rubbed and rubbed around her neck.

It was then that Gary opened the door and entered the room smiling, despite a swollen cheek and the bleeding scratches; war wounds he seemed to be proud of. "I'll show you both the ropes when I get back from taking Chester out for his morning walk. Missed it today because we had to take Jacko straight to the cells at the Magistrates' Court. Tommo's here if you need him. Harry and Angie are, too, so there's plenty o' back-up. He'll talk to you this afternoon, Holly, when you're both a bit more settled in. Bit of a stickler for procedure is Tommo. We do everything by the book."

That was when he brought the dog lead out of his pocket.

Wendy's eyes locked onto the dog lead, her face straightening, both eyes immediately taking on a dull lustre, eyelids almost completely shut. She raised herself to sit on her haunches, head down, feet tucked underneath her, arms straight, flat handed to the mat.

"What are you doing, Wendy?" Gary asked gently as the dog chain chinked in his hand.

With eyes still closed, Wendy replied in a tiny whisper; baby breaths of sound. "Her wants to ride in the cart. Only a good girl who is quiet and still as a dolly rides in the cart to Quinton. Her wants the collar on so she can ride out. Her wants the lead on the collar and threaded through the holes. Her wants the collar on so her can ride out with the lead on to keep her good."

Holly bit her lip. The child seemed to expect that the dog lead was used in conjunction with a dog collar, on herself. This was something else. This explained the red marks on her neck. This was weirdo beyond any weirdo she had ever known. In all her years of abusive behaviour against others she had never been treated like that. It had all seemed just a game to Holly. To the restrainers as well; "Holly's blowing again," they'd shout and then look smug when they had her pinned down on a handling mat. Holly had liked the physical contact when hugs were not allowed. No hugs, no kisses, no hands around you telling you; *You're alright, kid. You're safe!* Didn't the kid know her rights? What kind of person puts a dog collar on a child and uses it for restraint?

Gary let the dog lead slide back into his pocket. He would take Chester for his walk only after he had made a new entry chart for Wendy in the daily diary and reported the incident clearly. Later he would write everything up as a detailed report along with any other of his observations, sure in the knowledge that Tommo would go through it with a highlighter.

Holly thought that she had come to the very worst kind of place; far worse than any she had, so far, experience of herself. She might have been better off with the squat and the shoplifting than this. Even the launderette would have been better than this.

Too late, now, though. In for a penny, in for a pound!

Better get the child cleaned up. She'd wash her kecks for her. Just this once, that was. She would be showing her how to do it for herself, thereafter. Then she'd run the bath for her. Those finger nails would have to go, though. She'd be wearing the slippers even after she was provided with a pair of outdoor shoes if Holly Hargreaves had anything to do with it. Shoes were effective weapons to Holly, especially stilettos, so she wouldn't be leaving her own lying around, either.

Maybe she could show the kid a thing or two, too, but not anything she might use against Holly. Just how to get the best out of situations. Play the staff off one against the other. Stir things up a bit for the sake of having a bit of fun and for them to know you ain't as stupid as people might make you out to be. As long as the kid behaved herself! Maybe, her job would be easier if they were friends.

Fifteen

The brothers Kenyon held their communion at the altar of a long and tightly woven past, which was central to their relationships with each other, and caused them to be feared by most of the residents on the Dog's Bed Estate.

Hard men, each of them, they swaggered and preened except when being watched by the police when they merged into the shadows better than ghosts in a cemetery at midnight, so that long periods might elapse between them being seen. Benny and Woody living together with that Bull Mastiff, Sabre, to guard their patch in a dark house to the rear of the estate which was hard to locate. Mally having elected to have his own dishevelled pit for some reason which neither brother could understand. Something to do with his fetish for Magdalene they thought. A senseless obsession if ever there was one when the woman was these days possessed by religion. They also blamed her for Bass's death for no more reason than that she had been his wife. Reason enough in some men's minds!

The only time a Kenyon went anywhere near the church was when they had to beg for alms of Father Turner. Times being tough. Tougher these days than they had ever known them to be. Little money about and people selling off their fancy bits and bobs in order to treat their kids to things they had previously taken for granted. So break-ins on the estate were rarely practical. Nothing much to steal left lying about and the shops in the centre of Quinton, these days, tightening up their own security so that shoplifting had become a riskier business than it had ever been before. Easier to take cars and then sell them on to the backstreet dealers, though harder to break into these days with their owners more inclined to have a go than see their most expensive possession driven off from their own back gates.

Jobs even scarcer, too, though they all managed to get work on *the lump*; the Quinton expression for working for cash in hand. Just turn up and ask a bent foreman trying to pocket a few quid himself by taking on cheap, pay-as-you-go labour. Usually the hardest, harshest labouring jobs on the building sites and quarry workings about Quinton. They got infrequent work carrying palettes of cement up steep ladders to where the bricklayers laid their bricks when there was no hydraulic lift to save backs being injured. Sometimes, they barrowed brick; same again, when there was no forklift. Or cleared rubble by the ton into skips using large panned spades when it should have been cleared using a mechanical shovel to meet Health and Safety legislation. Hard work and poorly paid even when they avoided taxes. Rarely did they earn enough to support their expensive leisure habits which for each of them had to find money to buy cigarettes, booze and hard drugs. Benny's habits being the worst and most expensive. They had long ago given up on designer clothes and nightclubs. Benny was often to be found under a hedge, unconscious, when unable to make a disorientated way home. For Woody the drink was his greatest failing, his binges, once started, lasting for weeks. Mally dabbled but was rarely found to be incapable, these days. Ever since his twin had been found dead of an overdose he had drawn back from the edge of the precipice himself. These days he spent a good deal of his time mooning after Bass's wife from a distance.

Time and a lack of opportunity to move away from the Dog's Bed Estate had seen them keep together yet remain as individuals, even after their parents' premature demise from the wasting effects of much of the same, hapless lifestyles. They shared a past that had plaited their close childhoods together within the painful bindings of constant and unremitting hardship; one mainly of hunger and neglect, beatings and humiliations. Home, school and community alike, they had come to regard themselves as the lowest of the lowest, even in a place like the Dog's Bed Estate.

Such impoverishment of self respect had become consolidated with the passage of time into a code of practice by which to live. Namely to prey upon the weak and vulnerable and never miss an opportunity for easy, material gain. They were each of them inured with the sure knowledge that while they trusted no one entirely they would rather trust a Kenyon than anyone else; but only when they had to. They were neither kind nor generous nor helpful towards each other because to show such weakness undermined their meagre strengths. What they did, in the main, was to guard each other's backs as much as possible but never to risk themselves should a brother pay the ultimate price of being caught and sent to prison.

While they might interlace and interact they remained each their own, separate beings. One of the same group of tightly latticed strands which made up an interwoven history of poverty, crime and long term unemployment.

Now, as men, while they might have come through the same early endurances of their childhoods their adulthood was equally as fraught with just as many dangers within the deep and dark brick and concrete alleyways of an urban jungle like the Dog's Bed Estate where they had become the oppressors, so as not to become the oppressed. They made up a street gang, all of their own.

Now only Woody and Benny Kenyon remained. Mally, as far as they could ascertain, having been detained at Quinton Police Station where he would be charged for no other reason than that he was Mally Kenyon whose criminal record wrote guilty through him like a stick of Blackpool rock. It was within their code of practice never to grieve for what could not be prevented though they both knew that it had not been Mally who had committed the crime for which he had been arrested. They knew it because it had been Woody who had been a participant to the events which had happened prior to the child being discovered in a sack, in the rancid canal waters under Bridge Twenty-Eight. Not that he had put her there. But, indeed, he had been the one to waylay the woman with the shopping trolley in which the child was being transported.

It had only been after Mally had been arrested; a surprise to them both, that he had informed Benny, before Benny might become too intoxicated with the contents of the syringe he already had prepared, of what had occurred the previous night to make him feel so excited, even while feeling angered by the justification that there was no such thing as justice in this world. No one knew better than Woody that his brother, Mally, was innocent. However, an unexpected opportunity had occurred. The luck of all those who live by their wits and look out constantly for passing opportunity.

So Woody had brought Benny away from the estate to the lock-up, early, as soon as the pigs had carted Mally away and before he could get himself so stoned as to be of no use to anyone. They watched Magdalene and her mother walk away with harsh looks at their retreating backs, sneers shared through the knowledge of where each of the women would be going. No need to even ask where Magdalene was heading, her head already covered, her candle purchased, her day ahead the same as all her others. Not even a backward glance as she went on her way. Nan Bartlett neither when her hostility to their lifestyle was open for all to see. As their own attitudes were to hers. She would be going to consult them cards of hers after all her talk of doom and damnation, burning towers and calumny; whatever that was! Stopping on the way to talk with anyone who would share her looks, shake their heads, and dally in conversation.

Woody and Benny knew themselves better to be out of the way of their neighbours for the time being anyway. They had had to shoulder their way through the angry, barging women lining the pavement. Square up to the men who soon got out of Sabre's way as the hungry dog made a path through the crowds for them. The dog had to live as they did on what it could find, where it could find it, as long as it took nothing from either Benny's or Woody's plates.

After Mally had been carted away they might have gone back to the black hovel they shared when there was no work available. They might have switched on the TV set while Benny stretched himself out on the filthy, rag-heaped pallet he used for a bed after strapping up for the injection; his veins hard to find these days. Woody popping cans of beer as he usually did from first thing in the morning to avoid the worst of the shakes, sipping all day until he collapsed to his knees purely because his legs would carry him no further. Money in used notes in his pocket today because he had mugged a defenceless woman and stolen her purse. He had a whole heap of cans lined up but not the mind, as yet, to start into them.

When Woody started thinking his fair eyebrows met over the same silver eyes as all the Kenyon brothers had. The only thing of any discernable difference between him and his brothers was a beer belly which protruded over his dirty jeans like the swollen abdomen of a pregnant woman. Benny, skin and bone, sore infested and numb as yet from yesterday's indulgence. His mood beginning to become surly as his needs deepened and his thoughts turned to the day ahead of him.

"Need a conflab," Woody had said and wouldn't allow a refusal when Benny would have followed his wants to the filthy kitchen sink where his satisfaction lay ready and waiting. He was only persuaded by the quarter bottle of Methadone Woody brought from his pocket; a lure to get his brother to listen. Someone's State-provided prescription taken in exchange for some of the profit made from his work of the night before. No other way to get Benny to where he wanted him to be because what he had spent the night planning needed sharing and talking over with someone he trusted not to do the dirty on him.

So Woody took Benny to where they often laid low when times got tough, driving the battered, builder's transit he had borrowed without the owner's permission for just that purpose, to where they stashed stolen goods. Kept a firearm, just in case. Three chairs round a litter filled table; one for each brother. A place long used yet never spoken of outside their brotherhood. Never seen a cleaning cloth or a sweeping brush. Litter everywhere. Three broken armchairs, sagging and dirty, smelling of urine. The insects living within the dirty mattress in the corner might have had some interesting tales to tell as they fed upon the dead skin flakes and left over stains of a thousand, out-of-focus binges only vaguely recalled. Cockroaches the size of fifty pence pieces crawling through the spillage on the rickety table. The lock-up being the family pile, so to speak, where the Kenyons could talk without being overheard. The long-tailed, brown sewer rats cowering in the shadows; the only living things with ears...or so they thought...to do any listening into this *conflab* that Woody would insist that

Benny wait to hear. When all Benny wanted was the comfort of what was ready and waiting for him on his kitchen sink; enough to keep him satisfied and happy for the time being. They might discuss it together, Woody said, because this was a big one. Better had be, Benny thought.

So Benny suffered to go along in sullen silence to the lock-up with Woody who even took the trouble to park the transit inside the arch and close the doors. Every few minutes a train rumbled overhead and shook the foundations, them with it; a disturbance hardly noted as they straddled seats about a noxious table in this their place of hiding, under the brick arches of the railway sidings. A paraffin lamp lighting their almost identical faces and masking other acrid stenches. The lock up secured by metal doors fastened with bolts. The padlocks off the outside of the metal doors the only change to note that anyone was in residence.

Benny controlled his shakings with a few slugs of the Methadone, his knees twitching constantly as his joints began to ache while his brother explained just how he had come across the stolen handbag that contained an opportunity to tap into a money supply that might be never-ending. All they had to do was turn on the tap and put their mouths under the flow.

"Heard all that before, our Woody. What opportunity?"

"First you listen to my tale," he said demandingly then leant in closer, over the table while his brother rapped his fingers with impatience. "Last night...when you went home and I got to hanging about the bridge waiting for the dealer that never showed...I sees this woman come up the steps from the Lower Quinton side of the canal and cross over to go down to the other banking. Near midnight. She has this big shopping trolley and a bag hanging off her shoulder, as well as a suitcase...easy pickings."

"So?" Benny accepting a cigarette from his brother and providing the flame for them both. "This to do with the kid, is it?"

Smoke coming from Woody's nostrils as he continued speaking, wishing his brother would stop asking questions and simply listen. His speech quickening. "I follows her down the other steps in the direction of Quinton. Takes her by surprise. Grabs the bag. She falls to the ground. I opens some straps on the lid of the trolley and puts my hand in. I pulls out a sack. A dog in a sack, I thinks, at first. Then this hand pushes at me through the sack. What's in there has arms and legs. Scares me shitless. I drops it. She yells it's a child in the sack. Then this sack makes one big hop and it's in the water. When I comes away, up the steps, its head's still poking up."

"Wasn't our Mally then. Wasn't nobody. Was it you called the police?"

Woody nodded. "I'm not daft enough to get banged up for

murder of a kid. I thought the woman would squeal …call the pigs. When she didn't do nothing to get the kid out, I rang 999...first time ever."

Benny tracked his words. "Why didn't she go in for it if she were so concerned?"

Woody shrugged, shaking his head. Part of the mystery he would make Benny wait for 'til the end of his tale. "No idea, then. Had to get away fast so as not to be connected when the pigs came. Had to make sure the kid got saved though. Get slammed for child murder and your life's over."

"Looks as if our kid will though. Our Mally will get slammed for it. Hit her hard, did you? This woman…!"

Woody shrugged as he drew deep on the smoke. "I'd given her a shove that's all. It shouldn't have done anything more than knock the wind out of her. To move on…After I calls the pigs to come get the kid, I goes back over the road to the pub...round the back…and looks over the wall down onto the canal banking. I can see her moving about but not the kid. The kid's still in the water. The pigs are on their way by the time she gets to her feet...a real struggle. She takes the trolley and the case and then beggars off to hide in some bushes by the greenhouses. I takes the purse and a crucifix and hides the bag in the trash bins, back of the pub, in case I gets stopped or something. I think our Mally must have gone out the pub the front way just as the police van comes and pulls up on the bridge. They were quick looking for the kid. Mally and Tock, with them. Heard it all. Mally doing what the pigs should have done. That's how he came to be the one to save her."

Benny, narrow-eyed now, leaning closer. "So this woman hides and doesn't show her face?"

Woody nodded. "She waits until the pigs gets away with the kid in the van. Our Mally and Tock goes back into the pub for a drink. Then she goes back the way she's come, taking that trolley and suitcase with her…crying like and talking to herself…saying some name, over and over. I seen her with a phone in her hand and talking to someone but not the police…hard and angry like, but quiet…real quiet. Couldn't see her face to know her but seen her before, somewhere."

Benny's expression was one of disgust. "Trafficking kids?" Even Benny's face was spread wide as the thought occurred to him. "You follow her?"

Woody shook his head in disagreement with the first suggestion because he'd since worked it all out and then nodded to his last question. "Not at first. I gets Sabre. I'd tied him onto the boot scraper by the back door of the pub before waiting for the dealer to arrive. I takes him down the steps on the Quinton towpath side and finds this wet tissue...seen her drop it. I tells Sabre to follow and find. He gets his nose down then. I knows he has the right scent because he follows her path back over the bridge and down the steps, same way as I seen her come. We goes tracking across the playing field and past the mere where we used to smash up the rowing boats. Remember? Same place someone speared the swans and they tried to blame us for it."

Benny nodded. "Past the old bandstand to the old park gates."

"Her must have gone through them gates and up by the park railings. Then crossed the road to number thirty-four of them old terraced houses. Sabre stops outside and sits down because we can't get no further unless we follows her in. You know what that means!"

"It's where the woman lives. So what? She has this kid in her trolley and doesn't even try to get it out the water. Scarpers when you calls the pigs. Nothing new in that! We're to blackmail her for that? Not much money if she's living there...probably rents, anyway."

Woody nodded, popping a can of beer and swigging deeply though he had plans to go easy on the booze, so to think straight. "Maybe not. But why avoid the police? No one wants to see a kid harmed unless they're twisted. Made no sense to me."

There was something in Woody's expression that caused his brother not to lose patience entirely with this long winded tale. "What then?" Benny was getting itchy and irritated. He hated guessing games. "Get to the point, our Woody, or I'm off." Some people laboured the telling of anything too much and Woody was always one of them.

Woody lowered his eyebrows thoughtfully before laughing on his memory. "I could have saved myself the trouble of following her, maybe, because what I finds in the handbag tells me why all right. I takes out what's in it and brings the papers home. You were flat out when I gets home so I takes them upstairs with me and looks through it real slow. Bills and papers mainly with her name and address... Serena Collins of the same address on Park Road." Here he removed a crucifix from his pocket and let the thin, delicate, shiny gold cross and chain catch the light from the paraffin lamp as he stared at it as if a prompt to his memory. "There was this envelope with the name of a school on the front. A girls school. Black something or other, over in Shropshire. There was an admission date on it for the following day...girl named Caitlin Collins, seven years of age...and guess what...? Look! See for yourself."

Woody now spread the papers over the table. He had collected them together in a plastic pocket to denote their importance; several folded utility bills and the forms with the name and address of a private school in

Shropshire. All carefully filled in, in royal blue ink. The hand of an educated person.

Benny was tired of waiting for the punch line. He wasn't reading anything when his eyes had begun to itch as if infested with lice as his hair was. He nodded at the papers and dragged on the last of his cigarette. "What...? What about them?"

After Woody explained, pointing out names, taking Benny along the pathways of his own reasoning, his brother began to slowly nod his head in understanding.

"Struck gold," was what Benny said as he ground the butt into the table top, aimed at a cockroach but missed it as it crawled over the rim and under the table. "Father named as C. C. Watson. Strikes a bell. Clarion Evening News. Wife that magistrate fined our Mally for kicking shit out of a copper outside the Jackerby, last Christmas. Rich farts. The kid's kept under wraps. Wonder why that is?"

Woody, satisfied now that his longwinded explanation had lit a light of greed in his brother, Benny's, dull eyes. He nodded at him. "Don't want folk to know about her, that's why. Kid's a bastard. More than that. She's been kept under wraps...no one knows anything about her...except her...and him...and us!"

In his excitement and agitation, Benny kicked the other empty chair over. Should have been Mally's. As it hit the floor, it broke into pieces. Looked as if he'd have no need for it anyway. They had yet to know that their dear brother had walked out of Quinton Police Station and was in their immediate vicinity.

*****

Mally Kenyon could see only one way of proving his innocence and it did not entail staying where he had been with the police about to charge him for something he simply had not done. He had not put the child into a sack and chucked her into the water, simple as that! It had been she who had opened the door for him at the police station so that he might creep away to his freedom. Her blessings were with him. Though she had inflicted the scabbing wounds on his head and hand in panic when he brought her from the water she had helped him to escape. He had simply taken the opportunity she had offered to him while the police station had been overwhelmed with all the arrests being made. It had been so easy to just walk out after losing his usual appearance under a flat cap and within too small a jacket while people he knew complained about their own unfair treatment at the hands of the police.

If no one had recognised him it had been because he had no wish for them to do so as he had pushed his way through the throngs of people after the teenage girl had so fortuitously held the door open for him.

Once out on the street he had stolen a bicycle then peddled down the backstreets, eventually to the railway station sidings where the brick arches of the viaducts would offer him some protection for a short time at least. There he would hide and wait, bide his time, plan his purpose; steal what he needed to survive as he had been raised to do. Maybe get some money from his brothers, if they had any to give, in order to leave the area. There was always itinerant farm work or what he was best at; labouring on building sites for a lower wage on piece rate. What was the point of staying around when there was only the child, herself, who could save him? It took him a long time of thinking in closed-in places to decide that he would have to get the bit of cash he had stashed behind a brick in the wall at the lock-up under the arches. Hiding as he did so in any dark place he could find. Making a slow and calculated journey in stages when he knew the worst thing would be to let the police catch sight of him for a hue and cry would then begin. Nothing like the pigs with egg on their snouts to get them riled up and out in numbers, looking for the one to have stained their reputations. Made to look stupid by a kid! So he took his time as he made his way; anything rather than give himself away.

When Mally came upon the bolted doors of the lock-up under the brick arches, he saw that the padlocks had been removed. That could only mean that one or both of his brothers either singly or together were within. The tyre tracks of a large vehicle would suggest that someone had recently driven a van inside. He could hear voices; Benny and Woody in deep conversation. If they were not alone he'd be better to keep low until he could be sure of it.

Just to be sure he placed his ear against the metal door which he had every intention of shortly opening, the stolen bike held upright by the handlebars and seat as he leant in to listen to the drone of his brothers' voices. He had every intention of wheeling it in with him. It would be his means of a quick escape should one be needed. Might have done so except that what they were talking about came to his ears clearly as an echo. Woody talking and Benny doing the listening. Even when someone passed in a car he continued to listen with his ear pressed to the cold, metal door.

So Woody had witnessed everything! Followed the family code. He had known all along that Mally was innocent of chucking the kid in a sack into the water yet had said nothing to the police. Not that Mally blamed him. It was the way of things in the Kenyon household…each for their own! He would have had to admit having mugged the woman and stolen her handbag, otherwise. The story unfolding slowly in that way Woody always told a tale when he had actually done what he had said he had done and it wasn't all lies; a slow telling of every detail to convince Mally that what he was sharing with Benny was the cold, honest truth.

By the end of his telling, Mally knew, too. Knew their plans. Heard Benny trying it on with Cubby Watson but giving up on it when Woody cancelled the call because the whiz-kid hadn't a clue what Benny had been rabbiting on about and wasn't in for that kind of money even had he had it. Knew that they would be after the person who really had something to hide…the newspaper owners themselves. Rich farts as Benny had called them. What was twenty-five thousand to them? Only, suddenly, it had upped to forty grand in used notes. Let them get on with it!

For a moment he stood in some confusion listening to them profit from his crucifixion. Mally, however, had committed it all to memory…names, addresses, everything. He knew Park Road well. Knew, too, that once Woody and Benny got their teeth into a road kill they didn't let go of it for anything or anybody.

Hoisting a leg over the crossbar, he looked about before setting his foot to the pedal. Then set on his way, again.

*****

It was shortly after ten-thirty when a rusting, white transit van parked up in a lay-by a short way after the wide bend in the road to Burden Village, where the gates to Barton Manor allowed a meandering, tree-shaded drive to offer access to the forecourt of the elegant house which could be seen from the roadway. The dilapidated builder's van standing close to the entrance of the extensive plot had gone unnoticed by the driver of the expensive, red Jaguar car, whose entry to the exclusive address had been allowed by use of a remote control to open the high, wide, oak gates before driving within. The gates closing again automatically as soon as the car was safely within.

Within the van had been Benny and Woody Kenyon and the short-haired grey Bull Mastiff which, due to the men's preoccupation and total lack of consideration, had yet to be allowed off the lead to go on a hunt in order to be fed. Its hunger lay in its eyes for all to see as it watched the men, through a dirty window, set up traffic cones, a wheelbarrow, spades and picks by the hedges to denote that work was about to take place on the root-cracked pavements which the locals had complained about for many a year. This was a select area of impressive homes in an area of outstanding, natural beauty. Rolling hills surrounded the sandstone house as if protecting a tranquil idyll from barbaric invasion, save for that which modern technology allows by the speedy pressing of a button, the parking up of the expensively distinctive car with barely a squeak from the handbrake and then the production of a set of keys with which to respond quickly to the shrill call of a telephone coming through the stout oak door to beckon the driver into the house with some haste, leaving the door open as the home-comer made to answer the telephone.

As the driver allowed an unusual patch of strong sunlight to play over the polished oak parquet floor of the hallway, the pale lilac hessian wallpaper, the bowls of fresh flowers on hall tables arranged below polished, ornately carved mirrors, not to forget a hall robe of antique value next to a locked gun cupboard, three moving shadows came to make silhouettes caused by the blockage of the sunlight as they made over the threshold without invitation.

As the householder raised the receiver to answer the shrill call of the telephone, in Woody Kenyon's hand was a mobile telephone. When he spoke the same words relayed themselves to the ear pressed against the landline telephone receiver. "Thought we'd ask for some water in order to make a brew."

In Benny Kenyon's hand was a battered kettle without a lid which he held out as part of the excuse for their unexpected visit. With his free hand he shut the door behind them so that the sunlight and their shadows disappeared.

Shock was evident.

Woody spoke for both himself and Benny. "Got a bit of a secret to tell you. Glad you're seated. Make yourself comfortable. I'll begin...." Woody liked nothing better than telling an extended tale with all the detail filled in.

The Kenyon brothers! Questions were unnecessary. It was a simple matter of putting two and two together. The house and car keys were deposited into a fruit dish next to the phone as the chair provided a thankful seat for legs suddenly incapacitated with weakness.

"Makes a change from only ever meeting at the court house, doesn't it? Clarion's made a mint from all the reporting you done on us in the past. That son of yours knows about the bastard, does he?"

Eyes were closed. A sick pallor had come upon their listener's face.

Benny nodded his agreement. "There must be a few pills for the having in a place like this. You explain the deal, Woody; I'll just take a look in the bathroom cabinets. A few Mogadons wouldn't come amiss."

Sixteen

Serena Collins was thinking hard with her already tired and pulverised brain working overtime. As she waited for the 39 bus on the opposite side of the road from Greengates House, having seen her precious Caitlin behave in such a despicable way, her tears swilled over and ran down her hidden face. Though she hated to give in she had had no choice but to come away.

It had become expedient to move away when the man with the camera had begun to take photographs and she had become frightened that he might take one of her. Under no circumstances could Serena allow that to happen. He was still there, in fact, conversing with the uncooperative caretaker who had opened the gate, yet again, for the lady in the Fiat Punto to back out and be on her way. While the man with the camera might wave the woman to stop she had ignored him. It had been the same lady who had handed over some carrier bags to the person who had opened the door of the house; a woman wearing an apron who looked the type to be kindly. Or, at least, Serena so much hoped would be the case for little Caitlin's sake.

The bags Serena had recognised as being from the store where she had purchased all of Caitlin's fine dresses and small clothes by mail order. The delivery man had never asked her why all her more expensive purchases were for a child, though she might have said that they were for a niece or the child of a friend had anyone asked her. Had the carrier bags bearing the Trimbles name indeed contained clothing for Caitlin it was unlikely to be of the Little Princess Range which Caitlin had come to expect as she had grown older. Or at least until her changing moods and unpredictable behaviour had made it impossible to understand exactly what it was that she wanted when she had become so very contrary, one moment wanting one thing and the next the very opposite. No matter what Serena had done it had been impossible to placate her. Her tantrums could be terrible. She had become dissatisfied with everything, even her own shadow. No words of explanation or attempts at discussion could comfort a child so afraid of going away to school one minute and then so positive towards the event the next. Nothing could explain the root of the problem concerning why she had become so unhappy, other than to link her appalling behaviour to Serena having told her as she would one day have had to be told, anyway, just who her real mother was. That had seemed to be the start of the end of their happy life together, on the day that her sister had played with the police band in the park and the carelessly chosen words had spilled upon a peaceful afternoon with such terrible result. It had been the same day that the swans had been speared and the signet trampled to death after they had made their nest in the reeds at the mere; the day that the swans had, despite their injured wings, taken to the moonlit skies and disappeared. Since then there had been no peace. Not a single peaceful moment when Caitlin had laid the blame and accusation to hurt Serena in a way that nothing in her life before or since could possible hurt her. The stress of Caitlin's increasingly horrendous behaviour was why she had become ill.

Now this! Exposure eating at Serena as her greatest fear. Worry assailing her at every turn because, above all else, Catty must never find out. Her sister must never know. That was another reason why she had, now, to admit defeat in her quest to get Caitlin back again. The photographs which had threatened to see her included as a background figure, being one thing. Her lost papers, another. The caretaker had, also, threatened to call the police if she remained to pester. What would Catty have to say if their relationship became public? If she was taken to the police station accused of unlawful trespass? They would take her photograph at the station if she was charged with breaking the law. They would strip her of her veil. She would be exposed. Her name would link her with Catty, also.

Why they could not let her inside the grounds remained a mystery to Serena but the need to go had, finally, become apparent with the man's cruel words. She had no knowledge of the significance of the place behind the big green gates other than that she had heard on the radio that that was where Caitlin...now referred to as Wendy Bridgewater...was to be taken; a place they had passed by frequently enough with herself on a bus seat and Caitlin safely stowed away in the trolley. With hope in her heart and her rosary beads in her pocket she had hoped to save the day. It would have taken little for Caitlin to have spied an opportunity to slip into the trolley; home again, home again. Now the risks were too great.

A total waste of time. She dare not allow her picture to be on the front page of the Clarion for her sister to wonder why she was hanging about the gates of Greengates House. As she awaited her bus she brought a tissue from her coat pocket and squeezed it hard into the palm of her sheepskin glove before setting it to the purpose for which it was intended, dabbing carefully at the wet facial skin which was so fragile that the slightest roughness could cause it to tear. She had spent a whole night weeping and worrying. Something she had done a great deal of late. Physically she was feeling the tremendous drain on her energies which her doctor had thought fit to have tested at the hospital. Her worst fears had been confirmed. Serena was seriously ill. She would have to consider some way of destroying all the evidence that she had raised a child in secret. Never before had it seemed wrong. How could it be wrong to have saved a child from extinction?

Now in the aftermath of so much worry the man who had attacked her had done far more damage than that caused by a simple push while her bag was snatched. He had destroyed her life. He had endangered her health even more than it was endangered already. A painful bruise the size of an egg had formed where the man had thumped her hard on her shoulder. Under an anointed dressing her head was bleeding still. Her eyes had already begun to blacken about the shallow lids. Yet even the soreness of her scalp and the blackening bruises all over her fragile body failed to distract her from her agonised thoughts concerning little Caitlin. Her white knuckled, right hand of three fused fingers gripped so tightly onto the handle of the shopping trolley through her thick glove that her paper-thin nails were breaking against the sheepskin lining. Her breathing was both shallow and rapid as she felt her heartbeat flutter and falter, flutter and falter before jerking sharply within her breast. Her legs were in danger of caving in as the weakness invaded her. She was tired. So very tired as she waited for a bus to come at a stop where there was no bench to sit upon. Looking across through the busy traffic at a house where her beloved child was now painfully silent. There were no other sounds than that of the cars and lorries whizzing by on a busy main road. Caitlin! Caitlin!

Her head lowered even more to look within the cracks between the paving stones for answers to unsolvable problems, a gasp of desperation escaping with a realization far worse than that of the night before. What hope, now, of getting little Caitlin back? None!

There was so much more to consider than all she had originally envisaged after a night without sleep. A night spent pacing the house. A night listening to the small radio in her kitchen with the sound turned down low, her ear pressed against it. A night when it would have been useless to try to phone CC again. He had been too drunk to be of any assistance in the first instance. She doubted that he would even remember what she had told him had happened to them when he awoke. However, she had agreed some of what should be done now that catastrophe was causing such havoc. The proof of little Caitlin's existence must be eradicated. For all was in the house still to point the finger of truth at Serena...her toys and clothing, the computer she had so desperately needed to try to teach her more of the world...her school uniform and so many other items with Caitlin's name upon them. There was nothing else to do, now, but another sad and very necessary thing. That was when she again found the mobile phone from her pocket. Time had come to ask a final favour. It had to be done. It took no more than a few moments to ask help of some other person.

The bus came. Its final destination being Whemley Cemetery; the very place where Serena sensed she would be on a day not too far distant from this, because there would, now, be nothing to live for as there had been nothing to live for, but hope, before her precious gift.

She paid her usual, single fare and took her seat to the front of the bus, her shopping trolley riding empty in the space provided in front of her. The pink leather dog lead with its pattern of rhinestones on the loop to match the collar which was within the trolley still in hand, but no dog to explain it. No questions asked, either, and not a single soul ever to ask her for an explanation of why the lead had been needed. Where's your dog, lady? No questions ever asked of Serena; a woman who might wander the Earth alone with her identity hidden under her headscarf. A faceless woman. A non-person in enveloping clothing.

She kept her head dipped low to hide what little showed of her face as her tears fell again. Known yet unknown. People knowing her by her dress yet keeping their distance, looking away, their discomfort never failing to hurt Serena. This even after a lifetime of being aware that people feared her suddenly revealing herself to them because of her difference. An accidental freak of nature if nature ever made mistakes, for in all other ways she had been healthy until the last few months when Caitlin had put so much strain upon her. Now she felt ill and old. Bereft and lonely. Now was the time, indeed, for her suffering to end.

Her tears dripped onto her sheepskin gloves and her sobs caught in her throat. Not a single person sharing the bus came to ask of her sorrow. Not a single one. They sat motionless and stared out of the window wrapped in their own thoughts. Caitlin was gone.

The walk from the bus stop where she alighted on the shopping street, took her through the shady streets of terraced houses to her own dwelling on the fringe of the park. Her house was one in the centre of the terrace which had been built from good quality Accrington brick. Over the quiet roadway the sycamore trees spread bright green hands over the park railings, their arms waving gently against the soft April sunlight. It shone through their foliage as her last steps turned the corner of her street so that their veins were clearly visible. She thought of her own veins and saw them weeping blood onto her white skin, just as the swans which had been so savagely attacked had bled from broken wings. Yet they had, nevertheless, managed their escape; flown against the moon to some other place of safety. Maybe she could do the same.

She noted that an old bicycle leant against the railings even as she opened the gate to her short path and carefully shut it after her, the bolt replaced. The spare key taken from under the flowerpot again. She opened her black and mint green, front door with its fluted glass circle where her hooded head was reflected darkly in discordant lines of reflected light. She consulted it not as her eyes always turned from any reflection of her form. There would be none inside her house.

The cat met her as she closed the door behind her its tail in the air; a ring-tailed Tabby waiting for five bolts to be drawn as added defence, the chain added, its own way free to go through a cat flap whenever it liked. She would allow her pet the freedom that she had denied herself and the child.

The vestibule door stuck and required an extra push to open. This she left slightly ajar as she pulled her trolley through behind her. Inside her lonely house all was neat and tidy. The good, old fashioned, brown wood furniture standing solidly on fat, clawed feet against the threadbare pile of a Turkish carpet. The mood of the living room still her parents' choice. Nothing had been changed since her father's demise eight years previously just as her sister had reached the proud pinnacle of her career. His death shortly before the child had been brought from her sister's womb. A foetus more mature than her sister had thought. Supposedly a pregnancy that was no more than five months but which must have been at least seven because the child was fully formed.

Her sister's photograph stood proudly even yet on the dresser as a testament to Serena's efforts to cast out the peevish envy which soured her own soul. Something to be prayed against because envy was against the commandment of her Christian belief. The photograph had been taken by the professional photographer at her sister's inauguration to her role as Chief Constable of Quinton, sent to her through the post, though no one to show it to, save for CC who came infrequently and only then when Serena had need of the money to spend on a daughter he had never wanted. Just as Caitlin's mother had never wanted her. Just as Serena, herself, had never been wanted by her own parents once her natal deformities were known.

Whenever CC's eyes had alighted on the likeness of the woman he had once considered beautiful enough to bed he sneered at it, turned his face away, denying the results of a relationship from which could be formed such a beautiful child. Her beautiful, proud, sister wearing the gold braided uniform so becoming to a woman of her dignity and stature brought nothing but cold envy to her own heart and mind. Who was she to criticise a man for his peevish ways? Serena resented her sister just the same. Everything about Katrina proclaiming her rightful place at the centre of the dresser on a delicate lace mat that their deceased mother had crocheted for just such display. Other photographs, too...Catty holding her trumpet...Catty at the School of Music...Catty as a newly qualified officer on passing out of the Police College with flying colours. The photograph of her in her role of Chief Constable had been taken a year previous to Caitlin's birth. While her affair with CC was just beginning and her deceit had yet to know its final result; a pregnancy that in a woman of her age had been confused with the symptoms of menopause and tests taken been faulty. Or so Serena assumed for a foetus aborted at seven months, instead of at a stage when its existence is unviable, is tantamount to attempted murder. The Chief Constable of Quinton Dales and District a murderess! Not so much beauty, now, within her beautiful sister whose face looked back at her full of pride and coldly haughty. Serena's heart contracted as she made herself look upon vain beauty even while she felt her own deformities; never to be looked at in a mirror. No mirrors in the house. Not a single photograph of herself. There were none taken as portrait. A back view, perhaps, stuck away in a pocket at the back of an old album, amidst the clutter at the bottom of a dusty drawer which Caitlin had liked to pour over in order to know the names of the people within.

She had always referred to Katrina as *the lady with the golden trumpet* even before she had been informed that Catty was her real birth mother. There were no portraits to be admired of Serena other than to depict a fearful left hand, never the grossly deformed right one, revealed holding down an untrustworthy veil as the snap had been taken in a blustering wind, the top digits of this hand's fingers missing also. Hands that had begun to suffer so badly with arthritis that it was at times impossible to cope with the pain. The left one, these days, had begun to curl back upon itself unless she restrained it in the special glove which held it firmly in place. The deformed right at least functioned without pain so that she could fasten even the most complex things; straps and buckles, shoe laces even with the three fused fingers. Her left leg dragged when she grew tired or upset and especially as she was, now, so near to rest despite all the operations to free the tendons. Some of the scars on her scalp where she had suffered surgery to her brain to try to stop the fits had failed to heal and were constantly tight, causing headaches and requiring a new, fresh dressing daily with gauze and ointment. Nowadays, her fits were controlled with medication but not always. Now the assault had added to her discomfort. She had run out of dressings for her wounds because her routines had become shattered. She had been unable to think of anything other than Caitlin ever since her behaviour had deteriorated and steps had

had to be taken to get her away.

Now that she was home the tears of self pity and anger wet her headscarf as the hurt swelled within her like a volcanic flow of hot fire and brimstone growing out from the solar plexus and searing through the ducts of her gut like a wave of physical pain, making her cry out, "Dear God. Why am I punished at every turn? Why take her from me just as I was taking her to her freedom?"

With a hopeless heart Serena put the trolley away in the pantry under the stairs, removing the dog chain and collar to hang up on the peg retained for this purpose. She removed her gloves and placed these in the pocket of her coat. Then the coat was peeled away and hung up also on a peg next to the collar and chain in the space under the stairs. Caitlin's winter anorak hung small beside it along with a warm winter hat, scarf and gloves. For some reason, she had forgotten to put them away upstairs; an omen, perhaps.

The figure revealed was curvaceous. The breasts large and well shaped, the hips wide, the waist trim and flat bellied though of late she had begun to lose some weight to make her grey dress hang loose. The soft fabric of her clothes lay gently against her smooth, white, tissue paper skin which tore and bled at the slightest chafe and thus had to be protected by thick outer clothing. Her legs once revealed from the soft lining of the sheepskin boots were finely shaped but thin, the feet lacking toes save for three on one foot and two on another. These she slipped into light, silky slippers with goose down feathers to hide away what she did not wish to see herself. Her gnarled, deformed hands straightened the headscarf, pulled it wide and tugged it out so that even within the darkness under the stairs her face might be hidden away until she was safe within the cellar space. She had been conditioned from childhood always to cover her face when above the cellar steps.

Now, she went down to the cellar using the door opposite the pantry, unlocking it with a key which was shiny from frequent use and then locking it behind her again from habit. It was necessary to flick the light switch because the windowless cellar had no natural light. Only here did Serena remove her headscarf completely and let it drift over the back of the armchair where, together, she and her little Caitlin had shared so much.

The cellar spaces revealed the four corners of the kingdom of her little princess. Here the cat which had followed her to the cellar door and then used a cat flap to follow her down the turning, stone steps took up its reign on a silken cushion with golden tassels hanging over its own chair, one eye opening, yawning, turning over and stretching. Tigwell purred and looked around as if reminded that someone was missing.

Here she might know nothing of her moon-woman appearance. The cat gave no mind to the watering, silver eyes which stared almost lidless from the corners of her face. Her barely discernible nose which had been fashioned using sinew and muscle and skin from her hip ran with cold. The hole upon which a mouth and chin had been fashioned after growing material from her shoulder and chest to make some semblance of a human face had a different hue to the white flesh above it. Teeth grew downwards from the roof of her palate. She had learnt how to use them or be unable to eat anything other than soft, pappy foods. For that reason she never ate in front of others and especially not Caitlin who would have imitated her. That would never do!

It was as if God had intended deafness, too, though in this He had been thwarted by the skill of surgeons who had introduced implants to assist her hearing. Her ears were as screwed up bits of flesh on the side of a bald and severely scarred pate that had never possessed a full head of hair, merely the white straggling tufts around the banks of scars from so many operations. The coarse National Health wigs she had been fitted with as a growing child had been impossible to tolerate. Given up on altogether when Serena had been taught at home. Given up venturing out, become a hermit within the family home. A blighted soul who could not bear to look upon her own reflection. To that end not a single mirror or shiny surface was allowed to reflect the images of the people who moved within this house.

Now with hunger within her she felt faint. The bottle of pills lay on the draining board. They had been prescribed by her doctor with the warning that too many were dangerous. Six would be enough to see her dead. They rattled in warning as she lifted the bottle. What was there, now, to live for?

She had no sooner gone to the place in the corner where she might boil water in the electric kettle, make tea, and find crockery and cutlery within the cupboards when the door buzzer struck through the silence of the house like a chain saw striking metal. She jumped, gasped, dropped the cup in her hand for it to smash into pieces on the floor before common sense told her that it was, most probably, one of the rare but usual callers; perhaps a Jehovah's Witness or a door-to-door salesman. It could be any of the meter readers or, maybe, the newspaper boy or the milkman calling to be paid though she could not have said what time of day or day of the week it was to know the routines by which they normally called. It was as if her mind had been frozen.

Her hands began to sweat but she dare not ignore it. Her neighbours might have seen her returning. Sometimes they took in a parcel though none was expected. If they did not see or hear her for several days they sometimes knocked just to ensure themselves that she was okay. If she did not answer they saw it as a sign that she required help. She had no choice but to answer.

At the top of the cellar stairs, she donned the enveloping lightweight robe she kept for such purpose behind the cellar door and placed her veil over her face. All this done from habit as another insistent ring of the insistent bell drilled into her objecting brain. She would let no one look upon her figure just as she would allow no one, other than Caitlin, to look upon her face.

Where yesterday she might have gone to the lounge window to peep out through the thick net curtains to see who her caller was, now such action had no purpose. She undid the many bolts and single Yale lock. As soon as she opened the door a crack there was a sharp, fast jolt which snapped the chain from its socket and sent her reeling against the vestibule door as the front door was rammed open. Her veil fell away. A man pushed his way in. She thought she recognised him as the same man who had waylaid her the night before. Fear grew within her.

His voice was desperate as he drew a shocked breath at her appearance. "God Almighty!" were his first words. "The ugly woman!"

It was Mally Kenyon.

Seventeen

Holly's induction to the ways of Greengates House, its policies and its practice, was a compulsory one-to-one seminar conducted by Tommo in a cramped office room where, to his rear, out of his sight but fully visible to Holly through the window, Wendy was, now, playing happily. The weather was bright and sunny. Gary was attempting to build a relationship upon which to make some positive observations about her character and needs through a common, enjoyable activity while not getting on the wrong end of her volatile temperament.

This while Tommo claimed ownership of a very tidy desk in the cramped space where shelves full of files and hefty, erudite tomes confirmed his profession to be, indeed, as Holly had predicted: Tommo was a Behavioural Psychologist.

Behind him several CCTV screens displayed different areas of the house; all of them specific to where the client would have access including the gardens, outhouses, potting shed, greenhouse and a set of garages where Holly had seen the caretaker; a man with a miserable countenance whose name she deigned not to remember, store the various consumable items needed by a residential establishment such as this. Items such as paper towels, soaps and cleaning products, pan scrubs and detergents which he seemed to resent her taking stock of. Miserable old git! He had even had the cheek to tell her to watch her heels on the rubber flooring inside the house. "Makes pit holes in rubber, them shoes do. You'll be polishing them out with the buffer, not me, if I see any."

First he'd have to prove it! Holly pulled her tongue out at him as soon as he turned his back. Not friendly like Angie. She had even given Holly a hug and offered to wash the kid's smelly knickers while Holly got on with supervising her bathing. The kid did okay so that was a relief, though half a bottle of bubble bath did the job of cleansing. She was able to dry herself. Holly didn't fancy having to sponge her over with a soapy flannel and then rub her dry, or help with teeth cleaning, because she'd be up to her eyes in all that when she had the baby she needed to get her to the top of the housing queue and double her dole money. Though she did cut the kid's finger nails...pity she couldn't trim them sharp, pointed little baby teeth of hers while she was at it...aware, while doing so, of that irritable hand that wanted to smack again; the right one. It was like one was floppy and cooperative and the other was tight and uncooperative. What she had said to the kid, was, "I can have paddies, too. Big ones. Smack me and I'll holler so much I'll have everyone come running. Bags all

199

the attention."

Holly had been impressed by the look of understanding Wendy had given her with that bright, glittery silver, right orb of hers before changing her lead eye to the duller, lack-lustre, left one. Holly was already on the suss to know what the child was up to. Spoilt little brat if ever there was one; able to control the heat like turning the knobs on a gas cooker.

Apparently, according to Tommo's big red bible, Holly was never to threaten or smack the kid....even when she deserved it...so she'd have to develop a few, cruel control tactics that didn't leave bruises behind such as sweet deprivation and favourite toy and activity management. Holly quite savoured the prospects of dreaming up some cruel alternatives. She had already started with making the kid work for access to the rag doll.

Pushing from behind and hauling by the arm were banned, too, despite Holly having seen the handling belts and movement mats hanging up in the exercise room. If kids weren't allowed to be propelled unwillingly what was the point in having the gadgets, in the first place?

As for poking...one of Holly's more favoured methods of deliberate enticement when she had been at school herself and wanting to teach some other little shit a hard-to-detect lesson...that was definitely a no-no. Nothing more winding than two fingers jabbed into the solar plexus, of course, and so effective when a point need be made.

Banned, also, was hair pulling. Short tugs in Holly's practised estimation could be a waste of time if the end result had to be to get someone on the move. However, Holly had it from the horse's mouth when it came to the practise of trapping the small hairs in the nape of the neck between two fingers, so to lead an unwilling steed to water, that it was as effective as any bit between the teeth.

As far as Holly could ascertain they were all inducements to good behaviour which would have to be shelved if she was to be considered suitable for the job. It seemed, in the main, that Tommo was telling her that any type of bodily contact that could leave a mark or a bruise was banned for no better reason than that kids have rights these days. Or what was said would make it appear as if kids have rights these days. What they really had in Holly's estimation was no cause for complaint. In other words, there were no negative behaviour management policies in action. Just rewards.

"We believe in positive reinforcement here."

In other words when the kid's difficult offer a reward as a tactic of distraction ...maybe a game of skittles or a chance to shoot some pool. They would not have been on offer otherwise, Holly knew, had the kid been good in the first place. All strategies which a clever delinquent might use to their own advantage...as she had!

"No shouting, either. Not professional!"

Come off it, Tommo! What a dumbo! Know a better way, Holly thought, of letting somebody know that you're angry and getting angrier and they better watch out? Nothing got her own dander up faster and further than someone who refused to be riled and smiled mockingly through provocation. Chinese burn stuff!

Then the most frustrating of reactions to temper and bad behaviour, in Holly's experienced opinion, was exactly what Tommo suggested to be the best of good practice...the *Let's talk if through,* tactic. What a Wally! If it was talkable about what was the point of not talking about it in the first place. Half the time Holly had not had a clue why she had been difficult, bad tempered and out of sorts with the world. Just was! Whether she was menstruating at the time or nor, she had tipped tables and sent chairs skittering across the parquet floors of school halls and classrooms because she had felt like doing something to clear her space of all the people who were doing her head in. Know her own power in the face of the implacable control of others, like Wendy shitting her pants and smearing. There are some things others cannot control and need to be told so in ways without words. Then the follow-on being: *we've talked about it now. Time to move on. Solved it!* treatment, as if concessions had been made, time expended, empathy provided, sympathy given, and you're still not being reasonable, you holy, little shit!

Well, thank you for all your compassion and understanding!

Tommo was proving himself to be yet another of the *reasoning* psychologists who thought the guise of a disturbed child merely masked the presence of a reasoning adult without the appropriate expressive language skills. The crowning glory of all his advice on how to manage difficult behaviour was the application of the theory of self government even amongst minors. Apparently the kid had a right to make choices even when being an obnoxious, little terror. Holly's eyes stretched slightly before she remembered herself and had to staple her lips together.

That so! What you know?

If the kid chooses to sit on the floor in defiance while throwing shoes in temper she should be allowed to sit on the floor and be defiant while throwing shoes in temper. Holly should justify her own time by reading her a story, either sitting out of range or under the protection of a golf umbrella, rather than to allow an opportunity to pass without meaningful activity to be attempted, Tommo advised.

Holly folded her arms in order to stop herself from removing her own shoe and flinging it at him. Was this man real? Nothing was more rewarding than someone reading you a story. Holly would have given her eye-teeth for someone to read her stories. All the more reason by Holly's reckoning to be bad when there was never any way of getting a true professional to come close enough to share such a worthwhile experience with a feeling of innocent intimacy. Holly had not been sat on a knee, embraced and hugged after being taken into care until she had become sexually active at the age of eleven and had sought out a few for herself amongst the male contemporaries who were as needy as she was. Like no one had any idea how much hugs matter. Just hugs. The rest of the groping had been an invasive deed merely to be tolerated.

Then one that Holly actually liked the sound of as Tommo spoke to the ceiling: if the child looked upset before a confrontation she should be offered some time away from others as self regulated avoidance. Called time-out. Quite different from thrusting a kid into the sin-bins, in lieu of a bedroom, which Holly fondly remembered because she could cuss and swear and rant and rave as much as she wanted. In Wendy's case her own room would be suitable where she might be locked in as long as someone was watching the CCTV to know what she was up to. Holly was all for that one. She had a teen-romance in her purple plastic bag and an eagerness to get on with it. She could curl up with her book and forget about the kid in an instance.

While he commenced and continued his information concerning the permitted, staff responses to attack by a she-devil who had no ethical ethos concerning fair play or even a shred of consideration for others...also a thorough run through of the very rigid staff rules and regulations...he kept on his desk a two-way radio which was tuned into the one that Gary Silvers had in his hand throughout the course of the outside play. It crackled annoyingly though not as annoyingly as Tommo, in Holly's non-esteemed opinion. Every now and again, Gary and Tommo would commune.

"All okay?"

Reply: "No probs. Over and out."

Response: "Good. Over and Out."

This even while they could be observed through a window.

What was the point? Holly stared with disbelief at the two-way radio she was handed, wondering if she might use it to ring out for a pizza to be delivered. Her joke, spoken out loud, was received with a gasp of admonishment. "Under no circumstances are the radios to be used for anything other than staff support purposes. You will as yet have no idea how vital it is to have these phones at our disposal. I will, therefore, let your remark pass. You will soon know how necessary back-up is in places like this."

Then onto hours of shifts, pay details, contractual responsibilities; his and hers, and a thousand other mind numbingly, boring aspects of her employment. As he talked in the flattish drone of someone who liked nothing better than to hear his own voice and was not particularly concerned if his opinions were agreed with…his vowels as flat as her own but uttered with a preciseness of language which suggested he said nothing unconsidered… Holly had her own psychological assessment under way. The way he dressed was an off-putter to a fashion queen to start off with. Then, there was the lack of eye contact as if he was talking to little Miss Brainless or, worse still, a presence in spirit only; either way she was not permitted comment if his remoteness was anything to go by. Seeming to prefer the opinion of the grey-rimmed wall clock rather than her bored face and folded arms. And the tilt of a head that should have warned him that in her opinion he hadn't a clue what he was talking about. Holly thought him a handsome-enough man with science degrees aplenty, but with the absentmindedness of a dreaming poet as he sat back in his seat and droned on with his focal point anywhere but on Holly. Chewed fingernails building moving bridges between the bottomless pools of his own very intellectual thoughts, as if his mind was a little speckled frog which dived from one to the other. The nickname of *Wordsworth* came to mind. She had never known anyone who could write eloquent poetry to have a grain of common sense. Someone in this same room was *wandering lonely as a cloud*. Holly knew it not to be herself!

The fact that he had bitten his finger nails down to the quick told her that he was a nervous wreck. His dark grey, brown flecked eyes…or were they light brown flecked with grey?…held the confused expression of someone at variance with the framed certificates about the walls of his domain from various Manchester and London Universities, which confirmed the most prideful of his accomplishments. The photographs people displayed always told Holly a great deal about the person who had put them up there. Tommo's chosen time warp, as suggested by the ones he liked people to look at and admire as representative of his desired character and most creditable achievements being visible in the large, framed snaps of him in cap and gown, sharing posed handshakes with people wearing velvet mop-caps adorned with trailing feathers, draped in full cloaks like pearly kings and queens. In all of them he held a big scroll of paper tied with a ribbon and exhibited a discomforted grimace which told Holly that he was as complex a mix of conflicting characteristics as she was herself. Holly being good at reading body language and situation before she took even the slightest notice of the messages being relayed from mouths speaking.

This man, she considered, was seriously lacking in what she had in great abundance, despite all the rough water she had sailed in a tough, short journey through life...namely an intuitive understanding of people. Holly reckoned that Tommo must, through his work, confront himself on a daily basis with that which frightened him the most. Anyone as compulsively tidy as he with such fixed and rigid opinions must struggle to understand the quick-fires and hail storms of their own emotions, never mind those of other people. How did a man who compulsively arranged and then rearranged the objects on his desk using so many different bases...sometimes shape, sometimes colour, sometimes size, sometimes pattern...cope with the disorganization of people who lived random, unplotted lives using a different mathematics for their reasoning and classified their perceptions and feelings in ways that Tommo could never even begin to understand?

He was also on a raft without a pole to punt with if he thought she was one to obey his every command. Holly felt like telling him to *Chill, man, chill!* Only it would have been her job's worth! Better to pretend that she was deeply interested in his commitment towards her becoming a puppet to his strictly applied methods of assessment and observation, as well as his clockwork approaches, while it was much more absorbing to watch what was happening outside as Gary, Wendy and an old dog with long ears that had to keep lying down on the grass for a rest played catch-ball.

Here, through the window, behind Tommo's untidy head...as every few seconds he swiped a hand through his floppy, brown hair and then used an index finger to shunt his glasses back up to the bridge of his nose again, his words having begun to perambulate as if he had lost the thread of his speech...Holly certainly had!...Gary and the child and the dog played happily on. Wendy, now, seemingly over all her upset, was clean again and dressed in the pink tracksuit from Trimbles with pink cotton underwear and white socks with frills on. Her feet were clad in Velcro-fastened slippers. Her hair was up in bobbles, as Holly had groomed it, while she laughed and skipped about within the pure enjoyment of the moment. She was trying to catch a furry, yellow tennis ball in that babyish way of hers, hands cupped together while Gary aimed an underarm toss to assure her success. To Holly's intelligence she was doing what all conniving, manipulative, little bitches do when they want to get out of trouble...flirt!

Gary; middle-aged, but going on naive...a fat, shiny, red cheek showing the damage he had suffered from contact with Wendy's hard head butt and his hands full of scratches from her sharp, little finger nails...looked as if he was foolishly believing that it was he who was the one calling the shots. Pull the other one, Holly thought! Throw-and-catch when the kid had been that naughty!? He would be telling himself that he was building a relationship. That the child was a victim and so should be forgiven. That she was incapable of controlling her behaviour when her feelings were riled.

As far as Holly could see there was only one person controlling all that was going on outside and that, sure as hell, was not Gary Silvers. Holly felt like opening her mouth wide and pointing two fingers inside as comment for this lack of intellectual appreciation of the little minx's cunning. Was it sick making, or was it not, that such a naughty little madam, who had just wreaked such mayhem, should now be being shown a good time? If the kid was getting mixed messages on how to behave, in Holly's opinion, there lay a good example in what was taking place outside. She thought that the kid would have been better served with a detention or the naughty step or the loss of something nice like that doll of hers, even if she, herself, had been the one to give it back. Or her new clothes being binned one after the other until she said sorry. Though, Holly considered, being made to say sorry was a waste of time. It had never made any difference to her. She always did the same things again that she had been made to say sorry for as a point of principle unless she'd had something taken away from her which had caused her considerable grief. Nowadays she apologised in advance rather than later, because when Holly Kenyon made trouble she meant every bit of it.

"You may go join them now," Tommo said affably, as if he considered that Holly's mute responses to his lecture to have been a sign that he had been successful in converting the ignorant and the unaffiliated to his cause. "Tire the child out as much as possible with exercise and fresh air. It should give us all an appetite for a hearty lunch. You will find the food, here, surprisingly good."

Thankfully, Holly saw her escape. She rose to go but then was halted by the sudden catch of his voice like a shepherd's crook about her neck. "Just one more thing. Fancy my forgetting the daily diary! Gary may have mentioned that I am rather a stickler for each member of staff to enter a daily record of their observations and activities in the book within this desk." As he spoke he opened the drawer and extracted a tome, bound in blue leather and embossed with gold print. "The bible from which I collate all that will base the profile and portrait of my assessment report. With some children it can be used to represent circumstantial evidence so it is extremely important that you sign and date what you write within. You must take every opportunity to write within it on a regular basis throughout the day. I do not expect full length reports from the junior staff. Just a few well chosen words, will do. Sufficient to describe her moods and responses to the demands placed upon her." Here, Tommo smiled as if he had asked her to do nothing of any great merit; Mr Consideration, himself!

Holly looked at the giant ledger placed before her with horror hardening upon her face. If she flinched she hoped that, at the same time, she had managed to hide the sudden shaft of panic without her usual narrowing of eyes into angry slits when challenged with the prospect of any task which demanded even an average level of literacy. She had not been told this by the man at the agency! His description of the work had been entirely concerned with looking after the child, seeing to her everyday needs and nothing else.

Tommo seemed to have no idea of her discomfort. He seemed to find this task totally trivial. "A sentence is all I ask for." He might as well have asked for a completed novel!

Trying to ignore the first frazzles of concern that ran down her backbone, Holly tried to be positive by thinking that she could get out of it. Conveniently forget, maybe. Get Angie to write it for her. She had a whole list of avoidance tactics to anything which required the written word from having forgotten her bottle-bottom spectacles, without which she was as blind as a bat, to having injured her writing fingers, to simply refusing to do anything asked because her reputation demanded it. Better to cause mayhem than be found out except that, here, she was on the other side of the tracks. Start slinging chairs and turning tables here and she would be out on her ear. Simple as that!

Finally, she was given a small, photocopied booklet with a pale grey paper cover. It had been stapled together and held the title *A Summary of the Greengates House Code of Practice*. As he flicked it out for her to take it from him, he said, "This document is important. Refer to it until we can arrange some inset-training for you." Tommo settling a pair of level, dark grey eyes upon her. "Anything you require explaining further?"

Holly felt like asking if he knew the time of the next bus out of Quinton for Manchester City Centre. Might have done except that she had earlier overheard Angie talking about someone called Mally Kenyon. It had been Mally Kenyon who had pushed past her as he had escaped the police station. Her deceased dad had had a twin brother called Marlborough...shortened to Mally. Memories were coming back. What she asked was. "I did tell Gary that I needed a few personal items from the shops. Sorry, but my appointment was very short notice. Just some lady's things. He said that if all was okay I might get to the shops if Angie can cover for an hour or so." It was worth a try.

Surprisingly, Tommo nodded. "Just this once and strictly because you were allowed no prior notice. I noticed the case. I take it you don't live in Quinton."

"I live in Manchester. I came because I want to look up some long lost relatives."

Tommo looked disinterested. "You have an entitlement to the usual breaks. You may go after lunch and be back by two thirty."

Holly smiled brightly. "Thank you, Dr Thomas."

He frowned as if the title was a pretention he disliked, despite the certificates of his importance being so openly displayed. "Call me Tommo. Everyone does. We favour informality here."

Holly sighed heavily.

Eighteen

Within his empty church Father Turner stood before the simple altar with his back turned to the gleaming chalices and burnished plate. Here he slowly removed the outer garments which declared his commitment to his faith, placing them with care on the choir stools set out for that night's practise. They were, now, unlikely to be used.

Once divested of his vestments he was a man who looked no different from any other of his flock, as he unfastened the neck buttons of his grey shirt. Making careful movements he rolled up his sleeves before resting his weary legs by perching on the altar step. From his vantage point he looked upon the straight, diagonal rows of dotted chairs; at the closed doors of his church; at his own reflection in the long windows; over to where, beyond the closed gates of his church, people now whooped and shouted, building zeal, heckling others to the cause which he understood but could not condone. What of a shepherd now when his flock was bound together as one but running with the maverick rams, unheeding of anything but their own bleating?

Slowly he stood and walked away from his altar to the back of the church so that he might consider thoughts without being in the view of others. What had been arranged and planned for with the bishop and the man who had come with him, following on from the Prayer Group Meeting, was a hard thing for him to bear. While knowing and understanding that a church has to be as politically cunning in its gamesmanship as any business if it was to rise above its competition, he did not like to consider that he was at one with those of little faith. The man of common sense within him had to agree with a bishop whose suggestions were intended only to protect the ministry itself. Trust in God would not pay the costs of a derelict church within an impoverished community. And a lawless one at that! Father Turner might see the necessity for the betrayal of his parishioners and the corruption of his own frail but questing honesty; but would they? This in light of the knowledge that only He was totally above the political lies and the necessary deceptions of a harsh, cruel, practical reality. Some things that otherwise bear not to be contemplated had to be done just for the sake of survival. The church was no different.

Father Turner was no more than any other mortal man either. Despite his attempts to lead his flock by the example of his own virtue he was about to abet a sin that had come about as the only possible way in which the desperate financial state of his church accounts might be settled.

He was, after all, a man of the world who had lived long enough amongst thieves so as not to judge them harshly. They had done little more than what they had been driven to do in order to survive. Now his church was in the same position. The intended default from debt had come about, too, through the suggestion of higher orders than his own, as a convenience by which the parish might rebuild and, in so doing, remain a focus of hope within an area which required as much spiritual guidance as was possible. He had the bishop's approbation and confirmation of such within the irrefutable faith that what he had done and would be doing was no more than to obey the demands of his calling; a priest was but the vessel of higher calling. Such had calmed the last pangs of his conscience. That and the assurance of the professional who would commit the final act that no one would be harmed.

What he had to do now would have to remain one of the few secrets he shared with the Almighty and his direct line manager on the committee route to God Himself...the bishop! The same man who had just left his presence, a final prayer shared before the kissing of the ring that sealed his own forgiveness, along with the man with the black briefcase who had already begun his final audit and would return later with what would be needed for him to carry out his task. His confession heard by His Holiness in total privacy. To remind him also that the work they had to do on this Earth was never easy. Concessions and forgiveness had sometimes to be made for what might appear to be acts of wicked calculation and stealthy accomplishment.

However, taking the final decision had been removed from his shoulders and placed with far higher authority than that of a humble priest. He should remember above all else that those whose job it was to ensure that the ministry survive...God's work on Earth achieved for the wider benefit... had need to work beyond the base rules and common laws of ordinary men. Towards this end they had the permission of the Supernatural Power that was, is and always will be. Their excuse being the furtherance of the spiritual wellbeing of the human race. Did they not work amongst the sinners where others would turn their backs and walk away? Was it not expedient that God's work on Earth should so be protected?

If they could but deny the debts of the church there would have been no problem. However the building was creaking with the dry rot in its timbers and the failures within its supporting foundations to defy the rivers of damp that ran beneath. The whole structure of the building was unsound from the shoddy workmanship of its erection and the foolishness of its placement. Its bedrock not of rock, nor even sand, but marsh. The crypt was now so damp as to be almost unusable. While he might keep it open for those who would seek shelter but not knock at his door, those that slept there would have found a healthier berth under the hedgerows. It was not cotton fibres growing on the wall down there but invasive dry rot.

The whole church and its outbuildings had been built cheaply to supply an immediate need upon the founding of a new, quickly raised estate. In keeping with its surroundings and in keeping with the contemporary culture of the day. In reality to stop the Protestants moving in. Now the roof could no longer be patched and the late stitches to its fabric be assured to keep out the rain. The hostel for the homeless and the playschool for the children within the east wing, where Magdalene worked her long, hard, restless days, showed their shabbiness in worn floors and peeling paint. The playschool was taking its toll on the whole as a herd of tiny feet bounced and clattered and pounded over rotting floorboards, day by day. The steam from the kitchen in the hostel, without extraction and sufficient ventilation, had caused horrendous black moulds to form and grow. The condensation within the poorly ventilated building had caused the same moulds to form on ceilings and in all the closed spaces so that the building, as a whole, might be condemned upon the next visit of the surveyors who would ensure that the hostel and playschool were up to trading standards. This while taking no money from the parade of pitiful homeless who passed through their doors, or the innocent children who sat with eyes wide, arms folded, ears alert at the unfolding of a story. For how could they pay? All he might ask in return for the fellowship and succour of his church was that they came to his door sober and gave themselves to prayer.

It had been the bishop who had shaken his head over the reminding lists of figures and had pointed the only way possible if the church was to rise above the swamp. St. Saviours Church was failing badly in support of itself. The debt could no longer be justified. The costs of the hostel alone were astronomical in relation to the grants and gifts of charity which had determined its support for the past fifty-three years. The bank of the Vatican had shut its ledger. Time had come. He should agree to be out of the church after the hour of three that very afternoon and then not return. He should take no clothes. He should walk away without plate or the cash that might lie within the safe in the vestry. He should allow no one into the hostel after the hour of two p.m., being careful in his accounting of the bodies coming in and going out, for it would not lie well with his conscience should he miscount and leave one unaccounted for, even be it one of the aimless tramps and vagabonds who came and begged for rest and their sustenance, freely given.

He should sit down with those he had cared for, loved, respected…a last supper, indeed, at lunchtime…and know that what he might do, now, he would be doing for them so that at some other time of grace and favour an edifice might rise to take the place of St. Saviours. Take over the work. Feed the hungry of the world, elsewhere. His prayers at parting should reflect nothing of his own wish to retire from his ministration within the flock that had taken his health.

Thereafter he should wait for his helpers to go, make one last investigation, make one last prayer but then know that he would be walking away from his life's vocation for the very last time. When the last child had been taken home…when the last of his vagabonds and pensioners had eaten their belly's fill…he should then retire to the fells with his dog. Banished to the wilderness as Christ was in His temptation and wait for God's work to occur in the midst of the chaos about them. Who would lose out anyway? Only those Pharisees gathered in a Zurich bank filled with safe deposit boxes. Another few pence would go on the cost of buildings insurance. Far less than a single donation to a collection plate, but sufficient for a new church to be built elsewhere, in a place of appreciation. God's work in continuance.

He need know no more about anything other than that his own conscience might be clear, for the man with the black briefcase would come back with his own keys after he had left for his walk. A man who would not thank him for a welcome. He would come with his case full of wires and junction boxes and screwdrivers. He would let himself in when the coast was clear. He would do the job that he had already been paid to do. It was important that after he had gone no one enter the building. Just to touch a single light switch would interfere with the detonation that would be timed for a slow, creeping trail of fire to take its hold and the evidence of its presence burnt within the wake. He was to open the door to the basement from within for access to the gas and electricity supplies, make sure the crypt door was locked and barred against trespass and be on his way.

Now, he stood and turned to go. At the door to his vestry Father Turner looked to the bank of candles which burnt in the dark corner under the picture of the Holy Virgin. His heart was heavy. His mind filled with a great sadness. Not just for what was to happen but for himself, an ordinary mortal once again. What would he do? Where would he go thereafter? Back to his family in County Kerry? There was no one there, now, but a Godless niece who would not welcome him. He would be returning with nothing but the clothes he stood up in, just as he had come.

As if sensing his distress the old, black dog came to him from her place where she had lain on the warm floorboards to soak up the sunshine pouring through the windows of his church. He had called her Alma for the word meant soul. Ever his faithful friend the dog followed him to his desk where he took the office chair, the desk cluttered with the bills that could not be paid, the letters of demand, the estimates that could not be afforded, the list of figures which the bishop had left for him as the justification for what he should allow to happen with the blessing of the Great Redeemer.

He made space for her between his legs and leant forward arms outstretched. She put her soft strong body into his embrace as his bare forearms came about her and pressed against his legs. His head drooped against the dog's steadfast head as he began to pray, her breathing a strong and steady pant of warm breath against his bare arm. The dog raised a paw to his knee, its eyes shining, the *now* of its desires satisfied and replete, knowing only the peace of the moment. Sometimes that was all that might be hoped for. Prayer was said but what could not be soothed was his knowing. He could neither pray for their mission to be successful as he could pray against it. He would let the day unfold with his eyes turned to Heaven. It would be God's decision in the end. For He who was all powerful and all seeing would in His omnipotence make the end His own. For that return of faith he was grateful. It was out of his hands and into His. For it was He who accepted the responsibility for man's sinfulness in the end; even his own.

Coming from outside he could hear the war cries building, the boots marching, the gatherings declaring that the underdogs would rise and bite the hand of oppression. They would not cow to the treatment metered out, the tinder of their determination so dry that a mere spark had been all that it had taken. They had started to build the barricade.

Wearily, he rose and collected his dark overcoat from where he had placed it on the pegs to the back of his vestry door. He would go bare of collar up the lanes to think how they, who would take his place in a brand new building, mayhap in a brand new place, might continue the calling. There would be nothing of community here, after this day.

As he took the dog lead out of his pocket Alma came waddling, tail wagging, sitting up and begging in the way that it had amused him to teach her to say please and thank you as a young pup. If only people were like dogs – stalwart and faithful – the world might be a better place, he thought. If people were as Alma they would not be roused to the flags of discontent which he could see as he stepped from his vocation; from his church; from his responsibility, for the very last time.

The chant rose in one communal, repetitive voice. "Leave the

Dog's Bed be! Police stay out!" He would no longer feel responsible for the policing of their spiritual souls.

As he went round the back of his church, the playschool and canteen finished for the day, he made one last investigation to assure himself that no one remained within the building. Here a grey painted door gave onto the crypt. It had never been locked unless by error in all the years that he had been priest within this parish. Just sufficient light down the steps to the cellar floor. A place that gave shelter when no other was available to those without choice. He had even equipped it with sleeping bags and the provisions of ring pull cans to satisfy a basic hunger and thirst. He had placed the holy book upon a small lectern and each day turned the pages so that those who came within might share also the essence of the teachings of that week. He had provided electric torches for they were safer than candles in the giving of light to a place otherwise in darkness. The dark space before him smelled of damp and decay. There were better places than this unhealthy domain with winter gone...an empty barn...a garden shed...the lee side of a thicket hedge...in which the homeless might rest.

The spaces beyond were no more than those where church lumber was stored and another space held the coal which fired the furnace in winter and was now spent. The gas and electricity meters and switches were located over by the base of the staircase. He had already unlocked the door which led into the church above as instructed.

As he brought the door closed again he took the trouble to drop the snip which operated the Yale lock on the door. It snapped shut. He tested it with his hand flat against the wood. Impossible for anyone to get in there.

This, his last job done he felt the warm body of his friend, as she sat waiting patiently for her walk, at his side through the fabric of his pants. She was smiling up at him still. "To the hills Alma. What say we take a longer walk than usual? Get away from all this. After that we'll take up Magdalene's invitation to join her and Nan for an evening meal. A truly good lady is Nan Bartlett. She might even lend me that spare room until I can make another arrangement."

Alma wagged her tail. As they set off they were in total agreement.

*****

Father Turner had passed from sight out through the back yard gates just as Magdalene came hurrying back to the hostel. Using the front approach she then made for the path to the rear of the building. She had left her front door key in her apron pocket and would need it to get into the house because her mother suffered from deafness. Conveniently so at times, as Nan refused to wear the aid her doctor had prescribed. She knew full well that Nan would be lodged at the table under her window in that dusty room of hers, with her Tarot cards spread out on the square of purple silk she wrapped them in, probably summonsing up a few witches and wizards and speaking incantations. Her concentration deep so that she had heard nothing as Magdalene had hammered on the front door of their shared home and shouted through their letter box to be let in. Little wonder when there was so much noise going on around them, living as they did so close to the canal bridge where the barricade was growing ever taller and wider. The journey back to the hostel kitchens at St Saviour's Church, after Father Turner would have locked up for the afternoon, being unusual but necessary.

It was necessary, too, to make for the other side of the church away from the congregational hall, the back way. No point even trying to get into the premises the front way. Nor to try to summon Father Turner by knocking. This was the time of day when he went off for his walk with his faithful, old dog, Alma. She had known that the church, itself, at this time of day would be locked against her. All their routines were fixed. Despite what was happening on the bridge she had no reason to doubt that this day, in terms of their routines, would be any different.

And each day Magdalene's routines were long and hard. Each morning early, shortly after seven, it had long been her habit to enter the church using her own vestry door key even before Father Turner rose from his bed. She would be walking through his vestry even before he breakfasted, seeing the unpaid bills and estimates which were prematurely whitening his hair and so on into the far side of the building where the hostel and the playgroup were housed. As she went she would be assessing any additional work required to maintain the appearance of the church...new altar flowers, perhaps...the application of a brush or two of emulsion paint to cover the patches of rising damp...the tidying of hymn books or the repairs to the prayer books because there was no money for their replacement.

Magdalene spent each and every morning assisting in the organization and supervision of the very varied, daily programme of an active church where parents and children came and went...people dropped in for coffee and a chat...groups of worshippers met to arrange fund raising events...the donations of food stuffs, clothes and saleable goods had to be sorted in support of the hostel, itself. In between, there was always the need to supervise the preparation and serving of the lunches and oversee the activities of the playgroup. Her weekdays were busy with a thousand and one practical things via a group of voluntary helpers. At the weekend the hostel was manned by volunteers. Saturday she cleaned the church, polished the plate and did the flowers in readiness for Sunday Service. Sunday morning she spent in worship and then in the afternoon she did her weekly planning for the playgroup before helping out at the Church Youth Club in the evening. When funds were low she asked Gina Mon for some gratefully received help to buy the provisions of paint and clay, glue and tissue paper so that the children might have the right occupations for them to learn. For how much longer the hostel and playgroup might be kept freely accessible to all and sundry was open to speculation. The debts of the church were no secret. For His help towards that end she prayed daily.

The days had gone when it was possible for the church doors to be left open to all those in need of its shelter and protection. All too often she had seen the damage caused by those unsupervised ruffians who came within its hallowed walls for succour, yet failed to respect its status as God's House on Earth. Its vandalism was as a crime unto herself. Its desecration was the worst of all to bear for one who truly believed that the spirit of the Holy Mother lived within her figurines and the suffering cross of Her Holy Son, as he pleaded with the world for their deliverance from evil. What wickedness must lie within the hearts of people who could do such terrible, wicked things as to harm even as much as the cover on a prayer book? Even the threads of the altar cloths were sacred. No matter its physical state, the church was blessedly steeped within the lingering aura of all the powerful prayers that had been uttered there by the faithful. It was the spell that bound her to the church. Such was what kept her to her ministrations, day after day, year after year, since her reformation. It was God's hallowed house. It was God's home. It was sacrosanct.

The walk round the perimeter of the building put just a couple of minutes on what should have been an unnecessary journey. It had been her propensity that morning to think and worry about Mally Kenyon which had distracted her from her usual routines; her final task always to soak the soiled tea towels, along with her apron; pockets checked in a bowl of hot soapy water. This final act, today, forgotten in the rush of having too many things to do. The prayer meeting had put an additional stress on her busy morning. She had flung the apron over a chair back in the canteen kitchen at the hostel and forgotten that she had left her house key in the pocket. It had not been missed until the moment she needed it. Her mother not answering her loud knocking. What mattered, now, was the retrieval of her key.

As she went round to the rear of the church she saw nothing to concern her. All was as it usually was, though a black car had pulled up to the front of the building. An ordinary looking man like a travelling salesman or even a Jehovah's Witness; God Forbid, had taken a packet of sandwiches out of a black briefcase and had started eating, his newspaper spread open, a flask to hand. So many strangers about! The place running with reporters since the press conference that morning and all that had followed it.

Mally! Mally! So much like Bass that sometimes she thought he was her dead husband returned to her. His voice, his mannerisms, so much the same. So very different from Woody and Benny. They were both good men who had simply made the wrong choices, just as she had, within the foolish misconceptions of their youth. As she walked she wondered what had happened to Mally after he had been arrested. He would be charged for no more reason than that someone would have to satisfy the anger inside the human breast when a child is abused. She felt deeply within herself that Mally Kenyon was incapable of that kind of depravation. He was Bass's twin; more than just a brother. Not as hard as people might think. It was too easy to ignore the fact that it was always the weak and the meek who went to the wall, while the strong and cruel took the centre pews and looked upon those less fortunate with deprecation because they had been stupid enough to relinquish the seat. Mally's sin was, mostly, that temper of his which worked even against his own best interest. His frustrations deeply felt but then deeply regretted when just to count to ten would be all that it might take before lashing out to see his problems solved. That and a job which would take him from that hovel he had been living in to a decent fireside. A woman at his side perhaps. If she sometimes let her imagination confuse Mally with his brother she dashed the thoughts from her mind. Yet she worried for him just the same between working hard to stop her own destructive tides rolling back in. So much to repent. The guilt of having given away her daughter never ever leaving the coarse grains of her thoughts for a single moment, wakeful or sleeping.

Magdalene had yet to listen to her radio or switch on a television as her morning had unfolded to hear that Mally had absconded from detention at the police station. She was always too busy in the kitchen to listen to the talk of others and discouraged those who might gossip at other people's expense. Her mother was the one for gossip not Magdalene. She avoided all those relationships which might allow her vulnerabilities to overtake her strengths. If she had no friends of her own age it had become a necessary fact of her life if she was to avoid what was still temptation. She was thinking, too, that she might benefit from some fresh air when she had spent the morning shuttered into airless spaces with so many people and children pestering her like squawking chicks. Then the prayer meeting had not been successful because her mother would insist on coming along even while ridiculing their faith. An odd one out to their practice of a faith devoted to prayer. Sitting there looking like a gypsy fortune teller. She did it deliberately because her mother, Magdalene knew, had a defiant, non-conformist nature.

Once her key was retrieved she planned to get out into the fresh air so to avoid a brewing confrontation with Nan when they were both feeling tetchy and upset with all that was going on around them. After she had returned home again and found a warmer coat from the pegs to the side of the front door she would go down to the canal and, perhaps, walk that way into town. Maybe look for a new dress as an indulgence to the vanity that lived quietly within her even yet. She would not admit to wondering what Mally Kenyon might think once he saw her wearing it. Then remembered once again! Mally Kenyon was unlikely to see anything but the inside of a police cell.

Despite the sunshine the wind remained cold and her short jacket unsuitable as she made greater haste. On her way past the outer crypt door she did what she always did in passing. She tested it to make sure that it was open. So many times in her disreputable past this same crypt had been a welcoming space where she need not feel as much a squatter as a guest. Its availability had saved her and Bass from sometimes sleeping in the open. She would not see it shut against anyone in need no matter their condition. For she had once been as destitute, lost and helpless herself.

It was locked! It sometimes happened when people thought it a requirement to lock up after themselves. They simply put down the snip and let the lock take its keeper so that either she or Father Turner had to open it again.

Taking her church keys from her coat pocket she undid the lock and replaced the snip into the off position. While the door remained tightly fitting, there being no outer handle, it would prize open quite easily with a small penknife or a slither of strong metal. The crypt invited entry only to those already initiated into its easy access. The news spread person to person on a need-to-know basis while looking closed to those who were unaware. Children stayed away because it was known to be reserved for the kind of person better to be avoided…namely the intoxicated homeless…sometimes the likes of the Kenyon brothers when they fell upon hard times and there was no bed for them at the hostel. Few disrespected its purpose or Father Turner's trust that they come and go quietly and leave no mess behind them. Access to the church itself; up the stairs off a central corridor within the crypt was, under normal circumstances, barred by a locked door. As Magdalene glanced within she failed to notice an increase in light upon the inner staircase to denote that the door at the top of the stairs had been unlocked and left ajar. The door to the congregational hall, and thereby all its inner spaces, stood wide open.

That done she walked on into the yard, let herself through into the hostel kitchen where all was old and worn but clean and tidy because she would have it so. She put the tea towels and her apron to soak after rescuing her house key. She would return later, in accordance with her usual routines – usually after she and her mother had eaten together – to rinse them through and peg them up to dry. Occasionally, as this evening, with Father Turner joining their company for an evening meal if he so chose, she would come back slightly later than usual to complete all her tasks. There was always work to be done; choir cassocks to wash and mend, hymn books to tidy, chairs to realign, the organ to clean when the organist had a habit of eating biscuits while playing and then complain that the instrument was faulty when the keys stuck on his crumbs.

If the streets were safe that was! People were out on the streets milling in groups and talking of rebellion. Mally Kenyon would not be there to look out for her. Riot was in the air.

Nineteen

Within her office, high above the town centre streets, Catty Collins prepared her battle plan. She was perfectly aware of what was happening on the streets of the Dog's Bed Estate. Like some reigning, bitter, snow queen she now regarded the building of a barricade as entirely predictable and totally unimaginative. The mentality of a lawless mob was overriding common sense. What could they possibly hope to achieve and especially if they were now harbouring a paedophile in their midst? Mally Kenyon had escaped his detention before questioning. A child had been cruelly abused. They would harbour him. Her chain of command had been informed to prepare for battle stations once again.

Upon this premise she had rallied her troops and justified her cause. Tonight, upon the first darkness, when public drunkenness would raise the profile of her response to an isolated incident of anarchy to even greater heights, her reinforcements would come to raise again the banners of law and justice which allowed people to live together peaceably where they might otherwise fight like dogs. The common good being what was now uppermost in her mind. There was a need to protect and maintain public safety above all else. The mangy, lawless few should never be allowed to contaminate the lives of the lawful majority. She had already gained a tacit approval of those she had needed to advise of her decision. That so, she knew that they would save their final judgement for the outcome whence they would land on whichever side of the barricade best suited them.

However, she could see nothing that would stand in the way of her victory. The child had become as nothing to the situation she now faced. The dog's bed was about to be cleared of all lice and fleas. The blankets would be washed. The basket would be scoured and placed in the sunlight to dry. Of that she was determined. Never, again, would her officers be unable to enter the estate for fear of being spat on or stoned. Never again would the warrens and high rises, to the rear of the estate, be considered to be no-go areas governed by the gangland barons with a power greater than her own. Never again would she be relegated to a position of no importance and her words ignored.

As she stood before her window she determined that the last bastion to the lawlessness of her order would fall. The only problem being that Serena, her sister, lived closer to its perimeter than Katrina found acceptable when riot had a habit of taking a predictable route. There would be much marauding and setting of fires this night. The youth would roam like packs of savage dogs looking for their reinforcement within the clubs and pubs and back streets of Lower Quinton which meant that they would cross the bridge despite the barricade, make across the park, passing close to Serena's door.

She wanted her sister out of her imagined scenes of social cleansing when the riot vans rolled onto the Dog's Bed Estate and the curs fled to other hiding places. She told herself it was for her sister's sake that she required her to be brought away and, perhaps, concealed within her own apartment until the affray was over and done with. She told herself this while refusing to heed the tugs of truth on the frayed edges of her concerned emotions. She paid mere nodding grace towards the fact that she would not want Cubby Watson, or indeed any of the gathering press, to know that she even had a sister, let alone one as shocking in her disfigurement as Serena. She cared not to acknowledge that Serena was the only other person other than C. C. Watson who knew that she had aborted a child. Serena was witness to her greatest and most shameful secret. One that bothered her still. It still came back at night to haunt her.

The memories of that day of raging gales and driving rain when the thunder had rolled across the heavens and the lightning had struck its blue forks into the painful, wretched tribulation of a self-induced abortion...just a few tablets taken with a glass of water...the invasion of her body dealt with and curtailed... troubled her even all of these seven years later. With the encroachment of her menopause she had failed to protect herself, believing herself to be well past the age of conceiving. She had had no one to blame but herself. CC would neither take nor accept any responsibility other than that forced upon him. She had had to include him in the act of abortion for want of anyone else. And, anyway, why should he escape when he had been as much a guilty party to the conception of an unwanted child as she had? Then when there had been so much pain and mess and blood he had shown himself unable to cope. That had been when he had gone for the only other person they might trust within such a desperate situation; Catty's sister, Serena, to minister to the agony-wracked, bloody process, where CC could not.

Sometimes she could feel again Serena's hand upon her shoulder, see the child and its placenta come away between her legs, still attached the one to the other. When Serena had asked CC to supply a receptacle, all he had been able to produce was a galvanised pail which Serena had carried away with her into the dark night, as he had driven her home again. Had a tiny, doll's foot stretched tiny toes against the air? A finger-sized arm been raised and a hand spread like a flag of truce? A cry; weak but accusing? To this day Katrina could not make up her mind upon whether the child had already faded away or time had been required after it had been expelled from her womb for the tiny lungs to fail. Easier to assume than ask when the incident lay between them like a secret crime for which Katrina must bear all guilt. Then there was the never diminishing curiosity: what had she done with her? It had been a girl, she knew, for Serena had told her so. Never again to be mentioned between them. Katrina might only guess at the mode of its disposal.

Now time had come to return the consideration towards a sister in need when the neighbourhood where Serena lived was volatile and Serena would be in need of some support. Taking the mobile phone from her pressed pocket she switched it on and scrolled through her contact lists for Serena's number, quite sure that Serena would answer because Serena would have little in terms of occupation to distract her mind. Wondering as she tapped impatient fingers to her desk top what she did all day in that cellar of hers. Within the solid walls and behind the shuttered windows where she had been raised also with so little changed from the days of their parents. On the rare occasions she had called to see her, always with a prior arrangement…save for that day, last summer, when Serena had seen her playing with the police band in the park and she had felt duty bound to call before driving away…the same evening that the swans had been attacked within the same park and their wings speared and broken…there had been little to talk about. Nothing to say because there had been nothing shared. Their lives had no bridge to span the differences in their daily existence. She, a woman who lived her job on a twenty-four hour basis. Serena, idle and incarcerated in that sheltered life of hers. In some ways a position to be envied. Catty was tired of the starch and boot polish and the strivings of keeping up standards. She knew what they called her; named her after a battle gun which fired cannon balls and moved on a ratchet that required a windlass to turn it. As if she was not made of flesh and blood the same as the rest of them. Indeed there were times when she wondered, herself, and required reassurance. Raising two fingers of the right hand she felt the pulse of her left wrist to feel it beating strongly. Of late her blood pressure had begun to rise. Some days she found herself vastly tired and with a tightness at her temples. As she waited for an answer to her call she rubbed where a pulse beat with the tips of her fingers and tried to close her eyes for a moment's respite.

No reply. Other things to do. Sandra bringing her the letters of authority to mark a day when to be cast out of iron might have been no bad thing. A few minutes later…this time seated as she signed out the guns, and the battering rams and the riot vans once again; the issues of her command at her own disposal and no one else's, to overrun the underdogs who would challenge the authority of the law itself...she tried to phone her sister once again. Her watch said that it was shortly after one o'clock in the afternoon. A time when Serena usually rested, she supposed. If she knew what was happening just a short distance from her home she would be disturbed and upset by it. The reports Katrina was getting constantly reinforcing her own understanding that tensions in that area of town were rising with the acts of public unrest. People were on the streets, windows open. Bonfires being built. The barricade was growing. No reply again.

She looked at her watch with some irritation. Her time was precisely accounted for down to the last five minutes on this particular day. Her deputy, who would have been in charge of all operations had she followed her initial timetable, would shortly be coming in for a debriefing. However she might find a half hour to drive round there, see her sister pack a small, overnight case and then drive her back to her own flat where she might make herself comfortable. She would tell her secretary, Sandra, that she would be out to lunch so that no explanations would be necessary.

Such decision made, she found Sandra within the outer office, her form almost obscured by a set of clear, see-through, plastic evidence boxes piled high on her desk. All stacked within another clear plastic bag to keep the separate items together. They were each case referenced as QPS/7, 4, 2010/857632; one box for each individual item. She could see the soiled clothing of a small girl within; a red spotted dress, red buttoned shoes, socks with frills. A pair of white cotton knickers and a lacy vest now a putrid grey colour. The sack had dried and was now folded within the blue plastic box which had the reference of the Forensic Laboratory on it. Another box contained a red handbag equally as badly soiled and still wet from its dunking in the canal. Saved apparently because of its newish condition as possible evidence. It was thought to have been deposited in the water at about the same time of day; a somewhat tenuous link with the child's situation. Indeed, to Catty it looked very much like her own Christmas present to Serena of a few Christmases past; bought expensively from Trimbles Department Store on Quinton High Street. What use she had made of it was questionable. Serena rarely went out of the house.

On the top of the boxes and inside the enveloping clear plastic bag were clear plastic pockets bearing photographs of the child and her rag doll. A child whose poses were barely glanced at. All were kept free of contamination by the application of the inch wide, plastic tape which had been applied as one might place string on a parcel and fastened off with a plastic tag so that only the next authorised person whose name was upon the tag...this one her own... might take a pair of scissors to cut the bindings to look within.

Her secretary's harassed eyes flicked over the tall, wide bundle as if it had been placed there deliberately to offend her. Though, more likely, not to be forgotten in the midst of all her other work. "For your consideration, Ma'am."

Katrina frowned deeply and looked at her watch. The child had become second in her list of priorities. "I doubt until tomorrow at this rate."

Sandra offered a disgruntled glance at the watch on her own wrist as she typed from the Dictaphone Ma'am used to direct all of her work, her ears plugged with the sound pieces. It had gone one o'clock and she had yet to avail herself of a coffee break. The internal and external phones never having stopped ringing all morning. In order to cope she had directed the switchboard to take messages so that she might deal with the pile of incoming correspondence on her desk as well as see to the Chief Constable's outgoing correspondence. There was a pile of memos to denote that the calls concerning what had been happening on the Dog's Bed Estate had been frequent and the complaints numerous. Most had already been passed through to a woman who had been planning what looked to Sandra as the biggest raid ever known to Quinton Police Station. They had not been read.

Catty continued her explanation as if time was a problem to herself alone. "I have no time, now, to see to anything but the latest emergency situation. I shall have lunch, shower and change at home. Place the boxes in my deputy's office. He will be in shortly. He may choose to look at them and read the reports to become au fait with the wider situation when all this has stemmed from the child in the canal. Tell him that I shall be just a few minutes late for our debriefing meeting."

"You'll be out for some time, Ma'am?"

"An hour. Perhaps a little more. Should council members or the area politicians choose to consult me about the latest developments I will be available after two-thirty. They may choose to be referred to my deputy instead."

"You won't be back till then, Ma'am?"

Irritated by her stupidity Catty snapped at her. "I have just intimated as much." Then regretted it. She relied upon this woman, at times, to fight her corner. "I apologise. I sometimes have to make weighty decisions which fall heavily on my shoulders. If the press call it's a case of no comment. Refer all important calls to my deputy. You may phone me if there are any major developments I need to be aware of."

She left behind her the usual sharp scent as she went, gloves in one hand, hat in place, bag over her shoulder, her briefcase in the other hand. Her private lift would take her down to the ground floor where she would brave the crowded lobby and the press presence for no more reason than that way was the quickest route to her four wheel drive car.

Sandra knew that she would find it badly scratched with a dent in the boot where someone had banged it with a hammer before running away. If she had not informed her it was because she had no intention of being on the receiving end of Ma'am's bad temper. Not that she thought the damage to her vehicle unfair. Sandra would have liked to jump up and down on top of it, kick off her wing mirrors, splinter the windscreen with her own beating fists and pull every lead out of the engine. All with Ma'am watching. The woman asked far too much of her on such occasions as this when the whole place was pulled to pieces. Ma'am had no family and so had no idea how hard it was for a divorced mother to manage home, work and children. Get in for seven every morning and not leave until three-thirty. Her hours at work merely the first shift in her combined roles of breadwinner and single parent. Her teenage children running wild half the time. She only hoped that they were steering clear of all the trouble brewing on the Dog's Bed Estate, yet knowing that they would be instinctively drawn towards it.

Only when she heard the lift going down, did she find her own mobile phone, her eyes flicking towards the evidence boxes on her table. She found the number, pressed for it to be dialled and waited while her hands pulled at the plastic tape so that it twanged against the plastic cover. So reminded she opened her drawer to bring out a roll of the same tape. This she placed with a pair of her own scissors and fresh tags from the bottom drawer of her desk to her right and placed them together on the top of the stacked and wrapped boxes, files and plastic pockets within the giant plastic bag

She did not need to introduce herself to the eager voice which made a swift, introductory greeting following the ring tone and then waited for her to speak. This was her third call today to the same person and was equally as surreptitiously made. Sandra kept her voice to a whisper. "I have what you asked for on my desk now. I'll meet you in the usual place. No more than one hour. Make sure its back before two. She won't be looking at it till tomorrow but it might be missed if anyone needs to look at it this afternoon."

"I can be there within the next few minutes. I'm on my way back to the office. I'll make a detour. Usual place."

When she terminated the call she found a capacious black plastic bag big enough to take the whole package and conceal it by pulling on the drawstrings at the top. She left the office but did not make her usual way floor to floor, using the same lift as Ma'am had just done, but took to the back staircase. The back door was on a digital lock with a pass number. She closed it behind her as she went out towards the dustbins seeing incoming and outgoing officers as they came and went from private cars as well as police vehicles from where their non-esteemed *guests* were still arriving in handcuffs. She could not recall in all her ten years on the job the station being as busy as it was this day. Joe Public was plugging up all the parking spaces on the backstreets. Angry looking people were out in numbers so that the area of streets about the police station was swarming with people intent on coming in to have their say. They were being made to file at a desk specially set up in the foyer where Ma'am just might get herself lynched if the crowd could be persuaded. They had to enter the station the front way which was the opposite way to the one that Sandra would take. She knew that her colleagues would assume that she was taking her paper shreddings for disposal due to Ma'am never allowing the contents of her own waste paper bins to be placed in the police refuse bins at the station along with everyone else's. It had been known for lines of type, even after shredding, still to be readable. Sandra thought the woman paranoid. Sandra was, however, cunning enough to offer to take the material home with her, supposedly to burn it in her garden chiminea as a courtesy to her employer...a woman she privately detested. Big Bertha had been the most demanding boss she had ever worked for. But it gave excuse for what she was doing now, for which she would be brought up on a serious charge if she was ever found out.

Nodding to her colleagues but attracting no undue attention she passed by the bins, through the open gate onto the street and then turned to the left, around a corner to a back street where she regularly parked her own vehicle. A place of relative privacy.

No one was about as she placed the plastic bag to the side of her car on the roadway and then made a display of finding her car key from the several on her ring. No one was at the upstairs windows or at the back gates of houses here as she fiddled noisily while looking about surreptitiously for the approach of the person she was about to rendezvous with.

The red, low slung, sports car came slowly towards her on the same side of the street and then stopped with engine running. The driver leant over, opened his passenger door and picked the bag up to place it on his passenger seat as if stealing it without her knowing. As he did so she looked the other way while opening her boot. Neither spoke or looked to the other. When the black, plastic bag would later be transferred back at the appointed time by the same method the bag would contain the same items and a brown envelope also which was intended solely for Sandra. Its content would pay the giant electricity bill which, as a single parent had been created in order to keep her errant kids warm and well fed during the previous, hard winter. *Panda* was not bothered where the money came from as long as she might manage to pay her bills. She had never been questioned about the contents of the occasional plastic bags she carried back in with her. Where that to happen she might say that she dare not leave the items unattended or Big Bertha would have her in front of the firing squad.

When Cubby drove off she looked to see the back of his curly, chestnut head before he raised a hand from the steering wheel. He made a V sign as if being rude to a passing motorist as he hit the main street again. Panda knew that she would need to return to her car for two o'clock. Plenty of time for him to inspect what little evidence they had and which might lead him to discovering the child's identity. Take pictures and photocopies, perhaps, which he would use discretely. She hoped, too, that it would be Cubby who would take the glory for finding out who the child belonged to. No one at the station had found anything of use as evidence that it had been Mally Kenyon who had owned the sack that the child had been near drowned in; the same, known villain who had managed to skip the station to freedom. It was to be expected that by now he was a hundred miles away and still travelling. His brothers gone to ground, also.

The child remained unclaimed.

Twenty

Holly went the way of the fields. Down the winding lane, taking the way that led through the thick hedgerows towards the viaduct which ran straight and true at a forty-five degree angle to span the renovated section of the Quinton canal where a wide basin had been scooped out with earth grabbers, then the hole lined and flooded in order to take a parade of flat-bottomed, narrowboats.

A train high on the embankment to her left shared her journey in a stop and start; waiting for the green light to take it over the one-track viaduct. It was moving slowly and clanking with each turn and stop of its wheels. An unexpectedly familiar sound to Holly as she walked along an initially unremembered lane and looked up at the passing train windows which were full of the unknown faces of strangers.

A child looking out reminded her of herself. She kneeled on the seat with a pensive face, nose pressed close, one hand to the window as her breath wreathed a film of condensation about some disappointed thought, as if wanting something other than that which was to be. As if wanting her destination to be a different place.

I know that child, Holly thought, as if the child was floating above this same cinder path, breathing in the same air, wanting to stay and not be taken away; the ghost of the child she had once used to be when she had been carried away against her wishes to an unknown place. Smells in her nose reminding, too, of wild garlic and sappy grass, ginger cakes baking in a factory somewhere. Sounds calling through the funnel of her memories; cows lowing, traffic grumbling, dogs barking, the sounds made by the wind whistling through the trees and hanging valleys of the rising, distant hills. The taste of the air; a flavoured sharpness within the chilly sunshine as a stewed infusion of the tart scent of each and every budding leaf on each and every tree and shrub. An undercurrent of all the vibrations travelling through the earth's surface, rising through the rock, soil and vegetation, before it travelled through the thin, flat, hide soles of her plodding feet with each step that took her closer to the Dog's Bed Estate. A stench on the breeze, also, like the familiar, stagnant waters of her memories having been disturbed. A sluice gate opening in her head. Her sudden fear for the child who was still watching Holly walk along a cinder path back to her own childhood on a return journey; the train moving from behind then past and away as it picked up its pace. Another child; the one that lived inside her head screaming out as she had used to do; lost and bewildered, separated from her parents. *I want to come home!*

Her mind had been relatively calm, until that moment, even if she was going to see what frayed, unravelled ends she could find of an earlier life. She had been concentrating on what she saw about her, little expecting the sensory triggers which brought picking scissors to shred the insulating sheath which she had placed over her memories of long ago childhood...the abandoned monkey in the play house in the beer garden...the sallow-faced woman with the bleary, sunken, eyes...her own, small hands and questioning eyes to the rear passenger windows of a car which was taking her away...*Where am I going? Where am I going?* The suggested meaning within the *clickety-clack, clickety-clack* of the creaking, turning wheels of the train as it began to pick up speed and go on its way.

She had become that child at the train window which was now gathering speed as it crossed the viaduct over the canal waters, travelling too fast to catch. One moment visually large and loud and then growing ever smaller and quieter as it picked up speed and travelled off on its unknown journey. It was so very quickly gone from view, eaten up by the landscape until it had no sight or sound. Something tugged at Holly's insides. *Run after it, Holly!* her own voice advised. *Save the child!*

And so she picked up her heels and ran. The cinders crunching under her pounding heels, more chased-by now than chasing that which must not be lost, now that it was recognised. She was being propelled on a wave of panic to follow her own journey back to this place which tasted and sounded and smelt and felt like home. Tears cascading but she knew not why. A stitch in her side when she was not used to running. Her heart bang, bang, banging in her chest as the frazzled ends of her emotions unwound. Holly's eyes streamed with tears as she ran faster and faster to get away from the restraining thoughts which were chasing her mind. What if they rejected her yet again? *Go away, Holly Hargreaves, and don't come back again!*

Holly ran faster still. She had to catch that train before she, like the travelling child, was gone forever, over the hills and far away. For she was going home and no one and nothing would stop her. She dare let nothing snatch her back as her feet pounded the cinder path and splashed through shallow puddles spraying up bitter black water. It was as if her own better judgement was grabbing at her clothing from behind in an effort to stop her headlong dash after her own dangerous runaway train as it careered back along the same, steep, mountain tracks to the flat lowlands of a disaffected childhood. Trying to bring this thing inside her head to a halt; to stop the unstoppable.

Where the viaduct crossed the canal, the path turned abruptly to the left, under brick arches. Holly did not slow her pace, her inner head of steam driving her on. No need to look about her because she knew where she was going.

The old lift bridge was down, its paint rasped and curled on rotted wood, barely affording her a balanced passage over its stretching arm. So much junk still remaining in the greasy, yellow, rancid shallows of the fetid pond it skimmed over, her own reflection upon it along with that of the sky and the clouds and wheeling birds and the golden pennies formed of the sunshine. Holly was yet to realise that this was the place where the child had been found.

She crossed her own divide to the other side. Knew the broken fences and the sagging sheds and the greenhouses with panes of broken glass which bordered the towpath on this side. Knew each and every one of its buildings and what each contained. To her right was the church tower of Quinton; its clock chiming the hour of one; its green slate steeple bright within the midday sun. To her left the brick road bridge, every brick accounted according to her memory. A place where now piles of junk and silt from the canal bottom had been heaped over the towpath to cause the acrid stench. It had been strewn under the brooding beak of a long-necked crane which looked down in abandoned silence upon all that was happening. It hung a sorry head as if in judgement of the men and women barrowing, sorting, taking, passing, carrying away the rubbish and the filth to some higher place. They went up and down one set of steps loaded like a parade of ants working to a purpose. Cameras rolled and snapped to catch the scene as it unfolded. This was Quinton history in the making.

The woman had her back turned as Holly slowed her pace; a woman with the same tall slimness as she had herself. A woman whose dark head of braided hair was held high and cocked to one side as if she was struggling with her own thoughts as she watched what was happening; a mere bystander. Holly saw her profile as she turned to look upon the soup of yellow water from where the stinking, slimy litter of a hundred years had been brought, as if to ask for a better understanding of all that was happening before her. She hugged a warm coat about a figure which was so like Holly's, then wrapped her hands within its sleeves against the cold as a shiver passed through her. The profile of her face was identical to the face Holly recognised as her own. Holly knew, just knew, that this woman had been set by some higher force to wait in this very place, at this very time, for Holly's coming.

Upon the back of her memory Holly knew who this woman was; the sores healed; her mind sharp and bright. The veils gone from her keening, dark brown eyes as she turned to look who had come up so close behind her and then stood expectantly as if Magdalene was blocking her passage. Holly saw the light of recognition dawn in her mother's eyes. Knew, too, that this was the place where she belonged; right there, within arm's reach of the woman who had given her life.

The catch of anguished guilt within Magdalene's breast spoke to them both of her shock at being face to face with the same child, now grown, who eleven years before had been taken away from her own, selfish neglect; the pain of memory within her face for Holly to see clearly. Time later to spurn and rail and blame. "Mum. It's me. It's Holly. I'm home."

*****

Nan Bartlett was at her own upstairs bedroom window within the terraced cottage which backed onto the canal, no more than a few metres from the road bridge and the Dog's Bed Inn where she had once been landlady during her marriage to Tock Bartlett.

Her ex-husband still practised the trade of publican in the same public house where she had gone to live as a young bride. A trade which today was feeding the sustenance required of the people building an illegal barricade, a milling crowd of onlookers and those gathered members of the press whose fondness for alcoholic beverages was ringing his till with a regularity not heard at this time of day for many a year gone by. The alcohol was flowing from what Nan had already seen. People loud in drink, who otherwise went about their more usual business in quiet peacefulness, were now rallying others to join their cause. It was frightening the very life out of her and that was a fact. Something sinister had popped over her horizon and Nan didn't like it at all.

While she might not be able to see the low towpath under the bridge she had a full view of the frontage of the public house which would soon be blocked off from the rest of the estate, as the more militant of the residents worked in unison with only one intent. That being that their protest would be seen and broadcast nationwide. Their feelings would be aired whether Catty Collins listened or not. The bullying and provocative behaviour of the local police would be protested against in a way most guaranteed to draw attention to the victimisation they were all suffering because of the evil, wickedness of just one person. Their whole community was being persecuted, hounded and vilified for the wrongdoings of someone they now considered not to be the one arrested in the first place. That person not necessarily being a resident of the estate. They now knew that there had been no evidence against Mally Kenyon. They had arrested him purely on the strength of his involvement in her rescue and his previous record. The police had used such excuse to make an unlawful arrest as far as they were concerned. As they were continuing to do with the husbands, sons and daughters who had been hauled down to the police station, thrust into cells and were being asked to declare their innocence instead of refuting the evidence of their guilt.

Then there had been the insult of all the rotting garbage from the canal being deposited on the towpath and left there to stink worse than it ever did when it was covered with water. It was as if Catty Collins was using it to illustrate a point when she regarded the whole of the estate as a human rubbish dump; the lawful and the lawless, alike. That attitude had fired tempers more than anything else. What better way to make feelings apparent than to use the stinking rubbish, which the police had dredged from the water, by building a barricade to illustrate their own point.

However, Nan worried that, such being the case, the gesture of the barricade was inappropriate. It would work against them all. Even her cards said so as she sat at the desk under her window in a dusty, untidy room to which her daughter was forbidden entry as she shuffled them well. She then selected five by which to make a confirmation to the ten card Celtic Cross she had made earlier.

She was not a happy woman as she lifted each of the worn Tarot cards to reveal the symbolic imagery through which she reflected upon her life, the lives of those she loved and cared for, and the lives of the wider community where, this day, anarchy and anger lived. Nan looked down from her window to relate the scene she saw to the cards she spread in a fan, while asking questions concerning the wisdom of what was going on before her very eyes and which seemed to have sprung up out of nowhere. It was more a spread of wands and swords rather than cups and pentacles. Justice, Judgement and The Devil being the cards of the Major Arcana leading the way. The prospects of defeat by strength, change, renewal, devastating outcome...lay in the random choice of these cards to support the spreads that had gone before it. This day, while it might have some hope, was about to know an unhappy end. Not that such might be a difficult prediction to that suggested by the activities outside, but to Nan it was a confirmation that her own reasoning was correct.

As she looked back through the window, it was clear to see that a direct match with the cards was taking place. Some people had already taken their vehicles to the far side of the bridge before it became totally impassable. Others would bring them later to stay on the estate side of the bridge, for back-up to their protest; a way of extending the barrier which had grown, now, to almost span the whole of the bridge.

A large urn had appeared on a table set up at the side of the road. Children were secretively preparing sling shots and catapults and piles of stones. Youths were, unknown to their parents, putting rags into glass pop bottles in school playgrounds and pouring in petrol for the material to soak up. Knives were being brought out from under floorboards and long-barrelled, pellet guns from the backs of wardrobes. No one intended to use such dangerous weapons but they would be prepared for self defence. Look-outs had been set. Bonfires were being built. The Dog's Bed Estate was bunkering in.

As she looked from cards to window, to cards, and back again, her thoughts were not immediately transferred upon the two, female figures who emerged from the front door of the Dog's Bed Inn, arm in arm, though Magdalene was immediately recognisable. Nan was, after all, after snubbing her daughter for the way she had spoken to her after she had left her door key in the pocket of her apron at the church hostel. As if Nan should have known! How had she been expected to know that Magdalene had been knocking, fit to break the door down, when she had come upstairs to take advantage of the view from her bedroom window. It was not Nan's fault that she was becoming as deaf as a post and could hear nothing going on downstairs with the door closed. After which, her insolent daughter had gone out again in a sulk, telling Nan in no uncertain terms that if she didn't clean her room soon then she would have to come in and do it for her. Flap dusters everywhere. It had been disturbing the dust that gave Nan bronchitis. Spoken to like a naughty school child, too. And it being her name, not Magdalene's, that was on the rent book! Nan hated folk who carped and criticised as if they had every right to be self-righteous. That's what religion did to some folk!

Like her father was Magdalene, too, in that he could sulk with self-righteous stubbornness for days on end when it so took his fancy. Which, talk of the Devil, himself; there he was to be seen, too, as if an invite had been made by just thinking about him. Wearing that baggy old jacket of his that his new wife kept putting in the bin and Tock kept taking out again. He was walking out behind Magdalene and the tall, young girl. In fact they seemed to be coming her way. She saw his hand go to the shoulder of the young girl who walked before him. For him to leave the pub to the ministrations of his light-fingered barmaid meant that something momentous was taking place. Then he was looking up and waving, a smile of happiness lighting up a lugubrious face.

Nan stood, her hand travelling from the cards to her quivering lips. She gasped again. This she had not predicted. For there before her was her family...intact! She bowed her head in grateful thanks and closed her eyes in prayer to whomever or whatever it was placed blessings upon this world. "It's our little Holly come back to us," she breathed. "Thank you."

Twenty-One

Meanwhile, Ma'am was drawing her battered and scratched vehicle into the kerb outside her sister's house, on the opposite side of the street, closest to the park railings. She had already stripped off her cravat and uniform jacket and deposited her distinctive hat and gloves into the boot along with her shoulder bag and briefcase. A remnant of the sharp wind of the night before had caused her to adopt a warm, plum coloured, padded jacket over her uniform skirt. The coat had been taken from the case which still lay on the back seat of her vehicle. It had been shrugged into during the time that she had been parked in a leafy lay-by along the way; a delay which Catty considered to be worthwhile when she had no wish to be recognised alone in Lower Quinton.

The change of clothing had delayed her by a mere few minutes. With her top blouse buttons undone and her collar raised, the uniform-look had disappeared. She had removed the net which contained her natural blonde hair and let it fall about her cheeks and shoulders. She had pocketed the light responsive spectacles so that her silver eyes shone bright. Thus changed from her professional appearance and without the formality of her hat and cravat she could be assured of the anonymity she desired prior to visiting her sister. She was almost unrecognisable now from the same woman who more usually paraded her importance in pressed blues as she locked her car, crossed the narrow road and went to ring the bell on her sister's front door.

Like most rare visitors anywhere her conscience pricked. Sight of the black paint with its mint green beading and the round of fluted glass never failed to bring a pang of guilt with it. She might count on two hands the number of times that she had been back to visit the family home over the thirty years of being an ambitious policewoman with tall ladders to climb; never satisfied, always moving onwards and upwards. It had seemed best at the time for her appointment not to broadcast her links with the local community. Not that there was anyone of closeness other than Serena to compromise her role.

However, to Catty it always felt a bit like going back to square one on a board game. The house looked exactly the same as it had always done, the upstairs windows boarded over and the thick drapes on the downstairs window concealing all that went on within. Whenever she knocked on Serena's door these days she was reminded of her teenage, urgent wish to get out of Quinton so that she could live in the light, take people home with her and not have to be ashamed of having a sister whose face was ever hidden from sight. The Manchester School of Music had been a blessed relief. Later, her job had been all the excuse she had needed.

It was the curtain moving that told Catty that Serena was, indeed, at home. She heard the bolts being drawn back, counting five hard clicks as she waited. Finally a veiled head appeared through a crack where a safety chain remained. It was entirely as Catty had expected.

"Serena, I need to speak with you with some urgency. It might be necessary for you to vacate the house for a day or two. If you will allow me in I might explain."

The safety chain was removed and the door opened. Catty Collins stepped over the threshold as the lock snapped home and then the bolts were drawn; one, two, three, four, five to make all secure again.

Then confusion! Ahead of her through the open vestibule door she saw her sister standing, head uncovered, a look of abstract fear on her face.

Catty turned abruptly to look who had let her in. Mally Kenyon stood behind her, veil removed. He was grinning widely. "Well, well, well!" was what he said. "But for the photograph, I wouldn't have recognised you out of uniform."

Catty's eyes followed his glance. Her clothes and hair might be different but the faces were the same. Tigwell came up through the cellar cat flap and entwined himself about her legs.

Serena's face spread. "Dear God in Heaven, what are you doing here?"

Catty's mouth dropped open. "I should ask what he is doing here, Serena. He escaped from custody at the police station only this morning."

"Tell her then. Tell her!" Mally's voice was grave.

"This is all my fault, Katrina. Please forgive me!"

Initially, Catty wondered if Serena had been having an affair with Mally Kenyon! A woman so gravely disfigured could not be choosey.

*****

The invasion of her house had been swiftly executed, the locks replaced and the broken chain mended, even as Serena had swooned and gripped onto the vestibule door for support.

He had wasted no time then looking around, searching the house, poking his dirty hands into each and every nook and cranny while she took herself to her sofa to collapse on its length. He would have seen Caitlin's room; fit for a princess with her suitcase abandoned upon her empty bed. He would have wondered why a child should have the same black boarding with drilled holes at the windows from which to look out. The same as all the others which robbed the upstairs rooms of light. She even possessed smaller versions of the same veils as Serena's. He would have taken note of the thick nets and the lined drapes, the thick blinds and the lack of mirrors. It was too late now to plead that these had merely precluded her own presence in the house from being seen. There was too much of Caitlin about to be openly seen. Serena had become so very careless of late. Too tired to remove the evidence on a daily basis. Her pictures and stories were displayed on the cellar walls. Her hand-washed clothes drying on the clothes horse over the bath upstairs. Her books and toys spread about above and below. Her little coat on the peg under the stairs next to the shopping trolley. The child's presence was everywhere as he had invaded her fridge and stolen her food to make a sandwich. He had mused over what he had seen. "No one knows the kid lives here, do they?"

Serena closed her eyes, unable to rise, for his eyes were upon her face. Her veil on the floor by the door. She was exposed. What had he called her? The ugly woman!

"She yours?"

Another shake of her head. "No."

"Hers then," nodding to the photograph.

"She mustn't know."

"How does someone hide a noisy kid? Lungs on her like bellows she has. You know it was me as saved her. It weren't me as robbed you either."

Serena had nodded. He was looking at her face. Saying nothing but looking.

"She's your sister then? Same name as our illustrious Chief Constable. Same woman as the one in the photograph."

Serena had winced.

"You can tell her the truth. You needn't get into trouble if she's your sister. Thick as thieves when they want to be, is the law."

Prevarication very necessary, desperate measures needed. "I will be able to get you a lift if you want to get away. My friend has money."

"Mr Watson I presume!"

"How do you know this if it wasn't you who stole my handbag?"

"It was my brother, that's why. Overheard it all. He's gone the other way to try to milk the situation I think. The magistrate's husband of the Clarion Evening News. That Cubby Watson's father. The toff as always wears a big cowboy hat and struts about Quinton, half drunk, most of the time. Laughable ain't it?"

The description fit well enough. Her worst nightmare realised. One step nearer to Catty finding out. "I will phone him. He'll get you away from here. The last thing he will want is for his wife to be told."

"But I ain't done nothin'!"

"Please....!"

"Now speak of the Devil's bride. I recognise the car and her. She parks it outside the police station with her name on the space. Come incognito methinks. What's the matter with her? Doesn't want to get strung up round here or is she ashamed of you? No one knows you're her sister. I know that much."

"Please Mr Kenyon, help me!" Serena begged. "Some of us know what it is to be guilty without having committed a crime. I've lived my life suffering other people's perceptions of whom and what I am. Please. I beg you, don't let her in."

He took no notice. "Just the person I want to see. Why's she here I wonder?

"I have no idea. Unless...Unless Caitlin has told her things."

Mally frowned. "Why they put her in that Greengates place then?"

"It's a most unfortunate fact that Caitlin gets very angry at times."

"Not surprised. She never go out?"

"Yes, but hidden inside my shopping trolley. She became used to being restrained."

"Tied her in did you? That's why she did what she did when the copper flapped that dog chain at her." His face spread with disgust.

"You make it sound so cruel. I cherished her so. I cherish her still. She was the child that....!"

A ring on the doorbell.

"Please do not let my sister in!"

He picked her veil up from the floor. Too late. There was no charity within him to listen.

"You could have hung about to explain."

He was thinking that there had been insufficient charity within herself to make even an unnamed call from a telephone box to the police so to declare his innocence. Not for a moment had she thought of anyone other than Caitlin and herself.

Katrina's ring brought Tigwell back up the cellar steps as soon as she pressed at the bell.

Indeed, what was Catty doing here, now? And so easily brought within in her urgency to speak with her sister. Something about taking her away for a few days. The bolts and lock fastened again after her and the chain replaced. Katrina's eyes upon her uncovered face; so rarely glimpsed that it stunned Catty into silence for a moment as the shock and horror of her realization that it had not been Serena who had let her in.

With nerves of steel he had smiled smugly. "Well, well, well! But for the photograph, I wouldn't have recognised you out of uniform."

Catty's eyes had followed his glance. Her clothes and hair might be different but the faces were the same.

Yet her presence to Serena was hardly believable. "Dear God in Heaven! What are you doing here?"

Catty's mouth had dropped open. "I should ask what he is doing here, Serena. He escaped from custody at the police station only this morning."

Her eyes had been so accusing with suspicions Serena might only wonder about.

"It is Mally Kenyon, isn't it?"

Mally spoke again. "Tell her then. Tell her!" Mally's voice was tinged with self-righteousness innocence. He was usually guilty while claiming his innocence. Not this time!

How could she not tell the truth even if the words of explanation would not spill from her lips just yet. " This is all my fault, Katrina. Please forgive me!"

Katrina had been roughly propelled within, the door sticking on the ruck of carpet as he brought it closed behind him. Serena had to watch as her sister was shown a seat. "Couldn't be better. Tell her...tell her that it wasn't me as put the kid in the water."

Catty looking at her sister questioningly. "I assume that he isn't here by invitation, Serena. Your veil....!"

"She really don't know nothing does she?"

Serena felt faint. She shook her head. Then hung it in shame.

"What don't I know, Serena?"

Then when her sister remained mute, speaking to Mally as if the very sight of him was an offence to her eyes. "You won't get away with this."

"Don't want to get away with anything, Ma'am," was his insolent reply. "She'll be the first to tell you that I've nothing to get away with 'cause I've done nothing wrong."

"You'll be speaking of the child thrown into the canal in a sack."

"You better tell her now."

Was he threatening to harm her sister, for some reason to do with the charges that had been about to be made against him?

What he had to say further made no sense. "She's had the kid hidden here in the house since she was born. She was taking her somewhere when someone mugged her. Not me. But someone who got the shock of his life when he put a hand in her shopping trolley and brought out the sack tied at the neck. Kid inside it. It just takes off...splash!...into the water and the rest is history. Maybe, if you ask her nice she'll let you in on her little secret."

Then to Serena who looked catatonic with shock, her face hanging like an abstract Picasso painting. "No point in lying. You've been hiding the kid away. Her clothes and toys are all over the place. Upstairs. In the cellar too. Her coat's under the stairs. A bit small for you I'd say!"

Catty let her derision show. A man obviously of limited intelligence. Surely he was misconstruing the situation! Serena had always hidden herself away. What child? Serena had no child. She was incapable of conceiving, or so her parents had been told. Serena's female anatomy had been deformed from birth. To Catty's knowledge she had never known any man to even as much as look upon her face, never mind touch her. What child was he referring to? It was her sister's silence that was most telling. Catty felt herself grow cold. "Have you stolen a child, Serena...the child in the canal? Is that what this is all about?"

Then Serena spoke, her eyes as hard as flint, her mouth and nose dripping with the never-ending phlegm. Her head rose as she looked at her sister with blame. "I didn't steal her, Catty. I was given her...remember? You gave her to me...the child you aborted because she would have got in your way! I was asked to dispose of her if you remember. There was some miscalculation of dates I think. Or so CC said. Your self-induced abortion took place later than it should have done." Her strange, scaly silver fish eyes stretched even wider with accusation as she turned her face on her cornered victim. Her sister, perhaps for the first time in her life, was speechless. Time to drive the knife home to the hilt. "Like me, your daughter refused to die when others would have considered it to have been for the best. The child you aborted, Katrina, was fully formed. Small and weak but fully formed. I brought her home in the metal pail from under your sink. I cleaned out the old fish tank and lined it with silk. I laid it with her inside here on the rug by the fire. I tried to afford her the dignity of willing her to live not to die. I fed her drops of milk through a straw; hour by hour...kept her tiny body clean... blew air up her nose through a straw gently. She was so very tiny dressed in my old doll's clothes. You never phoned to ask did you?"

Her sister's face had slowly drained of all its colour.

Serena sensed her moment of fulfilment as the dam of spite inside her spilled over. "Your daughter didn't die, Catty. She lived to celebrate her first birthday on the twenty-first of June, two thousand and three. And then her second. And her third. And her fourth. We were so happy together until her seventh, after which I foolishly told her about you." Such agitation present that Serena had begun to shake. The words would not remain unspoken. "Her behaviour changed with that. Time had come for her to go away to school. Little Caitlin was so very afraid of that."

Now her sister was rising, her hand fluttering to her throat, her face stretching.

She has silver eyes, Mally noted, like her sister. Like he had. Like the child! The Chief of Police was a Kenyon! "It's like she says is it? She's your kid only you never knew about her!"

She didn't answer him, just stood and stared, eyes locked with her sister as a bright red tide now washed her pale face and her breathing shortened. "Dear God in Heaven!"

Catty's voice had lost all the crisp edge of the woman who had spoken so eloquently to the nation on the news just a few short hours before. She would never be the same again and she knew it. "CC knew about her, did he? He brought you home with...with what was in the pail. He has known that she lived even while I assumed her to have faded away. He let her stay with you here in this house with her hidden from view for all these years."

Serena nodded. "What else could her father do but leave her with me?...I who refused to let her die purely for the sake of his...and your...convenience. It suited us both to remain quiet as long as it was easy. I had to have someone to help me to raise her properly if she was to have all that she needed to thrive. Even someone as unwilling as he. I could not have kept her without the money he paid for her upkeep."

"It was wrong, Serena. It was wrong."

"To save a child is wrong? To love a child is wrong? I cannot see what I have done wrong. She received the same care and attention that I did when my presence was an embarrassment to our parents. To you, too. She failed to conveniently fade away as you put it. Just as I refused to fade away. Little Caitlin grew up in the cellar as I did. It was good enough for me. Why not for her? This house was where I felt safe. So why shouldn't she? It was only the threat of inclusion that caused her to become insecure when faced with Blackstone School. CC had arranged it."

Cellars! Mally hated them. It was to do with the dogs he so detested.

Catty wanted to know more. "When did you tell her the truth?"

Serena sighed heavily now. There had been no lasting joy in telling Katrina. Her voice shivered with weakness as she found a tissue from her dress pocket and attended to her wet mouth and nose. Just a strange light-headedness as if her brain was alive with shoals of swimming fishes. "We had gone to hear the police band playing in the park last summer. I didn't expect to see you there playing your trumpet. She rode in the trolley so very quietly then."

Her sister shook her head over and over with disbelief. "I recall the day last summer. I called to visit afterwards. Why…how…have you managed to keep her secret from me for so long? Seven years…almost eight. Why did I never guess?" Before answering her own question. "I suppose because I have always been too busy." Then she was recalling something that she had read only that morning. "Am I…?" Then rephrasing; "I am the lady with the golden trumpet, am I not? The one that the child kept asking to speak with. She knows that I am her…her…!" Her…what?

"Birth mother are the words you are struggling to find, dearest sister. Yes. She knows that you are her birth mother. She recognised your uniform but does not know your position. She has it in mind that you live at the police station. The very place that she was taken. She expected you to want her where she thinks that I didn't. Anything rather than be sent away to Blackstone School. That was where I was taking her when his brother…because it was your brother, wasn't it?…pushed me to the ground and stole my handbag. My darling child hopped into the water. She had been safely wrapped in the sack and lightly sedated. Secreted merely for the sake of escaping detection on a difficult journey, when it was imperative we get away without drawing undue attention to ourselves. It was the contents of the handbag that allowed him to trace me."

Catty gasped on a flashback of memory from that very same day. The red handbag in the evidence box that had been dredged from the bottom of a filthy canal. The one that she had thought so like the one she had bought for her sister two Christmases ago. Why had it seemed so preposterous a thought at the time that it might be the same?

Serena continued. "I had filled in her forms with my name and address as her contact. I had named myself as her mother though I have never sought to take that place. I required merely to protect her…to be her guardian as well as her saviour. CC was named correctly as her father. He had been the one to visit the school and then make all the necessary arrangements. I was to take her. He was to pay her fees. Caitlin and I were to holiday together at school recesses somewhere away from here. There should have been no repercussions. I should have been allowed to remain her guardian at least for as long as I…as I am able. My state of health being something else that had to be considered…another reason why she had to be sent away to school. Only my darling Caitlin did not understand. Neither does she understand even now that her mother does not want her either. They took her and put her in that dreadful place. I saw her struggle so hard against it."

"How can you say that I would not want her now? I never knew about her, Serena. You are ill?"

"You aborted her."

"I aborted what I considered to be a five month foetus. Not a child."

"How ridiculous that sounds. Do you know how stupid that sounds?"

Mally considered the difference between a foetus and a child. How could anyone not want a child as beautiful as the one that he brought from the water? Yet how could a child who would seem to have been so loved and cherished be put into a sack and tied within? Who would believe any of it? This part...yes. The child's genetics was a simple matter of DNA but the circumstances of her entrapment here? He would still be thought guilty unless she would speak for him. Then he considered her sister not to be a blessing but an added difficulty. She would want to hide the truth not reveal it. What to do now?

"Who else knows of her existence other than CC?" Catty asked her sister.

Serena hung her head momentarily. When she brought it up with sharp defiance Catty suspected that she was lying. "No one."

Mally replied sneeringly. "Only the whole world, Ma'am. And my brothers. Your sister is right. They think they have won the lottery. You might expect to be blackmailed, Ms Collins, should they find out that you are the child's mother, not her. You won't get away with this one." Then to Serena. "Think yourself lucky it was me and not them come ringing your bell. They'd have milked this for every penny they could screw out of you both. Only they've gone first for the side of the kid's family they think can best afford their purpose. What her ladyship, the magistrate, wouldn't pay to keep all this off the Globe's front pages!" Then his eyes to the window. "Maybe that's why he's here."

They all looked to the window towards the hazy figure getting out of a taxi through the thick gauze nets. The one in the large brimmed Homburg hat and the overlarge, beige, trench coat: C. C. Watson, himself.

Serena cringed.

Her sister swore.

Mally Kenyon took up Serena's veil again. "We'll see shall we? Maybe you might think about which one of you is about to declare my innocence. Or at least get the child to speak for me. It was her that let me out of the cell at the police station. Who the hell put her in a place like Greengates House?"

Catty hung her head. "I did!"

The bell cut into their cold expectation like an ice pick.

Twenty-Two

It was shortly after one when Cubby Watson brought the black plastic bag into the front, downstairs office of the Clarion Evening News offices which were round the corner from the police station, took it into the receptionists office and told her that he required some privacy so he would appreciate her making herself scarce for the next ten or fifteen minutes. She reluctantly left her half-eaten lunch to do his bidding and heard the door to her office shut after her with one thrust from Cubby's right foot. The fact that her cardboard wedge of mature Cheshire cheese, pickled onion and mayonnaise on brown bread, had already been opened, the crusts drying in a shaft of hot sunshine, mattered not a jot to Cubby. As usual, his own needs would come first as he spread the boxes on the floor and delved within, using a pencil shaft to move them or turn them:-

Clarke's red, buttoned shoes.

A small red and white spotted, smocked dress with a label that said that it had been made to fit a child of four to six years of age of the Little Princess range of clothing.

The underwear was thick cotton with frilly lace bits and recognisable as of good quality, despite the black silt that had discoloured it.

All items had dried but still retained the canal stench.

The handbag he discounted as something which could not possibly belong to the child. He could see no reason for its inclusion in the same batch of evidence. He assumed, after recalling seeing it come out of the water at roughly the same point of the canal where the child had been rescued, that such was its only significance.

The sack held no interest for him other than to cause him to wonder again what kind of human animal tried to drown a small, innocent kid. Mally Kenyon? Now skipped from Quinton Police Station; a fact which seemed to point to guilt rather than innocence.

With thirst he sipped at the cup of coffee on the desk and mewed at the taste of sugar while he looked at the small items of underwear, realizing that he had not a clue about children's clothing. There was no cardigan or coat. In a small, clear, plastic bag he saw some red hair clips and bobbles. He would have to take advice on all the garments from someone who might tell him where the items had been purchased. Where people shopped was indicative of their social status. His mother thought the Queen lived on the top floor of Trimbles with her second home within the buyer's offices at Marks and Spencer. Even as he started to pare through the files of reports and photographs he found his mobile from his pocket and rang Marjory's landline number. The fact that she was not answering at home and not answering her own mobile, either, was typical of a woman too old to depend on one for total balance in her life. She always switched it off, anyway, when on the bench at the Magistrates' Courts. Today she would be passing sentence upon the lad called Jacko, who had escaped detention at Greengates House; so much for high security. Wherever she was she was not answering her phone; not even on voice mail.

Failing being able to ask his mother about the clothing labels on the child's clothes, he mentally trawled through the list of his old girlfriends for inspiration on who he might ask for an opinion concerning where the clothing might have come from. It would have taken too long to have rung round the local shops; patience not being one of Cubby's virtues. He knew no one with small children. He kept coming back to Gina Mon as a woman who would be his biggest fund of knowledge over a wide range of issues if he was to discover the kid's identity and be first to publish it. He still harboured a hope that she would join him for a late lunch at the Italiana.

He was reminded, again, of Gina's undoubted attractiveness and the fact that he still had the smell of her in his memory...hospital antiseptic mixed with pear drops. It had attracted him like a pheromone. She had radiated body heat, too, which he found pleasant to recall. Would not, in fact, have minded getting closer. Even the fact that she had been taller than him in trainers had not been off-putting.

All this a momentary lapse in concentration as he dropped his phone back into his coat pocket and picked up a full frontal, colour photograph of the rag doll with the head of orange, thrums hair which had been set beside a metre rule to show that it measured, when lying flat, roughly fifty centimetres from the tip of its hair to the tip of its shoes. It had a tag sewn into the seam of its trousers but he could not read the words without his glasses. He too vain, most of the time, to wear them.

So much to ponder other than the source of the clothing. Where the hell were rag dolls sold in Quinton? However, while he realised this as a valid point he realised, also, that time was getting on. He just had sufficient time to photograph or photocopy a cross section of the evidence and file notes and steal one of the red hair grips which he slipped into his pocket before parcelling everything up again. By the time he left the receptionist's office he had eaten the receptionist's sandwiches, emptied her coffee cup and pinched two filter tips out of her packet of cigarettes.

Taking it all with him he dropped the bag only long enough to take her in his arms, waltz her twice round behind her counter, smile cheekily, deposit a fiver down her cleavage for a replacement lunch, and then make off with his booty. The fact that she was a plump matron of forty who had worked for the Clarion for twenty-two years and seen him grow from short pants to short length trousers allowed him a certain measure of forgiveness.

"I need a new office chair," she complained as he took to the other side of her counter and made on his way again.

"Try asking my mother." However, before the year was out he planned to have the shabby offices repainted and the worn, rubber floors carpeted. Maybe his dad put out to grass. Some of the junior staff were baying to take Cubby's place. He might appoint himself Editor, with his mother's blessing, as long as he could find a few hungry bloodhounds to track down local news, write it with the gore still on their teeth and get it out there with bloody paw prints staining the paper in imitation of his own inimitable style, of course.

It was while Cubby was getting into his car, the black plastic bag on his passenger seat once more, that he saw his father leave the Clarion offices, stand for a moment to turn his coat up at the collar and hide his face under a new, stylish Homburg hat. He seemed to be shaking his head on something as he set his leather-shod feet in the direction of his usual parking place ignoring the next-door, public house where he usually enjoyed a largely liquid lunch before returning for the final editing of the day's edition of the newspaper at the Clarion offices. Cubby had, in fact, already divested this responsibility elsewhere.

He had no sooner found his car keys from his pocket, however, than he stopped walking with sudden abruptness, turned about just as Cubby slipped into his driving position and switched on the engine as if changing his mind yet again. CC seemed not to be aware of his son watching him.

For a moment Cubby wondered why he should suddenly seem to change his mind and start to walk quickly the other way again towards the station taxi ranks, where a parade of black cabs waited for the incoming trains. By the time he had hailed and got into a cab Cubby was already pulling out into the traffic and heading in the same direction as the cab his father had commandeered. Cubby found himself a very discreet two cars behind him.

Where was he going? His father's sudden change of plan intrigued him and especially when it was almost unheard of for his father not to start his afternoon stint without a lunchtime session in the pub next door. When he looked at his watch, Cubby measured that he had ten minutes or more to spare before his arranged meeting with Panda to return the evidence boxes. If his dad had taken a taxi he could not be going far. It would be somewhere where he would not like his distinctive red Jaguar sitting like a beacon in some street or car park where he would prefer not to be recognised. Another mistress somewhere? A case of Viagra accomplishing what the body dissipated couldn't, Cubby thought?

Better to be prepared! Something troublesome was brewing between his parents if his father's worried face was anything to go by. He could feel it instinctively. So Cubby followed the cab on the same route that he had made twice already that day, passing the locked gates of Greengates House, continuing under the train bridge and then keeping on the same, main road after where he had twice earlier that day turned to gain access over the canal bridge to the Dog's Bed Estate.

He stayed two cars behind until the cab came to Lower Quinton High Street then turned right down Fenton Street. A strange way for his father to go, he considered, as he signalled right, himself, nipping dangerously in front of a bus in order to follow. Seeing the taxi turn left at the last street directly before the park railings.

Cubby slowed his distinctive car to a crawl in fear of being noticed should his father turn to look through the rear window of the slow moving cab. He had not been along these streets since he had played league football long ago on the playing fields bordering the Whemley canal. Close, in fact, to where the child had been found, he was reminded. Not that he could see his father heading for the municipal park and its playing fields. It was light years since his father had played football from anywhere but an armchair. The park was derelict almost, save for the occasional use of the bandstand for civic functions when they tidied it up and brought a few planted tubs to hide the broken down appointments. A mere full of reeds and sunken boats; the same place that two swans had been speared through their wings and their signet killed before the swans had somehow managed to fly away. That event had horrified the people of Quinton even more than the issues of child neglect he frequently raised as part of his criticism of the local social services provision.

Not that Cubby had the time to ponder much on other things as he realised that he would have to get a move on if he was not to be late back with the evidence boxes. Panda had a grave dislike of being messed about. She would be in a lather of worry until he got the evidence boxes and files back to her again. If he wanted to retain her as one of his more useful moles he had better not be late for their meeting.

Throwing caution to the winds Cubby followed as far as the end of the street leading down from the High Street. With curiosity calling he hopped from his car and, with great care not to be seen, peeked round the corner to see his father ringing at a doorbell roughly half way along the terrace. The cab now turning the far corner of the street. He saw him then step over the threshold as if someone had opened the door for him. As if he was expected.

Cubby counted down from the number of the corner house, removing two from the start number all the way when he saw that it was number forty-two and the next one down, number forty. The house his father had entered was number thirty-four, Park Road, in the middle of the terrace; a house with a black and mint green gate and flowering azaleas in the small garden which separated it from the pavement. A brown and black, tabby cat sat on the wall in front of it. Then he set back the way he had come. Panda was waiting. It seemed as if trouble was brewing at home. Cubby could only guess that his visit to this down-at-heel area was to do with his father having another woman.

Twenty-Three

How much a man might curse himself makes little difference to the outcome.

C. C. Watson stepped through the gate of number thirty-four, Park Road, and back into his disreputable past as the door was opened by the veiled figure he barely cast a glance towards. His familiarity with the interior, as well as his anger, led him to push hard on the sticking vestibule door as he went through it. It was the frisking from behind that caught him mid-stride before even his stunned eyes alighted on Serena and her sister together, when he groaned and raised his hands in cooperative mode.

It was obvious that he had initially thought that Catty was there in her official capacity but undercover. Most probably the police had used the contents of the red handbag to trace little Caitlin's home. It was with some shock and an increased trepidation that he saw that the man who had removed Serena's veil from his head and was now removing something other than his phone from his own mackintosh pocket was none other than Mally Kenyon; a villain well-known from his mug shot on the lesser pages of the Clarion. That he had escaped detention had become public knowledge and was now a matter of the police appealing for help on the local radio.

What he removed along with the phone Mally Kenyon might find to prove most useful to a man on the run; a small Derringer pistol. "What you plan to do with this then?" Then he laughed dryly in Serena's direction. "Maybe I was sent by fate to save you."

CC hung his head. He had turned from a greenish grey to grey white at sight of Mally Kenyon. He knew that whoever had mugged Serena might have made all the connections. However he had fully expected Mally Kenyon no longer to be in the vicinity of northern England never mind in Lower Quinton. It was all over the news that he had walked out of Quinton Police Station before being given polite permission to leave. He was compounding the belief that he was the one who had abducted and abused little Caitlin. Which served him right in CC's eyes merely for whom and what he was; human vermin.

Mally Kenyon was now being hunted with a vengeance by the police cars roaming the streets. They had already turned out all the dodgy businesses under the railway station arches and found no trace of him. CC had passed by and seen them as he had ridden in the taxi cab. The cab had followed the riot vans on their way out to the Dog's Bed Estate. They were, perhaps, expecting one of his family or some sympathetic person to be sheltering him. Never here. Here was the last place CC had considered that a man fleeing arrest would come.

His eyes strayed to the sisters, guilt and secrecy smearing his face. It was the first time he had seen Serena unveiled. His face spread with distaste. Then his eyes lowered away from Catty's. Now she knew. He couldn't give a damn about her. It was just Marjory whom he dare not allow to find out about his bastard daughter. The very thought of it caused him to go cold in his innards like an arctic tundra freezing over. He had switched off the phone, which Mally had taken from him, because he could not face Marjory's wrath even on the end of a telephone should she find out. Should she find out! God alone knew how his life would go if she cut him from her apron strings. He needed a drink. He could not think straight. His hands were shaking.

"You were hiding her from Marjory I gather."

"As well as you. What else was I to do? Don't forget that little Caitlin is as much your daughter as she is mine. Equal responsibility. At least I protected her."

When an argument threatened to ensue, Mally quickly shut them up. "Not now. I need to think." He extracted Catty's car keys and stared at them.

CC knew better than to argue further. He wrung his hands together. He felt like falling to his knees to beg. Why had he brought the gun? He would have been too cowardly, anyway, to use it.

Catty spoke in a whisper to her sister. "Just do as Mally says. Perhaps, Serena, I was sent to protect you, too. Let us please start again. I promise not to leave you no matter what he does to us. We will walk out of this together. I give you my word that this time I will not fail the child, either. Or you!" Her hand reached out imploringly.

Serena allowed her own misshapen one to be taken. "Your job...! You'll be missed! You will be implicated!"

Catty shook her head as she assessed her own worth to those she had had to dominate into obedience. A vast relief washed over her. "Good riddance most probably. My deputy will simply take my place when I don't return. I should have been away this weekend anyway. On leave. They'll not think to question the fact that I am not there. What do they care? It was timetabled as his rota. Time has come, anyway, I think."

Both hands were cold yet they sought whatever warmth might be collected between them. They leant into each other as they were required to sit to bide out a bout of thinking time as he prowled restlessly about from sitting room to kitchen and back again, while the clock on the mantle shelf ticked endlessly on. The one thing that they all could be sure of was that Mally Kenyon was not a man to make quick decisions, unless his temper was riled, when he thought not at all.

CC sat as far away from them as he could over by the window on a straight backed chair, hands sunk deeply into his pocket, his Homburg hat; so very trendy looking, secreting his face.

Catty found herself looking at her sister's face in a way that she had never done since the horror of seeing her shortly after her birth when there had been little more than a hole where a nose and mouth should have been; nothing to smile with. Her eyes on the corners of her forehead as if something had disturbed the formation of her face, the final development of her digits, fusing the three fingers of one of her hands together. Her mother convinced that it had been the fright of a dog which had jumped at her during her pregnancy having caused the developing foetus in her womb to curdle. Indeed, as Serena had claimed she had also heard her mother bemoan with shame the daughter she hid from the world within the cellar spaces, while her father had taken boarding to the windows and put up shades and thick drapes to hide her away. Leaving Serena behind when they went out into the world, shuttering her in when they went out to the shops, veiling her on the rare times that they had no choice but to take her with them. Her parents preferring to take only Katrina to show to the world. Enhancing all her talents with pride while Serena was contained and buried alive as if she was worthless; a reject they could not remould into the patterns acceptable to social expectation. In this very house. In this very same place. Was it any wonder that Serena should know no different?

How come that she had never thought of her sister as a thinking, feeling, disappointed woman, flesh of her own flesh, of equal mind as herself? Someone with rights and needs and hopes and dreams. Someone who needed compassion but, more than that, to be respected rather than blamed. Indeed, part of her own unwillingness towards motherhood had been the fear that Serena's afflictions lived in recession within her own genetic make-up only to come out again in future generations. Such responsibility was hers as much as it was Serena's. Knowing too that every human being carries a genetic potential which when combined with the same recessive gene may produce a mutation.

That it was the expectation that was disappointed and not the damaged child itself suddenly became apparent to Katrina. Serena had been herded ahead of them all down the dark passages of her childhood, roped and blindfolded as if she had been the cause of her own afflictions and, thereby, fully responsible for them. She had been unfairly made to accept full responsibility of her own abnormality by her own family; her own flesh and blood as if she had fashioned it through her own making. She had been blamed for being what she could not help but be. A blight from God. A punishment on her parents. There had been no empathy or kindness within their own hearts for a child so subjected to their tyranny that they would hide her away. She would accept their tyranny as that which she deserved for being as nature had made her. There had been no loving hands to draw her sister into the bosom of a caring family; into the sunlight to know a different life.

Even so, Catty had entrusted her sister to take away the bloody pail of her guilt and do with it as she would. There had ever been a strength about Serena that defied the deformities and the delicacy of her physical existence under her enveloping clothes, under the veils. A quiet but determined character which had allowed her to survive and overcome. To have in the end that which her sister had denied herself; a child. There was suddenly within Catty a painful need to see the child she had rejected and try to make amends. To be the lady with the golden trumpet. To play the notes loud and clear and pure for her sister, also, because those who can be piper might hide themselves within the cunning of the music for a short time at least.

The time had come to face herself. The memory of the tiny hand and tiny foot waving in the pail; indeed, no bigger than those of a doll, shamed and humiliated her. She had not solved a problem but instigated a guilt that had lain within and hidden. Her guilt was not biodegradable and would never go away.

And now Serena's head was bare. Catty found a scarf from her coat pocket and offered it. The offer was genuine.

Serena shook her head. "No thank you. It's time I was done with them." Her mouth was raised and puckered with her stubbornness. "I will not be ashamed."

"You are ill?" It had to be asked again.

Serena nodded, shrugged, and sighed. "I need to have her future settled." Her eyes were asking quietly. They were not begging for Catty to help but merely beseeching some higher force than hers. Not for herself but for the child that bridged the gap between them.

Catty understood that Serena was stating her terms. Was it blackmail or persuasion? Something stirred unbidden; a deep and lingering regret, not concerning her child but more her sister. They had never known each other. For what time remained unto them she would strive to change that situation.

Catty's phone rang in Mally's pocket; a trumpet fanfare. This time he switched it on and whispered breathily; a man used to deception.

"Yes?"

What he heard caused him to frown deeply. A voice gabbled quickly and urgently into his cocked ear where a rim of canal silt had dried as dirt. He disconnected without saying anything. Whoever had spoken would have thought that Ma'am was in one of her moods again. He looked at his watch. It was shortly after four thirty in the afternoon.

Then he found his own phone and Benny's number which he scrolled to. He pressed the command for the number to be rung. It was answered with a muted tone as if in a place closed in and full of echoes. The voice that answered was deep, low and strangely satisfied. It travelled to all their ears in a satisfied mumbo-jumbo without what was being said being understood by anyone but the man with his grimy ear pressed to the phone.

Mally's reply came down hard on the voice stopping any further rambling. "Where? Tell me and I'll meet you there."

Laughter was heard loud and silly like someone on drugs. Above themselves.

Then, "I need her, Benny. She can vouch for me. She can get me off the wrap as no one else can. What?" His eyes settling on CC as the satisfied mumble explained something further. Mally's lips pursed white and as tight as drawn laces, a square chin of bristle prominent, his nose flared wide. The Mally Kenyon who might be feared when his temper broke. He covered his mouth to stop his angry, tightly spoken reply being overheard, but his eyes were threatening a lightning strike even as he spoke, fast and harsh. Most of what he said in a language not fit for the ears of gentle folk. "Fuck you, then. So much for family when money calls." This overheard clearly as he disconnected the call and rammed the mobile back into his pocket, hearing the cheap seams split to denote his strength of feeling. "My brothers are bastards, the pair of them."

Whatever had been said to him was not repeated for the benefit of the whole company. His face was sour. He roughly took hold of Serena's arm and pulled her towards him, anger inside him still yet blaming someone else, not her.

What he would not tell them was that his brothers would leave him to take the can yet again for what they had just done in the furtherance of their own aims. He was on his own. Such was life when the rent man knocked at the door and the foolish one who opened it up to him would be the one to pay. Mally had opened that door when he had been the one to stupidly bring a child from the water, save it from drowning, put himself forward only to take the wrongful blame for having caused the situation in the first place.

He might have been better to disappear altogether with a one way, worked passage on a cargo boat to Outer Siberia or South America, as Serena had suggested, but such would abet his guilt. For once in innocence, betrayed by his brothers, they would steal that which might harm most the man who stood staring, now, deep into his own regretful thoughts.

What he had achieved through his phone call to his brother was a confirmation of what the interception of Ma'am's phone call had just told him. Some woman called Sandra, thinking him to be the person she really wanted to inform; Ma'am herself, had blurted out that the situation had changed drastically. A new development had taken place and just when all their resources had been directed elsewhere. The child and her minder had been kidnapped from Greengates House and whisked away.

When Dr Thomas had been unable to get through on the telephone it had been Brian Ghould who had taken himself into the station and was awaiting her pleasure to discuss the occurrence in her office. She was late. Ms Collins being urgently required to return to the station to liaise with the unexpected head of Child Welfare. "Can't be anyone other than Mally Kenyon's taken her either," she had argued despite the fact that an opinion had not been asked of her and she was unqualified to give one. "The child's life is in danger again he says. Mally Kenyon will shut her up for good rather than let her give testimony against him. He'll go down good and proper this time."

Mally had disconnected and then spoken directly to Catty as if he found her personally to blame. "The child's been abducted no more than a half hour ago. You'll know it's not me as has taken her this time. Can't have a better alibi than the Chief Constable herself." Then with greater deliberation; "Decision made. We're going to get the car. Me and Serena. Me and your sister together, arm in arm like lovers in case anyone's watching. Do anything stupid and I'll make her pay for it. Understand?" Then he thrust two keys into Catty's hand. "One for the back door. One for the back gate. Meet me out back in the alley in a few minutes. I'll drive round that way. You're going to help me save the child. If it's the last thing I do I'll prove my innocence. I'll save the child. I think I know where they might take her."

Then to CC who was looking inward at his own fear with knees knocking, his hip flask empty after he had drained it deep on the taxi ride, his life being wiped out before his very eyes. Mally Kenyon spoke with vehemence and distaste. "Do whatever you choose. Go to the police and you'll know what it is to have your name all over the front pages. Who knows you're here unless you tell them? Won't suit a beak will it to be implicated in scrubbing away the filthy skid marks on them fancy kecks of yours?" Then he removed CC's little gun from his own pocket and for a moment pointed it at him. Enjoying watching CC's face pale. "Like I said...do as you please." Then he handed the gun back to him carefully. It was on a safety catch but it had been loaded. Still was!

CC looked totally confused as he took it back.

It was Catty rose and taking the scarf she had offered to Serena once more from her pocket she snatched up the gun from CC's palm and wiped it clean of all prints before giving it back to him. "From this day forth, CC, I will accept full responsibility for the child. As I will for my sister. Come anywhere near any of us ever again and I'll take my own gun and blow your fucking brains out. That I promise."

It landed back in the same, soft, open palm; the hand of a man who had never done any physical work in his lifetime...never dug his own rose beds...never cleaned his own windows...never tidied up his own shed. Now only his own prints might be upon it. He was being told to go. He was free to go. He could not believe it as he scurried out of the house like a frightened rabbit. Even before he heaved the vestibule door open he was running. He would not stop until he got to the Glass Barrel Inn.

Mally Kenyon was an enigma because he would be trusting Catty, too. He would trust enough to leave her alone within the house where once her sister had been so poorly valued yet now held the key to her doing as he asked. The place where so many erroneous tributes concerning her own importance had been formulated at the expense of an unfortunate sister...the same furniture...the same half light...the same stuffy air made toxic by the gas fire which ate up the oxygen and fuddled the brain. Her thoughts upon what he had said and which she believed in, now, as a kidnapped convert within a cult sect might believe after indoctrination. Her own future abandoned. All her commitments changed. A hollow space inside her, now, as if the coarse sand of her existence had filtered from a cold hollow which she required to be refilled, again, more warmly. The hollow being Wendy Caitlin Bridgewater Collins. The child had been abducted once again. He said that he was going to save her. Something in his face told her to trust and hold that faith. For the first time she had seen within Mally Kenyon a gleam of integrity within the tarnish and the grime. A bad judge of men she, even so, believed his intentions to be honourable. She did not understand why a man like Mally Kenyon should thus change himself about but she believed his intentions...that he would help her and Serena's situation by saving the child...as well as to prove that he was innocent.

She determined to do all she could to abet that situation as her only course of action. Serena must not be harmed, also, and strangely she trusted him not to do so. Serena had seemed to have come to her own conclusion by allowing him to look upon her and not cower from his stare. He seemed to have some idea of what might be done to save the child whom she might come to recognise as her own. It was as if she had not only stepped out of her uniformity she had also stepped out of her old life; her old existence. Her old self had died. What she said came with honesty. "I will help you all I can."

He nodded back at her. "I think I know where they might have taken her. The last place to look."

A pact had been made. She tried to reassure him of her faith. "Not under the station arches. I approved a search of those earlier on. They're now under guard."

Mally shook his head. "Contrary to opinion, Ma'am, Kenyon's aren't stupid. But Father Turner is. Too trusting. The church crypt where he allows the tramps to sleep. Even equips it with an ever open door and a sleeping bag. Bottles of water and a tin of corned beef. Stores his church junk down there and the coal for the church furnace. The inner basement door kept locked when he values his gold cross and silver chalices but the one to the outside from his cellar kept open and off the snip for years. No outside handle though. Just a screwdriver is all that's needed to get inside."

Serena nodded with a look of defiance in her silver fish eyes, as she raised her chin against her sister, because what she was about to do she doubted that Catty would approve. She went to a kitchen drawer and brought back exactly what he required. She mewed at her sister as she handed it over; a small but strong screwdriver as if to dare her to question. Mally put it in his coat pocket, his pants already bulging with phones. She spoke with the high, prim voice of justification. "Are you not going to call the station as soon as we are gone, Catty? There's a phone box on the corner which answers to nine, nine, nine."

Catty's snort spoke of her change of allegiance. "Not yet. Not while you and our child are unsafe and Mally is still being hunted for a crime he did not commit. I swear."

Serena nodded in gratitude, but she could not yet trust that which she had never been in receipt of previously. Only hope for the situation being saved might be contemplated. "If we can get her back no one need know…we can even yet see her off to school…we can be happy…she will learn that it isn't a bad place given time."

Catty saw her naivety formed from her sister's separation from the real world. Then shook her head on what had yet to be. "It will have to be legally dealt with if she is to be allowed to live a life without secrecy,

Serena. We will cross that bridge when we come to it. It will be enough for the moment to know that she is alive...unharmed...as I should have ensured in the first place. You have done too much to keep her alive for all to be wasted. Also to know that Mally is cleared of the charges that have been made against him falsely. I admit to being responsible for that miscarriage of justice in the first place. That has, now, with her disappearance become compounded by her having been taken. Your brothers I take it?"

Mally nodded. "They'll sell her to the highest bidder."

He allowed Serena to tarry only long enough to don an outside coat and the thick sheepskin boots and gloves which she needed to protect her fragile skin. His rough hand leaving her arm only long enough for her to slide into her coat, don a headscarf, at his insistence. Under her dress the skin on her upper arm had already started bleeding as it tore like tissue paper under the rough handling which his ignorance failed to understand was more than her fragile constitution could withstand. If she said nothing it was because he had become her only hope of saving the child she cherished so dearly. As if no more an afterthought he took hold of the handle of the shopping trolley and carried it with him. Then he chucked little Caitlin's coat and scarf within. Gestures, Catty thought, towards his own determination. But strangely she trusted him.

As he offered her her phone back she shook her head. "I will do all I can to help you. I have said so. I have given my word. Better I am not informed of what my colleagues are doing...if indeed there is the manpower available to do anything!"

Serena looked with gratitude towards her sister. She spent a moment giving thanks. All her life she had been alone. All her life she had had to help herself to stay strong and brave and hopeful, save for those small mercies which she asked of Him. Despite what Katrina had said she could not quite believe her though her actions now suggested that she might a little. She had no choice. But the man; this Mally Kenyon, she believed in totally as her only hope of salvation. The fervour in his eyes told her that her faith would not prove to be displaced. Her only other hope had evaporated within the wastage of the situation. When she had seen the Homburg hat come out of the taxi...! But that had been too much to hope for no matter a promise made.

"We'll get the car. Meet you by the back gate. Don't tarry to lock up. Leave the keys in the doors but close them. We may need to return."

Catty nodded. "Hear me, Serena. I shan't leave you," she called after them as they left the house, her sister being dragged yet not unwillingly towards her own vehicle. What Serena did not hear nor anyone

261

other than herself was her last, deep whispers as she closed the door and looked at the cold keys in the palm of her hand... "I...I need you...I need you both. Dear God help us. Help Mally Kenyon. Cherish the child. Bring her back to me. I will never let her fade away from me again."

Twenty-Four

It was just after two-thirty when Holly got back to Greengates House. She was late! Her mind was reeling. What she had found was a warm and welcoming family but one, she had discovered, of relative strangers. Even so she had made a good beginning. Her reception had warmed her heart. Her mind was dancing. She could never recall in the whole of her life, before, crying tears of joy and happiness. At the same time the Devil inside her refused to trust what most people might trust completely...their own flesh and blood family.

She had felt emotionally flattened by the time they had waved her on her way with promises to meet again soon. Her grandfather seeing her safely through the ever growing, stinking barrier which was now so high and so wide that even the tallest people had a job to see over...and back to the broken lift bridge. There was so much agitation to see and feel that Holly felt glad to leave it behind, at least for the present.

"Whatever you do stay away from here tonight. There's trouble brewing. It's never safe for a female to roam the Dog's Bed on her own, anyway, after a certain time of day. At least where you're working couldn't be safer. Nobody likely to want to break in there even if they could get over them big green gates and high fences. Safest place in Quinton I reckon."

If she might have been tempted to abandon the work she had accepted at Greengates House, she had become reminded that while she had braved the emotional turmoil of a reunion they were all in need of a period of time for reflection. It would serve them all better for Holly to withdraw so that they may all take some personal space. Perhaps talk between themselves. Maybe Holly could talk it over with Angie.

Though her identity could not be doubted by any of them. She looked to be a spitting image of her mother but also had something, too, of the man whose face Magdalene showed her within a gold locket which she wore around her neck. "That's Bass, your dad. If you see someone who looks exactly like him walking about it will be Mally, his twin brother. Although at the moment that isn't likely."

That name again! He had been the one at the police station who had simply walked out when Holly had held the door open for him. She had heard Angie speaking about him to Harry. He had been described as a hard man who had been suspected of being the one to try to drown the same child she had been employed to look after and then repented enough to be the one to save her. Holly was beginning to think that anyone on the receiving end of Wendy Bridgewater's temper might have good reason to want to drown her in a weighted sack!

However, not the most reputable of families were the Kenyons it would seem. Something in the genes! They had yet to know Holly's track record also. Best to take time. Think about the situation. Be better prepared the next time they met to discover some truth about each other, Holly considered, with wisdom greater than her years. She could not give her trust freely to people who had let her down so very badly. Time was needed for the truth behind the masks people use to fall away. She had seen such within the adoptive and fostering families she had been placed with. People were rarely as they seemed on the surface. Not just Holly Hargreaves who used to be Kenyon.

Also Holly was frightened that once they knew everything about her they would no longer want her back within the family fold. Especially when she had several faces, herself, to cover all her own shortcomings and guard her most sensitive feelings. She was adept at making people believe that only they knew the real Holly Hargreaves... a school dropout...a girl with a past...hard as nails at eighteen years of age...a cheat, a thief and a liar. Someone who had come to Quinton with a bogus set of qualifications to help her get a job she was definitely not qualified to do. Someone who had no right because of her previous *disaffected* history to be working with a vulnerable child like Wendy Bridgewater. Or maybe...because of who she was...she was better qualified than even Tommo was, as long as her intentions were above board and in the kid's best interests. If she could get the kid to trust her, too, and read her right maybe she might find out who she really was. Get to the bottom of the mystery surrounding her. It made Holly feel better to think that, for once, she might do something that had someone else's benefit instead of always her own to the centre of her motivation.

She had told them almost nothing of herself just as they had spent their time together apologising to her, making excuses, justifying their actions to the young adult who, as a vulnerable child, they had allowed to be taken into care. They had been unable to cope; stressed out and keeled over her grandfather had explained. Holly could recall, now, some of the angry feelings. They had been a family in crisis. Would she have fared any better if she had been allowed to stay? Holly's unspoken, angry reply to such a question was, *Yes, I would!*

Full of pretence, too, as Nan had brought out her best china as if they used it every day. Magdalene had poured steaming, golden tea from a china teapot with rosebuds on the lid. Tipped milk from its relation. The best biscuits had been put on a gold rimmed, china plate. Those tiny, wafer thin ones with the chocolate barely covering the edges. They had melted on her fingers as she ate.

They had taken their refreshment over a white linen tablecloth in a very tidy parlour of crowded, highly polished, old fashioned furniture where only strangers were entertained. They had conversed in stilted fashion after the initial shock and surprise had been accepted with a lot of polite apology for speaking out of turn. Showing their manners. Her adoptive mother had had a thing about Holly *showing her manners*. No elbows on the table. Prayers of thanks before a meal. Asking politely if she may please leave the table at the end. Always saying thank you and adding the person's name. No slouching in each other's company. Sitting back straight and knees together. They, too, had all spoken politely with each other in the way of strangers.

While her mother might grip her hand under the table and they had hugged and kissed and cried, they were no more than people meeting for the very first time after a lapse of several years. Trying to impress each other shyly. All of them feeling, perhaps, after the first half hour that Holly had charged at them all too quickly when she might have warned them of her coming. Truth being that Holly had charged at herself in order to find the courage to come here.

Holly needed some personal space to reflect, too, for it had all happened too suddenly for any of them to absorb the reality of it. She had come to Quinton on a whim to find her family purely for the satisfaction of spurning them. That bitterness still remained under the sugar coated pretensions they were all intent on sporting. There was still the hurt to contend with, too. She had not yet forgiven and forgotten. Not time yet to move in with them though her grandmother had been all for it. "We have a spare bedroom. It's a bit cramped. We call it the box room because it's over the stairwell but it'll be big enough for a tiddler like you. We need to get to know each other again, Holly."

A tiddler! Holly towered over Nan Bartlett just as Magdalene did. They all looked down onto her gypsy-dressed head. Only Holly seemed to be amused by the fancy dress of an amateur fortune teller. Tock, her granddad, with a drooping moustache, towered over them all. He had, also, offered her a room at The Dog's Bed Inn. And a job. "I'll teach you all I know. Bartlett's have been pub landlords for three generations past. Get rid of that damned barmaid, too, whose fleecing me rotten. Fingers in the till. I have a feeling she's in with the drug runners who keep using my toilets." The rejection making him feel obliged to make up for his failure to support his granddaughter once he and Nan had parted company. Maybe it hadn't occurred to him that he knew more about his barmaid than he did about his granddaughter. Such was where blood ties made people trust, sometimes, where trust was not warranted. For all he knew she might have been as deep into drugs as her parents had been. Looking at Magdalene, now, though, all that was hard to believe.

It was as if Magdalene, drinking tea and not smoking like a chimney like her dad did had read Holly's thoughts. She had smiled at Holly with the same shape and colour of eyes that Holly painted and preened and flirted with every day of her life. She regarded them as her greatest asset and especially when rimmed with taupe eye shadow and black liner and mascara. Magdalene needed no make-up; wore none. Her face was open, calm, and serene. "These days, I'm clean. No men in my life either."

Her mother rolled her eyes at her. "Enough dogs at the gate though. You have enough sniffing after you, Magdalene. Mally, for one. Another Kenyon! As if his twin brother wasn't enough." Then realizing what she had said, her hand reaching out to pat Holly's arm. "Oh, Holly, love! He was your dad! I shouldn't have said that. It's just that he led your mother off the rails."

Now it was Magdalene's turn to roll her eyes. "I did that for myself, Mum. Just as I brought myself back onto the right track again. With a bit of help from my family and friends."

Tock had winged his moustache and looked concerned. "Let's not start a family row just as our Holly's come back into the fold." Then to Holly. "You'll not be used to the way we let it all spill out and hold nothing back...Dog's Bed folk!"

Then his eyes had been at the window glass though he could see out to nothing more than the tidy yard which backed onto the canal bank. There was plenty of noise going on out there. Sufficient to be informed of the anger within the community as people milled about the bridge and worked to their common aim. "What a time to arrive! Maybe we'd better continue all this when the place is all a bit more settled. My pub's full of press. Drinkers too intent on stirring up trouble. No stopping them from building that stinking barricade though it's all good for trade. War always is. What good's it going to do is what I keep asking though? The police can get into the estate down the lanes if they have to."

"It's the symbol of protest," Nan said with some defiance even though, like him, she disapproved of what her neighbours were doing. "The police had no reason to start pushing their weight about like they did this morning. Heard it on the news, too, that Mally managed to escape. Mark my words...they'll be back again looking for him."

"What?" Magdalene had looked shocked and surprised. "Mally's escaped from the police station? Why? He would have been better to have stayed and let the truth speak for itself. It always does in the long run."

Tock disagreed. "It would if everyone was as honest as you're naive, our Magdalene. Trouble is most folk aren't. But let's not put our Holly, here, off the Dog's Bed Estate as a place to live. Ninety percent of the neighbours are friendly and helpful and lead decent lives. There are actually worse places to live."

Nan would argue against anything. "Oh aye! Like where?"

"Like African villages in drought and famine...places where there's no fresh water on tap...little food...disease and no doctors or medicine...civil war going on to divide families, year in, year out... whole villages wiped out...limbs blown off by landmines...children as young as eight given drugs and guns and set to fighting..."

"Alright, alright!" Nan snapped. "No need to tell me. I know already. But does our Holly when she's been brought up in a leafy street with a garden with a proper family who dine together every evening and never quarrel."

Holly was aware that all her family were looking at her as if they had been taking tea with an alien. Time would come she knew to tell the truth but not yet. She was not ready to tell it. It was all too soon. Too fragile. She would have to plan all the lies that she was tempted to tell or simply abet the incorrect assumptions they were making in order to allow her mother and her grandparents to know some pride in a daughter who had nothing prideful to tell about her life since leaving the Dog's Bed Estate. They were of the opinion that she had been carefully nurtured as an adopted child within a loving home when such had been their justification for her abandonment. Holly was unable to find the words to set them straight.

All her possessions were still at Greengates House also. She had to return.

And so with joy and trepidation failing to settle comfortably together in her confused mind she pressed at the bell for entry through the small, side gate at Greengates House, feeling as if she had been caught up in a dizzying whirlwind which had whisked her off the planet to a different place and then, just as dizzyingly, deposited her back again at the same spot it had taken her from.

For how long the work would last had yet to be revealed. She would not be accepted into their fold, to be trusted with keys, codes and magic numbers until they had put her through her paces and she could demonstrate a sense of responsibility towards the care of the child. Tommo had already told her that she would not be allowed to know the numbers to operate the digital locks in order to come and go freely until her work had been assessed as efficient in other ways, too...that dratted writing in that damned, big, blue day book being Holly's main nightmare! After which he would make the decision of whether or not to retain her services for the duration that the child was at Greengates House.

Holly was already aware that Angie knew her birth family, too. What she had had to say about Mally Kenyon in passing conversation at the lunch table had not been particularly commendable. Too easy for Holly to be tarnished with the same brush before she had had opportunity to set a different first impression. If she made a better job of looking after the child than she knew that she had intended, hitherto, maybe she might redeem herself sufficiently to find some self esteem to share with her family when next they met. It had never seemed more important to Holly that she consider what others thought of her than it did now.

Back to Earth, it was Gary who came to let her in with a worried face and more bleeding scratches on the backs of his hands... so much for the nail cutting unless the dog had been the one to make his hands bleed again. "Thank goodness. We had begun to think you weren't coming back. All hell's broke loose again. Where's your packages?"

Holly passed through the gate realising that her excuse had been rumbled. She had gone without as much as a handbag or her purse. She could see Angie with her face at the kitchen window perhaps wondering, too, where she had been if not into town to shop. Harry was sweeping up after the last of his gardening and passing her disparaging looks as he deposited a shovel full of sweepings into a black bin bag. Tommo was probably with Wendy when she could not see him anywhere. He would be annoyed with her for returning a few minutes late. "I didn't get anything. I went to the shop on the Dog's Bed Estate..." not altogether a lie when she had walked past it. "...but it was closed. There's a lot of trouble going on. People are building this barricade across the bridge as a means of protesting about some police raid this morning. I met my mother." Holly was making revelations and knew it. She would have to try out this personal honesty thing some time or other. "Not seen her since I was seven."

Gary looked at her face with some concern registering on his own. His daughter had already told him what was happening on the estate. She and her mother were panicking because they lived close to the clubs and pubs on Lower Quinton High Street. When trouble brewed on the Dog's Bed they always seemed to suffer from whiplash. His own family was fractured by divorce, too, so he knew how easy it was to lose touch, become distant; different when the children are older. More complex than it had been when they had been young and welcomed him with open arms. These days he didn't even know where his son was. Could be dead for all he knew. He'd turned out a bad 'un, too. "Things okay otherwise? Family, I mean."

Holly nodded. "I think so. Early days...but I think it might be. If we all make an effort...maybe!"

"What's her name? Maybe I know her."

"Magdalene Kenyon."

Gary gasped. "S'truth! You're Bass Kenyon's daughter? Mally Kenyon's niece? Benny and Woody's also! Christ! What a pair they are!" Then he looked as if he regretted speaking. "Sorry kid but you should have told us all this earlier."

Holly was genuinely surprised. "Why? I'm just here to look after the kid. What difference will it make?"

"If Tommo knows he'll have you packed and out of here as soon as look at you. Your uncle's thought to be the one to have abused the kid in the first place. It's what's called a conflict of interest. Your treatment of her might be affected by the family link. Tommo's a stickler for doing things by the book. You didn't tell us you were a Kenyon. You told us your name's Hargreaves."

"It is. I was adopted. Put into care at seven. Does he need to know?" That seemed to bang all her ideas concerning personal honesty on the head. But then why should she be blamed for what other people did? "I can't remember him and he certainly didn't remember me when he pushed past us through the door at the police station. Besides, he saved the kid didn't he? Or so it's thought. Guilty until proven innocent."

"That's what being a bad boy does for you! Kenyons suffer because of their reputations more than their surname. Most deserve a bad reputation though. At least them that live on the Dog's Bed Estate." He thought for a moment. "Tell you what, kid. We all deserve a break sometimes. I'll play conveniently deaf as long as you don't go telling anyone else about you being a Kenyon."

"Compromise!"

Gary nodded. "But keep schtum! We won't get any other cover for the present. Not at this time of day...not someone to start straight away without any notice to get their things together. I'll keep schtum as long as you don't go telling Tommo you told me. Whatever you do don't tell Harry. He'll be counting all the garden forks and spades like he does when our usual clients are after digging their way out of here with anything they can get their hands on. Kenyons...other than Magdalene...have a bit of a reputation you might sooner not want Tommo tarnishing you with. Not until he knows you a bit better."

Holly's laugh was harsh. If Gary but knew she was already tarnished of reputation. She felt like saying that she had already begun to follow in the family footsteps then thought better of it. Instead she thought it time she got out her own polishing rags. Buffed herself up a bit. "Thanks, Gary. I want this job. I'll try not to let you down."

Then Gary made his confession, eyes rolling upwards. "This one is harder to handle than any oversized, angry lad. We can't work her out." They were now passing the white mini-bus and close enough to the house to be aware of the din. They could hear screams and crashes coming from the room which had been appointed as Wendy's bedroom.

As she looked up, shaking her head at her own lack of understanding for this latest temper tantrum, something smashed through the window glass, splintered itself against the outside bars and landed not too far from Gary's feet. They both looked down at the remains of a bedside clock, totally smashed to smithereens. "We need you. Big Boss is here to see this one. Just leaving. Seen enough, I think."

Holly looked to see a thin, white-haired stranger coming out, shaking hands with Tommo who stood in the doorway. In contrast to Tommo the man wore a matched suit, a very neat blue, striped shirt and a tie pinned with a gold clip. He nodded to both herself and Gary in friendly fashion yet remained slightly distanced in his manner, shaking his head from side to side. "Got your work cut out I see. Let me through the side gate, Gary, please. I'll leave you to it. My car's outside on the street."

Holly saw Tommo look at his watch as he stood in the doorway noting the time. Then shut the door after the stranger had left the house most inconsiderately when Holly could not get into the house without someone punching in the number on the digital lock on the front door for her. She had no choice but to wait for Gary knowing that she had a late mark, already, against her.

After Gary had come back from his mission he explained the strange man's full name and identification. "He's the big boss. Brian Ghould. Head of Child Welfare at Social Services. Used to work here in Tommo's place. Come just to see the kind of problem we're having to deal with, with this one. Worse, she is, than even our usual adolescents. She's in her room wrecking the place."

"Why's no one with her? Is it because I haven't been here?"

Gary shook his head. "Because we can observe her better from the office on the CCTV screen. Battered us enough, too." Looking at his stinging scratches which Angie had just bathed with antiseptic. "Never seen a temper like it. Strong little thing she is. The film lets us see things that the situation doesn't because of our involvement. Gives us a better incite to what triggers her bad behaviours too."

When they got to the office Tommo was watching the first screen on the right dispassionately. Holly was appalled. She had never witnessed anything like it in her life before. "She's smashed the room to pieces."

It was no exaggeration. Holly's mouth dropped open just to see the damage that the child had done. The plastic mirror had been attacked and now lay on its front where the frame was broken. The strong, single bed had its back broken also, its headboard collapsed, its duvet ripped to shreds and feathers everywhere. Now the child was doing something utterly disgusting and smearing it over the flooring. It was then that something tugged at Holly's heartstrings. The child was badly frightened and terribly angered by whatever was frightening her.

"She suddenly saw her reflection in the window glass and went crazy," Gary explained. "Kicked Tommo where it hurt most. Head butted Angie when she came to help and stabbed Harry in the leg with his own garden fork. I take it all back when I said that handling a seven year old girl between the four of us is a bit like cracking a walnut with a sledgehammer. This child's more trouble than Jacko ever was."

"So you just put her in her room and left her there." Holly felt herself becoming angry, her cheeks reddening. "No wonder she threw the clock at the window."

Tommo turned round from his note taking. "Her temper will cool once she has no one to spark against. She's on her own for that purpose. I have made note of the fact that you're five minutes late."

Twenty-Five

Wendy was not alone had they but known it! She was not only with Caitlin but another child, also, who had appeared with great suddenness to spoil all that was turning out to be such glorious fun. It had been a shocking state of affairs to realise that there was, in fact, another little girl at Blackstone School which was now called Greengates House. One who had stared back at her through Angie's kitchen window and had been doing everything that Wendy did, including looking for all the interesting things to be found in the grass and the newly dug soil as she had crouched on her haunches with everyone's attention upon her.

They had already eaten a very delicious lunch and gone out into the garden, again, because she had so wanted to smell the air and feel the sunlight on her once again. Tommo had found a large, mesh riddle in Harry's shed with which to isolate all the amazing things that Wendy was noticing in the strange medium she had never handled before. They did not complain as Serena might when her hands became dirty and her new pink track suit became grubby with such a new and interesting activity.

Wendy's curiosity had been insatiable. Gary had been helping her to use a small gardening fork to turn soil and put her findings into a bucket including the wriggling, pink worms and old leaves and stones and creepy, crawly things. After a short time, when Angie could take her place, Holly had gone off to do her shopping. Or had she gone off somewhere to bring the other little girl back with her? The one who Caitlin recognised as the first of many others in pink tracksuits. Just as Holly had been the one to bring Wendy. There was still so very much to be confused about.

When she had seen the other little girl holding up a wriggling worm and mimicking Wendy by doing exactly what she was doing, Caitlin had reacted with a suddenness that had startled even Wendy. It had, to Caitlin, been a frightening, overwhelming shock when she had considered herself to be the only child along with Wendy at a place she had started to discover was not as bad as expected. Wendy had been unable to hold back Caitlin's fear long enough for Caitlin to be introduced to the other little girl as Wendy might have advised to be the sensible thing to do. Her reaction had been immediate, inexplicable to others and violent. That was when she had kicked Tommo between his legs and scratched Gary's hands when he would have come to lift her up and away from what he had assumed had frightened her...something in the soil, perhaps!

Then Angie had come to comfort her and been attacked too. Gary had laid the gardening fork on the ground. Naughty Caitlin had

273

picked it up and used it to stab the bad tempered, surly man in the leg when he had come running towards her like the giant in one of the fairy stories which Serena had read to her, who ate little girls for breakfast. He would have lifted her up by the armpits and carried her away into his dark shed to put in his oven with some of the carrots he had said that he would be planting when she had stopped getting in his way and he could get on with planting his vegetable garden.

Caitlin's unpredictable tantrum had been enough for them all then because she had hurt them all in her violent struggle to get away from the little girl who had been looking at her through the kitchen window. Tommo, who had been struggling with a funny limp and Gary, with blood running down his hands again had lifted her between them, brought her up the stairs, put her into this strange room full of sunlight and strange furnishings, shut the door again and left her there. They had ignored her screams and terrified panic. They had ignored her beating fists and kicking feet as she had begged for them to come back and rescue her from all that Blackstone School represented in Caitlin's fearful imaginings, for she had come to think herself as a little princess again just as she had been with Serena in the cellar.

They had ignored her screams and terrified panic. They had ignored her beating fists and kicking feet as she had begged for them to come back and rescue her from the other pupils at Blackstone School. Tommo had told Gary as they left her alone that he was going to ring someone up and ask him to come to see what they were having to deal with, but it was a man by the name of Brian and, therefore, could not be the lady with the golden trumpet. Caitlin's anger had turned to seething frustration and then a huge and monstrous fear because she had never been inside this room before. She had only been in the bathroom. Too short of stature to have seen herself in the bathroom mirror earlier Caitlin was confronted with the very worst of her very worst fears...other girls! All that had ever happened before was that she had seen them through the eye of the cart as she and Serena had travelled around. Sometimes they had been pleasant to each other but often they smacked out and screamed. They had frightened her. Caitlin did not like other little girls and especially after she had been informed that her wonderful, happy world with Serena would soon be coming to an end. She would have to go to a school where she would have to share everything with other little girls. The very thought of that unknown terrified Caitlin. She would not go! She could not go! She could not share! She could not compete at games and in lessons because she did not know the rules and had no idea what would be expected of her. If she refused to go what could Serena do about it? Not with the brown ring to keep her safe. She would then be allowed to stay with Serena in the cellar and have the best of everything just for herself. For was she not a little princess?

Wendy, for her part, tried her best to teach Caitlin to be patient and wait. To have faith that the lady with the golden trumpet would want her back once she knew that Caitlin was alive and was such a clever little girl. That they would find her eventually if they looked for her hard enough. If Serena did not want them then the lady with the golden trumpet would. She would want even the naughty Caitlin who screamed and smacked and smashed and smeared because she came paired and was inseparable from the placid, cooperative Wendy whom anyone could love. The one who was trying so very hard to be a good girl and show Caitlin the right way to behave so that they might all be happy again; Serena, included... *We have to be like Oswald, Caitlin, and make ourselves fit the cracks and the spaces in the toy box with everything else. Then we can both be happy because we will be loved for ourselves.*

Yet Caitlin would have nothing of what she did not want or did not understand. And so, once again, the child was in distress. Wendy submerged under Caitlin's greater, short-term strength. All those who might have protected her, even now having left her alone in a room of strange shapes and shadows, with big, windows bringing in the light despite the metal bars of a prison being on the outside.

Was this the dormitory that Serena had told her about? Only one bed not several that, maybe, had to be shared? A big room where the other little girls were hiding ready to jump out at her and frighten her witless...under the bed...inside the wardrobe...behind the curtains! Where were the hateful little girls in the same pink track suits hiding themselves?

Caitlin's fear started to escalate within the room where they had abandoned her. Then she saw what she had never seen before in the whole of her life; a dressing mirror... a looking glass...a thing forbidden at 34, Park Road, Lower Quinton. It rose from the floor in a mount of pinewood on balled feet so that the same child she had seen earlier with a red and tear stained face floated in the air ten inches from the floor, her chin high, and her eyes wide and fearful of Caitlin. She wore the same clothes; little school girls all having to dress the same. This enough to strengthen the haughtiness which came naturally to Caitlin when she had a huge insistence inside her that she would have her own way. She would not be made to do what she was told just because Serena had told her to do it. She would not dress the same as other little girls even while Wendy tried to persuade her that she looked pretty in the pink tracksuit with its rough fabric and chunky zip. She would not allow all her cleverness to be spurned and ridiculed. She had not been asked kindly like Serena usually did for a preference as was the right of all princesses. *You must choose carefully, my precious darling, so that you may be sure that what you have is your heart's desire. There, now, my little princess...look at all your choices. Which one would Caitlin prefer?*

Was that not the way that things should be? It seemed to Caitlin that there was a conspiracy for her to cooperate. They were all closing in on her. All the strange people in this place and Wendy, too, who would try to draw her out, reassure her, explain all that was merely new and different. She would soon get used to all the changes.

She was afraid of losing herself; becoming lost, not understanding, her perfection ruined. The other little girl would have to go and Wendy told in no uncertain terms that Caitlin was mistress of their destinies, not Wendy. So there!

To those who watched this on the TV screen in the office, one floor below, they observed a child who stood before the looking glass in her bedroom and took objection to what was her own reflection as she smacked out a hand to strike her own likeness in the face. They knew nothing of Caitlin's total bewilderment over the newness and strangeness of her own body image to the two minds that lived within her head, for Caitlin could not see Wendy just as Wendy could not see Caitlin. They existed in their wholly different personalities with a shared awareness, as one.

The child looking back at her through the glass of the mirror was a total stranger. Her hands might be the exact size and image of her own, she noted, when the ones that moved in the looking glass came to touch, right with right and left with left, in the same mocking way as her counterpart had done in the garden, but she could not allow it.

Caitlin could not allow the touch as she pulled her own hand away to refute a friendship. Caitlin would not have her right hand held by any other than Wendy's calming left one. She would not be touched by anyone otherwise than Serena and later, when they found her, the lady with the golden trumpet who would listen to Caitlin and make Serena do what Caitlin wanted her to do. Just as Caitlin could make Wendy do what Caitlin wanted through her cleverness and superior strength, with the magic of the brown ring so disliked by everyone. The brown ring had become so very powerful in its protection and shelter of Caitlin's indomitable will. The same rigid and impenetrable strength which Wendy would see Caitlin abandon...*We must learn how to be like Oswald, Caitlin, and the swans which despite all that had happened to them managed to spread their broken wings to the sky and escape to a better place. If we are more like Oswald in his cooperation then we will find the lady with the golden trumpet. She will go to get Serena and together, like the injured swans, we can go to a better place.*

Those watching on the screen below frowned at each other as the child smacked out, again, at her own reflection in the looking glass, pouting and posturing, drawing back as her hand hit the hard surface of the safety glass, the reflected hands clapping in cold symmetry with her own, as she repeated her action leaving behind their misty shapes which disappeared magically as quickly as they had been made. Then she leaned her body against its length as if she would barge the other girl out of the way. To those watching from below it was as if she was trying to merge herself with the image in the glass. Both images hostile, the one to the other, as in a stand-off when the one with the weakest disposition will stand down in favour of the other. Neither girl budged.

Then some of her curiosity seemed to overcome her fear as the nails which scratched the glass failed to penetrate the same soft flesh she was trying in her anger to hurt. She let the tips of her fingers stay on the faux-glass to rub over the surface, feeling and looking, watching them wipe back and forth as she moved her own the same. She stretched her face and put her tongue out to see the other little girl do the same letting her own tongue lick against that of the little girl's in the mirror, tasting only polish and dust, sharing an eye and the misty breath they breathed onto each other's faces. She bent and stretched, high and low, this way and that as she started to understand the cooperation of the other child to do as she did. To imitate; to show her willingness to be her friend, to allow Caitlin to have her way because Caitlin had to be in command of all they did. Yet when she looked down the other child had no feet, her own being under the tilted edge of the mirror's frame. She went round to the other side of the up-stand of the frame to its rear, thinking that the little girl was standing at the back on the rim of the frame, ready to take advantage of Caitlin's compliance and strike her unexpectedly, maybe.

There had never been anything like the magic of the mirror inside Serena's dark house. At last she began to understand. It was a magic of the light shining on the shimmering, silver surface of the looking glass. The third little girl was not like Caitlin and Wendy together inside one body with their one pair of eyes to see all that was before them...their one set of hands to reach and touch...their one mind within which to argue even while knowing that the one must protect the other if they were both to survive. The reflection in the mirror was but an image of both Wendy and Caitlin superimposed on a surface. Wendy and Caitlin together. There was no second or third person. Reflections being something that Serena had failed to teach her about in their science lessons in the cellar.

However, unlike Wendy, Caitlin did not like what she was now understanding to be what other people saw of herself. This little girl was ugly and not beautiful like Serena whose eyes could shimmer so brightly when she laughed and her funny face became a lantern. This child did not smile and had no soft and charming graces. This child was such a gross disappointment as Caitlin came to realise that she was different from the woman she had always thought herself to look like. She wanted to be so like Serena whose smile was like the morning sun. Whose soft and gentle voice soothed the fractious Caitlin and made the cheeky, saucy, brave side of her nature which she thought of now as Wendy, laugh and smile also. Serena was truly beautiful and that beauty shone from within. For Serena was kind and gentle. Serena knew how to love. Serena would tell her that it did not matter what she looked like on the outside. It was what she looked like on the inside that mattered most.

For the first time in her life she had a sense of what she looked like to others. She now knew where her minds and thoughts and feelings lived in relation to the rest. She was no longer merely the bridge of her own nose if she crossed her eyes. Or a navel with a belly button. Or a torso with bumps at the back and with the orifices which Caitlin invaded with angry hands because the smelly brown stuff was sometimes the only way of making a space for herself where she might talk and Serena listen. Only no one listened when Caitlin shouted and screamed and smeared and Serena became upset. They only listened when Wendy tried to speak for her quietly so to try to show the angry Caitlin how to cooperate. If only Serena and these others would understand that all that she wanted was to feel safe again.

So that's what she looked like to others she thought, as she stripped off all her clothing and then looked at herself upside down, head swivelling backwards, head ducking under through her legs. Turning and frowning so that she might see every bit of the body that was herself. Trying to work it all out. Matching herself against the pictures and the diagrams of human anatomy she had used to bring up on a computer screen when Serena was not around; male and female. She had worked out already for herself that because she did not have a pipe and two small walnuts in a sack that she must be female. Understanding now what the word *gender* meant. Serena had a bee in her bonnet when people should refer to the *gender* of a person and not their *sex*. For some reason the latter word offending. Caitlin always knew because Serena would cock her head and mew.

It was Wendy, not Caitlin, who aspired to live as one with others. To be part of a group in a real and challenging world of new experiences. As it had ever been Wendy even before she had a name who would seek to be the child that Caitlin in her stubborn haughtiness and clever pride could never be. It had ever been Wendy to ask the questions which Caitlin would not aspire to answer in her curiosity to know the truth: Who am I? What am I? Why am I? Questions relative to the abstract spirit-self who lived as one with Caitlin inside her head. For a long time she had thought of herself as a cat like Tigwell; slinking, arching, purring, scratching away at its own soft fur, licking itself. To be always as quiet as Tigwell was as he crept about the house. Then and until now as a clone of Serena with her fizzy-funny lantern face which could grow bright as sunlight or become as dim as shadows as her moods and feelings changed. She saw her own silver-grey eyes like those of the tropical fishes swimming round and around in the non-reflective glass tank by her bed, in the glow of the lamplight, in the perpetual darkness of a house starved of natural light. She could see them now but in a different shape. Matching herself against the forms of other little girls she had seen through the eye at the upstairs window or from behind the gauzy veil which made her part of the nets at the downstairs window. Looking through the panes of frosted glass onto a distorted world of bits and pieces, moods and urges, all collected together by a confused mind's eye.

It was Wendy who understood that their divided mind with all the differences of their shared perceptions would not bode well for either of them as long as such confusions reigned. Their irrevocable differences could only deepen and widen and become unbridgeable as each character developed differently from its other self. There could be no conformity, no unity, and no agreement because it had become impossible for them to coexist. *Time has come to choose*, Wendy said softly to the other reflection in the mirror glass; the one in perfect unity with herself. The only one to share her new existence with from this time on because they were of the same mind, the same opinion, the same mode of reaction. From good and bad. From fears and happiness. From clever facts and stupid fantasies. From placid acceptance and angry demanding. Wendy; only Wendy...the child who would seek to cooperate with the strange and frightening world about them...must choose herself. For Wendy was now certain that she was the one upon whom their adaptation must depend...their real strength...their means of survival...their dignity.

"Me Wendy now."

Caitlin's anger was immediate and extreme. *No!* Wendy stood firm even as her own right hand smote her right cheek. The left smote back. Then battle commenced.

Below stairs, Tommo stood with Brian Ghould to watch her slap her own face hard with both hands and bite down on her own thumbs until the blood ran red. Then she began to pull her own hair and bang her head against the mirror glass. Soon the mirror was toppling to the floor. There was a loud crack which shook the ceiling above their heads and made the light fittings jangle as the wood and reflective plastic split before the child rolled away, miraculously without bloody injury from the splinters, over and over, across the carpet, pinching and nipping herself. The men watched, appalled and shaken despite having witnessed such self harm in other clients so many times before, as she pulled on her own ears to haul herself up onto the bed where her skull began to hammer into the headboard, repeatedly, as if she was being propelled as a battering ram against the padded wood by an unseen person. Her screams of pain and upset came as Banshee cries to the ears of those watching below. It was if she was lifted by invisible hands and then slammed back down on her back again as her legs thrashed and kicked against the fabric of the duvet while her hands clutched and tore the seams asunder with ripping sounds as the material rent.

"Leave her for a moment to see if she can resolve her inner conflict for herself," Brian advised, though his face showed the distress her behaviour brought to those who had to stand as witness. "It's like a fever breaking...a crisis inside herself...a deep and abiding unhappiness which only she can resolve for herself. Sometimes all there is to do is to give space and stand as guardians as a battle rages within. This is her fight, not ours. It's safety glass in the mirror I take it."

Tommo nodded, his hands curled into fists as he watched a child as young as seven strike and beat and harm herself as if wanting to tear out her own heart from an acid bed inside her own breast, his own hands then feeling out the scars on his forearms where, as an angry youth, he had used razor blades to pare a stinging pain sufficient to overwhelm the anguish in his head. Even to this day the exquisite agony of self mutilation could tempt him to do it again when there was need to confront his own fears and trepidations. For the scars within his mind would never heal completely. It was a compulsion he had to fight against just as he would swallow back the hot, welling tears; his compassion fathomless, his understanding infinite. He would try to package up such pain in an insulated sheath so that those who will place themselves as judge might be protected from the overwhelming tide of hostile feelings. When it came time to write it down he would couch his reports in cold, professional syndrome and legal platitude instead of wrapping them within this raw, unadulterated emotion running as molten chaos inside him which he and Brian were witnessing. He would cool it down to cinder, sort and order it, straighten and compartmentalise while knowing that those who have never known anguish can have no empathy with emotional riot, save through the bridge of words. For who, otherwise, would follow the way into a burning house to recover whatever might remain, save for the compassionate? Just as his own emotions would now remain as stone. He dare never love again as he had loved his frail mother. Not when he had hated his father sufficiently to raise the brush to batter down his own insistent pain.

They watched her as her self destruction took her off the bed and had her crashing headlong into walls, flinging open empty drawers and sending them flying through silent, unresisting air to splinter like matchwood against the papered wall. It was as if she was pushed and dragged back to the bed by someone other than herself where she began to roll from side to side, from back to stomach, all the time her hands pinching and scratching at her own naked flesh.

As she started to pull at her own hair again her bare left foot stamped against her right foot and both in turn flexed against the baseboard of the bed, slamming it over and over again with the soles of her bare feet. They saw the inevitable happen as her strength caused the bed to begin to shake, lean and then the baseboard collapse under her onslaught. The child had done this before of that they were certain. They saw her get off the bed to complete its destruction, her anger red hot upon her cheeks, her growls those of a wounded animal in pain. Her bleeding hands tossed the mattress as if no more than a pillow in her demon strength. With the same awesome purpose she turned over the broken bed frame with a loud cracking sound.

"There won't be anything left in there by the time she's finished," Tommo said. "She'll have thumped herself black and blue."

Brian knew that Tommo would have to summon help before taking any action to prevent her doing both herself and her environment more damage. He was these days beyond coping with anyone's anger other than his own. "I'll go now. Let you get on with it. There are some things about the job I don't miss and this is one of them. She's started tearing up the duvet now. Feathers everywhere."

"Now she's battering herself again...punching her own chin...pulling her own hair. Where the hell's Gary and Holly?" Tommo looked angrily at his watch. "She should have been back five minutes ago. Let's hope in the meantime that the child doesn't kill herself...lots of sharp edges in there."

Brian Ghould was leaving the house, let out through the digitally locked door by Tommo just as Gary was returning to the house from having his scratches bathed. He was walking with Holly. That was when the clock came smashing through the window from Wendy's room on the first floor and almost landed on them both. Angrily Tommo shut the door on them. He would have something to say later concerning the importance of punctuality when situations like the one he was watching on the office screen could flare up in a moment. He went to observe her on the screen again, shunting his glasses up his nose and repeatedly sweeping back the curtains of his hair. The child's anger was building, not lessening. They would have to get in there but not until the staffing was right. They had their own vulnerability to consider.

Outside still, and only just realising what was happening within, Gary and Holly stopped only long enough to have a word with Brian. Holly had to wait while Gary let Brian through the side gate to his car before he might let them both inside the building. The office door was open and an angry Tommo cast her bald glances as she went within. Gary behind her. Holly's eyes widened in appalled disbelief as she watched Wendy fight with herself over possession of the rag doll. Why was she being allowed to do this to herself? Why had they left her all alone? The child had gone beyond all self control or the ordinary control of others. She was throwing herself like a bouncing bomb onto the floor now as she made deep sounds like whale calls. Getting up naked and animal-like in her caged dementia she went to fling herself against the window bars, doing the same self-harming actions as a repeated sequence over and over again. It was only the metal bars that prevented her from crashing through the space where the smashed shards of glass remained in the window frame, offering a very real danger to her threshing wrists.

Tommo seemed to blame Holly's tardiness for the situation. After some complaint he spoke directly to Gary. "Time to get in there."

Holly was afraid that all that would be achieved was a repeat of what had happened earlier. They would try to calm aggression with aggression; overwhelm her. For some reason it mattered greatly to Holly that she make up for some shortfall of prior commitment within herself. "Can I try first on my own to calm her please? Please...please?"

Tommo's hard eyes lost a little of their granite polish though they flashed at her brightly. Both men looked at her questioningly. "Not alone. We follow policy on such issues in these circumstances."

"That's right," Gary agreed. "We have to ensure our own safety first. Place shuts if Tommo and I get injured. God alone knows where she'd end up then."

"Look, she's stopping, now. She's all tired out. Please let me try to comfort her before she's restrained again."

Their eyes went back to the screen. They watched the child crouch as the brown ring was made. They saw her stretch her hand and arm out as if to draw someone else within the ring. What Wendy was doing was absorbing her alter-ego. Caitlin had been defeated but she would, henceforth, live inside her one true self.

When finally she collapsed to the floor in the stench and the mess of her own making, breathing hard, her tears now falling as heavy rain, her screams silenced within the fetid stench of excrement and within an environment laid to ruin, her tiredness overwhelming, only Wendy remained. Her grief and sorrow were as tangible as a voile curtain which Holly had to step through as she entered the broken room. For Caitlin had gone as far as a mind-voice was concerned.

A child of seven had done this! This destruction. Holly's own history found a comparison with the devastation around her though she knew that Wendy's trauma was much deeper than anything she had ever experienced during her life in care. There was fear too in her approach when she had begged Tommo and Gary to allow her to face the child alone. If she had gauged this incorrectly the child would attack her also. So she walked slowly, breathing softly and evenly when she felt the need to gasp, slowly reinstating the room as she made a wide journey about the child who crouched still.

As Holly spiralled in upon her Wendy watched her warily as she cleared a pathway quietly and gathered up the child's clothing. Until her nakedness was covered the men would not be wise to come close to her. Such rules were more for their protection than the needs of a distraught child who more than anything else required comforting.

While the men lingered outside on the landing, listening, the house now totally silent, Holly felt her way, coming closer to the sobbing, wary, frightened child, thinking that Wendy too might be that same child she had seen on the train being transported away from all who cared. That child, come full circle after a long, arduous and circuitous journey. This child needing what Holly, herself, needed in that moment. That being the comfort that only the arms of another human being can bring.

Her face did not complain as she took herself into Wendy's contaminated space. Her hands were not rough as she put them under the child's armpits and drew Wendy to her feet. She did not drag her, or push or pull or poke as she propelled the distressed child by her clean hand to the only chair that still remained standing. There Holly dropped the child's clothes and sat, allowing Wendy to see and feel her understanding in a caring face before she wrapped her sobbing form in the ripped coverlet from the bed. Binding the soiled right hand within, letting the gentle, left hand dangle free. Then she brought her up against her chest and hugged her tightly. "It's alright," she whispered against the fiery heat of Wendy's cheek; no shouting, either. "I know...I know...I know how you feel."

As Tommo and Gary with Angie and Harry following came quietly into the room the child wept with relief and tiredness against Holly's breast. Only Holly knew that she was comforting the child that she had been, herself. Her own tears brimming deep and running free down her youthful cheeks. She felt so very sorry for the Holly she had once been. Now changed and never to be the same again. She had lost the moorings of her anger and was floating free as she and Wendy cried together.

Twenty-Six

Holly had bathed the child once again. This time taking the trouble to kneel at the side of the bath next to where Wendy sat naked, deep in bubbles and doing what a child of her age should be doing; playing! This time, Holly joined in the fun. If she had committed herself to the job she might as well enjoy it as much as possible and at the same time see if she could make the kid feel a bit better.

They had both cried themselves dry, though Holly had denied to Tommo and Gary that her own tearful state had been anything more than a case of coming out in sympathy with the anguish little Wendy had been suffering. This had led, of course, to one of Tommo's sermons. Apparently she should not have sat her on her knee as this was against European Regulations. Tommo had had that po look on his face. "However, I might turn a blind eye when touching was appropriate to the occasion. I can see that the child has benefited. She's relaxed in a way that she hasn't been since coming here this morning."

Gary had looked shame-faced.

Not that she could have allowed Wendy to go to sleep on her knee. "Got to get you clean, kid," she had said when Wendy would have closed her flickering eyelids and slept. Then when Tommo and Gary had gone: "Something's changed. Both your hands seem happy now. Your eyes are more alike in colour too. Anyone ever told you that you're a cute little thing. We'll have you looking as pretty as a picture again in some more of them new clothes that lady brought for you. Best not spoil these, though. She might not bring you any more if you do."

Wendy had nodded and spoken through trembling lips, in a whisper. "You is a kind lady, Holly. Me feel better, now." That baby voice again.

Oh well! What did it matter how the kid talked? Holly thought they might both start again. Wipe the slate clean. So the kid had probably given Gary a blood disease through all the scratching he had suffered. And serve that nasty Harry Groves right if he went down with a case of tetanus poisoning after being stabbed in the leg with a garden fork. Tommo was saying nothing about being kicked in the nuts, though Holly had frequently savoured the disarming results of this particular mode of female defence when faced with a dog who thought he could swarm all over her. She'd take her lead from Angie who was too soft-hearted to bear a grudge against a distressed child and especially one as young as Wendy. It had been Angie who had found Wendy an old colander, a ladle, some plastic tubing, a huge pink sponge and some different sized, plastic containers and a bubble ring to use as water toys. She was obviously enjoying the change of having a small child to cater for despite Wendy's quixotic temperament and her recent distressing, violent and destructive behaviour. She'd shed a few tears herself before going back down to the kitchen to finish the washing up. Later she promised they'd bake some gingerbread men. Holly felt just as excited at the prospect as Wendy who jumped up and down in the bath and wet them both through with all the splashing that went on.

Holly was enjoying playing with Wendy as they explored the properties of the water. They had used all the equipment to see how it worked. The child was relaxed and happy as she squealed her delight and joined in with wafting bubbles as big as teapots and making waves in the bath water which she referred to as tsunamis....whatever they were! She seemed to have totally forgotten about her earlier bad temper.

Afterwards she allowed Holly to dry her hair with an electric drier and then find a nightdress for her to wear as the prospect of an afternoon sleep was considered. There was the matter of a destroyed bedroom to consider also. The one that had been trashed and soiled was now sealed off and would have to be stripped of the broken furniture and steam cleaned before it was habitable again; an extra task which Harry was most disgruntled about. There had been an argument between Angie and Harry about the nature of their work. He had been one-eyed as he looked askance at the terrible state of the bedroom, his nose wrinkling. With a bucket of hot soapy water in his hand, his words had been angry, his disgust apparent. "If I had my way she'd be carrying this and getting down on her hands and knees with a scrubbing brush. If you ask me she does what she does because she's been spoilt rotten in the first place. She wouldn't if she had to clean it up herself."

"No child does this kind of thing unless driven to it as a last resort. It's severe emotional distress that makes people this destructive. Tommo will get to the bottom of it and make sure that she gets the right treatment so that she becomes happier in herself. It's what we're here for in the first place," Angie said tartly. "So shut up and get on with it. The child has to have positive experiences. It can't all be punishments."

It had taken him a full hour to empty the room of all the broken furniture and ripped linen and then scrub it clean. "Bah!" he kept saying over and over again.

"Bad tempered old beggar!" Angie muttered to his departing back.

"I'll get the spare room ready on the other side of the bathroom. It'll mean that you and her will be sharing after this. You'll be better to leave your things where they are but be prepared to sleep in the other bed in the same room. It might not be a bad idea this time for one of us to take her in there and let her have a good look round so that it isn't a shock to her. Distressed children find change even more difficult than all children do. Where are her parents is what I keep thinking. Poor little mite. Can't you tell us who they are, chick, and what your real name is?"

Wendy had replied in her usual manner of clamped lips with arms crossed as an extra insurance that she tell them nothing.

"Maybe this lady with the golden trumpet knows who she is," Holly suggested. "When she reads about Wendy in the paper she might come get her."

Wendy's response was to deeply nod her head.

While Angie took Wendy to look all about the new room before she was put to bed to sleep Tommo confirmed that Holly was now to share a two bedded room with the little girl because they had seemed to have begun to develop the basis of a relationship. "She'll need constant attention after breaking the mirror and the window. We dare not allow another situation where she might harm herself. I read her medical report," he told her with a serious expression. "It might be concluded that those red marks about her neck are the result of being restrained with a dog lead after her reaction when she saw Gary with Chester's lead in his hand."

Holly didn't mention that she had seen them already but had refused to broach the task of writing about what she had noticed in the big blue, daily diary in the office. The alternative he offered, however, was more to her liking than writing.

"I'll give you a body outline so that you can put crosses anywhere you might see old bruising or signs that she might have been regularly mistreated. After what happened before I think we might assume that she's been used to being restrained using a dog collar and chain. Unfortunately she will have some bruising caused by her own self-harming behaviour and our need to manhandle her earlier. However I will write about that in my own comprehensive report."

Holly was able to breathe a sigh of relief. Diagrams caused her no difficulty. She was quite happy to make crosses on a body map. As it was, now, they would be considerable.

After a short sleep Wendy seemed to wake in a positive mood. Her dirty clothes had been taken away by Angie to be laundered. She allowed Holly to choose a new set of clothes for her to wear from the Trimbles carrier bag and then do her hair using Holly's own hair products. By the time they went downstairs to make use of the Activities Room Wendy was wearing the second set of clothes from the three sets which

Gina had provided only that morning. Now she was dressed in blue patterned tights and a short denim, belted dress over a pretty, frilly mauve blouse. Holly had put her hair up again into a sideways ponytail. This time with a blue hair band to keep her hair off her face. She looked so much like a small, happy angel that it was impossible to imagine her behaviour of such a short time earlier.

Within the Activities Room was a box full of play equipment and story books which were suitable for a little girl. Angie had rummaged them all out of somewhere she referred to as the School Room where she had informed Holly, come the following Monday, the child would be provided with her very own teacher so that the legal aspects of her detainment might be met. Poor, little thing! Holly would be expected to help her with her writing and scribe for her where necessary. Holly's cringe was noted by Wendy, though the child said nothing as Angie went back to her work. She would give them a shout when she was ready to start on the gingerbread men. At present she had bones on the boil for a pan of fresh soup. She was also baking bread as judged by the smells emanating from her kitchen. Holly was beginning to think that she had landed not in a secure unit but in paradise.

A bit of quiet time suited Holly nicely. Here, together at a small table, they sat drawing and colouring. Holly provided a piece of white paper each and both the pencil and the wax crayons which Angie had brought for their use. Holly provided herself with some of the same as she watched Wendy draw a big eye shape in the middle of the paper using the sharpened pencil crayons. She coloured it blue. She drew two swan-like creatures on its rim causing Holly to assume that the eye was a lake. They had blood coming from their wings and something that looked to represent feathers over a grassy banking. Then she drew something which looked like a wedding cake next to the water. On the other side of the lake she drew some trees. Underneath the lake she drew two figures. One a female figure, identified as such because she wore a blue jacket and skirt. She had yellow hair and was holding a trumpet in her right hand. The other had no face; just a triangle shape, coloured grey. The cloak was long and enveloping so that only her feet stuck out. Her hands were represented by mitten shapes. Between the two figures was a black oblong on two, sturdy looking wheels with a handle.

Holly did not make the connection. She was busy drawing herself. She had drawn a house shape with four figures within; one at each window, and one outside the house, the same as she had always drawn as a representation of her family structure from being a child of seven. The sky had clouds not sunshine which she might once have coloured black before obliterating all under big black blobs. The sadness was again within her. She resisted the urge to colour her picture as history prompted but instead drew a big sun and left the clouds white, colouring a blue sky round it. She put flowers in her garden and drew a path about herself which connected her to the house. On the door she drew a number seven. She did not know why other than that to Holly it represented good luck. She coloured the door blue and the number yellow.

This while Wendy had taken up another pencil crayon and was writing words which Holly failed to become aware of until after Wendy had found the black, wax crayon and had begun to use it thickly to cover over all her work. By the time that Holly realised that Wendy's picture was significant she saw that the child had obliterated the words, the wedding cake, the figures, the long necked swans, the sky and the trees, leaving only the shape she had started with surrounded by thick, black wax. It looked like a giant blue eye.

"Can I have it? I'll give you mine if I can have yours."

Wendy spent a moment thinking and looking. Then she nodded. They made the swap. Holly folded it carefully and tucked it in her pocket. As she did so, through the back of the paper she could see the pencil outlines of Wendy's picture. She intended handing it straight to Tommo only when he poked his head through the door where Wendy now sat with a fairytale book on her lap he was not after listening. The rag doll was on Wendy's lap and she had started to read to it quietly, only stopping as Tommo's head came round the door.

As Holly extended the piece of paper towards him for him to take he shook his head at her. His attitude was coldly warning and his voice sharp. "I told you earlier that all information should be written first and foremost into the daily diary. Her drawing can be slipped inside the diary for me to collate along with anything you might write. All our observations are important and should be put into the diary before the details get forgotten or minimised by the opinion of others. Before supper I expect you to make clear notes in the daily diary concerning your observations."

Holly in her newness was in some confusion. Also her panic was rising. "Such as?"

Tommo shrugged his shoulders and spread his hands as if to gesture to all and anything. "Her responses to being bathed and played with. Anything which allows me to build a comprehensive picture of her needs and character. Her drawings are useful because I can gauge her intellectual maturity from the detail she provides within the figures and buildings."

"I is seven," said Wendy with her shoulders rising and flashing a look of insult. She went to stand by Holly and took hold of her hand. "My birthday is twenty-first of June, two thousand and two."

Tommo got out his notebook and wrote it down. "Your name being?"

"Is Wendy Bridgewater now. Only Wendy now. Her lives at Bridge Twenty-Eight, Whemley Canal, Lower Quinton." Then she folded her arms, found one straight index finger, squeezed her lips shut and placed it against them.

Holly had managed to hide her discomfiture at the prospect of writing in the day book even though it filled her with horror. She remained unheeding of Wendy who was standing next to her, watching and listening and seemingly alert to the fact that Holly had suddenly physically tensed and her palms had begun to sweat profusely. The prospect of writing anything, to Holly, was stressful enough to cause her to shake and tremble. Even her name if it had to be written in front of others was daunting. Though that had now been correctly spelt for her, under a small photograph taken and printed off a computer screen by Gary. It was attached to a Greengates House staff badge and pinned to her sweatshirt. If she had to she could always copy it. Her signature deliberately disguised the spelling anyway.

When Tommo had gone off again with a fly fishing magazine rolled up under his arm Wendy tugged at Holly's hand. Her eyes, which looked levelly at Holly, held a very knowing look. "Wendy help," was all she said. "You is kind to Wendy. Wendy is kind to you."

Holly glared down at her then relented. What did a kid know? She was more like four than seven. Maybe there'd be a dictionary that she could use in the office. Or she might find something to copy from things that people had written before about other clients. Often she had to choose her words according to her ability to spell them rather than to use a more complex vocabulary. It made her look stupid.

After she had put the crosses on the body map which also indicated the rough, ring of skin about Wendy's neck, she allowed Wendy to lead her along the corridor and into the office where she shut the door behind them. They could see from the CCTV screens that Tommo was feet up in the lounge engrossed in his magazine. Gary was writing his own reports concerning the garden games in the Exercise Room and Harry was cutting the grass outside, taking off the first inch of spring growth. There was a pile of broken furniture ready to be taken to the tip waiting by the gates. Angie was collecting together her utensils and equipment ready for baking the gingerbread men which, after mid-afternoon tea, both Holly and Wendy would help with.

With a heavy sigh Holly used the key in Tommo's top drawer to open the one that held the sacred daily diary. She made no exception when Wendy took Tommo's chair and she stood behind her. What Wendy did next was to find a ballpoint pen and shake her head when Holly would have wrested it from her. "Caitlin good at writing. Me left-handed. Caitlin help Wendy now with her right hand."

Open mouthed Holly folded back the cover and the pages of the large, gold embossed, blue book to see that it had, indeed, been ruled into sections of the day; morning, afternoon, evening and night time. Wendy looked up at Tommo's grey rimmed clock and noted the time. She wrote the time and the date correctly in the appropriate space and then on the top line, her name, correctly spelt despite it being unpractised; Wendy Bridgewater. Holly was amazed and shamed.

"You say, me write it."

Holly was gripped by a strange weakness and a terrible knotting in her belly as Wendy waited with her pen poised in her right hand for Holly to start the dictation. With deep embarrassment she nodded a final agreement to Wendy that she might write in the precious ledger and only hoped to God that the child had the skill to match her confidence. She would have to make some feeble excuse if Wendy messed up. So what was new in the life of Holly Hargreaves cum Kenyon? Nothing much!

Holly began tentatively. "Wendy trashed her room and smeared faeces on the floor."

Wendy wrote. "She trashed her room and smeared poo. Naughty girl."

Holly continued. "Wendy played happily in the bath and then had a short sleep."

Wendy wrote. "Wendy played happily in the bath and then had a short sleep."

"Wendy drew and coloured a delightful picture as supplied."

"Wendy drew and coloured a pretty picture, as inside."

Holly handed it over with the body map. Wendy tucked them both within and leant out of the way for Holly to read what she had so cleverly written.

The script was cursive with correctly formed letters and of a copper plate appearance. In fact just as Holly so wished she might write herself. Under the column headed; Reporting Staff, Wendy had written *Holly Hargreaves*. Outdone by a child of seven!

The entry completed, Wendy placed the pen down, left the seat and went to stand in a corner of the room with her hands hanging limply by her sides just like a switched-off robot. Her eyes almost shut. She slumped to the floor cross-legged with her back to the outside wall. The rhythmic banging of her head against cold, hard plaster sounded like a reverberating heartbeat. Holly slid down the wall to sit next to her thinking that at least she was no longer so violent in her self-abuse that she might hurt herself.

With tears in her eyes Wendy looked up at Holly. "Wendy miss Caitlin...and Serena. Holly help Wendy look for the lady with the golden trumpet?"

"I'll try to. Who is she this lady with the golden trumpet?"

"She my real mummy."

"Is she the lady with the blue clothes and the yellow hair holding a trumpet in your picture?"

Wendy nodded.

"Where are you in the picture?"

"Is riding in the cart of course."

"In the shopping trolley? With the lady wearing a veil over her face?"

Wendy nodded. Then she laid her head on Holly's knee and closed her eyes again. "I miss Serena."

How do I spell the words golden trumpet? Holly thought. It should all have been so very easy. But it wasn't!

Twenty-Seven

At going on for three-thirty, Cubby tried phoning his mother again. He had eaten alone at the Italiana; a simple Tuscan Salad, Ciabatta bread and imbibed two, small glasses of Chianti to wash it down with. It was what he ate and drank at the same time each weekday; a light meal with only sufficient wine to allow him a half hour sitting in a relaxed mood, planning the rest of his day. The waiters had his meal ordered in advance so that not a moment of Cubby's valuable time was wasted. He was usually the last person in the restaurant as they laid the covers for the evening trade, that day's lay-outs already having been passed on via the internet to the printer. The hard copy should by now be spewing forth as newsprint and combining to make today's issue. Cubby had used his own photographs of the morning without his parents' consent. Before they brought his meal he ordered a pepperoni pizza and a bottle of good wine to take out with him. He was planning to make up for the fact that he so very rarely called at his parents' home these days. Time, perhaps to soften his mother up a bit.

As usual he enjoyed his meal, even while keeping an eye on the door just in case Gina Mon changed her mind about joining him. Between bites of food he phoned his mother once again. She answered on her mobile number. He told her that he intended popping home for a chat over a glass of wine and a shared pizza. He'd bring the food with him like a nursery tea; the only time they had ever sat down at the table together in his formative years. "Maybe we can snack together and Dad can join us. I've got some photographs I'd like you both to see. He in?"

"I have no idea where your father is. I'm still at the Magistrates' Court. I was late arriving so someone took my lists. Where your father is only your father knows. Look at what photographs?"

"Just the kid's clothes. The things the kid was wearing when she was brought out of the canal. A photo of her rag doll too. You might know where they're sold; if they are sold locally. I intend tracking her down and being the first to publish her identity. One in the eye for Catty Collins. It will be a scoop for the Clarion that will have even the nationals sitting up and taking notice." The determination in Cubby's voice was intense. "The woman's stirring up a right hornets' nest on the Dog's Bed Estate. People are seriously pissed off with her using the excuse of the child to increase her standing with the CPS in terms of crimes solved. The identity of the child or catching her abuser seems to be the last thing on her mind."

Her voice changed then, deepening with anger. She was obviously extremely annoyed with him. "Is this sensible, Cubby? Why have such a bee in your bonnet about something that is not relevant to selling newspapers? Both your father and I have asked you to stop this, please. You do not know what you're meddling with." Her voice was shaking. His mother never shouted. When she was most controlled with her voice lowered instead of raised he was warned that she was seriously upset about something. "For the last time, Cubby, leave it be."

Cubby dug his heels in. "I disagree. It'll be the best scoop we've had in months when I'm able to identify the child and the whole of the Quinton and Dales District Police Force cannot."

"You are tampering with an unexploded bomb!"

"That's ridiculous. Are you alright, Mum?"

"Of course I am alright. Why should I be otherwise? I am alright I tell you!"

Cubby was taken aback. He was certain that trouble was brewing between his parents once again. "I'll come round."

"You will do no such thing. I have things that I have to do of great importance."

"Such as?"

"Settle something that should have been settled long ago if you must know." Then she disconnected the call.

Cubby was frowning even as he accepted a very warm box and a bottle that had been gift wrapped in tissue and stood up to go. He made his own interpretation of her words and sighed heavily. It did not do to even imagine what would become of his father if his mother threw him out of the house. He would have liked to pretend that it didn't matter to him that his parents were always at loggerheads but it did. Christ! It was like he was the father and they, his parents, were the children. In light of what he had seen that very afternoon it begged a question: Had his father gone too far this time? One mistress too many? Despite his age and maturity Cubby found his parents disparities greatly upsetting. He did not blame his mother for being angry if she had discovered that CC was playing away from home again. Thing was, too, he could not find it in him to blame his father when his mother was not the type to serve dinner with a rose between her teeth or dance on tables. Their compatibility was zilch!

He was also thwarted from his intention to gain some intelligent information regarding the child's clothes and her rag doll. He would just have to find out his information elsewhere. There was only one place he could think of. He hoped that Gina was hungry and had managed to forgive him. Cubby smiled as he left the restaurant. He knew precisely where she lived.

Twenty-Eight

Angie had had that strange feeling again that she was being watched through her own kitchen window for most of the early afternoon. All the while, as Wendy had been at play and then later when the child had been getting in Harry's way while she had been exploring the garden soil under Tommo and Gary's supervision, Angie kept looking out onto the garden wondering why she should feel so certain that there was an audience to what was going on inside the high, chain link fence.

It felt as if there was a Peeping Tom out there, though other than the workmen filling holes in the lane there was no one to be seen. They seemed to have no interest in anything other than the job in hand. The white builder's van had backed onto the lane about an hour previously which did not explain her feeling of being watched from shortly after eleven that morning. The two workmen had started some patching up of the rutted lane at shortly after three, after some considerable time sitting over by the hedges, eating from plastic trays and paper bags while popping cans of beer. They could not be accountable, she thought, for the occasional movement she had seen in the bushes at the bottom of the garden where Harry had made such an untidy job of cutting them back.

Later on she had thought that she had seen a dark, moving shadow over by Harry's shed to the front of the grounds. Then she had thought that she was really allowing her imagination to work overtime when she could have sworn that she heard a strangled cry and something fall heavily with a crashing noise. It might have been a case of Harry hurting himself when he lifted that fly mower of his onto the hook in his shed. That bad back of his not being up to lifting it so high. Serve him right for having no kindness in him for the poor and unfortunate of this world, she thought. He'd probably come telling her tomorrow that he'd dropped the damned thing on his foot, wanting tea and sympathy as he showed her a black and blue, swollen big toe and expecting her to bandage it for him. Not the sense to take himself off to the hospital to make sure that it wasn't broken and get it strapped up. That heap of broken furniture still being there, too, an hour after he'd piled it up by the rolling gates ready to take it the tip. Tommo wouldn't like it when he saw that Harry hadn't taken it to the tip already. Tommo believed that it was seeing furniture broken in a heap which made people feel concerned about having a secure assessment unit for naughty boys and girls in their midst. That and the noise when their usual adolescent clients could scream just as loud and long as Wendy Bridgewater had done. They saw some sights at times did the neighbours, Angie thought. Boot camp wasn't in it!

Then again there had been a lot of public curiosity about this particular child. Harry had spent a good deal of the day, while getting on with the garden, talking through the railings with all manner of folk who had simply wanted to know if her parents had turned up to claim her yet. There had been several phone calls from the press, Tommo had said. The only thing he would allow any of them to say about little Wendy was *no comment*. The child was a real strange how-do-you-do when, even so late after she had been discovered, no one had come forward to claim her.

Oh well! None of her business, she thought, as she arranged the trays and carried them loaded from her collection points to the kitchen table; flasks, plates, cups and saucers. Everything ready for them to help themselves as and when they wanted. She was off home early. Chester would finish off everything that wasn't eaten. Eat anything would Chester then sleep all day in that outside kennel of his. Though, come to think of it, she hadn't seen Chester since Gary had brought him back from his mid afternoon walk when he'd barked his head off at a growling Bull Mastiff in the van which belonged to the men filling the holes up in the lane. If those workmen had let that grey beast with a head like a Spanish bull out of the transit, Chester would by now be dog meat in all senses of the phrase. Dog walks being something Gary did as a ritual every day of the week unless one of their clients was blowing when poor Chester would just have to wait. Strange for the dog not to be scratching at the door, though. She had been boiling up raw bones for the soup after bathing Gary's scratched hands; raised welts they were that if they became infected could see him with an arm amputated. Brian Ghould had come especially to see it all unfold but stayed well away from any affray. He had left them all to it, of course, when the worst came to the worst. *Heads of Anything* always get too full of themselves to be bothered rolling their shirt sleeves up when times get tough! Or was it another case of old dogs getting past it? Poor Chester! She had insisted he stay out in all weathers through the winter which had probably made his arthritis worse. Maybe she should check on him before getting home early? Then decided against it. She couldn't do everything! Not with the heavy trays to carry and no one thinking that she might need a hand to carry them. Men! It was nice to have another female worker for a change.

Funny little girl, that Holly, though. Her upbringing did not seem to have engendered any domestic skills. She had not a clue about baking the gingerbread men which now lay on plates ready for serving. It had been Holly instead of Wendy who had seemed to have no experience of the absolute basics of food preparation. Maybe like a lot of young girls in this age of convenience foods she had little idea how simple it is to combine a few cheap ingredients and have a far superior product to those with little taste but a long shelf life, bought from the supermarket. Yet another of Angie's silent criticisms. Even Wendy had managed better than her helper when it came to handling the ingredients. Holly had found it difficult even to sprinkle sugar off a spoon into the balance pan of the scales. She had not understood about rubbing-in or how much ginger spice should be added. She had been covered with the flour when she had finished and smelt exactly like the gingerbread men they had cut out with the shaper. And laughed as much as Wendy when she had seen the state of her shoes. Even when it came to taking things out of the oven it had been Wendy who had understood about the safety of oven gloves when Holly would have used the tea towel. It had been Wendy showing Holly and not Holly showing Wendy in the end as they had iced and decorated the warm biscuits, personalizing them with different clothing, different expressions. Holly sharing all the fun like a kid of seven herself.

She had to write in the daily diary though, as her client comment for the day, that Holly was making some progress with building a good relationship with the child which was what mattered more than anything else. A rapport was growing between them that was allowing the child to feel more comfortable. Something had changed within the child, Angie thought, after Holly had shown her some love and affection. It just proved Angie's case when it should be common sense to understand that children reflected whatever attitude they were approached with. While she had to admit that all these restraint procedures they were trained in had to be standardised and approved for the sake of the staff involved, nothing had the desired effect the same as straightforward mothering. They had a worthwhile product, also, to show for all their trouble now set out on trays so that they might help themselves to supper as and when their late afternoon or early evening dictated. Something to be proud of!

With the food laid out on trays, Angie's work was done and dusted a bit earlier than usual. She was off home and had no wish today, of all days, to be on the streets of Lower Quinton longer than it took to get a few bits and pieces from the shops on Lower Quinton High Street. She had already had plenty of warnings that trouble was brewing on the Dog's Bed Estate from several of her acquaintances, Nan Bartlett included. She had phoned Angie with the news that her granddaughter had turned up unexpectedly and taken them all unawares. There had been a long pause which Angie thought Nan had expected her to fill before Nan went onto a different subject. The conversation turning eventually of course to all the trouble brewing on the bridge which Nan could see from her bedroom window.

Angie was horrified to hear that the barricade stretched right across the road to stop all traffic getting in or out, unless it went by a circuitous route through country lanes. The protesters had built bonfires on the lanes, too, and were passing out handmade leaflets. In panic, Angie had phoned to ask her husband to head home early from laying tarmac upon the main highways of Britain in order to meet her off the four o'clock bus just in case the trouble started earlier than expected. They intended getting in some extra supplies and then going home together to batten themselves in as they might, had they had prior warning of a tornado approaching. So all those who lived in at Greengates House would have to help themselves to homemade tomato soup from a flask, ham and cheese sandwiches and the iced and decorated gingerbread men. Everything ready, cut and placed on plates. Four trays laid, one half the size of the rest. All they had to do was to come to the kitchen and pick them up, carry them off to their own eating places and then get stuck in.

As Angie went to take her coat from the peg she imagined again that she saw movement in the garden where a second look assured her that she had seen none. Down beyond the bushes at the bottom of the garden where the undergrowth was thickest, in front of the chain link fencing. The white van was still on the lane with the Bull Mastiff, a ghost behind all the condensation its breath made on the windows; probably stank like sweating feet. She could not see the two men working to mend the holes, but there was no way that they could get into the garden. She was seeing things. Floaters at the back of the eye she told herself. All part of getting older.

As she shouted farewell from the kitchen doorway with a casual, "I'm off home. See to yourselves. It's all on the kitchen table," flung in the direction of the other downstairs rooms of the house where Tommo, Gary, Holly and Wendy were in the lounge watching the telly. If she hurried she would be able to catch the four o'clock bus so she didn't tarry as she dragged on her winter hat. It was still too cold by late afternoon to wander about without protection from the chill and the damp.

They shouted back as she dragged her gloves on, her weekly Saveaway between clenched teeth ready for the bus driver. Even little Wendy, who now sat with the orange haired rag doll on her knee instead of tucked down her own neckband, bade her farewell. "See you tomorrow, Angie."

"You will as long as the buses are still running. Don't forget there's soup in the flasks. Bye now."

When she went, Tommo went to watch her through the window

as she went out of the side gate and crossed over the road to the bus stop. "Time to make a few deductions of my own I think. I assume that all reports have been made in the daily diary, Holly? Yours too, Gary?"

Holly stopped the cringe from showing on her face.

It was Wendy who nodded. "Clever girl, Holly is."

*****

Shortly after Angie left the house, Tommo was within his office working on all the baseline information he could gather on his new client. He had several different reports spread out in front of him. These he would use to provide the initial psychological profile of Wendy Bridgewater which had been commissioned by the Chief Constable on behalf of the Crown Prosecution Service. The hefty bill for this service would come out of the public purse. Her future placement would need to be paid for expensively by Social Services. There again out of the public purse. Children cared for by the state were very expensively provided for. However, he had the feeling that the child might soon start talking of her family for herself. There was no doubting that she was calmer and more comfortable with them all. Holly especially.

So he shut himself into his office to work knowing that the sooner an appropriate care establishment could be found for Wendy the better it would be for all concerned. Once completed this initial profile would assess the effects of the violence considered to have been carried out against her, the exact basis of the Crown prosecution against her assailant and a description of her character with its own propensities towards reacting with violence towards anything that frightened her. What he would not do would be to corrupt the truth out of empathy for her situation because that would help no one in the long run and in particular the child herself. Finally his report would finish with his recommendations concerning any observed trauma and the post traumatic effects she might have been left with from an undoubtedly cruel assault. From such comprehensive information he would form the basis of a prognosis regarding her future support needs, social welfare requirements and the predicament of her continuing homelessness about which he would make recommendations in conjunction with the local child welfare department and, in particular, because this was a high profile case, with Brian Ghould. What he would present to Catty Collins would be only a small portion of the final, very comprehensive assessments and recommendations which would accompany her application for her to be accepted as a Ward of State, should no responsible relative come forward to claim her.

A Statement of Care would then be written which would follow her through the rest of her schooling. Whether such would be a benefit or a blight would very much depend on her own attitude towards her special status as she became older. He had used his own special status as a youth convicted of manslaughter to maximise his opportunities and gain the kind of education his family status and circumstances would probably have denied him. A wheel of fortune had begun to spin on the repercussions of horrendous circumstance. Had Tommo not been too young to face the same trial as would have followed a case of patricide by someone of adult years, he would probably have turned out little different than Mally Kenyon because opportunity would never have come his way. What would happen to Wendy would be something of a lottery situation, also, many of the decisions being influenced by his reports.

He had already taken into account the medical report submitted by the doctor who had seen her upon admission to the police station and the reports of the officers who had taken her in. That she was fit and strong, even if small for her age, could be supported by a healthy appetite, energy and good gross mobility.

He had a brief but succinct report on his desk which Brian Ghould had passed over to him earlier from Gina Mon, written apparently while awaiting treatment at the hospital in the early hours of the morning, concerning her own observations, with a description of the actual attack on her person. Apparently due to the child's behaviour on the mini-bus he had missed speaking with her personally when she had brought Wendy some clothing. That he had caught sight of a very attractive woman as she had stood by the gates awaiting entry to Greengates House in the company of Cubby Watson, his mind shied away from as an impression best forgotten about. Tommo had spent his adult life cowering from any relationship which would threaten the tenuous hold of his peace of mind. He thought of himself like a blinkered cart house; his work being his life. Self being permanently buried beneath the tragic needs of his clients, their needs and wants considered at all times instead of his own.

Work to get on with now if Wendy was to pass on before she became too comfortable and she could begin to think of the staff as some form of family which would never do. He had his own notes to remind him of his personal observations concerning the deviant behaviour he had witnessed at the police station, her fearless aggression, the smearing which had prompted him to accept her as a client when such behaviour was usually indicative of severe emotional distress. And, of course, all that followed. A notebook and pencil were at all times somewhere on his person for that very reason. He added his own observations to all those before him and began to read, collate and make notes to bring everything together into one succinct report.

Gary's detailed reports supported his own and were equally as thorough. Angie had written in the book, too, about her cooperation and pleasant involvement while making the gingerbread men. She had also remarked on Wendy's relationship with Holly who was helping to make the child feel more secure. Harry had reported his stabbing as if his own pen was the weapon of revenge for the plucks to his overalls, though she seemed to have left no lasting injury unlike the scratches to the backs of Gary's hands which would probably leave scars for a lifetime.

From such he had decided that the sooner he devised a structured handling programme for her the better. One which would allow himself, Gary, Holly and anyone else attempting to control her violence a way to coordinate their approaches for their own safety as well as hers. Also to pass on with her to those who might experience the worst of her behaviour later; a forewarning that this sweetly smiling child could in the space of a moment turn into a Tasmanian Devil. Such a handling programme would, perhaps, prevent as much as possible a physical closeness to those biting teeth, scratching nails, kicking feet and that butting head of hers.

He would have to think up strategies which all his staff and any future staff would, thereafter, have to comply with in order to calm and restrain her rather than alarm and incite her. Wendy had the strength of a writhing anaconda when physically manhandled. The lion tamer's chair and whip might have been the most appropriate way of solving that particular problem, had he been able to get away with employing such tactics as a behaviour management strategy, but in this day and age the child had rights and those rights insisted that she be, at all times, treated with dignity. As it was they would have to make do, as much as possible, with handling belts and handling mats, approaches from the rear and head-down tactics which would keep her from biting and kicking. They would not be allowed to use cuffs or straps or have her behaviour calmed by medication for the sake of making life easier for themselves.

He had before him, also, a copy of tonight's Clarion Evening News with its damning criticisms of the way Greengates House handled its more vulnerable clients. It had been brought to him by a very chastened Harry who had seemed to be as appalled by the reporting style as Tommo was and Gary would be when he saw it later. The photograph had been printed in colour so that the red on the child's face could not be interpreted as anything other than blood. Tommo also believed that it had been doctored to let the blood stand out and emphasise the way she was being carried. Cubby Watson had totally sensationalised the situation from the one he recalled himself as a participant. It had been selected to show her being handled in a way that looked as if she was being further abused. That it had been Gary's blood on her face and not her own had not been mentioned in a harrowing and extremely vitriolic report written by Cubby Watson, which then went on to arouse rebellion and riot on the Dog's Bed Estate because it was considered by the police to be the breeding house of all evil; the home of her assailant and the source of all the crime ever committed in Quinton, ad infinitum. This twisted reasoning being at variance with all that Cubby Watson had written in the past when he had suggested that the Dog's Bed Estate should be razed to the ground and its residents housed elsewhere; divide and conquer tactics.

Cubby Watson, was nothing if not quixotic of opinion if it sold newspapers when he was suggesting, now, that his readership should side with the feelings of victimisation and discrimination on the part of the police and in particular Chief Constable Catty Collins. In his opinion they were doing nothing to try to discover the identity of the child or the whereabouts of a child abuser who, most likely, would strike again. What Cubby was promising the Clarion readership was that he would try, where the police were failing, to solve the mystery of the identity of a little girl who remained nameless except for that given to her as a reference and who was being cruelly treated further at the hands of the monsters at Greengates House.

Tommo threw the paper down in disgust. He felt outrage, not only for himself, but also for Catty Collins. Who the hell did the man think he was if he considered himself qualified to write a published article in a way so unfounded by knowledge and experience? He had no way of understanding how hard it could be to manage wild-fire situations which blew up unexpectedly and with clients that one had yet to get to know how to handle with least damage to any of the parties involved during a physical confrontation. If Catty Collins was using the opportunity of searching for evidence of the child's abuser on the Dog's Bed Estate and question on other wider issues as she did so, to solve other crimes, who could blame her? She was simply killing two birds with one stone. As far as Tommo could ascertain Mally Kenyon had only been taken in for questioning. He had not been charged with anything, so where had it come from that he had been wrongly accused? Knowing Mally of old, the man had a problem with controlling his temper so would not have responded in a way that suggested cooperation. Not that Tommo considered him guilty of child abuse from what he knew of him. His brothers neither, as disreputable as they were.

Grievances against Cubby Watson aside, by Monday morning he hoped to have a comprehensive report sufficient to call for a Multidisciplinary Review Meeting along with Social Services, the Special Needs Team at the Education Department with Catty Collins, herself, as the area's Chief Child Protection Officer in charge of a high profile case which was being extensively reported on the local and national media in order for the child to be passed on to a more suitable care institution. Though an institution at this time was all the child was likely to get, due to the violence she had shown herself capable of inflicting on others as well as towards her own person. That and the smearing which no ordinary foster home would tolerate. Wendy was still a collection of confused characteristics which had yet to be assessed by people better able to deal with the lapses within her developmental profile and the trauma created by an isolated existence.

For Tommo was now sure that she had been displaying all the characteristic behaviours of a child isolated from play and social contact with other children.

She had demonstrated an inappropriate response as a stimulus to a dog chain to suggest that she had been restrained using such methods and had suggested as much, herself.

She seemed to have no perception of self in terms of an internalised body image. It was as if she had never played dressing up in front of a mirror using Mummy's clothes or been used to seeing herself reflected in a wide range of surfaces, as she travelled about within her community.

She had, probably, never known face paints or the delight of seeing herself pull funny faces in a mirror before she had been terrorised by her own image in a dressing mirror. He had noted that she had since spent a great deal of time looking at herself, which was not in keeping with the usual play practises of a child of at least seven. The gaps in her development would have to be filled in before she could use her perceptions as the stepping stones to her future. It was simply not possible for any child to make developmental progress without the earlier stepping stones being planted firmly for such progress to be made.

Yet her reactions to adults in her play had been appropriate from what Gary and Holly had reported. She could read, write and draw. She could sing and dance. She could even play the small, toy keyboard which Angie had provided for her amusement. She had asked if there was a computer she might use to play games and find information using the internet. She knew the rules of games and had been able to take turns and share. She had not therefore been uneducated.

She had been well fed, showed no greed and knew how to make appropriate choices when these were offered to her. Apart from her violence when thwarted she had understood the role of the adult as educator and guide and organizer within social situations. Who was this lady with the golden trumpet, she constantly asked after? As long as she would tell them nothing of her previous life the child would remain an enigma.

There were other points he noted as of equal importance in her confused perceptions of self. The child had seemed not to have developed dominance of hand or eye and had demonstrated different ways of presenting herself, sometimes demanding, sometimes placid, sometimes exceptionally eloquent and at other times so immature that he had occasionally suspected that she was intellectually retarded. Conversely, he had known a lot of confused adolescents with sufficiently good language skills to appear to be intellectually bright and yet have very little actual understanding of the social rules they constantly offended. Lads who could read and write and yet had little comprehension for the meaning of words both spoken and written. Lads and girls with warped perceptions as if they looked at themselves and all around them through fairground mirrors. They were victims of their own distortions and lateral thinking.

Yet now, for some indefinable reason, she appeared to be greatly more settled, as if whatever she had feared had diminished somewhat. For that reason he decided that he might perhaps interview her without causing her to erupt into violence yet again. He could attribute nothing of the deviance in her behaviour to be directly associated with her having been placed in a sack and thrown to drown in putrid water other than to note the reaction she had made towards her rescuer. It was not unknown for extreme shock to trigger the same reactions. Yet most of her anger had seemed to be directed at anyone who failed to comply with her need to be given access to this lady with the golden trumpet. Her trashing of her bedroom seen as something else. Tommo saw that as a direct reaction to not understanding the science of reflection, though why it should also lead to self harm he did not yet understand. Time to do a bit of investigative questioning himself.

To this end, he had Holly take her to the Activity Room again where they might all share a common activity. He took with him the big, blue, gold embossed daily diary which he might use himself to note his observations through a few succinct, key words which would inform the first of his formal conclusions and recommendations. Also, to give an example to Holly of how he liked the entries to be made. He had noted already a childish hand, though he was reasonably impressed by the way she had expressed herself and would therefore be satisfactory on a temporary basis. He thought to use the drawing Wendy had done earlier to start a conversation. It looked as if all she had drawn was a giant eye surrounded by thick, black, wax crayon. He removed it from the diary, noticing as he did so that the pencil she had used to make her original drawing now covered with the black wax had come through to the back of the paper. He turned it over, looking from front to back and seeing the hidden drawing beneath. There was also some writing which she had covered over, also, as if to hide it away under the wax. His gasp was discernible though neither Wendy nor Holly seemed to take much notice as they waited for him to begin. Wendy sat happily on Holly's knee though she had her arms crossed and one finger over pressed lips. Her body language said that she would be saying nothing. Her eyes were level as she stared at him. She had the rag doll on her lap which she gripped onto with blue patterned knees. Dressed so and with her hair done as Holly had fashioned it to one side of her face she looked pretty enough to discredit her behaviour of such a short time before.

As he held the picture up what he saw was immediately recognisable to him. An outside scene; a lake with swans, trees and a bandstand. It was a place he recognised immediately from her childish drawing for its characteristics and their placement, each one in reference to each other. As a boy he had used to roam the same open places, drawn the same images. As a boy there had been rowing boats on the lake which the local ruffians liked to sink on a regular basis. Each year a pair of nesting swans came to produce a brood of signets, nesting within the reeds and shady trees of a central island; the pupil of the eye she had drawn which was all that had been left visible in Wendy's drawing. They had recently been attacked with spears. It had been feared that their broken wings would mean that they would never fly again. Yet they had flown again. They had flown away to a better place, hopefully to breed again, somewhere safe.

Tommo recognised Lower Quinton Park, the bandstand, the mere and the playing fields without question. It could be nowhere else, though the bandstand looked more like two tiers on a wedding cake. He had used to go there and hide himself away, put himself into solitary confinement in order to avoid a beating from a father who had made his and his mother's life one of continual Hell. Until Tommo had struck the blow to the back of his head with a sweeping brush that had killed him. To this day he could not decide whether or not he had intended to commit patricide or merely stop his father from hurting his mother further. For this reason he feared what lay within himself. That potential for harming others which lay within the breast of all mankind when it was human nature to protect that which it loved and, like any animal, will attack under provocation.

The child fascinated him, too, for she was a fighter, determined to gain her end in any way she could. Only her years held back what he considered to be a formidable ability for self preservation and self determination. If she had decided that she would not speak then she would not speak. However, what she had drawn was speaking to Tommo loud and clear of things she had sought to keep secret by making her drawing look like an eye in a sheet of black wax. The impression of her original drawing came clearly, even if back to front through the back of the paper, as he held it up for all their admiration. To the foreground two figures and between them what he assumed to be a shopping trolley; an oblong shape on wheels with a handle which the lady with the blank, triangular head was holding. Not a single part of her body was showing. She held the end of a chain in her hand which looped about her hand in a single line and then attached itself to the shopping trolley.

Immediately, Tommo made the connection with the same woman who had stood outside the railings as they had brought Wendy through the gates that same morning. He had noticed the shopping trolley. He had seen her before, too, when he reflected deeply, out and about the shops of Quinton with the same trolley in tow. He had earlier that day listened to Harry's bleated complaints concerning her requests to come into the grounds to look for a timid dog that would be hiding away in the shrubbery because it would be frightened of Chester. All his life Tommo had some distant and occasional familiarity with this woman who covered herself from head to foot, wondering why her face was hidden, but then quickly forgetting about her again. Wendy had seen her standing outside Greengates House, just as he had moments before she began her mammoth tantrum while still strapped into her seat on the mini-bus. This, the tantrum that Cubby Watson had got such mileage out of. Could the shopping trolley be the cart which Wendy had referred to as a vehicle she enjoyed riding in? The same as depicted in her drawing, too, as far-fetched as it seemed? It had certainly looked to be big enough to carry a small child hidden from view with the lid down. The woman had been holding on to a pink dog lead, too. This, the same as that depicted in loops of circles in her drawing which went from the woman's hand to the lid of the shopping trolley. She had tapped at the window of the mini-bus with the clip end to draw Wendy's attention. That had been when Wendy had gone ballistic, as she had screamed and screamed and made tantrum to see the lady with the golden trumpet. And there she was in the picture, also!

The drawing and writing, seen through the back of the paper was back to front, right to left, but clearly visible as an impression under the cover of black wax. That side being all that Wendy and Holly would be looking at. He could see a name and an address written clearly at the bottom of the paper. He was about to read it out when suddenly Gary interrupted him, bursting in suddenly as if something had arisen which would not be waited on.

"Out everyone! Evacuate the building. There's a bin on fire by the front door. Pressed up to it and ready to set the house aflame. I've phoned the fire brigade."

Ever a stickler for procedure Tommo slid the drawing back into the large book, stood, issued the same order to Holly and Wendy and went as pack leader to show them the safest way out. It was his job as head of the unit to account for all staff. "Where's Harry?"

"No sign of him. He's our back-up, too, after Angie leaves for home. It might have been him smoking again under the porch because he's frightened to death of Angie seeing him. Just carelessly discarded the butt and then the wind blew the bin hard up against the door where it suddenly ignited."

The men looked at each other knowingly. It was all wishful thinking so as not to alarm the young ladies present. Men being macho he privately considered it to be a personal attack on himself and Gary for recommended procedures carried out against previous clients. They each shared a similar thought that it was one of Jacko's gang members, or one of the same, never-ending, disaffected youths back on a mission of revenge. Not the first time that they had come under attack, despite the locked gates.

As he gathered up his precious daily diary they started to move in unison towards the side kitchen door. Holly had Wendy firmly by the hand. They had yet to avail themselves of the refreshment that Angie had left for them. Holly grabbed two gingerbread men as she passed a plate where they now lay juxtaposition one on top of the other, ever so prettily decorated. Not to be wasted after all the work of making them. At least the kid might have something to stop her getting peckish if they were unable to get at their supper for some considerable time to come. Holly had a lot of experience of watching the effects of nuisance calls made to the fire brigade and the thoroughness of their search when they came hoses ready to douse non-existent flames. It was getting time for the hole in her belly to be filled again so she hoped that they would not be long in going so that they might enter the house for the soup and sarnies which she could smell;

the kitchen was full of lovely food smells. One day she would have a go at cooking instead of living off junk bought from supermarkets and fast food establishments in plastic or polystyrene containers.

"Take her over by the fence down at the bottom of the garden," Tommo called to Holly. "Quick as you can just in case there's some kind of explosion. The gas comes in the front way off the street. Better to be safe than sorry." Then, organizing his command of just the one permanent conscript, "You try to find Harry. I'll go to open the gates ready for the fire engine."

They could already hear a siren. Passers-by were gathering as the smell of smoke drifted towards them and was blown by the wind in a swirling, grey screen to obscure the potting shed. The dog's kennel was empty as they passed. Gary checked as he went past it towards the front of the house calling Harry's name as he went. Where the heck were they then? Both Chester and Harry seemed to have disappeared. Not that Chester was, these days, any use as a guard dog.

There were no lights on to indicate that Harry had already retired to his self-contained, dimly lit flat in the basement for a bit of a skive and, maybe, taken the dog in with him. Maybe to refresh his bowl of water or find him a few biscuits. Though such actions would have been much out of character when he thought the dog a blasted nuisance most of the time. It was unheard of for Harry Groves to miss a single meal, also, and like the rest of them he had yet to avail himself of the soup and sandwiches left by Angie for their supper. Dishes washed for him, too, via the services of an automatic dishwasher which he did not have within his flat. Why dirty plates in his flat which he would have to wash himself?

So where could he have got to? Gates locked and the heap of broken furniture still visible, he had not taken himself off to the tip. The mini-bus was still to be seen, also, and Harry no vehicle of his own. It was also getting on for his knocking-off time. Harry worked not a minute longer than an eight hour day if he could help it. If he was not in the flat or the house then where was he? He would not have left the grounds unless telling them first in case they needed back-up.

Gary, fired with his mission, went to the potting shed first because Harry had last been seen cutting the grass with the fly mower. He always took his penknife to the encrusted grass around the cutting blade as one of his last tasks, usually seated within his potting shed, so Gary fully expected to find him there completing this task.

The door was closed and the padlock fixed to the bar which secured it when not in use. However, the key remained in the padlock hole and the bar was fastened. Harry turned it hearing the dog begin to whelp within the shed. One mystery solved. When he opened the door the dog bounded out barking. Harry Groves groaned where he lay on the floor.

At first Harry assumed that the aging man had suffered a heart attack. Then he remembered the lock had been fastened on the outside of the shed. Then he saw the blood on Harry's skull and a claw hammer lying against the back of his overalls where it had been discarded, presumably after applying a sharp smack to the back of Gary's head.

Only then did he realise the implications. "Tommo quick! Harry's been attacked. The garden. Leave the gates. Someone's attacked Harry and put the dog in the shed with him. They can only be after the kid."

The gates were unlocked even if not rolled back as the fire engine came to pull up outside still with lights flashing in front of the closed gates. A fire blazed merrily in a green, plastic bin on wheels hard up against the front door of the house. It had been over by the railings close to the small side gate. The leaping flames which the smell suggested had been ignited by a dousing of petrol had not yet caught a hold of the yellow paint which was fast blistering.

"The child...!" Tommo yelled back, still with the diary tucked underarm even as he began to run back round the side of the building in the direction of the rear garden.

When he got to the bottom where the bushes screened the fence all he could see was grass, trees, bushes and hedges. No Holly. No Wendy. He tripped over a large pair of industrial snippers discarded on the grass. They had been used to breach the chain link fence by cutting through the plastic coated metal. A piece as big as a table top had been prized open behind the screening bushes. Whoever had done it must have spent a long time silently cutting each individual snick.

There was still no sign of either Wendy Bridgewater or Holly Hargreaves even as he called their names and hoped that a reply would come from somewhere close by. The hole might have swallowed them up as if through a time-warp. The lane was deserted. There was no sign of a car or indeed any kind of vehicle to suggest in which direction someone might have spirited them away.

On the grass, however, lay two pads of cotton gauze. When Tommo lifted them to his nose he could smell solvent. His stomach churned to think that he had directed Holly to bring the child to the very place where someone had been in wait, their decoy placed, knowing something of the regulated procedure of a fire drill at Greengates House.

The dog sniffed about at the deep footprints in the soil and over the grass. It ate the foot of a gingerbread man that had fallen to the ground.

In the distance the smell of burning petrol was in the air. Another train slowed in wait for the signal to take it over the single tracked viaduct. The distant sounds of screams and shouts and pandemonium and destruction filled the air. Kick off had started at the Dog's Bed Estate.

Then Gary was behind him. "Harry will be okay I think. Took a nasty bang on the head though. No sign of them?"

Tommo shook his head. "Not that I can see. You don't think that Holly was planted do you?"

"Why?"

"To get the child away. To stop the child from talking I would think. It has to be Mally Kenyon who's abducted them." Then he looked at the diary and thought about what it contained. "I think that I might know where the child previously lived."

They walked together round to the front of the building. The fire in the bin had been put out quickly by the fire brigade and a cursory inspection of the building made. No time however to make an occasion of a bit of house fire, as far as the fire officers were concerned. Not when it was all tenders to the Dog's Bed Estate.

"I'd better inform the police that we've let another client escape," Tommo said wearily. "The second in as many days."

Even after a couple of minutes of attempted phone calls Tommo was still unable to get through to the police station. The lines were continually engaged. Instead he phoned Brian Ghould and told him that a Ward of the Authority, most likely soon to be a Ward of the State had been kidnapped from the most secure establishment in Quinton, save for the holding cells at Quinton Police Station. Someone had made a hole in the chain link fence and spirited her away along with her nursemaid. For the time being he would keep his suspicions to himself concerning Holly Hargreaves.

When they got back to where a very dazed and rambling Harry Groves was blaming Wendy Bridgewater for attacking him again, his head running with blood while he leant back against a bag of potting compost, Tommo shook his head. "Can't get through to the police, Harry. After the ambulance has seen you off I think Gary and I had better get over to 34, Park Road, Quinton."

"Why there?" Gary asked. "That where the child lived?"

Tommo shrugged. "It's an address she put on the bottom of her drawing and then tried to obliterate by colouring over it. I would think so, but we'll only know when we knock on the door and ask. It can only be Mally Kenyon's taken the kid so that she can't give evidence against him."

Then Gary paled as his brain began to clear of panic. Finally, what

Holly had told him earlier came back to mind with an unpleasant suspicion that he had goofed big time. His eyes grew wide.

"What?" asked Tommo, seeing the look of guilt on his face.

Gary was contrite. "I should have told you earlier. I didn't because I thought to give Holly a break. Tommo...she's a Kenyon! Holly is a Kenyon!"

"She can't be."

"She is. She's Magdalene Kenyon's daughter as was taken into care."

Tommo's face was a picture of offended accusation.

Twenty-Nine

He got her up out of bed with one, long, persistent ring on her doorbell. The pizza was still hot in its box and the wine well thrashed about in its bottle after a very speedy ride in Cubby's sports car to the flats where Gina Mon lived.

From her bedroom and lounge windows she had a top floor view out over the Dog's Bed Estate towards the higher fells which rolled bitter green and purple in the haze of the late afternoon sunshine. It was yet to turn four in the afternoon.

She lay awake but not yet ready to get up out of her rumpled bed. At first ring she had thought that her caller might be her mother come to take a look at a wound which now throbbed and smarted as her head lay against the pillow. Gingerly she had washed her hair in the shower before getting into bed, and then blow-dried it with great care. She had the worst, most undeserved hangover of her existence.

Most irritatingly she kept thinking of Cubby Watson. She had been unable to get him out of her head as she soaped and rinsed and dried herself and then composed herself for sleep. In his own inimitable fashion he had forced himself into her personal space. His grasp was still to be felt like a locked bracelet about the fine bones of her wrist. He had impressed her with his body heat as if she was made of wax. His vapour had somehow wrapped about her and sucked her into the genie lamp where charismatic people like Cubby Watson live. He was the type of man to offer promises as any genie does. She had missed his offer of a free lunch even while knowing that there was no such thing. She was hungry and in some discomfort. Feeling sorry for herself. If she had three wishes the first would be to indulge herself shamefully with pizza, the second to open a bottle of good red wine to drink with it and the third to have her headache disappear.

Part of her had wanted to accept his invitation. The common sense part of her brain told her to stay well away from him. It did not stop her from recalling the strength in his fingers or his black-pea eyes which could soften to so many different shades of brown from sweet toffee to dark, bitter chocolate to black coals when the light penetrated them. A temptation that presented itself as a magnet twisting over her head which drew her irresistibly towards him. Opposites attract. Like to like repels. Was body chemistry the same?

She could not be thinking straight if she was attracted by a man like Cubby Watson. Perhaps the child's assault had caused more damage to her brain than had been revealed by X-ray. There was a hair line fracture to her common sense.

When the bell persisted she considered that the button had become stuck in. Her mother would never so rudely insist on her answering the door bell quite so expediently by leaving her finger on it.

Rising with some stiffness when her ribs were sore she wrapped her semi- nakedness in a belted gown of cerise silk with a quilted collar as she went to know what the urgency was about. Even before she had opened it a crack she wished that she had put the safety chain on before opening. There was simply no way of stopping a man like Cubby Watson from bowling in, relinquishing his gifts to her coffee table, removing his jacket and looking about. He had his sleeves rolled up and his pockets bulging as he availed himself of the view through her lounge windows. His camera hung about his neck. His chestnut curls gleamed in a shaft of sunlight, though he had the scent of a man in need of a shower and a deodorant spray. When he turned to look at her his face was pensive.

"You can see over to the Dog's Bed from here. My informant tells me that the stone throwing's started already. The barricade's complete. Waste bins full of missiles. Beer's flowing too. The men are all tanked up on best Thistlethwaites and it's not yet teatime. The women have seated themselves in a line behind them in charge of the rally call while nipping at a shared bottle of gin. Or so I'm told. I'll get all the pictures I need later when it's well underway."

Gina looked at him expectantly. He had yet to explain what he wanted.

He looked back to the window, eyes darting, thrusting hands deeply into pockets where they had limited space. "It's like it's all been choreographed for them. History repeating itself. Like one of them mock battles by historical societies. The police are on stand-off at the minute. She's troop commander placed there to settle the uprising. She's after building the tension because it all suits her own ends. All I am is the little drummer boy. Catty Collins will be waiting on horseback, well back from the fray for one of her men to be injured. That will be all the justification she will need. There's nothing unlawful about protest for protest's sake, as long as it's harmless."

He turned back to her, explaining the plot of an event that might have happened long ago. All he was doing was recounting. "I doubt my columns make much difference in the long term. All I do is create debate. It's fact that people act upon...an injured officer will be all the excuse she needs to really show her colours...batons...rubber bullets...tear gas, probably...the lot. There's riot vans already lined up all along the road to the bridge for just that purpose. Or they were when I left there earlier."

Gina squared herself against him. "I take it that this is the bare bones of tomorrow's lead story. You're a fund of information, Mr Watson. People will only stand so much pushing around before they retaliate. Personally, I don't blame them." Then as he flung himself into her favourite armchair, "Please feel free to make yourself at home. Brought your own afternoon snack have you?"

"Thanks. So I have! Enough for two. It had to happen sometime. You missed a late lunch at the Italiana." He brought his folded copy of the Clarion out of his coat pocket and waved it at her. "First off the press. Front page spread. I still intend to find out who the kid is."

After he had placed it on her coffee table he found his own bottle opener on his key ring and started to skewer the cork and wind it out. He had had two glasses already and work still to do but a sip of hers would help to wash down the slice of pizza he intended to enjoy. He had not had his usual leisurely breakfast. He felt hungry just looking at her.

The bottle in the main was for her. Soften her up. Make her more mellow. God she looked gorgeous. The dressing robe showing her panty line left little to his fertile imagination. She looked entirely unaware which added to the pleasure of noting it. The last thing she was doing was flirting with her arms folded under her well endowed bosom and that look on her face. Whiplash lady! He doubted she was aware that her hair was sticking up at the back and the rest was all over the place. A mouth made for kissing.

"Help yourself to pizza. I'll get a glass for you. Kitchen this way?"

Gina let her eyes roll. How did he know that when she was down she was always a glutton for pizza and red wine? Or, maybe, he hadn't as it was standard Italian take-away.

When he returned he had two plates also. The pizza he intended to share in equal quantity.

Why not? She took a corner of the settee and folded her legs up under her, tucking her feet away and picked up the paper. The photographs horrified her. Mally Kenyon being led away in handcuffs, his head covered, his torso bare, was bad enough when he had yet to be proven guilty but the lead caption printed in bold, extra point, was a damnation of the police themselves; *arrested for child abuse and then allowed to walk free. Suspect still on the loose.* It was scaremongering at its most sensational.

The photograph of Wendy being delivered to Greengates House made the child look as if she was being abused for a second time. She was gripping onto a doorpost with a terrified look on her face while being dragged by two unfriendly monsters. She had what looked to be blood on her face. Gina knew differently because she had witnessed it just as he had. The child's vulnerability was what was most striking about the picture. "For goodness sake she's seven years of age. What are you trying to do? Get Dr Thomas in trouble! They don't deserve this."

"That's what the camera saw. That's what my readers have a right to know about. I've brought these."

"You're a man with very big pockets I see."

Cubby nodded as he took the photos and photocopies out of their folded, plastic protection and spread them out on the table.

Gina accepted a slice of pizza and a glass of wine as she appraised them. The photo of a red polka-dot dress with a smocked top intrigued her. She assumed that this was what the child had been wearing from the staining. Definitely part of the Little Princess Range. She had avoided that very rail of designer children's wear at Trimbles only that morning because of the price labels. The underwear, too, was top of the range at Trimbles. The pretty socks had silk butterflies on the frill with diamante spots on the wings. The shoes were the moderately expensive type for which children's feet were shod after minute sizing from narrow to wide fitting. These looked to be small for a seven year old and very narrow of width. "Where did you get all this? The police don't release this kind of thing mid-investigation. I'd say they were bought from Trimbles Children's Wear, if that's what you're asking. The Little Princess Range is expensive."

"The shoes?"

"Any good shoe shop. The rag doll's different. I recognise it because my mother has a lot to do with fund raising for St Andrew's Church. It's a charity doll. VAT exempt as long as it's sold for that purpose. The firm who make them offer a donation from their profits to doff a cap to their own charity status. Can't remember the company but I can soon tell you. I'll phone my mother."

"How do you know it's a charity doll...the same range?"

"Its hair. I saw the full range for sale at the Christmas Fair last December. I helped sell them. They all have that same kind of thick, orange wool hair and the same faces. It's just the clothes that are different."

"Any way of finding out who bought it?"

"I think there might be. Mum told me at the time. Every purchase has to be recorded quite meticulously because of the doll's charity status. Names and address taken for the guarantees. Each doll numbered."

"What?" Cubby had a string of mozzarella and a splash of tomato sauce on his teeth. "Numbered?"

"That is her doll is it? I recall seeing it drying on the radiator at the police station but that doesn't mean it's actually hers...bought for her specifically. If she's off the Dog's Bed a lot of toys are second-hand or donated. It might even have been chucked into the canal and she'd just brought it out with her."

Cubby shook his head. "Came out of the sack with her according to the police reports. I've read them. Has to be hers and no one else's. Numbered?"

Gina rose after laying down her glass and her plate. Her gown had fallen open to reveal good legs, white skin, a triangle of white silk and lace. She quickly brought the parted opening together and fastened the belt tighter before going to the phone. "Soon tell you."

Cubby brought the picture up to take a closer look. Looking round he brought a pair of spectacles from his inside pocket and slipped them on the bridge of his nose. The label showed up more plainly. If he had looked earlier wearing his spectacles he could have saved himself twenty quid and a good deal of time. On the other hand he would not have missed this for the world. Her flat had the kind of homely quality and order his own lacked. Oswald Charity Doll: Item No: 397 was made by Stuffed Dolls Limited. The manufacturer was, he now realised, next to the unit where they printed his newspaper on the Whemley Industrial Estate.

After talking in the hallway, Gina returned. "That one with the blue pants is Oswald. There's also a Marcy...a Daphne...and a Frederick. They sell well every Christmas at Mum's church. At Easter they do bunnies and hens. In the summer, frogs and scarecrows. In the autumn it's witches and wizards and then back to rag dolls. Mum said they aren't available to shops, only to registered charities with a share of the profit going strictly to registered charities. If you know the number on the label the company can tell you who the doll was sold to."

"Simple as that!"

Gina nodded. "The factory should still be open." She placed a piece of paper on the coffee table. "Mum doesn't know the telephone number but that's the address of the factory on the Whemley Trading Estate. They might not be willing to give the information over though. Confidentiality and all that!"

They would if they thought the VAT man was checking up on them, thought Cubby. "Save me another slice. I shan't be long."

Gina watched him slide into his jacket again and put the paper in his pocket. He left his photocopies as if sure that he would be returning. Then a request in his eyes as he spoke again. "Maybe a glass of wine for later."

After he had slammed out of her flat, Gina considered it. It was still a case of only maybe! He left behind him an atmosphere of disturbed air. There was no doubt that he had strummed against her strings and left her vibrating. Somehow she knew that Cubby Watson would be her own downfall because there was that something indefinable about him which turned off the red light and changed it to green.

*****

Cubby Watson was on a roll as he went up the outer steps to the upper floor of a factory unit, following an arrow to *Reception*. To the ground floor a late afternoon shift was presently working to produce its latest batches of charity dolls. Through the windows he could see orange thrums and boldly patterned material everywhere. They now seemed to be onto scarecrows and frogs as the machines hummed and the bobbins turned on industrial sewing machines. The things some people did for a living! The sunlight coming in through the big windows was shimmering with the cotton dust from the stuffing.

He caught the woman just as she was about to lock the office and go home. She looked tired and harassed as if it had been one of those days.

"Whatever it is it will have to wait until tomorrow."

She looked as if she meant it. Cubby revised his plan slightly. "Police. I need some information with regard to the child they found in the canal last night. Radio and TV is full of it."

The woman's face suggested her horror. "God Almighty! What a way to treat a child. Had one of our dolls did she?"

"How do you know?"

"Why else would the police come here? It's all we make. Charity dolls are our business. She's a child. Dolls and children go together."

"The Oswald, number 397. You'll be asked to say nothing concerning this by the way. It will be regarded as a breach of confidentiality if you as much as breathe the name connected with the purchase of this doll to anyone but me. In particular the newspapers."

"As if I would. People buy our dolls for all kinds of reasons. Presents mainly. We're only obliged to take the information because we have charity status. We allow a small percentage of our profits to charity and we only sell to registered charities. That's what makes us competitive with all the foreign rubbish that gets imported in at two thirds the price."

She opened up again, inviting Cubby in to stand before her

narrow counter, side by side with a Marcy as tall as he was. If only women came as cute and as mute he would be a happy man.

"Three, nine, seven you said?" She opened up a hand written ledger with the name of Oswald on the front. "Our most popular because it appeals to both boys and girls. We ask for them to be sold in strictly numerical order if at all possible, allowing no more than batches of twenty five at a time. Batch three seven five to four hundred went to St Andrew's Church for their Christmas Fair last December. Let's see…the person who purchased that particular one paid us with a cheque drawn on Abby Bank…a C. C. Watson."

Cubby frowned. He had been about to point out a mistake. Then decided his ears were faulty. "I beg your pardon?"

"Why not write it down. We always ask for a note of the bank details and take an address should the cheque bounce or the guarantee need checking before we make a replacement. Mr C. C. Watson of thirty-four, Park Road, Lower Quinton."

For the first time in a long time Cubby felt the wind punched out of him. It was as if someone invisible had landed a fist in his solar plexus.

He did not know why he went back to Gina but when she answered her doorbell it was to two short, polite rings. She had changed her clothes to a short, denim skirt and a blouse of red chiffon with gathered sleeves. He looked to be a changed man.

"Er…I need to speak to someone."

"Then I'm your man."

"I'm serious."

She saw the blanched look and the curve of his lower eye lids. Cubby Watson shocked? She found it hard to believe. "You had an accident or something?"

He shook his head, coming in, turning to face her. She allowed him to take her in his arms. She could feel him trembling as he laid his head against her ear. She allowed her own arms to come around him.

They stood together like that for several moments before he moved his head, lifted it, a pain in his eyes. "You have a father as well as a mother?"

Gina shook her head. "A big family though."

"My father's an asshole. I've always known it. Can't keep his pants zipped. Caused my mother hell. I don't want you to think that I'm like him. I'm not."

Gina frowned. He was trying to tell her something important. "You found out who bought the doll?"

He nodded.

Her wait was painfully long but she quite liked the hug being in need of one herself.

Eventually as if a decision made. "My own father. There can't be all that many C. C. Watson's write cheques on Abby Bank in Quinton."

Gina pulled her head back and gaped at him. The implication he was making was obvious. "Are you thinking what I'm thinking?"

He nodded. "I only hope to God that it's not right." Then he lowered his head again so that his breath was tickling his neck. "Pigeons coming home to roost. Supposing it's true? What do I do now? Lie to my readership or tell the truth?"

"First discover the truth. Then decide. Do you want me to help you?"

He nodded. "We have to get over to thirty-four, Park Road, Lower Quinton. I have to know why dad has that house as a second address...which my mother and I know nothing about. I even followed him there today so I know it's correct. He was acting strangely. Had been all morning. The kid's picture holding the rag doll seemed to mesmerise him. I thought it was a case of too much of the hard stuff. Both my parents warned me not to chase the balloon. They both begged me not to pursue her identity. I didn't listen."

"Shouldn't you call the police with his information?"

"I don't know. I don't know what to do any more."

Gina allowed him to bring her closer again into his embrace. She always had been a sucker for damaged children.

Cubby raised a right hand to stroke her face.

Thirty

At shortly gone four-thirty in the afternoon, half an hour after the Quinton bus arrived and which Angie Meadows had boarded, a battered transit van drove out of the side lane that wound between the train bridge and the side of Greengates House. It was indicating to cross the traffic and make in the direction of Lower Quinton. Two men were within; one driving and one seated on the passenger seat. There were no back windows. The name of a local, Lower Quinton builder had been hand-painted on the sides and rear doors. The men within were talking animatedly before one, the one in the passenger seat, took a call on his mobile. He was laughing loudly as people do when their usual reticence is overwhelmed by certain types of drugs. Full of himself!

Between the men the huge head of a mottled, grey, short-haired Bull Mastiff poked through between the seats over the gear change, its studded collar shining in the sunlight coming in through the passenger window. The dog's invasive head was roughly pushed back to the rear of the van. Its rapid breaths had already caused the windows to steam up as the van pulled out into the traffic and then went on its way in the direction of Lower Quinton. The person watching this egress stood on the pavement opposite the house, following its receding rear doors and the black smoke coming from the damaged exhaust pipe, until it was out of sight.

Unlike those round and about there was no gasp of surprise or shared concern as an injured man was carted out of a shed on a stretcher and put into a waiting ambulance. Just a brief shaking of the hat. There was no request for an explanation from the next person within the milling crowd standing round about as Tommo and Gary ran back and forth like scalded hens between the front and the rear of the house, a sure sign that someone was unaccounted for.

The dog that had come out of the shed before the stretcher was now chained up on a lead next to its kennel before the hole in the back garden fence was roughly repaired using a roll of wire as a temporary stop gap. The two unit staff waited for the fire engine and ambulance to be on their way before they got into a white mini bus. The man with the glasses who wore an odd mix of clothing constantly trying to contact someone on the phone. A big blue book deposited behind the seat when at last they were ready to go. His hand kept sweeping the air as if he was trying to make an explanation that was not being listened to.

People began to disperse after the ambulance carted away the man brought from a garden shed where some form of accident had occurred. The fire engine having done little more than attend to the fire in the bin before going on its way again. The person at the bus stop dipped a head covered by the big, fashionable Homburg with a beribboned brim sporting a pheasant's tail feather which gave the hat a racy look. That it was handmade and expensive was obvious. The coat was a beige mackintosh with buttoned, shoulder epaulettes and a wide collar turned up and button fastened at the neck. The shoes were brogues of fine brown leather, light and supple on feet which raised themselves together onto tip-toes as a prelude to a clipped walk to the red Jaguar, which was parked a short distance up the road.

The person so attired flicked the automatic button on the gadget in gloved hands to release the catch on the door, got into the driver's seat, looked into the mirror to judge the traffic behind longer than was needed to make an assessment of the wisdom of pulling out. It waited only long enough for the white mini-bus to turn itself about from its parking space via a three point turn, nose its way through the open gates and then wait as the man in the odd clothes jumped down to close the gates and lock them again. The figure knew that the only evidence that could make a connection with the child was the rag doll and the rag doll had been taken also. Thus all was accounted for...the child, her minder, Dr Thomas and Gary Silvers. The caretaker had gone to hospital and the cook had gone home.

With a murmur of satisfaction the car was put from park into drive as the mini-bus turned right and passed by the red Jaguar. It pulled out into the traffic as the mini-bus passed, following behind all the way to Lower Quinton. It turned down Fenton Street and seeing the mini-bus turn at the park railings at the end of the street parked up without being seen by those it was following. There could be only one course of action, now. One already considered. One finally decided. One agreed.

The figure got out of the car with the same quick decisive stride and went to the boot. Lifting the heavy lid it removed two large, white plastic containers with moulded handles and screw tops; identical containers even to the brownish fluid which swilled inside them, save for their quantities. Supposing that they had shortly before been filled with the same measure one was now depleted of a fifth of its contents.

A drip soaked into the palm of the brown leather glove as they were brought out and placed on the tarmac road while other items were sought from the boot interior. The funnel was placed underarm with the plastic tubing which was attached and trailing more spots of clear fluid onto the pavement.

The first thing to catch sight of was not the men getting out of the mini-bus but the low slung, red sports car bearing two people and slowing down as it came to park opposite the house. The gasp was audible as the person retreated back again quickly.

This was now a case of anxious wonderment and some considerable worry. How had Cubby found out about the child and the goings on at thirty-four, Park Road, Lower Quinton?

The people in the red sports car and the white mini-bus had the same destination.

*****

They met face to face: Tommo and Gary; Cubby and Gina, with only cold air and disapprobation separating them as they stood on the pavement in front of the black and mint green painted gate, though Gina recalled her gratitude over Tommo's well-timed intervention of only that morning. Tommo, for his part, would have wished for her to be in the company of anyone but Cubby Watson.

Cubby offered an olive branch. "I'm here to discover the truth. I have every reason to believe that the child lives here."

Tommo stared back coldly; standoffishly. "So have we. The child has been taken from our care."

Cubby's eyes widened. "Kidnapped?"

Tommo nodded. "For want of a better word. Her care worker too. Though we have some suspicion that she may have been involved. She's a relation of Mally Kenyon."

Gina offered a solution. "Then maybe we should work together. We need to find her. We want to get to the bottom of this…."

"So do we," Tommo said. "In fact, I think I have some idea. It's the same woman who was standing outside the gates to Greengates House this morning. She said her dog had strayed into the grounds. I've seen her about Quinton but don't know her name. A woman who covers herself from head to foot because of some kind of disfigurement."

Cubby and Gina looked at each other and nodded. They had both noted her being there. It was too late now to try to protect his father's involvement with the child even if his suspicions had yet to be proven and a relationship identified. Cubby offered his suggestion for action first. "We might have been seen already. If anyone is after avoiding us and wants to escape there are back entries to these houses onto a shared alleyway. Might

323

I suggest that you knock at the front and Gina and I will go round the back to watch the back gate."

Tommo nodded, looking up at the frontage of number thirty-four. "The house looks empty. It's boarded up upstairs. Okay then. We might as well help each other when we're after the same thing."

An agreement was made for want of a better suggestion, Gary agreeing with everyone because he considered his opinion to be of lesser importance. He also blamed himself because Tommo would have sent Holly packing as soon as he had known that she had a link with Mally Kenyon.

Cubby and Gina ran back along the pavement in the same direction they had driven in to the end of the far corner of the street, round the corner and up the cobbled, rear access to a gate marked with a number thirty-four; mint green paint, on black gloss.

Meanwhile, Tommo and Gary went up the path and rang at the bell. No reply was forthcoming so they rang again, standing waiting. A neighbour appeared. They began to chat over a low, dividing wall.

Round to the rear of the house, Cubby did not wait on invitation as his hand went to the gate. He found it to be open as he pressed against it and, despite Gina's reluctance, trespassed within. Cubby had no reservations about going where he shouldn't! Gina held back.

The yard was tidy and cleanly swept. The back door open by a few inches. The weather not clement enough and the neighbourhood certainly not friendly enough to make this anything other than a statement that someone seemed to have left the house in a hurry.

He went in with Gina lagging behind still. He could hear a familiar voice on local radio talking softly from the next room. The house held a fetid warmth. He went past the open door to a toilet into a kitchen, into an inner hallway where a tabby cat with a ringed tail was coming to investigate. It had seemed to walk through a closed door until he saw the flap swing back with a click. Its green eyes looked wary. It arched its back at his gasp and hissed at him but then went out the back way, rubbing past Gina's legs as she followed Cubby timidly into the house.

Before entering the lounge Cubby called out. "Anyone at home?"

No reply.

He moved into the lounge area where a gas fire was set to a low flame, the cause of an airless atmosphere in the room. Its mantles glowing gently above a tidy hearth. He went to the old fashioned radiogram and turned the dial to switch the radio off. Then the fire. Also the TV set, no sound but its picture showing an afternoon soap. The tick of the clock on the mantle immediately annoying him. How could anyone listen to that all day? No sign of occupation though as he went through to open the front door, having to tug hard on the vestibule door which had rucked up the carpet. He let Tommo and Gary into the house.

"According to the neighbour, no child here. Serena Collins. A lady with a severe disfigurement," Tommo said. "Very reclusive. Quite a lot of unusual noise in the house of late. When questioned she said that she was becoming increasingly deaf and had taken to having the television and radio turned up too loud. No relatives as far as they know."

Then Cubby saw the photograph. "Look at that. Our noble Chief Constable herself. Some relation perhaps? Collins you said. Same surname." Cubby was beginning to feel extremely sick. Her likeness to the child, too, was unmistakeable. As was the child's turned up mouth so like that of his own father. The evidence was substantiating rather than refuting his suspicion that his father had been hiding a love child away. The Chief Constable too! He recalled something of the despising way she had looked at him when she had poked him with her stick long ago in a manner sufficiently offensive to arouse his antagonism. She had singled him out for an obvious discrimination...an undeserved dislike...even before Cubby's challenging questioning. The probable reason why was becoming increasingly apparent! It would not have been the woman with the disfigurement his father would have been having an affair with. Not CC! But if Catty Collins was her sister she was exactly representative of the kind of woman his father liked to chase: cold, haughty, beautiful to look at with independent means. Where was the evidence though of the child living here? As he looked around there was nothing to give that indication.

What they found upstairs told them differently. In the child's room Cubby found a red hair slide which exactly matched the one he had kept from those the police had removed from the child's hair at the police station. He took the purloined one out of his pocket and replaced it in the dish with identical ones of various colours.

Tommo following. He saw the suitcase of a child about to be sent away to school lying against the quilt cover of her bed. A child with no experience of what she would have found when she arrived there and severely frightened by her ignorance. His theory was proving out. She had, it would seem – if the holes in the window boarding were indicative of being hidden away – been entirely isolated from social situation. She had never played with another child, rarely gone out of this house and when she had done so been secreted in a shopping trolley and held mute and restrained with a dog collar and chain. Never seen her reflection in a mirror; a constant blank missing from her view on the world when seen as reflections from shop windows. She could even have believed herself to be the shopping trolley! Suddenly it all made sense.

No such school uniform or crest in the area. He had never heard of Blackstone School. The clothing was unworn, much of it wrapped in tissue paper to stop it creasing. The case had been prepared in readiness for an event about to happen. He imagined the thrust of emotional terror in a child who had no experience of social communication with the outside world. He also, from somewhere at the back of his memory, seemed to recall that their Chief Constable was a talented musician. Angie had once told him that Catty Collins played a trumpet. This child had been able to pick out a tune on a simple toy instrument as if she had inherited the same musical talent.

The trespassers gathered together on the landing for discussion. Tommo, the one holding forth. In his usual authoritative manner Tommo made his opinion known. If he assumed that Wendy had inherited a musical ability from an aunt and said so, Cubby and Gina did not correct him.

Cubby was unusually mute because he found himself strangely affected by the fact that this child was most likely his half sister. Cubby was finding what he saw within this house difficult to cope with emotionally. It was worse than a case of his father simply having fathered an illegitimate daughter that no one knew anything about. Catty Collins was implicated in some sort of conspiracy. But why had she not recognised the child when Wendy had been taken to her own police station and photographed? She would hardly have banged the drum for a hue and cry and begun such a massive criminal dig-out had she been aware that the child was a member of her own family; that was for certain. He had to assume that this Serena was her sister or at the furthest relationship to each other, a cousin. That being the case, Catty Collins had family in Quinton and most probably strong links via her upbringing. A well guarded secret! Secrets upon secrets! He preferred not to think of them as skeletons in cupboards. Instead of sensationalizing he was trying to find a banal explanation which was less shocking personally to the one jumping up and down inside his head, like a vandal who was running riot through his mental alleyways and trashing all his preconceived ideas.

Some personal blame had to be admitted to here. Why hadn't he listened to his parents' sensible pleas, even if his father had a great deal to hide by wanting Cubby to keep the child's situation off the front pages and most certainly would not want her identity revealed? What he had done though was undeniable! He had not just set the cat among the pigeons this time to send feathers flying. He had sat a lion amongst the eagles, sharpened claws and clipped wings and begun a fight to the death. He felt like banging his own head against a wall until he learnt a much needed lesson. The strange, sick, feeling in his stomach was the same as that he had always felt over his father's indiscretions. It was fear because, while he might not like his father, he loved him. The ground beneath his feet was moving with earth tremors because he loved his mother too. The volcano about to erupt would blow them all to smithereens. They would be a family no more for nothing would be able to patch this blown-up house together, that was for sure. His family had never felt more important to him than in that moment. His emotional security was threatened.

Gina put her hand through his arm. While she felt tempted to crow her compassionate generosity as a caring human being responded to his pain. It was obvious that Cubby had had the wind knocked out of him. His balloon had been pricked. He looked deflated of all arrogance; an unusual attitude for Cubby. If she kept her voice low it was because Tommo and Gary would not know anything of C. C. Watson's involvement with the women linked with this household. "What will your mother do when she finds out?" she murmured.

Cubby spoke into her ear for her hearing alone.

"Shoot him probably. Either that or chuck him out." No denying some things. His dad had bought the child the rag doll. It had to have been specifically for her because of the address he had given. He did not explain this to Tommo and Gary. Just let his disappointed message pass silently to Gina who seemed to appreciate his feelings and took his right hand in hers. He might always have known that his father was weak and a liar who cheated on his wife but it was never pleasant to have it proven.

Tommo looked away from them as he saw the intimate look pass between them... their entwined fingers...the way that Gina leant against him. He went instead to look out of the spy hole cut at a child's eyelevel into the boarding over the window for which he had to crouch, close one eye and peer. What he saw was the parkland over the railings; the bandstand, the trees and the mere where he had used to come to feed the swans; always a breeding pair. The mere looked back at him in silver light with its central island like an all seeing, all knowing, eye; the same colour as the child's. Where had the swans gone to after their wings had been speared? They must still have been able to fly even with broken wings. Could he be the same? Could damaged creatures heal themselves sufficiently to fly again?

They moved on to the different rooms, Tommo noting the absence of mirrors and reflective surfaces to explain little Wendy's lack of self image.

All came to the same conclusion after a quick inspection of the cellar spaces; the child had been hidden away. Though this was not a child who had been uncared for. All her clothing had been properly laundered, neatly folded, of the best quality; better quality than the social status of the dwelling would suggest. They were also of the right size and the same style as those she had been wearing when brought from the canal. Indeed a little princess!

So much evidence to show that she had been deeply cared for as they investigated beyond the surface. Her drawings had been placed into scrap books. There were tapes of her voice to provide a more definite evidence as she sang sweetly and someone played along on a piano in clumsy, two fingered fashion. There was a recording of her reciting poetry but with an intonation quite different than the immature restricted phrases of Wendy Bridgewater. This child had been in receipt of lessons in elocution. All stored as if these artefacts had taken the place of a photograph album.

It was as if the child had morphed into someone else. Tommo considered her adaptation as the adoption of a series of coping strategies needed to venture out into the real world. The drawings had been signed by Caitlin Collins. Tommo's eyes rolled. He recognised the handwriting! It had not been Holly Hargreaves's handwriting in the big, blue diary, but the child's.

They could belong to no one other than the same Wendy Bridgewater whose behaviour had been so terribly difficult to handle until that very afternoon when she had seemed to have begun to settle.

Following discussion, everything they saw led them to think that the woman who lived here…whom they now understood to be the same woman they had all seen standing outside Greengates House that same morning…to be the person to have kept her in secret within this very house. She had brought the trolley and the dog lead to bring her contained, back home, to this very house once again.

"Maybe it was Serena that set fire to the bins and had Holly and Wendy kidnapped by Mally Kenyon." Cubby suggested. "Either that, or…" He kept quiet on that one! His father now seemed a very obvious suspect.

Gina shrugged. "Whoever she is she's not here now. Long gone by the look of it and especially if she's seen this afternoon's Clarion. Where do we look now?"

"It's a dead end." Gary was not hopeful.

Tommo disagreed. "There is one lead we can follow."

All attention was his. He knew that he was giving Cubby Watson cannon balls to fire but there seemed nothing else to do if the child was in danger. "We have reason to believe that the girl we took on as Wendy's carer is implicated somehow. We only found out after she had been hired. She's Bass Kenyon's daughter who was put into care. If Holly Hargreaves is really Holly Kenyon…if she is really Magdalene Kenyon's daughter…that's where we should go next. To Nan Bartlett's house on the Dog's Bed Estate. If anyone knows where Mally's likely to be it will be the widow of his twin brother."

This was indeed news to Cubby. He nodded slowly, carefully digesting the information and having to agree that it would be their only possible lead other than to try to dig his father out of a watering hole somewhere. Even if he hid the truth of his father's relationship with the child, which had been named within this house as Caitlin Collins, he could not ignore that she was something more to him now than what had been a retaliation…egg on the face of Catty Collins…a scoop for the Clarion. Now he would have to find her for her own sake. If the nursemaid was the daughter of Magdalene Kenyon he would save judgement for another day. Unlike Tommo and Gary, who believed that she had been pivotal in the child's kidnap, he was not so sure. His father, he knew, would do anything to keep this situation from his mother. Anything!

There was nowhere else to look, anyway, but on the Dog's Bed Estate.

*****

They had gone when the figure in the Homburg hat and mackintosh reappeared carrying still the large plastic containers, the funnel and its attached tubing…walking with calm confidence, attracting no questioning attention as this person took the back way into the same house at thirty-four, Park Road, Lower Quinton.

The clipped strides were heard clearly, even as the brown leather shoes took to the alleyway, entered the yard and banged closed the gate. The person entered the unlocked house without calling out a name, casting the funnel and its tubing onto the cluttered kitchen table because the intention to pour the petrol through the front door letterbox, using the funnel, had been altered by circumstance. A more thorough job could now be done.

Starting at the front door the figure began to flood the vestibule and then the lounge area with the accelerant, taking the utmost care to douse the soft furnishings and the wooden surfaces that would most quickly burst into flames. The photograph of the Chief Constable was removed from its frame, ripped to pieces and would be left to burn. Upstairs the child's room, in particular, was doused inside the wardrobes and out. Within the inner hallway petrol was poured through the flap to run down into the basement to pool deeply by the foot of the stairs. The kitchen was last to be doused before the figure stood by the open rear door. It turned on the gas jets, matches in hand. One strike and the air exploded into flames.

Quickly the arsonist fled the scene, locking the back door and then the back gate, which still held their keys in the locks to delay the fire fighting before the blaze took good hold. Before it had reached the red Jaguar car, smoke was billowing. It was not the only smoke, however, to be seen rising above the rooftops of Lower Quinton. Lower Quinton was beginning to turn into a hotbed of trouble all over the place.

Thirty-One

Holly had taken Wendy down to the bottom of the garden where Tommo had asked her to go to wait while they put the fire out. Probably kids messing with waste bins and matches. Nothing more than a junior science lesson, in her opinion, followed by a wild goose chase. She considered herself to be too old for that kind of escapade these days. But just kids being kids!

She saw the smoke drifting across to screen Harry's shed from view. She could not give a toss about where Harry Groves was. He was zilch in her people rating, while Angie was tops. Next Gary. Tommo not much up her listings from the nasty little man she thought of as a bad tempered bogeyman. Maybe Harry came up through the drains at first light on a bubble of sewer gas and then at dusk glugged back down them again. He lived in a cellar under the house like a black slug under a stone.

Angie had done a bit of whispering already about Harry Groves. He had glossy magazines under his pillow apparently. Kept complaining about his wrist being weak and could Angie find him a bit of support bandage. "I wouldn't touch that right hand of his even if he scrubbed it with Dettol and wore a rubber glove. Some nasty habits has Harry Groves. One of them men as services himself. Done some poor undeserving woman out of a well-paid job that right hand has."

Angie made her laugh. She had seen her hopping on the number thirty-nine bus as she had watched TV with a much happier Wendy before Tommo had asked them to go with him to the Activity Room. Wendy had already whispered that she wasn't telling Tommo anything more about her search for the lady with the golden trumpet. Holly had been unable to spell the words and so had not written about it in the daily diary. Stubborn, little madam Wendy was. She had had her finger over her lips and an arch to her back that told Holly that she meant it. Then during the interview, while Tommo prepared himself by showing the drawing to Wendy, as a point of discussion, maybe, Holly's mind had been elsewhere. She had been thinking only about getting the number thirty-nine to Banks Circle in Lower Quinton, herself, sometime soon to where Angie had told her was where she should have gone to get her bits and pieces instead of ending up on the Dog's Bed Estate. There was a club there called the Jackaby, she said, where the young folk hang out. Sounded real cool to Holly. Got raided at least twice a week. Flats there for rent too if she had the money. She'd blag her way around the deposit. By the time next week came round she'd be in. The landlord would have to start again in the search for another tenant if he tried to get her out so he'd grin and bear it unless he was one of the bastard rat-slum types, when she'd be out quick as it took to find another place of her own volition.

Otherwise she'd be bedded in like a deep splinter and nothing short of a surgeon's knife would get her out. No other way would she leave willingly, at least not until she'd made her mind up about this newly found family of hers. That would take a few more visits before she'd agree to come under scrutiny in Nan Bartlett's spare bedroom. Nan Bartlett would not be fooled by her faked school certificates. It would all be come-clean time. That would test them as nothing else would!

Till such time though she could get over the canal easier when she visited the Dog's Bed Estate by going through the parkland and then using the bridge steps where that barricade was being built. She hadn't told Angie about being Magdalene Kenyon's daughter because of the infamy that went with it, but she would tomorrow because she didn't like to think that she was trusting Gary Silvers while not trusting Angie Meadows. Angie would be a fund of knowledge too. Men didn't know how to bitch, that was the problem. There was nothing like a good bitch-together for feeling close to someone.

Things were turning out better than expected, she thought, with a deeply satisfied breath. To celebrate she broke a bit off a gingerbread man, his foot to be precise which Angie had iced with winter boots and looked about expecting that loopy dog to come dragging its long ears through the grass because it could smell the sweet ginger. Stupid faces had Cocker Spaniels; all squashed in as if stood on at birth. Any dog that could tread on its own ears can't be all that bright, either. Or was it a King Charles? Over-bred like all royalty! It liked rolling itself in its own muck, too, which was why Angie said she wouldn't let it in her kitchen. Been jumping up at the window most of the morning and doing her head in she said because Tommo, Gary and Harry were too lazy to feed it. They were as capable of taking the trouble to give it some food and water as she was. Only they were all men and men only ever thought about their own belly, never anybody else's.

Holly noted that the dog wasn't about. It was probably flat out in its kennel catching up on Z's. She was ready for a nap herself. Damned exhausting was emotional turmoil! Yet a dam had been breached and a few sluice gates opened. She'd start totting up the insurance claims for life damage against her birth family later when she was more established, her eyes flitting about as she delayed giving the bit of gingerbread-man boot to Wendy who was standing ever so good and quiet next to her.

What were those two men doing on the lane with the battered

transit van with its rear doors open? They had a rusty, cement encrusted wheelbarrow and shiny spades as if they had been working in the lane. Don't say that they were Kenyons also! It was just something about them that snagged on a memory. Her dad's other two brothers perhaps; the ones with the bad reputations, while Mally, the man she had seen at the police station, was her real dad's twin brother. Looked exactly like the man pictured in her mother's gold locket and these similar. These the bad 'uns…the ones best to avoid, her dad had always said, though it was more because they'd take her sweets and comics for themselves if she allowed it.

When she caught a flash of the silver eyes she was sure of it. Big belly on one of them like a Sumo wrestler which hung over his pants, while the rest of him was thin as a string-bean like that Mally. The other, a smack-head if ever she saw one. A gaunt head and sores all round his mouth. How pathetic could people get? She could tell from the cotton wool in his mouth when he started speaking to his brother; something about it "being time" that he'd tipped a few pills or swigs of something. He probably hung around hospital wards at visiting time looking for anything chemical. She turned her eyes away from his when his head turned in her direction. If there was one thing you didn't do with a druggy it was allow eye contact when they were rambling because it snapped them off from their happiness and spoilt the pleasure they were chasing. Just to let them see you looking was enough to remind them that the high was about to be followed by a deeply agitated low. They were often sensitive little souls with fragile egos. Wouldn't look anybody in the eye without the drugs to embolden them. Once they had the drugs inside them they thought themselves invincible. That's when they'd come round, that acrid smell about them, stiff limbs like their legs and arms were locked with keys, spaced out of their brains but worried about where they'd get the next bit of crack or smack from.

When she saw a giant pair of wire cutters on the grass she didn't link it with the men, more with the bogeyman who had been cutting grass, which she could smell strong and sappy. It sort of tickled the hairs in her nose. The cuttings were covering both hers and Wendy's feet. The rag doll's legs were trailing and covered with the grass clippings also as it dangled from the kid's hand. Awe! She was being good.

Even when they came to the rear of the big, chain link fence, Holly thought they were only nipping behind the bushes for a pee. There was some cracking of twigs from behind her but she didn't think much of that either. Nature sounds were not much up in Holly's Big Book of Important Reckoning and never had been. The child's probably even less because she had begun to think that the kid had no idea what grass was like after her antics in the garden. She had kept on getting her slippers stuck in the hummocks and falling flat. When she hadn't got up once Holly had gone over to find her cross-eyed as she lay with her head on her hands watching an armoured, black beetle work a mouldy leaf through some stalks. "What d'at?" Always babyish when wanting favours, Holly noted, same as she could be herself. Never anything like feigning incompetence to get others to shift for you!

"I wouldn't let it get into your ear," Holly had replied. "It'll get into your head and eat your brains up."

"No it won't," came the reply. "It's a member of a pop group Serena said. Is a Beatle. What's a pop group? Bands is better."

Holly had intended telling Tommo about that and the name and the address on the bottom of Wendy's picture, but then couldn't be bothered because he'd get on his high horse about everything having to be written down in the book or some report or other with a reference so he could dig it out of a file somewhere. Why was life all about writing? Human beings, she thought, were hunter-gatherers, cave dwellers, tool makers, trouble shooters. She would have been good at all that. Her life blighted by this lack of two-dimensional ability to write about three-dimensional things.

Tommo worshipped books. She'd dipped into his bedroom to take a peek. He had a book on his bedside called *Psychological Barriers to Free Thinking*. Took her ages to decipher. Is that sad? Or is that sad! Just for the sake of it she had opened his underwear drawer and taken a peek at those within. Y-fronts. Holly kicked Tommo into touch as a possible slave. Too old anyway. A fuddy-duddy! God! Wasn't the man a pain for making sermons of things that made no difference anyway? The only thing that would affect the kid would be the things that Holly understood without ever having read a book from start to finish. But she had experienced them!

When she looked down upon her pretty, blonde head Wendy was nibbling at her own gingerbread man. There was indeed something far happier and more settled about her. Holly patted herself on the head for that.

Wendy, chewing at the head of the clutched brown, iced, ginger flavoured shortbread looked back with a smiling face, showing the mashed biscuit about her milk white, baby teeth. "Loves you, Holly!"

"Awe! Stick with me, kid. Okay? Me and you together. Do what I say and we'll both be alright. Right?"

Wendy nodded. "I's helps you and you helps me!"

Holly nodded. "First rule of survival, kid. Use other people before they use you."

Wendy considered this seriously. "What I give you if you helps me find the lady with the golden trumpet?"

"Easy-peasy! Money. Lots of it. This love bits all very well. A family is important because they'll always have you back even when your bad and you get chucked out. But put yourself first, kid. Savvy…?"

Wendy thought deeply and nodded. Her smile held cunning.

"…because being mushy won't get you a duvet day when you need one…or that glittery top from Top Shop…or that pair of shoes I saw in Bags and Boots with the seven inch heels and the platform soles. Metallic purple like my shoulder bag."

Wendy began to frown. "Money is the blue and brown paper the man and the lady gives to Serena for me to come here."

Holly nodded. Then thought again. A man and a lady? Mum and dad? She wouldn't call her mum Serena would she? "Is this Serena the lady with the golden trumpet?"

Wendy shook her head. "No. Serena not the lady with the golden trumpet. Is a lady meets Serena on the street corner sometimes. She no come in the house like the man. I sees her through the spy hole when it's dark and hears them whisper under the lamppost. She wears a big cowboy hat and a big, floppy coat. Her toes go clip, clip, clip. They goes over to the bandstand in the park where no one sees them. Is a secret. I have to wear the collar to keep me still and quiet because I's alone in the house when Serena goes over to the park with the lady. Not old enough to be sensible yet, see."

Holly was thinking dirty. "Does Serena go over to the park with the man when he comes?"

Wendy shook her head. "Serena no like him. Caitlin no like him. Wendy no like him big time. Him my daddy but him a bad man."

Then thinking back to how Wendy had managed to catch sight of this woman. "The spy hole! Was that the eye in your picture? Like your peeping through something."

Wendy nodded. "Wendy wants to go out. Caitlin is frightened. Wendy wants to go to school. Caitlin no like it."

"So who was in your picture?"

"Serena and the lady with the golden trumpet who has the blue uniform and the yellow hair in a bun."

"Were you in the picture?"

Wendy nodded. "In the cart."

"There was no cart. Just a shopping trolley."

Wendy nodded. "Me inside the cart…the trolley. I has to be as

335

quiet as a dolly."

"Why wasn't this other lady...the one with the big hat in your picture too?"

"Her not my mummy. Her Serena's friend. Her only comes now and again. She gives Serena money like the man. Serena says that's why I'm a little girl as has everything."

"How can anyone have everything?"

"Everything! Caitlin has Little Princess dresses from Trimbles and only the best toys and computers and books and has..."

"Alright! So you're a spoilt brat! No need to rub it in, kid! But this lady gives Serena money?"

Wendy nodded. "Hush though. No tell Tommo or Gary or Harry or Angie. I's helps you. You helps me find the lady with the golden trumpet."

"Your mummy?"

"My real mummy as didn't want Caitlin because Caitlin is a clever, naughty girl. Her want Wendy though because Wendy is sweet and good and kind and...dumb."

"Where's Caitlin now?"

Wendy pointed to her head.

"Where's Wendy?"

Wendy put two hands to her chest.

Holly shrugged. "A bit like me when I can't make my mind up about something. I'm two people too. I'm Holly Hargreaves and I'm Holly Kenyon. But I'm Holly Hargreaves when I'm with you. Got that, kid?"

Wendy nodded. "Me no tell Tommo was Caitlin as wrote things in the big, blue book. Wendy can keep a secret. Wendy likes secrets." With which she wrapped her arm about Holly's leg and winked up at her, biting again on the sweet confection. She brought the rag doll up and hugged it.

She was a funny, sweet, little thing away from her tantrums, Holly thought. When Holly had the baby which would get her to the top of the housing list for a Salford high rise flat, if she had a girl she would want one as quirky and funny as Wendy...as nice looking too. Keep them fat, ugly brats as cries all the time! Nice looking gets you where water can't. She knew because nice-looking had stood her in good stead for all her life so far. When she got into trouble all she had to do was play-act innocence and in combination nice-looking, somehow, got her out of the shit.

That and quick thinking, looking for the main chance, spying the opportunities, thinking one ahead. If she possessed the same gene pool as her mother, Magdalene, she would be quids in by the time she was forty with her looks still an asset. Her mother, not that old yet she didn't think, but still ancient! But she would have used her head not like her. Stayed away from drugs. Found a man with money as well as a good job to bleed dry of every penny in his bank account.

Smug was a suitable description of Holly's thoughts of her future when the white pad with a spirit smell just like the stuff the school nurse used to remove sticking plaster residue from tender skin came about her nose and mouth. Tight hands over her mouth and digging into her chest like grappling hooks.

"Ger-off!" she wanted to yell but a weakness assailed her as the stuff swirled into her head and then she was away on a fairground ride as the same hands hauled her back and up and waltzed her around and then threw her onto the cold metal of the back of a transit van. Even with her eyes shut she knew the hollow sounds well after a good few occasions of being ridden by some Lone Ranger on the hard, tinny back of his metal steed after a few too many Bacardi and white wines up some back alleyway where cats sat on high walls and watched the windows steam. They probably wondered what the face to face bit was all about.

For some reason there was always a full moon on such occasions. Her chosen one having left Tonto and the rest of his doodle-headed friends somewhere else in order to ride the range with his little pistol cocked, snooker balls hard as iron. He usually dismounted without his wallet. By the time he realised that, Holly was miles away. A bit sore about the crotch especially if she got a bit carried away herself but worth it if she gained another condom for her purse for the next ride, a few credit cards to buy something nice from Top Shop and could afford a better pair of tights to replace the ruined ones. If she had gained any pleasure from it herself it had been a bonus. Where did people get this strange idea from that prostitution was a modern transgression from the holy pathway? The body sacred! Nothing sacred about Holly Hargreaves' body thank you very much. It's what women have been doing from time immemorial. Oldest profession on Earth! Though she didn't like hers being taken without permission. It made her mad, see.

By the time her senses stirred she realised that they were rattling hers about in the rear of this transit van because it was already in motion. When she opened one eye it was to see the sky whizzing past. Her clothes were covered in building dust and her back was hard up against the rubber wheel on a wheelbarrow. She and Wendy had been stacked like two spoons in a drawer with the rag doll tucked under Wendy's arm. When she looked at the small body curled up next to her she guessed her to be feigning sleep just as she was herself. Her little silver eyes were roaming behind the slits. They both had their feet warming on a great big, fat, dog's bum. It had a short narrowing tail that stuck out like a spike, a coat of fine, grey hair and was wedged between the passenger seat and the driver's seat. Holly assumed that it was the dog's hair that coated her tongue. One of them British Bulldogs you couldn't shift off sofas and always nipped the sausage off your tray of chips and gravy given half the chance.

Two rough men in the front seats and one talking on a mobile. She could tell by the backs of their heads they were the same Tweedle Dumb and Tweedle Dee that she'd seen mending the lane next to Greengates House. What Holly could not understand was what possible use she and the child were to them. Weirdoes roamed alone usually, rarely in pairs and never brother with brother, because brothers were usually always at each other's throats, worse than sisters sometimes. If they wanted Holly for her body they might have to fight her for it, but that being the case what would they want with the child? Besides which, druggies were not known for being studs. Too much relaxed tissue!

Without moving much more than a finger she poked the child in the back and then wagged it against the arch of her back, feeling her stiffen with awareness. Then she let her hand stray over the kid's mouth. This to discourage any speech until she had devised a plan of action. When Wendy looked at her, eyes questioning, Holly clamped her lips together and sealed them tight. It was Caitlin, Holly noted, not Wendy who was looking back. The kid was angry! So was she! Between them they'd manage it!

Then the dog got shoved back from where it had its head between the front seats. Probably dripping long strings of saliva onto the gear stick where the driver had his work-grimed hand. It was punished with a chastising slap across its ears. The dog's whelp was barely discernable but Holly heard it. Wendy too.

Holly saw its ears drop and then recognised its cower as it turned its head towards them with a sad look on its broad, thuggish face. Down it went on all fours and laid its head on them giant paws that had never had their nails clipped. Sad brown eyes looking at her which reminded her of her own. It curled itself about a rumble of its belly. The dog was hungry. It began to lick at the crumbs of biscuit on Holly and Wendy's clothing. Holly put her hand out so that it might gently take the broken part of the gingerbread man still clutched in her fingers.

This dog was really a pussy cat, Holly thought. Without moving or making sound, Holly began to make a friend of the dog. Gather another troop. Never known a dog to bite the hand that fed it. She'd consult the dog, too, about the possibility of a deal similar to the one she had made with Wendy. First a finger for it to sniff. It got licked not bitten. Then good, lingering eye contact. Dogs were pack animals and needed to feel inclusion just like people. When the dog began to lick her hand without the lure of a crumb of biscuit Holly slowly let her hand settle on its huge head. Slowly, almost indiscernibly, she began to tickle a spot behind its ear which she found when the dog inched itself closer. A spot just behind the right ear. Her eyes and its eyes communing deeply. Holly filled her head with thoughts of lampposts and doggy chews, bowls of leftovers and lappy-splashy water because she suspected it had a terrible thirst. The dog spoke back to her of long walks and its own kennel and a kind owner. A bit of flea powder would not come amiss either. There was a patch on its side where it had scratched itself raw. Holly saw that it was a dog not a bitch. She always preferred women to men but would have to settle.

When Wendy's hand stretched to turn the dog's head towards herself Holly realised that she only had herself to blame. She had *asked* her to do what she did! As the trade of dog seduction was being witnessed by an apprentice who wanted a bit of a go also, Holly would have no other option than to let Wendy in on her secrets. Dogs were no different than a whole parade of boyfriends. Not that Holly had ever considered sharing before. She wasn't letting another woman in on her trade secrets. However, the kid was different…not old enough to be in competition!

Between them they took an ear each while Wendy found a few extra crumbs for the dog to lick. Some serious love making in a threesome was taking place despite the slime of nose to nose contact, licks over a whole face by a piece of pink, dry sandpaper, its breath stinky because its last meal must have been fish.

When Holly pulled her hand away its huge head came upon her chest, eyes sorrowfully pleading. When Wendy did the same a giant paw stretched out to scratch at Wendy's clothes insistently. Here was a dog with serious emotional deprivation. They resumed their therapy session and the dog relaxed again. Bliss! Pure bliss!

Wendy winked at Holly. Holly winked at Wendy. When Holly sat up. Wendy sat up also. The dog followed, smiling at them both because they each kept a hand on its studded collar.

The driver nearly jumped out of his skin as Holly tapped him on the shoulder. "Well, well! Fancy that."

Wendy put the rag doll into Benny's neck and jiggled it about. "Fancy d'at!"

He turned to stare at her with a dazed expression, not seeming sure if the doll was real and not an hallucination.

Holly brought Wendy round to her side to be close even as they continued to hold onto a dog which was licking at Wendy's denim skirt. She knew that the first thing they would notice would be her silver eyes.

"This here is Wendy Bridgewater," she said brightly.

"We know she is. She's the one we want not you. So watch it!"

"She has silver eyes like a Kenyon. Real name Caitlin Collins." Now for the next surprise. "And my name's Holly Kenyon. I have brown eyes just like my mother, Magdalene. I'm your brother, Bass's, daughter. Not seen either of you for how long is it now…eleven years at least?"

They were on some lane or other. Holly could see that they were taking a roundabout route but were heading towards the Dog's Bed Estate by the back roads. No traffic about. Black, toxic smoke beginning to billow from a bonfire they passed which had been built out of old car tyres by kids in Wellington boots. She braced herself and Wendy for the slamming on of breaks. The white van came to a screaming halt.

"Who did you say?" from the one driving, the one with the clear head. Eyes as big as organ stops.

"I'm your brother, Bass's, daughter. I'm Holly. You'll remember me."

They stared at her gob-smacked, the pair of them. Even the one who couldn't balance his head straight.

"I's the daughter of the lady with the golden trumpet!"

Holly smiled. "Too true. Let's start some negotiation."

Thirty-Two

Woody drove up to the church with a strange sense of being five minutes late for an important occasion. Kick off had started. The noise coming from the bridge was full of clangs and screams and battle cries. No way that Benny and Woody would ever get involved in anything as crass as an assertion of their human rights. Public demonstration? Keep it mate! A fool's game! They had plenty to fight for, but strictly for themselves. Like forty thousand quid in used notes. The deal had been struck with remarkable ease. The money acquired as if it came off a printing press. Probably did when the Watsons had a print factory all to themselves.

All it had taken was a proposition followed by a trip to the bank in Quinton where they could see the cash assembled into a plain, brown envelope. However, it would only be handed over on certain conditions. If they tried to take it beforehand the police would be informed; a publish or be damned attitude. They would have to snatch the kid and hand over the papers that had been so telling in the first place. At least they could see that the cash was available. *Struck gold* had been the right expression.

They were to meet at five in the afternoon but they were all running late. What with the shock of finding themselves in the company of Bass's kid and the detours and the time it had taken to make a hole in a chain link fence they were running seriously late. Not that they automatically believed the kid, despite Holly being the spit of Magdalene. They'd need a bit of proof first.

They had turned off the main road and come round the back way because there were not only police in riot gear everywhere, but Lower Quinton High Street was being pillaged like a supermarket dash and grab won on a lottery ticket. However, the spread of unrest was good for taking attention away from themselves despite the old rust bucket they were travelling in having been stolen from one of the builder's yards where they sometimes worked shovelling sand and stacking bricks. They had been on the back lanes between the High Street and the Dog's Bed Estate when they had realised that they had actually kidnapped a member of their own family along with the kid.

Then the girls seemed to be entirely unaware of the danger that they were in. Benny looking at Woody and Woody looking at Benny in a shared state of confusion because the girls behind them were laughing and singing, tickling the dog, throwing the rag doll about, behaving like anything other than subjects of ransom. "We go look for the lady with the golden trumpet," the kid shouted gleefully.

"I can't believe it," the tall, slim teenage girl kept saying. "You come to get me special because you heard I'd come back to Quinton? Tired of that dead-end job anyway..."

There was no doubting that she was a dead ringer for Magdalene.

"Uncle Woody and Uncle Benny! Fancy meeting like this!"

"It's not you we were after," Benny slurred. "Just her!"

"It's the kid you're after is it? Is it so that she can't testify against Uncle Mally for putting her into the water?"

Wendy was busy shaking her head. "No one put Caitlin in the water. Caitlin jumped in all on her own. She not go to Blackstone School. No, no, no, never!"

Woody was concentrating on his driving, bedazzled but nodding.

Benny took a snort of something in a small brown bottle, a wave of pleasure immediately apparent as the vapour hit his brain. "Whooooooooooo!" Then with some malevolence. "Help Mally? That Dick-head! You're joking right?" Then to Holly, as his eyes rolled in his head, "You should be au fait with family policy if you're a Kenyon. Kenyons stick together until the crunch. Then we go our separate ways. That's the rules. Mally's on his own. If he's any sense he'll be miles away."

"So what you want the kid for?"

"You for real?"

"Sure am! I'm a Kenyon. Been about a bit too. You can trust me. I want in. I'll take care of the kid for you. What's going to happen to her?"

"Forty grand in cash is what's going to happen to us in exchange for her. I wouldn't give a two-pence piece for her but someone will. The kid's an embarrassment to...."

"Shut up Benny. And leave that shit till later!"

In reply, Benny took another slurp of the liquid in the brown bottle. His repeated whelp was an orgasm of delight as the drug hit home again. The dog's head went down. Holly got onto the job of scratching its back. Wendy got on with the job of tickling its chest. Then she spied some screwed up white paper in the back pocket of the passenger seat and brought it out. The dog sniffed and let go a couple of mucus strings which sucked onto her denim skirt like glue. Wendy opened the paper up to see the crusty rims of the meat pies they had probably shared for lunch and a splodge of greasy, gravy covered chips in the bottom of a polystyrene tray. She let the dog feed, seeing its pleasure. It smiled at her and put out a gentle paw of gratitude. It had probably not been fed for days.

"Why did you take me as well as her?"

"You daft! Then you can't describe the van or us. Why else? Least not until we've legged it. You seemed to be watching us. That because you recognised us?"

Holly nodded. "I remembered you from when I was a kid. I used to live with Nan and Tock at the pub."

"Where you play then?" Like they were testing her out.

"In the play house in the beer garden. Tock told me today that the brewery sold it off for allotments".

"What was your favourite toy?"

"A stuffed monkey. I used to always be changing its nappy."

"Seems kosher," Woody said.

Benny shrugged. "Will she keep her gob shut though? That mother of hers!"

"I know why you might think that," Holly said. "But me…I spent my life in care. They didn't want me. Been in trouble too. Got sent to a remand school and then later a residential special school. Nothing to thank her for have I?"

The brother's looked at each other.

Woody shrugged again.

Benny nodded. "We'll see. After the handover when the kid's gone you can stay with us. You can do some slaving to show you're in with us. Run a few errands. You use?"

"No, but that means you can trust me with the packets. Not likely to skim off the top am I?"

"You can always sell it on."

"So I could. Don't want to have to start heading off back to Manchester yet though, do I? Got more sense. Don't fancy staying with my mother or Tock and Nan either. Party poopers if ever there were any."

"She can be useful," Benny said encouragingly. "Missed having a slave since Christy went."

Woody's eyes rolled in his brother's direction. "You shouldn't have hit her over the head with that melon, Benny. If you want people to stay around you have to have some consideration. The back of your hand would have done the job just as well, even if the whiplash did get you an insurance payout." Then to Holly. "You cook?"

Holly was about to tell the truth. She could burn water. No point in pretending that she could. Besides she was nobody's servant. Liked baking though. The gingerbread men had come in useful also.

Wendy spoke before her. "I's can make sandwiches and bake cakes." Artful already, Holly thought, at seven. The little madam was a future Madam and no mistake!

Then Wendy nipped over the seat back and sat on Benny's knee taking the rag doll with her. Their rough play had started a seam coming open into which Wendy stuck the tip of an investigative finger making the hole bigger.

Benny looked at both Wendy and the doll with great distaste, his arms held wide as the doll divested its stuffing over his greasy black denims. Nothing doing there!

So Wendy tried the other brother. She poked Woody in the ribs even as he drove. "You's the man took me out of the trolley. You's not the man that saved me. But you's the man that took me out of the trolley. I hear your voice. You phone the police station to tell that Caitlin's in the water. You speak to the lady with the golden trumpet?"

Even Holly was surprised at the child's lack of fear for the situation. She had just been forcibly kidnapped yet she had no fear of anyone.

"Don't know who you're talking about kid."

"Her name Katrina. Her live at the top of the police station. Serena Collins's sister. You's take me to the lady with the golden trumpet."

"The only person lives at the top of the police station is our own lady Chief Constable, Catty Collins…evil bitch!"

The child dipped her head, cocked it, and looked at Holly. She was thinking carefully. "Is my mummy!"

Holly risked being seen in the driving mirror as she put a finger to her lips. Whoever this Catty Collins was had created some impression. Woody whistled. Benny looked with a new interest on the kid. No wonder they had hit jackpot!

Wendy was on a continuing adventure and quite unaware of the danger she was in as she looked up at the man with the wobbly head who was looking down at her with renewed interest. She smiled fetchingly. With pride, she said. "She my mummy! She the lady with the golden trumpet."

Holly found herself cringing with utter dread.

*****

At first they could see practically nothing through the darkness of the crypt under St Saviour's Church. Woody had parked the battered transit van under trees to the rear of the church and then the brothers had frogmarched them quickly along the path to the crypt, prised open the door with a screwdriver and then poked the girls down the steps. In the background, over the rooftops, came the noise of beating drums. Voices were shouting and people were chanting some kind of battle cry. A siren was blaring. Someone was honking a horn like they do when their team scores at football matches. Overriding the sounds was the smell of burning rubber from the bonfires as well as the smoke from burning sheds and garages, as evidence was incinerated perhaps. Here, however, the peace of the church had been respected. If pillaging was going on elsewhere St Saviour's was guarded by its holy grace. It seemed to be deserted.

Still not taking anything seriously, Wendy was of the opinion that her search was soon to be over. The church seemed to be a fitting place for her to have her wishes granted because Serena came to this very place occasionally. Though more often than not the man with the dark clothes and the big cross and the gentle voice came to visit her and together they knelt in prayer. Caitlin, as long as she promised to be quiet, had been allowed to listen from the cellar steps with her ear to the cat flap. However, Serena had brought her once to the church itself inside the trolley so that she might know what a church looked like. She had told her that this was the place where God lived and God was the person to grant all good wishes. Here, she knew, was where she would find the lady with the golden trumpet when she had not been at the police station. Wendy could only think that the person who was about to buy her back for forty thousand pounds could only be her real mother. Serena had no money other than that which she had been given. To Wendy's limited awareness it had to be the lady with the golden trumpet who was about to save her from Blackstone School and had thus arranged to have her kidnapped. This was why Holly's uncles had come to get her because Holly had said that she would be the one to help her. They had pledged to help each other.

Holly had also been huddled, despite her precocious familiarity with her relatives, into a dark corner of the crypt lit only by the light from the slightly open door at the top of the inner staircase, which gave a vague illumination to their silhouettes. They could just make out their shapes in otherwise almost total darkness. The brothers had shut the crypt door as they waited. Though through the darkness, as the brothers sat at a rickety table, Holly and Wendy could hear all that they were saying.

"You still in touch with that dealer down in London, Woody?"

"Nah! Save for the occasional spliff, drugs give me the shakes. Don't mind a bit of weed now and again. I'll be drinking best cognac by the litre bottle instead of cider or beer after we get paid. Start at eight in the morning and not give up till I pass out. Sleep, vomit and then start all over again. If that ain't how to live I don't know what is."

"We'll deserve a good time after all of this," Benny agreed; his brown bottle empty and his voice even more slurred. "I'll be trying a few of them designer drugs. The ones that make you feel as if you're walking on mile high stilts and your arms are ten times as long."

Woody guffawed. "Anyone ever tell you Benny that all you have to do to feel like that is hold your breath and do some fast spinning. Don't last though. Prefer the booze myself."

"It's all that arm lifting though. Too much like hard work!"

Holly shook her head as she let their voices fade and tried to see Wendy through the darkness. "Knob-heads, the pair of them!" she whispered in Wendy's ears. "What a daft way to live. You see anything through this gloom, Wendy?"

"Stop talking, the pair of you. We're listening out for the ransom coming. You, Holly, make yourself useful." Something got dumped on the table and the voice was beckoning. Holly was required to get up and go see what it was her uncles were expecting of her. "Got the technique I hope. Lets us relax with all this tension."

To that end Holly made herself useful, as required, and rolled her uncles, both of them, a joint the size of a fat Havana cigar from the drawstring bag full of crushed brown leaves. The more the better Holly thought because the drug was renowned for slowing down the thinking processes and mellowing even the worst of temperaments. Already Woody was warming towards her when he had occasionally made reference to his dead brother with some affection showing. However she was a long way yet from being trusted. They trusted no one, not even each other.

Wendy watched the ceremony involved in the rolling of a toke as her eyes became accustomed to the dimness and then the brother's accept the light from the lighter which Holly produced from her own pocket, as they wrapped pale lips about the fat, leaf-filled tubes of paper. When the flame lit up their faces from below they looked sinister. She thought it all rather strange that people put tea leaves in rolled up tissue, set fire to it, drew the funny smelling smoke in with lots of air, choked it down into their lungs with frog-like faces and then let it out slowly through their noses with their eyes turning up in their heads before settling low on glazed faces.

Holly, as she came to rejoin Wendy on the pallet, rolled her eyes at them again and circled a finger around her temple. Then she got on with the corruption of one of their number as she stroked her fingers over the dog's head. The dog having been set to mind them both as if a third member of their gang. Obviously the trained behaviour of a thug on lookout duty was what it was kept for, its bared teeth were as good as hunting knives in the dog's insistence that they stay where they had been asked to stay on the pallet. Menace wasn't in it as it lowered its head to a fixed stare to keep the girls herded together. The brothers had had enough of their previous antics. They should now remember that they were being forcibly detained. The kid especially, though Benny looked as if he could not have detained a butterfly in a jam jar. He was stoned out of his skull. It was Woody taking care of business, but even he was getting jittery. They had spent all day planning their blackmail. It was now to come to fruition. He was nervous. The drug would calm him down, let him think. This was when they missed Mally most because he was usually the one to think things through to a satisfactory ending, even if it did take him all day.

The brothers were drawing deeply again on their giant tokes even as they heard the car approach and set to the steps quickly…the tokes momentarily forgotten about. Holly cursing as her plans to overcome them by their own intoxication were left to smoulder on a big plate on the table. "Pay out time."

"At last."

They both went out to meet their visitor.

While the brothers claimed a torch to light their own way up the crypt steps, Holly and Wendy and the dog had to let their eyes adjust in order to see each other. They had been pushed over to a pallet in the corner and then made to sit. Wherever they were in the church, probably the cellar spaces, the brothers were familiar with the layout of the place. There was a wooden table and some chairs as well as a bible on a lectern. The dank, dark place was also equipped with a box of refreshment which required no cooking; tins with ring pulls and bottles and cans of drinks. As their eyes adjusted they began to make out each other's shapes in the darkness from the bit of light shining down from above.

The dog was set on guard duty by Woody with a growled order to "Keep them pinned," purely as an afterthought before they both went out to greet the clipping stride of the person they were meeting.

The dog's head went down and it let out a low, menacing growl. However the stance lasted only long enough for the brothers to close the door behind them and begin an inaudible discussion. It turned to look after its master with a whimper, legs as bowed as a Sumo Wrestler with rickets, teeth hanging visibly like the incisors on a white shark. Then it stared longingly at the cans of lemonade Holly was popping open, one for herself and one for Wendy, whimpering with thirst as they drank deeply. The place stank of peppery damp, the walls dripped; a white fungus grew on all the brickwork. Only the sleeping bag afforded a glimmer of warmth as they, waiting in the cold darkness, huddled together, the rag doll still clutched in Wendy's hand with its stuffing falling out. Holly helped herself to a tin of corned beef. Wendy said that she had never eaten it before.

When given a chunk of the greasy meat she fed it instead to the hungry dog which licked her hand with every grateful mouthful.

"Me no like."

"Never lived, kid! That and luncheon meat are the staff of life when it's Thursday and there's no money left for proper food from the chippy."

"Is the lady with the golden trumpet come, Holly?"

Holly shrugged. "Most likely not," she said with as much kindliness she could muster. "Whatever you wish for most has a habit of going the opposite way. Best not to wish for anything then you're never disappointed. It couldn't be this Serena, could it?"

Wendy shook her head. The mumblings she could hear were indistinct but she would have recognised Serena's dulcet tones anywhere.

Holly shrugged and tried to be reassuring. "Not to worry." If the kid was of the impression that her birth mother was about to pay a hefty ransom for her Holly considered it to be highly unlikely. And especially when her uncles had talked of this lady with the golden trumpet being none other than the Chief Constable of Quinton. Then, voices had been raised. "Hush! Listen....   something about handing over the papers and there's mention of that crucifix Woody keeps digging out of his pocket. Who's C. C. Watson? They want the forty grand now or something will...Oh, nothing!"

"Will what, Holly?"

"Nothing, kid. Forget it."

The promise of forty grand being a huge temptation to Holly. What Holly would not have given for just a tiny nibble of a small part of forty thousand quid! Maybe with a bit of man-management and more of the stuff that was beginning to dull the brains of both of the brothers, now, she might manage an odd handful down her own T-shirt. Forty thousand pounds in used notes! She could imagine exactly what it smelt like; wet dog and stale tobacco. Utterly gorgeous! All she had to do was to get close enough to it.

Next thing, the dog was on the pallet with them and lying down after doing that tail chasing and then a heavy flop that made the pallet creak. Wendy raised the can of lemonade and allowed the dog to lap at the liquid which she kept swilling onto the top of the can. Poor thing was seriously in need of a drink. Its eyes paid grateful thanks as it lapped, seeming to like the fizz where she hadn't.

Then Holly had an idea as she looked at the forks in a tray close by them. "Weapons. Here, open up that seam some more on that rag doll of yours and take out the stuffing. We'll put a couple of forks inside in case we need to protect ourselves."

"Why Holly? Wendy a good girl now."

"This is self protection, noodle head! In case they start to get punchy. Something to use to scratch their eyes out with. I'm not breaking my finger nails! Or if we have to, fork them in the nuts. What else? I forgot to bring my pepper spray in all the rush. Lay a finger on me and they'll know they're men alright. I know all about fighting dirty."

Then she took a chance. She half expected the dog to object as she crept up the steps behind them to lay an ear to the closed door while Wendy kept the dog happy.

She crept back down and took her place on the pallet again with her finger to her lips. "Money changing hands I think."

The dog had shown itself to be extremely thirsty. By the time Holly arrived back on the pallet it had finished the whole can and was burping happily. After which it was further seduced by tickles to its belly. It rolled onto its back and placed its legs in the air. Wendy's arm wrapped about its huge head. It was smiling with happiness, a fat tongue hanging out with its eyeballs roaming between them as if it considered itself to have died and gone to Heaven with two blessed angels.

Holly looked at the teeth and hoped not to be on the receiving end; great fangs caked in cream cheese. She whispered to Wendy. "Maybe they called it Sabre because it's got teeth as sharp as swords but it's breath would improve if them gnashers had a bit of a clean. Needs its coat brushing too and that sore healing. We'll be scratching next."

Wendy nodded. Blithely unaware of the danger they were in and better kept that way as far as Holly was concerned. She wrapped a foot over the dog. The dog wriggled in closer. If a dog could laugh it was chuckling.

Then the men were back with a brown paper bag. The dog shot off the pallet even before the door opened. The person they had been talking to did not come with them but stayed outside. They could hear the brown leather shoes pacing up and down…clip, clip, clip. Benny and Woody sat down on creaking chairs, their faces up-lit by torch light. Their bad reputations seemed suddenly much more deserved to Holly in the sinister light with upside down shadows on their faces.

The dog let out a low growl in their direction but the menace had gone from it. If only it could have winked, Holly thought, she might be more sure that she had totally undermined its training.

"It's alright, Sabre. I forgives you," Wendy breathed while Holly rolled her eyes. Holly took up the rag doll and got on with picking the seam and removing the stuffing. She let the fibres fall to the quarry tiled floor as Woody let the contents of the brown paper envelope slide out onto the surface of the table. Holly saw the plastic packets of real money gleam with the small amount of light coming down from the partially open door at the top of the inner staircase. They opened one to check it. Twenty fifties, at least, together in one sachet. At least forty sachets, still wafer thin. The brothers were already laughing and rolling their heads together, talking of heading down to London. Maybe finding out where Mally had gone and joining him.

Holly wondered why they weren't handing over Wendy yet. It seemed that whoever had handed over the cash was waiting for the contents of the brown paper bag to be checked before the deal was finalised. She had no idea whether they had asked for more money or not. Maybe they had been wise and settled for the bird in the hand. It sure looked a lot to her spread out in a fan of plastic sachets over the table top.

As they began to put the money back into the envelope Holly's face took on strange contortions. Her nostril flared, her eyes changed shape. Wendy watched her face become ugly as Holly stared at the money and was overtaken by wanting the promises it made. "Where we couldn't get with that, kid!" she breathed, shaking her head from side to side. "I'd be on a plane to Hollywood as soon as damn it. They named the place after me!"

Wendy was looking to the stairs and thinking that she might make a dash for them.

Holly was acting strange over the money.

Now that it came to it she was no longer sure that the lady waiting outside was the one with the golden trumpet. She recognised the clip, clip, clip of her shoes. It was Serena's friend. If she was going anywhere it would be back to a cellar. Wendy could not countenance going back to the cellar and living her days with only Serena for company. She knew now what it felt like to explore in the sunshine and be out in the fresh air to play. Wendy thought that maybe if she made a dash to get away she could find somewhere to hide; upstairs in the church where she could sit perfectly still like a statue where no one would find her. She took the now very thin rag doll back as Holly passed it back to her and stuffed it down the belt on her denim overdress. Holly seemed to have forgotten about her intention to find something they might use as weapons with which to protect themselves.

The brothers had put the money back into the envelope a different way. It just looked like a loaf of bread to Wendy; no bigger than a small, sliced brown loaf of whole wheat. Then Woody got something out of his pocket. The bunch of white papers all rolled together were very creased and very dirty, along with the crucifix. Benny was laughing to himself already, so high that it seemed unlikely, to Holly, that he would be going anywhere but on a slow slide under a table.

Woody had the papers in his hand as he came to take Wendy from her position on the pallet. What he did was to haul her up roughly then he shoved the roll of papers down the neck of her clothing. "Right kid. Sold! Out! Your handler's here. Got a dog collar and a chain at the ready to take you away."

Wendy wasn't going back to the cellar! Wendy was going to school now! Wendy was still out to find the lady with the golden trumpet!

Maybe it was the roughness of the hand with which he started to drag Wendy away which made the dog go for him. Its low growl was warning but Sabre gave Woody no time to realise that he had forfeited his hold of hungry terror in favour of kindnesses given. The dog now had a different allegiance.

Suddenly Sabre had him by the leg and was dragging him backwards, shaking him down, going in on him like a teeth threshing machine just as Woody had trained him to do. Woody screaming as the sharp teeth bit into his leg and no amounts of shouts and cries would get the dog off him.

He had already let Wendy go. The door opened from outside and light flooded in as Woody's screams filled the cellar. Benny seemed to have lost track of everything that was going on around him. Wendy realised that she was about to be taken again, against her will, by the figure in the big hat coming down the stairs. All she could see was the dog collar and a lead. Wendy would never wear one ever again.

Petrified more by the dog lead than the person, she stood quickly and started for the inner staircase, pulling the papers out of the collar of her blouse and letting them fall onto the pallet. She began to make for the inner staircase, away from the approaching figure with its identity shrouded in the large hat and enveloping coat." Holly did likewise. On the way Wendy snatched up the brown paper bag holding the money as if picking up a bag of sandwiches. If she was going to find the lady with the golden trumpet she would need Holly and Holly would need to be paid for her services. She was at the foot of the stairs and calling to Holly to follow even before Holly could wonder what was happening. She had been as stupefied with greed as Benny was within his chemical intoxication.

"Wait, you stupid girl. Wait!" the figure shouted, running after them but then falling over in the darkness. They heard a chair crash as it tumbled into the pallet.

Benny didn't seem to know what was happening. "All right, our kid?" He was already off with the fairies. "London here we come!"

Sabre kept a hold on Woody's leg and was chewing until the blood ran; shaking his head on his master's clamped leg while Woody screamed at the torture he was receiving. He had trained the dog to bite and not let go until it became exhausted.

Benny looked on as if watching the unfolding of an hallucination. "We're rich." Then finally, his responses on a delayed switch, he stood up, reeling. "What's going on?"

Wendy and Holly waited for no one. Up the interior stairs they ran. At the top Holly slammed the door shut behind them. She turned the key in the lock even as the figure in the Homburg hat had got up quickly and made up distance. They were almost caught. Even as Holly removed the key from the lock the person who was still calling them to wait was starting to pound upon the door with a clenched fist from the other side. "Wait you silly girls, wait. I've come to help you."

Holly was waiting for no one. Grabbing Wendy's hand she made for the vestry, off the large congregational hall that smelt of polish and reminded her of her mother; a dark expanse of exposed space that led onto an even darker interior corridor. Doors, any doors, if only she could see them might lead them to freedom. She wondered, now, why Wendy was bothering stuffing the money into the belly of the rag doll, having regained her common sense. No amount of money was worth dying for, she thought, just as she made through the doorway onto the dark, interior corridor. Knowing too that they had not been followed. Her hand went out to snap on the light. The whoosh came with a flash of a spark and suddenly all about them was ignited.

St Saviour's Church went up in flames.

Thirty-Three

Greengates House stood on the main road situation between Quinton and Lower Quinton with the Dog's Bed Estate forming an isosceles triangle where police cars, fire engines and ambulances ploughed backwards and forwards; lights flashing, engines thrumming and growling loudly into the quiet of the late afternoon.

By six o'clock sirens were shrieking and the air was contaminated with the belching toxic smoke which rose up from between the biscuit buildings as illicit bonfires were built on waste ground, on the smaller access roads and in the pedestrian precincts. Sheds and garages were going up in flames. This as number thirty-four, Park Road went up in flames also and the neighbours had need to evacuate the terrace before the fire spread through the roof spaces.

Marauding groups of youths were everywhere. They were bent on trouble as they kicked in headlights and took baseball bats to car windshields, smashed shop windows and carted away electrical goods and fashion clothes by the armful.

They would later be blamed for having started the fire which raged through the home of the poor, disfigured lady who lived opposite the park, but thankfully had been out, probably shopping in Quinton, when someone had invaded her home and poured petrol everywhere. So fierce and entrenched was the blaze by the time that the overstrained fire brigade arrived at the scene that all that could be done to protect the inhabitants of the whole terrace was to evacuate them to the local civic hall, give them blankets and thereafter expect them to feed and sort themselves.

The adults were shocked and the children traumatised. Riot and pillage everywhere. Old people had to remind themselves that they had never seen anything like it before. At least in war time they had not fought each other.

Within Lower Quinton the mob had free reign. The Jackerby Club and the Glass Barrel and twelve other pubs and clubs and restaurants emptied their own mobs onto the streets to add to the affray. It was by five-thirty in the afternoon already a mindless free-for-all directed at no one and nothing in particular, as even normally placid youths joined in missile throwing, started fires in derelict buildings, committing wanton destruction of the very buildings which represented the place in which they worked and lived, venting frustrations that had become steam engines driving their own vengeance against the nameless thing which was buggering up their lives. Something called poverty at the base of it.

Something called unemployment. Something called society and everyone against them. Something that felt like frustrated helplessness but had no name they wished to recognise, as its motivation was urging them on to wilder and wilder atrocities as they then turned and fought each other.

And so the whole of Lower Quinton became an uproar of indiscriminate fighting. The riot police were stemming stone throwing revellers at Banks Circle using two armoured cars and a phalanx of bobbies carrying riot shields who marched resolutely forward until the strategic tactics of a scout leader, high on adventure, took his troop round the back alleys and attacked them from behind. He and his young squad chucking the coke bottles which they had earlier filled with petrol-soaked rags and set on fire. They would not be telling their division commander or their parents when they got home.

Children as young as ten were on roof tops dragging the slates off the old factory buildings on Harcourt Street and flinging them down to shatter in the gutters. What Catty Collins had planned to be a slap on the legs for the bad boys of the Dog's Bed Estate, to impress the nation, had turned into civil war without a purpose. It was all being filmed, too, because the press were here already, pencils flying over paper, reporters speaking into microphones, sheet after sheet of shorthand, copy dictated over mobiles directly from the scene, black bands on their arms with the word PRESS in white lettering so that they were distinguishable from the mob. Even when being filmed and photographed the youths failed to stop their mischief. The people of Lower Quinton had taken up the fever of revolt as equal in its determination to get rid of its own anger as the residents of the Dog's Bed Estate. Those out on the streets were beyond all reason. Those who stayed within dared not show their faces but cowered under staircases with fingers in their ears. They would not be coming out until the battle was over.

The women were equally as bad as the men when the booty being brought out of smashed shop windows was too good an opportunity to miss. If they didn't take the clothes from boutique shop windows someone else would. So televisions and music centres were carted away, tools pilfered with which to prise their way into other establishments, this year's Christmas presents provided for and never a thought given to the abused shopkeeper. This was not an act of God but of man's frustration. They would get their money back from their business insurance. The ones being stolen from sat on the kerbs and cried because pleading had got them nowhere.

Youths had already raided the off-licences. Lads were already assembled in baying packs, bottles tipped for the raw spirit to trickle over chins, sleeves rolled up about biceps hard with the adrenalin pumping around their systems. At last some use for the hours spent at the gym shifting weights, howling like hungry wolves, feeling strangely united, empowered by their own battle cries, owning their own streets, evangelistic almost as they fought back against the outnumbered bobbies who were past caring who they arrested. The latter just ploughed in with swiping batons and head-butting helmets, dragging lads backwards in half-Nelsons to get the affray...any affray...into the back of drunk-wagons, even if whoever came into their path was guilty of nothing more than being there.

Over on the Dog's Bed Estate whoever had started the first serious battle cry of *Get the bastards back!* had sent flying the first petrol bomb to land on the pants of an innocent policeman. Sufficient to suffice, as far as Quinton Police were concerned, under the direction of the Deputy Police Constable. The Chief; the woman who had started it all had disappeared somewhere. When the firecrackers followed suit, the marksmen took their places on the bridge and meant business as the rubber bullets were fired with every intention to stun and cause pain. Pushes turned to shoves, shoves turned to smacks, smacks turned to punches and then in real fighting mode the battle cries rose all over Lower Quinton...on the canal bridge...in the back streets...on the playing fields...even the graveyard...no public place sacrosanct from affray.

On the street where Magdalene and Nan Bartlett lived trouble was rife also. Kids were dashing across narrow streets from house to house as if playing games of chicken or soldiers in warfare, as high as kites, when in their imagination they were play-acting a Rambo or Bruce Willis character. High windows were forced open. Roofs were accessed as scouts with binoculars and two-way radios relayed news of the incoming police reinforcements.

It was upon the bridge where the police focused their resources. They were determined to see the barricade brought down and people arrested then brought to book, as examples to others who might think that they could also behave in such a way. People were taking turns to throw stones at the phalanx of riot-shielded police, whose faces were guarded by Perspex shields, batons at the ready, hands in gauntlets, a frill of fireproof material hanging to the back of helmets to stop the petrol bombs from exploding down their necks. The Deputy Chief Constable, sitting safe in his armoured vehicle, was feeling privileged to be the one to steal the glory from Catty Collins. He had informed his men and the politically recruited lady policewomen who looked most intimidated that there would seem to have been a personal reason why their trusty leader had not returned from her lunch break. It was suggested that when it came to it Catty Collins had no bottle. However, they would cope, he was sure. He was already in her shoes, cramped as his toes might feel, elbows set to resist any suggestion that she be the one to hold the glory of this day. The glory would all be his.

The other person missing was the one who might have relished it most; Cubby Watson. Local people looked out for him because they wanted their own faces to front the next issue of the Clarion as they fought the just fight and would like to be remembered as social heroes. As far as the Deputy Police Constable was concerned he would countermand such foolishness with the excellence of the police in-service training which should have prepared each and every constable for what they should do this day. This was not a mock riot, but the real thing. Each and every constable was textbook-trained.

Nan Bartlett had shut her curtains and was seriously afraid. In recent hours this place where she had spent all of her days had become somewhere she did not recognise; somewhere to fear. Fear of her neighbours seemed as preposterous as it was real. People who had hitherto been staunch in their sameness to herself were, now, behaving in ways that were incomprehensible. What had started as protest had turned to warfare. Anarchy was before her in all its chaos and lack of order. Children were running riot. Fires threatened to burn down the very structures that people had initially wished only to protect. Even a hovel if there was nowhere else to live would give the shelter required to the weary in need of rest. Now even the hovels were unsafe from the inside out. Residents and police were fighting each other as if on separate sides of an iron divide, not something thatched by human hands; a barricade woven of rubbish was not worth all the destruction that it was creating.

For that loss of peace tears ran down through the deep creases of her face. She had changed into her dressing gown, her gypsy clothes abandoned. Beneath she wore an old washed-out sweater and a pair of nylon ladies slacks with an elasticised waistband. She had put her cards away in a drawer. She drank coffee instead of tea made with fortune-telling leaves because she would rather not see into the future. Now, each passing moment was all that mattered in a desperate situation where neither the past nor the future could hold sway. Should trouble come round the corner from the bridge, it might be necessary to flee and that distressed her. For that reason she had collected together a knapsack of her belongings. Her papers. She had five hundred pounds in cash and her passport. It would get her somewhere where peace reigned because she no longer felt safe on the Dog's Bed Estate.

For the first time in her life she was aware of her age, her aches and pains. Her corns were jumping as they had never done before. Her hands were shaking. She had removed the polish from her finger nails because the bright pearly purple colour offended her. The knock on her door was three short raps. She heard it clearly.

"Come in."

Tock spoke sharply. "Come downstairs and join us, Nan. You never know when a stone might be thrown to break the glass. Magdalene has made tea. None of us are hungry. Father Turner is here. Elspeth has gone to her daughter's house to help look for her grandson. He's in the midst of all this somewhere if not arrested." Elspeth being the new wife who had replaced her in Tock's life but would never be able to share the chest of memories that Nan shared with her ex-husband. As he came to put his hand on her shoulder she knew that but for Magdalene's troubles as a girl they would have been together yet.

She allowed herself to be led because his face was stretched and pale. He had trimmed his moustache. Never a good sign. Every time a finger touched his face there was nothing to wing. He was as bereft as she was in his ability to cope with all this fighting going on outside. Away from his pub which was now closed to all comers, no matter the money that they might spill into his tills, he was like the displaced captain of a steamer overrun by pirates. He had been ousted from his comfort zone. His customers had not listened to the voice of common sense. They had ceased to do that no matter who spoke it with the building of the barricade. He had shut down his bar. Brought down the old wooden roller shutter and bolted it firm, disconnected his beer taps, taken the bottles off his optics and emptied his tills. If there was anything left of his inn come the morrow he would be dearly surprised for tonight his livelihood lay in ruins. It was not the bricks and mortar he feared for but the soul of his community. It seemed unlikely that it would ever be the same again…could never be the same again…it had all gone too far. The Dog's Bed Estate had gone to wrack and ruin.

"Thank God our granddaughter is safe. What would she make of all this?" was all Nan could say.

As if there had not been enough emotional turmoil for one day they wended down the stairs to the small kitchen at the rear of the house where single, threadbare armchairs crowded round a blazing fire. This room was where they lived most comfortably as themselves.

Nan took her knapsack with her. Father Turner looked at it as she placed it near the door. Tock knew what would be in it. This was what Nan did when she was unsettled. She packed to go then never went. It had been he who had brought her knapsack to Nan's old aunt's house and thrown it in as a sign that he had had enough himself all those years ago.

Found a new wife. A cold one who did not argue back. Did as she was bid, never questioned. In return he paid the bills without quibbling. Never complained about his meals. Darned his old socks, himself, when she would have bought him new ones. They pilfered from each other rather than gave. What Elspeth had done was to go to the place where she felt safest. He had done the same.

The old priest and his dog sat before the grate. Magdalene stirred the pan of stew that had brought him there with her invitation. The smell of it filled the kitchen but raised no appetite in any of them. The table had been set for four people. She turned out the gas flame under the pan knowing that none of them were hungry. They would not eat until it became necessary and then they would pick at cold bowls so that they need not face each other at table, need not talk of the fear that lived within them all this day. A day of such quixotic emotion when she had been reunited with her daughter again. Yet knew her to be a stranger. It would take time. It would all take time. Bridges needed to be built, barricades brought down, as far as Holly was concerned.

As for Father Turner, he had set his guilt aside with the decisions taken by others. He had still to have someone come to say that the church was aflame. Indeed he had been given no exact time for the detonation. His dog and these welcoming people were more his staff of faith and place of comfort than his ministry had ever been. His personal altar their welcome into their home. The rampage upset him more than anything else. The arson of his ministry seemed to him to already have happened. The church in people's hearts and minds had already been destroyed.

Magdalene's eyes were full of pity for his distress as she put the lid on the steaming pan and left it to cool. This day was not about God but Godlessness. For her it had started with the arrest of her brother-in-law and gone on to put before her the course of her own life as the day had progressed from bad to worse. That she cared for Mally deeply had become clear to her and not just because he was Bass's brother. However, he was now someone seemingly lost to her forever now that he had walked out of the police station and had become a wanted man. Even her daughter's return had now come to rest like a heavy weight within her because she had come to see the blame in her daughter's eyes for that for which there was no redemption.

The knock on her front door caused each of them to look at each other just as Nan raised the teapot to the first of the four mugs set before her. The sounds outside were growing louder rather than receding. They were expecting no one.

"Holly?" Magdalene breathed because suddenly she was no longer sure that she was safe where they would expect her to be. Her father rose to answer it with a hand that waved her to stay behind him. The others crowded at the door to listen. He answered the door with the chain in place. Four people stood on the doorstep. He recognised Gina first.

"We need to speak to Magdalene, Mr Bartlett."

Tommo, as the one to harbour suspicion, was less pleading. "Is your granddaughter here?"

Gary tried to be less threatening. "We're from Greengates House where Holly was working. She went missing with the child...the little girl she was looking after. We don't know that it's her as has taken the child," he explained kindly. "It's only that she's related to Mally and he might have persuaded her."

While not recognising Tommo or Gary he did recognise the shorter figure who hung back at the rear. The man who had inflamed this mayhem with his careless reporting in the first place. Yet he looked different; chastened. "To put it as it is your granddaughter has disappeared with the child who was pulled out of the canal last night. We think that she might have been persuaded to take her but we're not sure. Holly Hargreaves is Mally Kenyon's niece isn't she?"

Nan and Magdalene came crowding the door to show their faces. Nan's face had blanched. "You're from Greengates House."

Then Magdalene spoke, her face deeply concerned as she wiped her hands on her apron. "Holly and Mally don't know each other. Why would she do such a wicked thing?" She felt comforted by seeing Gina hanging to the back of the group of accusing enquirers as if not wanting to be a part of their suggestions. They smiled thinly at each other.

That was when they received a shouted message from a boy on a bike who was playing town crier as he peddled furiously past. "Mally Kenyon's pinched the crane off the canal side. Tell Father Turner his church is burning and there's people on his roof."

They all looked at each other. The door was thrust open by Magdalene. They started to run to the end of the street as if their world was crashing about their ears to where a new kind of commotion was raging. The smell of fire was now intense. However, the fire engines could not get through. Father Turner was clutching at his chest and having trouble breathing. How could this have happened? How could people have still been within the church? He had taken such trouble to make sure that no one remained. Alma reared up to press her body against him.

As he followed on behind the streaming crowds now running in the direction of his church, his legs turned to marshmallow, his breathing stemmed by fear. On the church roof there were, indeed, the black silhouettes of a young woman and a child. He heard Magdalene cry, "Oh, dear God, no...Holly!" No one stopped to raise him up as he fell to his knees and began to pray, hands beseeching God to forgive him for he had turned his back, not on Christ but on the people of this his community. He wanted the earth to open up and swallow him whole...to have a heart attack...to have some excuse not to have to witness what may very well happen before his very eyes...a young girl and a child burn to death this day. He could see the licking flames rising, and inside huge black swathes of smoke above the rooftops of the houses. Seeing the church afire enflamed his soul for he had passed the buck instead of accepting his responsibilities. Why had he allowed himself to be persuaded when all he had had to do otherwise was to turn the key in the door and walk away?

It was Magdalene who sprang to her toes and ran ahead of them for she had immediately recognised the taller of the two figures on the church roof as they tried to distance themselves from the flames. Flames which were now licking up and around the shattered windows of the church, a wall of smoke all around them. There was no mistaking Holly. She even wore the same clothes that she had worn earlier. A small child clung to her back as she climbed up the steep, shingled roof with the smoke billowing about her as if God could pluck her off its pinnacle to safety. If only! She could only assume that the small girl clinging onto her was the child that Holly had been hired to care for.

Why had they been within the church? They had to have been within the church to climb the stairs into the attic spaces. Then from there up the access ladder and into the roof. They would have had to have used the ladder to the dormer window which gave access to the roof for maintenance.

Then she heard the rumble of the moving crane as it came from behind, out from Carlton Terrace, its hydraulic lift folded for a careless, bouncing journey over corner pavements and through narrow spaces as it turned towards the church. People running with it and shouting because the crane could only be heading that way for one reason; it would be the only way of attempting to get her daughter and the child from the roof. She saw that it was Mally guiding the big crane with its huge bucket, which had been used earlier to bring the barricade material from the stinking canal. Next to him was a woman she failed to recognise, but she recognised a unity in their expression; a fixed determination. It was vital to her that he know that it was Holly who was up there; Bass's daughter. She called even as she ran by the side of the high cabin running on clanking treads to leave scars upon the road's surface. "Mally! Mally!" And when she had gained his attention. "Mally...Oh, Mally!...That's my Holly...Bass's daughter up there. Please…bring her down safely. If she dies there will be nothing to live for."

Mally was thinking the same. What was there for himself to live for if his own innocence died with a small, silver-eyed child and his brother's daughter perished in flames. Magdalene saw his chest rise as he drew deep breath. What was there to live for anyway?

In the moment her faith was not with a distant God but with Mally Kenyon.

Thirty-Four

They had parked up before the bridge, Catty driving, Serena hidden within her clothing in the front passenger seat, Mally not to be seen but present in a hiding place behind her seat. Already three police cars that Catty could see had been set alight and the fire tenders unable to gain access because of the barriers erected against them, lights flashing, doors open, bombardiers waiting. Affray was untidy and upsetting and frightening. People with bloody heads and noses being led to the waiting ambulances in front of the Dog's Bed Inn. Children frightened and crying now that the reality was before them.

The sound was deafening as people screamed and cried and shouted. Faces pressed to windows with mouths wide open, fingers pointing. A tractor was coming up the road from Lower Quinton, its engine roaring. Press helicopters were in the sky overhead, circling and hovering. Catty cursed them as if each of them were being piloted by the man who had started all this incitement in her opinion. Only one to blame; Cubby Watson. Where was he now that all his weeks of poking had started the unrest in the first place? He had been the one to incite her own commitment towards doing something about the lawlessness of this place. Then again he had been the one to suggest that these people were worthless and the place was better razed. She had expected merely to teach a few lessons. Not this.

Everywhere she looked, people fighting people. Roofs were being claimed. Ripped-off slates crashing down, broken glass everywhere, occasional fires from randomly thrown petrol rags exploding from broken bottles which skittered fire and glass over pavements. It had become a free-for-all as the police swarmed the barricade from one side and the residents swarmed from their side of the big divide, meeting in the middle of the stinking barricade. Onto and over; no going round or through or under, legs forward as they kicked their way. Sticks, batons, poles, punches, kicking feet, flying leaps and foolish tackles. Everywhere was pandemonium and senseless violence. It had all got out of hand and it seemed as if no one was even attempting to bring it under control.

There was no getting into the estate by vehicle other than to take a circuitous route up and then down twisting country lanes. There was no getting off or onto the estate by the bridge, either. The other roads in had probably been barricaded also, bonfires burning everywhere. Confrontation seemed to be the only way.

Catty flung herself down from her driving seat and stared with incredulity at the scene before her. "This has to be stopped," she shouted. "It can't be allowed to continue."

Before Mally could pull her back, from his hiding place behind her seat, she had leapt down and was running into the midst of her own manpower, shouting and screaming at them to cease fighting. "Stop I tell you! Fall back I tell you!" Her words falling on deaf ears as she was elbowed by one of her own men in riot gear out of the way; floored to be precise. Rolled away to the side like a swatted fly. No one seemed to accord this mad woman in their midst the slightest attention as she tried to stand in front of the barrier with her hand raised. "Halt this minute. Fall back! I am your Chief Constable."

"Get out of the fucking way!"

Anger now replacing fear. Did they not know who she was? She would show them, she thought, as she began desperately trying to beat a way through her own ranks to get to her deputy, only he was insulated inside her own armoured vehicle, looking out with all the helpless horror that she felt herself. Wondering perhaps like her how all this could have developed from out of nothing more than protest.

As she ran towards him she was dragged back with a strangling jerk by an arm about her neck and thrust downwards. She was further set upon with a thrashing baton about her chest and hips then dragged and rolled through the stinking mud until it stuck to her face, hair and clothing. Her tights were ripped to shreds. Someone she recognised had her held by the foot and was intent on pulling her towards the open door of a van where people were being thrown in like dead sheep and the door slammed closed on them. The friction of being dragged was burning through her clothing. "Let me go you idiot!"

It was then that Mally Kenyon came to her defence. He propelled the policeman doing the dragging down by his clothing until he was flat on his back, taking Catty's black brogue with him. His foot pinned him down as he helped her upwards. "We've come for the child, remember," was what he shouted as he dragged her by the hand back to the car. Catty limping, as her bare foot was penetrated by a sharp piece of broken metal. It just would not have to matter.

"We have to get there quick. To the crypt of the church," Mally yelled over the din.

"They didn't recognise me," she shouted back, appalled that something as inconsequential as an absent uniform and a hair bun could strip her of all rank. If she could have seen herself in a mirror she looked wilder than the wildest woman present.

Serena was weeping in the front passenger seat when they got back to the car, unable to cope. "I started all this," she was crying. "Dear God in Heaven forgive me."

Hysterical women did his head in. "Stay there. Lock yourself in and then get down so that you're hidden. If anyone throws something at the windscreen get out quick. Go back home." He opened the door and gave her back her phone. "Call me on your sister's phone if you need me."

Then he began to drag Catty the opposite way, down the bridge steps and onto the canal banking; the side that would have taken them to Lower Quinton through the park land. He pushed away a man set there to prevent people coming and going freely. His eyes were flashing. They all knew Mally when he was angry. The man melted away. He then dragged her into the stinking ditch which was now clear of junk and then threw her like a bag of sand up out of the water and onto the opposite towpath. Catty Collins was unable to understand what he was doing. Above the din Catty screamed. "Where are we going? We have to get through. What are you doing?"

"We're getting on the right side of the ditch. We have to get to St Saviours Church. No getting through over the bridge is there? We can get the back way through the allotments." Then he stopped walking and stared over to his left, high above the rooftops to the flaming spires of St Saviour's Church. "Shit! Look! She's up there...the child is up there and the church is burning."

Catty's breath was sharp in her throat. Her hands fluttered like birds as she raised them to her lips. "That's little Caitlin. That's my daughter. The fire engines can't get through. What will we do? We will have to save them."

On the canal towpath the mechanical beast that had dredged the canal with its grabbing bucket at the end of its long, hydraulic neck was still sitting sorry headed, looking on. Mally pointed it out. "That's our only chance. Ladders will be no use. There's too much smoke and flames. If we can raise the bucket high enough...!" He was now running, dragging her with him. Catty had no choice but to go with him. Her one shoe was sodden, her other foot bleeding. They were both covered in the slime from the canal.

Then the dog was before him. The German Shepherd stood directly in his path as it came from under the tracks of the giant machine, darting at him, teeth bared but restrained by the neck so that it could not reach him. The terrified animal was trapped there by the lead trailing from its collar. It had got stuck between the overlapping gaps in the tracking plates. The noise and mayhem on the bridge rose and the dog made to spring at Mally again, fangs bared and snapping. It could not get free either to find its master or run away to where it might cower in a place of safety somewhere away from this war-torn place.

Mally stopped dead in his tracks staring at it as mesmerised as a petrified rabbit, the dog's eyes becoming those of a wolf called Timber, yellow eyes turning on him in a darkened cellar space, its teeth biting deeply into his mind still. His heart had begun to crash against his ribs. His breathing had shortened. His face had paled. Beads of perspiration appeared on his brow like crystals.

Catty was dragged to a halt also. She had noted his sudden pallor. His complete stillness. "What's the matter? It's only a dog. Let it loose and it will run away. We have to get to the church quickly. There is no time to waste."

Mally steeled himself against the shakes that suddenly passed like an electric shock through his body. He looked at what must be saved for a second time in the same span of twenty four hours. The child! And a young girl holding onto her. They were trying to scale the steep roof shingles to the very pinnacle. Suddenly the glass windows in the church popped and shattered. The fire within came licking out in smoke and flames.

"They'll never get down from there without our help," Catty shouted. "There isn't time to wait."

Then the shouts of "Fire! Fire! The church is on fire. People on the roof."

The fire engines were unable to get through, he knew. He could see them on the street ineffectually waiting for a tractor to barge the barricade out of the way.

His eyes went back to the dog's face as it coiled itself to strike. He had to overcome his fear. "Stay. Lie down."

The dog's ears went down.

He took a step towards it. He had to approach it and be the master. He had to deal with his fear. The child had to be saved. "Lie down."

It did.

Slowly, Mally moved to release the end of the tether that had held it fast between the plates of the caterpillar tracking. He had to move close enough to smell it, to know that it might snap at the hand that was a mere few inches from its growling teeth. The dog sat up again. Mally had its lead in his hand as he threaded it back through the plates. For a passing moment dog and man looked eye to eye. The dog's ears went down again. The growling diminished. Mally dropped the tether. As soon as it was free the dog bounded away.

Only he might know the relief that swept over him as he found the screwdriver from his pocket. He clambered up onto the caterpillar tracks and rammed the tool into the door lock to break it. The door came open with a single tug. As he took the seat inside he plunged the screwdriver into the ignition and forced it round to bring the wires together, to bring the engine to life. His fear over the dog barely receding as he used the levers to swing the cabin about to face the opposite direction.

Catty climbed up and shoved herself in by the side of him. She gripped onto the strap. "Through the greenhouses I take it."

As he swung the cabin about to face in the opposite direction he nodded. "You do realise that this is wilful vandalism."

"If that's what we have to do we'll have to do it. Straight through the shed. We'll just have to hope and pray that people hear us coming and get out of our way."

Mally used the levers to put the machine into gear. They took the fence and the shed down with the bushes behind it as if no more than matchwood. The tank tracks ploughed through the glazed housing estate with no resistance. Barrier fencing to each plot uprooted, pots smashed, plants mashed, bags of potting compost bursting open like peapods popping, glass flying everywhere. Then the hedges to the rear of the allotment were flattened under. All that they could hope was that anything alive and able to move quick enough had sense enough to get out of the way.

Onto Carlton Terrace he took down the fences of the houses which shared his own slum dwelling as he swung the creaking, clanking machine down the road, scraping cars and pushing them onto the pavement. When push came to shove the giant machine had the advantage over the flimsy, metal tea caddies people drove around in.

They passed the spot where he had been arrested only that morning. People fearing a stolen vehicle careering clumsily, of sufficient power to flatten them like ants under its tracking, they moved well out of its way. Those in the houses came out to stare, keeping their distance before noticing the clamouring calls of, "Fire! Fire! The church is on fire!" as the crowd grew in ever increasing numbers. The people running recognising Mally but not the woman with him as the huge machine turned another corner towards the back of the estate where more people were running, all heading one way.

It was then that Magdalene came running beside the moving crane. "Mally! Mally!" And when she had gained his attention. "Mally…Oh, Mally!…That's my Holly…Bass's daughter…Please bring her down safely. If she dies there will be nothing left to live for."

Mally nodded, only for a moment were his thoughts negative. For Magdalene, anything! For Bass's child, everything! He would not fail his brother, now.

She saw him nod briefly and stopped running, her faith not in God but in Mally Kenyon and the woman whose face was set with a determination which further raised her faith that there was yet hope in a desperate situation; a woman who had been already in the thick of the raging battle, her clothing ripped and her face smeared with filth.

Catty saw Magdalene's importance in Mally's face. His determination hardened. The breath that he took raised his chin, brought his chest high and tightened the muscles under the thin clothing. She saw a man worthy of her respect in the jut of his chin, even as her heart was in her mouth and she would be able to think of nothing but rescuing the child she had once sought to kill. This man, like herself, would risk his own life rather than see the child and her carer die for lack of trying.

She saw the child come into view again as her view of Magdalene fell away. Her beauty as fragile as the smoke that wreathed her as she clung onto the back of the tall young woman who had now pitched herself upon the steaming shingles with a rag doll pressed between them. She wanted desperately for her to live. She prayed for such as Mally wound the creaking giant round the back of the church taking the front bushes down as the giant tracks of the machine pressed them into the ground and rode over them. When she saw them begin to climb the shingles Catty realised that there was nowhere to go other than upwards to the pinnacle. Then the older girl became frozen to the spot with hysteria, fear upon her face as she screamed for them to be saved. She was on her knees with the child clinging to her back, the arms and head of the rag doll dangling down from where the child had tucked it into the back waistband of her skirt as if she would not lose it. Holly looked to be in danger of slipping.

"Hold fast," Mally shouted upwards as if above the uproar his voice could be heard. If they fell it would be to their deaths as the flames caught at the dry, paint-flaked wood of the clapboard planking on the face of the church. There seemed to be no other way than to jump. They had both begun to cough in the hot smoke billowing about them.

It was Catty whose voice rose even higher than his own, "Don't fall. We're coming."

*****

Catty had been planning the offensive from the moment Mally had planted the idea in her mind that the crane was the only way for the girls to be saved. With no more barriers for the crane to flatten she found her voice. "Not too close. We have to make sure that we can get the bucket into position and raise it high without it catching the building. When we're in position I'll climb into the bucket. You raise it up as high and as close as you can. Into the smoke if it has to be. If it extends long enough they might be able to climb into the bucket with me."

A moment's pessimism was all it took before Mally felt his twin brother within him. He felt him like a strong force of spirit inside him. Not really gone anywhere. Bass now strong. Repaired in death. Urging him on as he brought the heavy plant machine up at the side of the church with enough space at his disposal to raise the hydraulically operated bucket as high as he could. Tears began to wet his cheeks; they were rallying to his courage not diminishing. Even if he had to die for her, Holly, as well as the child, would live; a part of Bass that could live on in his stead and the child who, while she might proclaim his innocence, had his love and devotion still entrenched within his soul. Thinking this even as he noted the courage of the woman he had previously detested. She would do that which she said she would do. Not for a single moment did he doubt her.

Catty was already climbing out of the cab and onto the friction-hot tracking. She didn't hesitate as she began to climb onto the lower neck of the crane and into the giant bucket with its jaws locked to keep her within. She seemed fearless in her focus. A woman for whom a uniform had once denoted her authority had now relinquished her cold dignity in tights ripped to shreds, her hair and face filthy dirty, her coat torn, her hair hanging in rats tails about her face. She steeled herself into the deep concentration needed to overcome her fear. That she was compromised in her presentation was something she cared for not one jot. Her skirt rode up her thighs as she climbed. She had lost one shoe and her foot was bleeding. All this while her deputy sat in the comfort of an armoured car probably thinking a church fire to be his salvation.

As soon as she was in the bucket with its jaws locked Mally pulled the lever to start the slow rise which would take her upwards. He could see the figures of his brothers amongst the crowds of people. Everyone but them, necks craned upwards, dragging all they could from their homes to cushion a jump or a fall, working together. Benny and Woody had begun to fight over something in quarrelsome fashion. Even in this desperate situation they were both too sunk into their own concerns to concern themselves with others.

His head shook from side to side in wonder as he watched Catty Collins rise in the bucket upwards and ever upwards. Then he saw that the lift was short of length by over a metre from the parapet that ran around the roof perimeter. Smoke was beginning to fill the cabin of the machine. Catty was coughing as its vapour wrapped about her. The metal bucket was becoming hot but he could see that she was after trying to find some way to get onto the roof to save her daughter as she lifted herself onto its edge but had nothing to cling to, to rise further. Both he and Catty were in danger of frying unless the rescue was administered quickly. They were saved by someone below hosing them with water. People were working together now to try to find what they could to make for a softer landing should any of them fall....empty cardboard boxes, mattresses dragged from houses, a child's trampoline, anything and everything of give or stretch and softness was being placed in a ring on the grass and over the pathways. People with blankets spread between, looking upwards and waiting, holding their breath.

Under a spray of drenching water he left the cabin and climbed to the hot plates then onto the hydraulic shaft where the grease of years of maintenance began to cover his hands and his clothing. Heat and billowing smoke from the building pouring over him so that he could imagine himself roasting like a pig on a spit.

Still he climbed. The people below urging them on, Catty too, as she struggled to climb up onto the edge of the bucket once again, her height insufficient to make it when there was nothing in reach to cling on to. The desperation on her face would not allow her to give up now that she was so close to achieving what she had set upon doing.

Before reaching the bucket Mally saw the cast iron downspout as his only means of bridging the shortfall in height denied by the bucket. He leant across and placed a foot on what could just have easily fallen away under the tenuous hold of loose screws which had been driven into the rotten wooden boards of the dilapidated building. It held firm. One hand followed, his palms burning against the hot iron. Mally made his mind numb to all feeling. Then he passed himself over and began to climb. One swing of a leg onto the weed-choked, iron gutter allowed him to scramble up until he was on the parapet where he might look for Bass's daughter and the beloved child who would attest his innocence. They were directly above him. He saw that they were stuck with fear and panic. Holly incapable of moving. "Let yourself slide. I'll catch you. I'm your uncle. Trust me."

Holly was sliding anyway with the child clinging to her back and wrapped about her like a baby monkey. They were both brick red with the heat of the shingled roof beneath them. When his hands came about her she knew that they were not yet saved. The flames were now catching on the underside of the roof shingles. They could see them and had begun to choke on the smoke pouring through. They could feel the searing heat through the soles of their shoes, the child still clad only in the thin slippers bought for her by Gina Mon who stood below, next to Cubby Watson, her hand to her throat, barely breathing. It had been to her that Magdalene had gone to be embraced and comforted. Too frightened to look. Tock and Nan behind her. Father Turner nowhere to be seen.

He took the little girl first, flinging the rag doll away because it might impede his handling. The child cried out as they watched it float down, down, down like a parachutist might use the air currents to glide in free fall, limbs spread before pulling the rip cord. It hit the piled mattresses below in a belly flop, head down. He raised her high in his arms and held her suspended over the parapet in mid-air. She kicked her legs and screamed as loudly as she could as she was lowered, his back bending to the task, his knees spreading wide. Another pair of hands rising to take her then...her mother's, had she but known them, without a golden trumpet in her hand. Wendy slid down her length and crouched in the bucket.

Holly was next to be taken in his strong hands as if she weighed nearly nothing; a young woman almost as tall as himself. Slowly he lowered her with her eyes shut, until her feet felt the rim of the hard metal bucket and Catty's extended hands guided her inwards and downwards to safety.

Lastly he might save himself as he saw someone climb into the cabin of the machine, ready to bring the bucket away from the burning building. As soon as he was in the man would take the bucket away from the heat and the flames and slowly lower it safety. Mally stood rooted. Did he want to live? Was there anything worth the struggle and the effort of his daily existence? Now with himself redeemed was the time to take that decision.

It was Holly calling to him. "Uncle Mally...we can't go without you. Hurry. Jump in. Please, Uncle Mally, before we all burn in this heat."

Mally ducked his chin once, raised it again and jumped. Catty and Holly caught him within the limited space. The child scrambled up his length and placed her arms around his neck. It was obviously the safest place she could think of to be in that very moment. Never in his life had anything felt as precious as the child as she hugged him tightly. He lowered his head on glistening eyes because a Kenyon never cried in public. Catty placed her hand on his shoulder. "I will never be able to thank you enough, Mally Kenyon. I will make sure that your innocence is declared. I will make sure, too, that Wendy knows of your bravery and grows up knowing you."

Mally broke down as a dam inside him broke. Less than twenty four hours, one beautiful child and his life had changed forever.

Only when they scrambled out of the bucket did Catty take the child from him. She began to walk away quickly before people might hem her in...ask questions...want to know her name...already her own men were closing in as she slipped through the knots of people, walking quickly to avoid them. Talking to the child as she did so. Her voice urgent. Whispering for Wendy's ears only. "I am Catty Collins. I am the lady with the golden trumpet. I am your mother. You are the baby I gave away to Serena. Serena is my sister. We have come for you together. You must do all that we ask of you now without question. Promise me, cherished child...promise me. So that we can all be together."

Wendy's face spread with joy as she listened further. "I shall be as good and quiet as a dolly. I promise." Then she remembered. "My rag doll!"

Catty was not after waiting. As they ploughed on through the crowds she saw a man with chestnut chair bend to take her Oswald Rag Doll from the place where it had fallen. Inside it was where she had placed the loaf sized, brown envelope to keep it safe. She could see Woody and Benny standing close to him, looking about, dazed and bewildered even as the man with the chestnut coloured hair weighed the rag doll in his hand, with the package inside its belly where the stuffing had been.

Holly, in her mother's arms with her grandparents behind was unable to prevent him as he did the unexpected. He pitched it into the fire through the space where the stained glass window had been...into the flames. For a moment its limbs and head spread against the licking fire before its black shape was eaten up in the burning.

Holly collapsed on her mother's shoulders and wept for all that might have been. Anger on her face as she spoke to the man harshly. Wendy could only imagine her angry words. Wendy however was not sorry because she hadn't liked the Holly with the greedy eyes. It was better for Oswald to be sacrificed, she thought, as she saw the same woman that Caitlin had attacked at the police station come to speak with the man who had sent the rag doll to its cremation. Whatever she said caused him to hang his head. Wendy felt so sorry for Holly. Maybe she might make up for her disappointment when things settled down again.

Her arms went round the neck of the lady who was her mummy for she had achieved that which she had set out to achieve. Then she was being turned about to see Serena's joyful face and knew what she had to do as Serena opened the lid to the shopping trolley. Before the lid was closed she thought herself to be a very lucky, little girl indeed.

Both Wendy and the lady with the golden trumpet vanished. The Chief Constable in her state of anonymity simply walked away.

Thirty-Five

Cubby watched closely as the little girl came down in the large bucket in the arms of someone he had only slowly realised to be Catty Collins, though no one else did apparently. It was a fact that he found very confusing for she was after getting away without having to speak with anyone, even her own police officers who Cubby guessed had made no connection either between this child and the child who had been kidnapped from Greengates House. They had been too caught up with the other work of the day and perhaps had no knowledge that this child was the cause of it. Neither did they recognise the woman who was usually so smartly turned out in a braided blue uniform with her hair smoothly caught back in a hair net. The same as usually courted publicity like a film star at every turn. She was even avoiding being photographed as the child shielded her and the smoke drifted and people showed only relief that the young girl and the child had been saved, even while the building burned. Had he not been so very familiar with her he might not have realised who she was himself. She was nothing like the woman of the morning as she made her way quickly through the crowds of people, talking to the child, holding onto her so very tightly. Strangely, for him, his curiosity was more for his own confirmation than to make any kind of exposure. He said nothing to Gina as he followed. Tommo and Gary seemed to have lost sight of Wendy in the arms of the lady as they searched the crowd, waiting perhaps to take their ward back into their care.

That was when he saw the rag doll lying on the grass. He saw the child's nursemaid make a move towards it. Cubby got there first. Her cry seemed out of proportion to the deed as the doll plunged into the flame. "Do you realise what you've done?" she screamed at him.

"I'll buy her a new one," was all he said. "What's a damned doll for Christ sake."

What was a damned doll, indeed, if not damning! He would not see his father exposed when it came down to it. So much for publish and be damned where his own father was concerned.

He followed Catty, then, as she carried Wendy Bridgewater in her arms as if she would never let her go again. Her shoulders were heaving as she walked. If she was overcome with emotion it seemed out of keeping with all that he had previously known of her. He could only imagine that she was weeping. Whatever she whispered into the child's ear caused the child's eyes to light up and her face to spread into a smile sufficient to bring sunshine to the whole world. He saw the child place a kiss on her cheek and then listen solemnly to what was said to her. Wendy seemed to think about what was said before nodding.

Then there was Serena Collins standing before them and dressed much as she had been that morning, her face obscured totally by an enveloping headscarf. The child turned to the woman whom Catty Collins had obviously gone to meet. Serena Collins greeted the child with tears coursing down her hidden cheeks if the wetness of her scarf was anything to go by.

Feigning his attention to be elsewhere he looked on surreptitiously, his confusion deepening. He saw them embrace with the child between them and knew that he could not be mistaken. It was, indeed, the Chief Constable of Quinton who was wanting to avoid being apprehended as she passed the child over. A child who was one minute there and the next minute gone. Like a magician's act, the child had totally disappeared.

For a moment he looked around frantically. She had definitely not been put to the ground, there to be lost from his sight within the milling people. Next he wondered whether Serena had slipped the child under her coat. She looked to be no fatter in her clothing than she had a moment ago. Then he understood. There was only one place that she could be. The child had slipped silently into the trolley and the lid replaced. Serena fastened the buckle which kept it tied down. Catty had already gone from sight by the time Serena moved away.

Was there any point in confrontation when the child and Serena might implicate his father even yet? Yet still he required the satisfaction of his curiosity as she threaded her way through the crowd of people towards the front of the church. She went to stand at a spot where the branches of a lime tree had yet to burst into green leafy splendour, close to a parked, red Jaguar car; a car he recognised as belonging to his father with its distinctive, personalised number plate. He could see her clearly as she raised a phone to scroll for a number. Her call was brief and then she waited.

It was then that he saw his father come tacking through the crowd towards her with his own mobile raised to his ear. He was wearing similar outdoor clothing to that Cubby had seen him wearing earlier that same afternoon; a style often repeated in his father's wardrobe.

When Serena turned in CC's direction he was shocked to see his father go to her side and embrace her lightly as he might embrace a friend. If this relationship was clandestine, which Cubby doubted, he would have ignored her altogether. Instead he pressed something into her hand. It looked like a batch of crumpled papers followed by a crucifix on a chain.

These Serena brought to her chest and gripped tightly as if they were something for which she felt extremely grateful. They kissed cheeks then in the continental way of a farewell. Then Serena walked on. The meeting had been so brief that it was hardly noticeable. People were crying and hugging each other all over the place now that the storm of released emotions had come and gone. Faces amongst the crowd had been blackened, clothes torn, possessions dragged from houses were now being walked over and sat upon yet no one seemed to care. They might now have been watching a bonfire.

He saw Tommo and Gary scratch their heads as they walked in the opposite direction, looking about...looking for Wendy whom he doubted they would ever see again. They had not spotted Serena Collins. Had they done so a very different ending might have occurred. For once in his life Cubby Watson had not the slightest wish to expose the truth of things. What was he anyway, but the drummer boy; in this instance, his job over.

He might have let his father escape also except that the figure in the large Homburg hat with the pheasant feather in the hatband had noticed him and was beckoning him over. He was leaning on the bonnet waiting for Cubby's slow approach, while undoing the buttons of his coat. Cubby was thinking carefully in ways not usual to his character. Was it his place to pry in matters that did not directly concern him where his own parents were concerned? Whatever relationship they had was theirs and no one else's. There seemed to be no chance of his mother discovering the truth...that his father had fathered an illegitimate daughter and had been hiding her away in a house in Lower Quinton, cared for by the deformed sister of the mother who just happened to be the Chief Constable of Quinton. All this, of course, mere conjecture. Indeed was there any such thing as truth, for it all lay in the interpretation?

Of one thing he was sure...that being that the child would be in no danger. However she had come to be in the canal in the first place he felt sure that it had nothing to do with a deliberate abuse by the woman who cherished and adored her. It had nothing to do with Catty Collins either. It had not been Mally Kenyon who had put her there. Sometimes it was too easy for people to make assumptions; not just himself, either. He now considered it to be better to be cherished within an eccentric family with support than to know no family whatsoever. The prospect of a life in care, to Cubby, now looked so horrendously bleak that he could only be glad that the child had been returned to those who loved and cared for her. Such was important to him also. No matter his parents' disparity, he loved them both.

Trying to determine his politics, as ever, he walked slowly. He saw his father begin to remove the hat which he let drop on the bonnet behind him before starting to peel off the mackintosh with the epaulettes and the high-buttoned collar. Cubby could not believe what he saw! His jaw dropped open to see that the man he had assumed to be his father...assumed entirely because of his dress...turned out to be his mother. His senses confused further.

Marjory's face was sorrowful and tired as she drew a hand through the same copper curls so like his own. Her eyes were dark rimmed as she stared at him defiantly and knowing the shock that she was providing. As usual, she was wearing black clothes save for the brown leather boots which she tapped impatiently one against the other while looking at him accusingly. "I would ask, Cubby, for the sake of all concerned that you keep what you know to yourself. You are, I believe, one of the few to have recognised the woman who brought the child down from the roof and then handed her over to Serena Collins. I know that you have been to the house. I know that you saw where the child went."

"You knew about her?"

Marjory nodded. "I have known since shortly after the child was born. Your father was being difficult over money. Who else could Serena turn to? I should have turfed him out but...but then I would have been on my own. I have my reasons for accepting that which I cannot change. As inadequate as your father is he is all I have. You have your own life to live. It means a great deal to me to keep our family intact."

"You knew last night what happened?"

She shook her head. "Serena has only ever phoned me when things have become desperate. She phoned me only when it seemed impossible to get little Caitlin back and there was no other way. It became imperative that we find some way to get her back before the child gave away our family secrets. It has to be said that the Kenyons have their uses. They approached me this morning at the house when I went home to change for the Magistrates' Court. Needless to say I was an absentee when the court sat in judgement. There was so much to do and arrange. Then the evidence needed to be destroyed..."

Cubby's eyes widened. "Her clothes and toys...the contents of the house on Park Road. How? There has been so little time."

"Tomorrow it will be in all the national papers. You might save yourself the trouble of an investigation in order to report on what will be the effects of public affray. Arson by marauding youths in fact. A woman with severe disabilities...her home doused with petrol while she was away. Poor Serena. She will have to go live with relatives until another home can be found for her. Such a waste but no one hurt. Save for the gold fish by her bed. The cat has been taken in by neighbours."

"What's happening to the child now?"

"Why, school...what else? A private establishment in Shropshire. All the arrangements made already. In that, at least, your father acted responsibly. There was never any choice in the matter even if convincing little Caitlin has, at times, been extremely difficult. However, now that Catty knows, Serena will find it all easier.

"It won't be easier for Catty Collins though. There'll be questions to answer of a delicate nature. Like where she was today when the riot occurred."

Marjory smiled. "Oh more than that, Cubby. Evidence will all magically disappear in the course of a thorough investigation which will be covered up in order to avoid the police further embarrassment. It will be as if Wendy Bridgewater was nothing more than a figment of someone's fertile imagination. Stolen back to where she had come from and no one any the wiser. It can all be swept under the carpet if those in the know keep their mouths shut. You will, Cubby, won't you?"

"Her sister knows all this? She is willing to be a part of what is essentially a cover-up?"

Marjory nodded. "Tomorrow she will arrange for the charges to be dropped against Mally Kenyon. The staff at Greengates House will be informed that the child has been returned to her family and discretion will be necessary should the national press care to follow up on what has happened to her. It is the right of every child to have their identity protected where nothing is to be gained by exposure and where the legal guardians object and there is no reason to suspect that the course of justice has been corrupted. Dr Thomas will be eager to guard the reputation of his secure unit when a second client got out through a badly maintained fence...the second in two days in fact. It was merely unfortunate that she tried to hide in the crypt where her nursemaid found her before the place went up in flames. Holly Kenyon has her own family to protect. She will keep a low profile because she will choose not to become involved. As long as there is a mundane outcome to her situation the interest will be dropped in favour of more sensational press. What's news today is old hat tomorrow. A week from now and the child will be forgotten about entirely."

"Where's father?"

"Where he always is when there's a problem...drinking himself stupid somewhere...head in the sand as usual. The Glass Barrel Inn actually. He has been there since leaving the house in Park Road earlier this afternoon."

"What will happen to Serena now that she has nowhere to live?"

"She will return to Quinton after depositing Caitlin where she should have been taken first thing this morning and stay in Quinton only long enough to deal with the effects of the fire. After which she and her sister will retire discreetly to leafy Shropshire together. I gather that she has already spotted a house close to Blackstone School on the internet, so that Caitlin can become a day pupil instead of a boarder. All should work out well in the end I think. Now what I need most is a cup of tea before I pick CC up from where he is presently finding it a little difficult to talk coherently or walk in a straight line."

His mother had nerves of steel. "Will you tell him? He needs to know or he'll think he's got away with it all again."

"My darling, Cubby! Getting away with things is what your father has always done. I shall let him stew in his own worry and guilt. In return he will afford me someone to come home to. It's a compromise. It's how relationships work. I would rather have someone like your father than have no one. The prospect otherwise is to live alone."

It was then that the fire engines came; too late for the hoses to make any difference. By the time the fire was doused, leaving only charred and buckled remains which steamed against the cool night air, few people were left to look over the plot where St Saviour's Church had once been. Tomorrow there would be a great deal of clearing up to do.

Father Turner came with Alma by his side to look for what might be left of his few belongings, if anything. It was there, within the blackened ashes that he saw Benny and Woody Kenyon raking over the debris. *To what end?* he thought, so he turned himself about, found the dog lead from his pocket and attached to it his faithful friend. As he turned to leave through the back gate, the stocky, grey-haired Bull Mastiff followed. Little had he realised that Alma had started her heat. Next to his band of worthy pilgrims came a loping Alsatian; the same as Mally had released from its imprisonment. "Come on then, Sabre," he called, and from his pocket found a biscuit. It came to him then that he was homeless. "You too. Perhaps my new ministry should be for the stray dogs of the Dog's Bed instead of their owners."

When the phone rang in his pocket, it was Nan Bartlett. "I've made the bed up in the spare room, Father. You're more than welcome. Magdalene and Holly have gone with Mally to the police station. Just a formality."

Father Turner smiled gratefully. There were still some good people in the world. "You're a dog lover, Nan, I take it.

Thirty-Six

Almost fifteen months later, the twenty-first of June was a bright, sunny day. The Dog's Bed Inn had had a make-over. Its new restaurant had been built on part of the car park to the canal side and rear where Tock had used to have his waste disposal bins. The area had become a large conservatory filled with hanging plants and lined with shelves for the display of Willow Pattern plates, Toby Jugs and old curiosities. The floor was quarry tiled. The dining tables and chairs of stout oak. The glass panels afforded views of the Whemley Canal by Bridge Twenty-Eight which was now reclaimed, the water flowing clean between locks that had been renovated to work again. Here, the colourful canal boats might now make a slow and tranquil journey through pleasant countryside to Whemley and beyond. While it might not make a best food guide, The Dog's Bed Inn offered good value and a pleasant place to eat.

And such a change of scenery! These days people came regularly to walk their dogs along the canal bank to the renovated lift-bridge. If they took to the towpath in the direction of Quinton they might cross the smoothly flowing water by the renovated bridge to the lane which would take them under the viaduct, through the fields and so follow the train line into the centre of Quinton; the way that Serena had finally gone with her charge, this time stowed willingly in the shopping trolley, less than twenty-four hours after her intended journey.

It was here that Cubby brought Gina for a sunny, weekday lunch so to admire the boats tied up at moorings on the towpath side while their owners dined within. Their relationship was, as ever, an on-off affair of total devotion followed by angry partings; grief and passion, lots of laughter and lots of crying. Today was marked by a truce within yet another conflict of interests. Their plans to move in together could not come to any form of compatible agreement. Where to go from here? Neither would concede. Both too stubborn to part with their opinions.

They both saw the quiet man with a text book on his knee and recognised him immediately as he sat with his chair turned towards the canal. Tommo had taken to dining at the Dog's Bed restaurant at least once a week, usually after he had cast his line for a spot of river fishing either within the canal or the mere across the playing fields, which was newly stocked with trout, both banks only available to those with a fishing permit. The book he was reading was a catalogue of species of fish common to the inland waters of Britain.

He remained unaware of Cubby and Gina taking a table to his

rear. Or so it seemed when he remained with his back to them; only their reflections in the glass for him to see. Occasionally as he forked food into his mouth he dipped his head to read, turned a page or looked onto the reformation that had once been a stinking ditch now no longer filled with the detritus of past generations. Now the yellow, stagnant water had disappeared. Its flow was crystal clean. Dragon flies buzzed over the lapping surface and laid their larvae to the base of the yellow flags growing below the wall of the Dog's Bed Inn. Butterflies fluttered amongst broad, bitter green leaves and within the buddleia and lilac which was sprouting wild by the water's edge. Water voles made timidly through shadows cast by the verdant undergrowth. Frogs dived and newts swam amongst rocks covered with green beards for the water was shallow; never more than a metre deep. Wild life abounded with the turning of spring to summer. Today was Midsummer's Day; the longest of the year.

Gina saw Cubby frown in Tommo's direction and so Gina looked away. Cubby's jealousy could be unreasonable at times.

With little wait their order was taken by the same young girl who had so very nearly lost her life within the fire at St Saviours church. Gina knew her mother well. She knew Holly in a distant way, too, for she had been the one to take her as a child from a play house in the beer garden that had once belonged to this inn, before the land became allotments, all those years ago, for a childhood spent in care. Now she was back living with her mother and grandmother and working for her grandfather, setting tables and serving meals. She did not seem to Gina to have fared too badly, she thought, as the girl set a table with new covers. What she did not know was that sprouting healthily in Holly's womb was a female foetus which would probably turn out to have ginger hair. Holly was already planning how to spend the five hundred pound state hand-out for a pram and other necessities. She already had a claim in for a council flat.

The car pulling into the car park was a four wheel drive. It shed its passengers quickly; a woman walking with a stick and, by her side, slipping off the back seat, a small child. Only those who had known Serena Collins, of old, might wonder at the difference in her appearance. Wearing a wig of soft, real hair; expensively come-by, her face looked happy in repose. With eyes hidden behind sunglasses, she felt less of a sideshow. These days, she did what she had been unable to do before. She allowed people to look at her without hiding away. It was rare for their curiosity to persist beyond an initial inspection and a few embarrassed glances after which they stared at her no more. She liked to think, also, that a new dress of shimmery multi-coloured silk with a matching scarf about her neck flattered a figure that any woman would be proud of. She smiled at all and sundry and never failed to find that once having done so, they invariably smiled back and then entered into pleasant conversation. Something that her sister tried to dissuade her from. Serena paid Catty no heed on this point for she had discovered the key which might have caused her life to take a different tack from childhood. Serena talked to so many people as she went out shopping, these days, with her trolley in tow that it took her hours to do what had once taken mere minutes. These days, the trolley had but one purpose; to bring her shopping home. Her health while in need of attention was better than it used to be. The doctors had noted a huge improvement. Serena laid her improved happiness at her sister's door, for Catty had become what she had never been before; a trusted friend as well as a sister to be loved.

The child, too, was much improved both in manner and temperament since Catty had come to live with them and she had grown to like her life at Blackstone School. The only matter of lingering contention was Caitlin's fondness for being referred to as Wendy. When asked to state her name, she told everyone that she was Wendy Caitlin Bridgewater Collins. *Very posh!* they said when they also noted the quality of her clothing. But then little Caitlin had always had the best and would continue to do so for as long as Serena might influence her situation.

Today she was dressed finely, also, as she skipped over to the pub wall and looked down upon a place where she might so very easily have drowned but for Mally Kenyon. An incident that, to the child, seemed to have happened in another life, to someone else. For now, she truly had all that her heart desired. Her happiness shone within her eyes as she levered herself up to sit and look down onto the stretch of water where her life had changed.

"Not too close to the water, my darling. Mind you don't step in a puddle. Take care not to dirty your birthday dress." Serena fussing again!

The woman who got down from the driver's seat cast an indulgent eye over her daughter before smiling at her sister whose arm came to rest firmly in the crook of her own even while the walking stick took her weight. Catty had cut her long, fair hair into a fetching bob which hung about her face and shoulders. The sun had bleached it to a shade of platinum with darker roots. Since her retirement from professional life, she had put on weight. To those who might recall Chief Constable Catty Collins in a professional sense there was nothing left of the woman whose life now revolved around a family of dogs and cats and playing her trumpet in a local brass band. She no longer carried herself with self importance and no longer yearned for anything other than the simple life she lived daily with her sister and the child she had so very nearly missed having.

Her nails were jagged from working in her garden. She spent her evenings helping the child to do her homework, practise her scales, walk the countryside; learn everything there was to know about the wider environment in a new place where all was fresh and new and exciting. The child was, these days, settled and well balanced. The occasional tantrum was no more than any child might indulge in when learning the rules of social bargaining. She could scream and cry all she wanted, but unless Catty believed that what she wanted was beneficial, she would just have to accept *No!* for an answer, firmly spoken.

The man who came to join them accepted the hand of friendship each held out in turn. With him came Magdalene, who would shortly be joined by her daughter once their table was fully set and she was ready to become a guest of the house, rather than a waitress. They greeted each other like old friends, with smiles and laughter. Catty and Serena were filled with gratitude for the fact that he had left his work, gone home to shower and change, and come to join them in joyful celebration of what might not have been. For today, the child that Mally Kenyon had saved from death not once but twice was to know yet another birthday. For that he would ever be regarded as a person of exceptional importance in the life of the beautiful child before him. They owed him a debt of gratitude that could never be repaid other than to include him in Wendy's life as she grew and developed from child to woman.

Wendy cared not a bit for the cleanliness of her dress as she drew herself up and sat on the top of the wall looking out to the place where she had very nearly died. Her call for everyone to come look was accompanied by extreme excitement. "Serena...Catty...Mally and Magdalene...please come here, now. See what I see!" her finger pointing at something on the water.

And so they each went to look, leaning elbows, gasping with pleasure, a little unbelieving of the sight before them for they had been honoured by the presence of a pair of gliding swans which came towards them; as white as snow, necks arched, beaks a bright and vivid streak of orange below eyes as bright as jet.

"How magnificent they are." Catty breathed in awe of their majesty. "Such dignified creatures." Then she saw the missing feathers on their wings. An inability of one to fold its wing fully against its back. The scars that gouged a hollow into the other's chest. "They can't be the same ones to suffer at the mere."

Serena knew an affinity which caused her face to beam and her heart to swell with joy. "They are the same pair...their signet killed...their wings broken. They bear the scars still. A bit like me."

"Didn't stop 'em flying though, did it?" Mally asked, aware of an awe he was unable to express in words. "Wonder why they came back here?"

Magdalene replied. "Because this is where they choose to breed. Look!"

Wendy nodded. "Look over there...between the boats...their family," as two small signets came to join their parents. At sight of people the cob and the pen gathered their brood between them as they glided on, centre stream.

Within the restaurant Tommo watched them, too, with eyes that flickered over Gina's reflection in the glass before him, his mind reflecting longingly upon what could never be. If he recognised Wendy then he also recognised the company she kept and knew better than to question where happiness was apparent. His mind was elsewhere anyway. What he would have dearly given to be the one seated with Gina! Yet knowing, too, the impossibility of such yearning, for his own broken wings would never heal.

It was later with all assembled at table that Wendy slid a small, oblong parcel onto Holly's knee where they sat side by side. Holly took note of the look in Wendy's eyes which asked for discretion; the parcel was wrapped in waxed paper, the size of two slices of bread. Wendy winked. Holly's brown eyes widened hardly able to believe her thoughts as Wendy whispered; "Stick with me, kid, and you'll be alright."

Holly gasped because the contents of the parcel could only be one thing. "Is this what I think it is?"

Wendy nodded. "Greedy, greedy! Is for the baby, Holly."

Holly knew a sudden, deep regret. Committed herself, now, hadn't she? Hollywood would have to wait for Holly Kenyon. Instead she was headed for one of the high rise flats to the rear of the Dog's Bed Estate. "How did you do it?"

Wendy winked again. "Is a secret!"

Lightning Source UK Ltd.
Milton Keynes UK
14 October 2010

161294UK00001B/9/P